A CUP OF CONFLICT

Justice #10

SUZAN HARDEN

A CUP OF CONFLICT
Copyright © 2025 by Angry Sheep Publishing LLC
All rights reserved.

ISBN-13 - 978-1-64918-053-7

Published by Angry Sheep Publishing LLC
Findlay, Ohio

Cover by For the Muse Design
Interior by JW Manus

More books by Suzan Harden

Each series is in suggested reading order.

Bloodlines

Blood Magick
Zombie Love
Zombie Confidential
Zombie Wedding
Amish, Vamps & Thieves
Blood Sacrifice
Love, War & a Bulldog
Zombie Goddess
Ravaged
Sacrificed
Reality Bites
Ghouls in the Grocery
Resurrected
Bloodlines Shorts Anthology
Bloodlines: The First Boxed Set

Seasons of Magick

Spring
Summer
Autumn
Winter
The Seasons of Magick Anthology

Justice

Sword and Sorceress 28 ("Justice")
Sword and Sorceress 30
("Diplomacy in the Dark")
Justice: The Beginning
A Question of Balance
A Modicum of Truth
A Matter of Death
A Touch of Mother
A Twist of Love
A Virtue of Child
A Hand of Father
A Measure of Knowledge
A Hint of Thief
A Cup of Conflict
A Barrel of Vintner
A Sprout of Wild
A Glimmer of Light

The Justice Thalia Stories

Snowfall
Murder Most Fowl
The Sweetest Poison
A Granddaughter of Mine
Too Many Fish in the Sea

Tales of the Twelve

The Trickster Priestess and the Demon

Crossover Worlds

Invasion!

888-555-HERO
Hero De Facto
Hero Ad Hoc
Hero De Novo
A Very Hero Christmas
Hero De Jure
Hero In Camera
Hero Amicus Curiae
A Very Hero Wedding
A Very Hero New Year
Hero Ad Litem
Queer Eye for the Super Guy

Solar System Services, Inc.
Alone Is Not Lonely
Halloween Harvest ("A Place at the Table")
A Place at the Table

Millersburg Magick Mysteries
Spells and Sleuths
Fae and Felonies
Magick and Murder
Feline Navidad

Soccer Moms of the Apocalypse
Pestilence in Pumpkin Spice
Famine in French Vanilla
War in White Chocolate
Death in Double Mocha
Demons Run at Halloween

The Enchanted Bakery
Chefs, Shrooms, and Sherry
Cakes, Cookies, and Conjuring

Miscellaneous
Sword and Sorceress 31
("Pig-Headed")
Sword and Sorceress 32
("Unexpected")
Practical Witches
Revenge Served Hot
The Yule Switch
Chocolate for Dinner
Silver Shoes and Pigs' Ears
Snipe Hunt

For updates, news, and giveaways, join Suzan's mailing list or visit her website at www.suzanharden.com. You can also check her out on Facebook, @SuzanHarden.

PROLOGUE

No matter how many times Conflict sparred with Balance, He could never defeat Her. One day as They sipped cool, delicious water after practicing with Their weapons, He asked, "Why is it I can never beat You?"

"Because You think too much."

He laughed. "But You've frequently told Me I don't think at all."

"When You were fresh and new, that was true."

"But if there's balance in everything, Knowledge says I should win once in a while," He protested.

"But You are not Me." Balance chuckled before She rose to Her feet and held out Her hand. Conflict took Hers in His and accepted Her assistance to stand. "When I created Light in My loneliness, I set off a chain of events. By pairing Myself with Light, each of You are not balanced without Your counterpart."

"But I should be paired with Death," He protested. "Often mortals end in Her arms because of their service to Me."

"No." Balance sighed. "You are the counterpart to Love for a reason. You provide the elements to keep mortals from becoming lost in Her influence. The emotion of caring for another can cause a mortal to give too much of themselves, to the point where nothing is left."

Conflict frowned as He tried to understand Balance's explanation. "But You said I needed to steer My own aggressive nature and that of mortals to protect Our families."

"I did," She admitted. "But that's only part of the lessons You needed to learn. Too much of anything can destroy. Light feeds the World with his energy, but My Darkness gives the World a chance to sleep and dream."

Conflict frowned. "I am not sure I want to encourage mortals to be selfish. It seems to be counterintuitive to what You require of Me."

"Aren't You being selfish by pursuing Death?"

Conflict contemplated Balance's question for a long moment. "So, a little bit of selfishness is necessary to protect Yourself?"

"Death may be the end, but She is not everything," Balance murmured. "And You can be with Love without rejecting the whole World in the process."

He nodded. "I will consider Your wisdom. Would You like to continue sparring?"

Balance laughed and drew her sword. "I might even allow you to win this time, Youngling."

The Tenth Book of Conflict, Verses LI thru LXVII

CHAPTER 1

I watched as Sister Yin Li of Love threw herself into the arms of her lost paramour, who we all thought had died with Reverend Father Chen's doomed expedition. Their young son Yin Shang followed suit. The reunited family laughed and cried and hugged.

High Brother Shang of Conflict was quite a handsome man. I could understand why Yin Li was physically attracted to him. But the wave of emotion emanating from the pair was something far deeper. I leaned close to Luc and whispered, "So that's Shang?"

I could feel my love turn to look at me. *Could you tone down the level of lust for another man you're sending my way?*

That isn't amusing.

I don't think so either. At least, you've now confirmed you were never physically attracted to Quan.

"That's what it took!" I glared at Luc.

Behind him, the Skoloti Sister of Thief Darys looked at us in confusion. Luc's warden Yar smirked. I had a feeling my own warden Jonata wore the same smirk behind me. Sister Yin Li of Love and High Brother Shang of Conflict were too busy kissing to pay any attention to the rest of us.

The merchants, who had stopped here for the night on their way from the coast to the capital as we did, drifted through the courtyard of the caravanserai and took inventory of their wares and stock that survived the battle. Shop keepers who resupplied travelers did the same. If it weren't for the forethought of Darys, Shang, and the rest of their rescue squad, everyone at this rest stop would be dead.

Crown Prince Bao Quan Po, heir to the Jing Empire's Dragon Throne, walked over and stood at my left side, but his attention was also on Yin Li and Shang. "She never kissed me like that."

"You were a worshipper, not her true love," I snapped.

"But still, with the size of my donations, I expected more," Po complained.

"I should be the only one receiving your donations, my husband." Bao Shi Hua, the soon to be empress consort of Jing, stalked through the mayhem, her bow still in her hand. She glared at her spouse as if she considered using her weapon on him.

A sly grin filled Po's face. "You never kiss me like that either."

The tiny woman reached up, grabbed the edges of his robe, and yanked him down for a thorough kiss. When she released him, she also smirked. A glance at his silk pants said why. "What were you saying?"

"Not a blessed thing, my wife." He released a deep breath. "Should we rent a cell for Yin Li and Shang so we may have some privacy?"

"I'll take care of it." I made a shooing motion. "Please go back to your room before you feel the need for another public display of affection."

The royal couple held hands as they retreated to the spiral stone staircase leading to the second story. It was good to see them showing some affection. While Shi Hua was only interested in women and Po was interested in anything that moved, I was glad they were trying to make their political marriage work.

"Should we interrupt?" I asked Luc.

"Quan and Shi Hua or Shang and Yin Li?"

I eyed my own paramour. "If you interrupt the prince, he will ask you to join them."

"Unfortunate, but true." Luc shot me a wicked grin. "Maybe if we both join them?"

I held up my hand. "You're on your own for this one, High Brother. I'm going to take a soma tear and try to get some sleep." I turned to head up the same stairs the prince and his wife had just climbed.

"Wait, Chief Justice," Sister Darys called out. "Aren't you going to question me and my party? We could be renegades for all you know."

I pivoted to face her. "Sister, I already know you aren't a skinwalker. If you were a demon, you would have ripped out both my throat and the Lady Shi Hua's a few moments ago when we were standing next to each other. And if you're a renegade, all I ask is that you let me have a good night's sleep and a cup of Jing black tea in the morning before you poison me. Again."

I turned and walked toward the staircase once more. Frankly, Reverend Father Jin and Reverend Father Biming were responsible for truthspelling the newcomers in order to protect their soon-to-be crowned emperor since I was technically a foreign ambassador. And Balance help me, I was mightily tired of doing their job.

"Excuse me!" Shi Hua's shout from the third-floor balcony actually broke Yin Li and Shang's embrace.

I looked up to find the empress-to-be leaning over the balcony railing. Everyone in the courtyard quieted.

"Can someone please remove the dead assassin in our bed? The crown prince and I are trying to conceive an heir!"

CHAPTER 2

The next day, folks from the area farms started arriving when they noticed the billowing smoke from the funeral pyres. A dozen dead renegades and nine dead guardsmen would have attracted attention in other ways if we hadn't burned the bodies. The caravanserai director explained the situation an equal number of times before he finally posted a sign at the gates.

Which only triggered more questions from the locals. Apparently, a good many of them were illiterate.

Which prompted me to ask Shi Hua, Po, and their family about the education situation over our morning meal of porridge and boiled eggs.

"The Temple of Knowledge has been trying to continue educating the children, but many of the civilians protest against it," Shi Hua said.

"Why?" I laid my spoon in my empty bowl and started cracking the shell of my first boiled egg now that it was cool enough to touch.

"They don't see the purpose of it." Po shrugged. "There wasn't a known demon attack during my mother's entire reign. Reading, writing, and sums were only important against demons."

Shang snorted. "It didn't help that the School of Sorcery wanted an ignorant peasantry to help them gain power."

"An ignorant peasantry?" I asked as I peeled off the last of the shell of my egg.

"It's part of the various philosophical schools attempts to discredit the Temples," Yin Li explained. "The farmers complain there's too much work to be done. The wise men of the philosophical school commiserate and ask why are your children not helping in the fields or with the herds? Because they are at the Temple of Knowledge half the day, the farmers complain. The wise men clasp their bosoms and say reading isn't necessary to pull weeds and learning the continents and seas means nothing when one never leaves their province. Or even their village."

Yin Li's exaggerated manner of portraying both the farmers and the sorcerers of the various philosophy schools was hilarious. But the actual contents of her speech concerned me. It sounded like one of the renegades' whisper campaigns. Encouraging people not to listen to clergy placed a major wedge in the civilians' trust of them. And with Jing losing clergy at a similar rate as we were in Issura, this tactic would sorely affect the next generations of humans.

This tactic might even help the demons to win the war.

While most people considered Knowledge to be the weakest Temple, they were the bedrock of our civilization. They compiled and disseminated nearly all information. The brothers and sisters analyzed every report from the other Temples and bureaucrats. They saw trends in harvest and weather long before anyone else did. And their predictions were often correct.

It wasn't a matter of precognitive talent or pretending the heavens could foretell the future. Knowledge paid attention to the cycles around us. The rhythm of the earth. The song of the universe.

And it made me wonder if Yin Li and Shi Hua had been held back from being tested for their talents by their own village elders. Granted, Luc's father Itzel hadn't presented him to a Temple until he was eight winters, but as merchants, the family was often on the road between nations. However, Itzel did so as soon as he saw Luc entertaining his sisters with animals he fashioned from firelight while the family was in Standora. Shi Hua had told me she hadn't left her village until she was seven, but only because her aunt Yin Li had pushed her sister over Shi Hua's distance speaking talents.

"But surely the recent demon attack on Chengzhou would convince them—" Luc started.

"One would think." Shang's emotions felt . . . haunted was the best word out of all the languages I knew. "But not even the wardens and soldiers with us could conceive we were under a demon attack until it was too late."

Yin Li laid her hand on his shoulder, lending her strength to him. "You need to tell the emperor what you told me, my love. He needs to know what he faces."

The porridge and eggs curdled in my stomach as the Conflict priest related how Reverend Father Chen and his army encountered our foes in a desert valley. Realizing his people were outnumbered, Chen signaled a retreat, only to be caught in a pincer attack from the rear. However, the Reverend Father didn't panic. He ordered a charge in a desperate attempt to break through the demon lines. Shang estimated that twenty percent of the expedition fought free of the enemy, but most of them had been wounded, and they lost all but one healer.

For the next two weeks, the demons chased the remnant of the Jing forces. People and horses died because there was no rest. They ran out of food and water. They couldn't even stop long enough to burn the dead. Then, they had the demon-animated corpses chasing them as well as the demons themselves.

When they encountered a defensible stand of rocks, Reverend Father Chen ordered Shang to take the few able-bodied priests and wardens west to seek assistance. An animated corpse had stabbed the Reverend Father in the gut. He knew it was a matter of time before he and the other injured survivors would die. Shang left the last canister of flash powder with Chen. The survivors heard something two days later, but they couldn't be sure if it was an explosion or thunder.

Eventually, Shang and the last dozen survivors encountered Darys's army. The Skoloti had been warned of the demon army by their Reverend Mother of Balance, who was one of their seers. The talent to see the future was incredibly rare, even amongst those of my order.

"The Skoloti fed us before transporting us to their closest Temple of Child." Shang scrubbed his face with his hands. "Their army encountered scattered groups of demons and eliminated them. They never found any more Jing survivors."

Grief filled all of Po's party. I never knew the Reverend Father, but Shi Hua had told me of her encounters with him. However, he must have been very imposing to a fourteen-year-old Light novice. To me, it sounded as if a devoted priest had chosen the only path he could after losing thousands of people.

Fat yellow tears rolled down Shi Hua and Yin Li's faces. Po rolled the beads of his moustache so fiercely, I fear he'd twist the blue hairs out by their roots.

"Your Majesty?" I murmured.

Po's head jerked up. We had so rarely addressed each other by titles for the two months we were at sea. "Yes?"

"You need to speak with every village elder and Temple clergy on the way to Chengzhou." I stared at him. "You need to tell them what happened to you in Tandor. The renegades. The skinwalkers. The demons. All of it."

"You truly believe tales of my torture and our starvation will entertain my people?" he mocked, but I recognized the flicker of fear in his visage. I was sure my own countenance held it from time to time.

"He can't," Shang protested. "Doing so will make him look weak."

"He survived the demon siege of Tandor," Luc said. "He helped us save our citizens. Without him, Issura would have fallen last year."

"Twelve help us, was that only a year ago?" Po released the beads on his moustache. "It would be an excellent task for Reverend Father Biming." He smiled. "And an excellent use of his particular talents."

"He might deem such a task as an insult, my husband," Shi Hua said softly.

"Which is why I'll address him personally about the matter." Po raised her right hand to his lips. "If you'll excuse me, my empress and my guests." He rose and strode from the room the caravanserai director had assigned Po for meeting the local leaders.

Shang eyed me from across the table. "You hold a great deal of our emperor's esteem."

"I also noticed you didn't mention reporting to Reverend Father Chen's replacement in Chengzhou," I replied.

"Ah, the vaunted logic of Balance." He nodded. "We did, along with an emissary of the Skoloti. However, no one in Jing besides Reverend Father Feng, his head of household, and his chief warden are aware of our survival." He shrugged. "Until now."

"If it needs to remain a secret, speak with the empress's head of security Mataqai," Luc suggested.

"Do not worry, High Brother." She Hua grinned. "I already have. As far as anyone else is concerned, High Brother Shang, Sister Darys, and their party are part of the Empress's Guard."

CHAPTER 3

Wu Sunshu sat cross-legged on the floor of his cell, his eyes closed against the Knowledge paper lamp outside of his reach. He kept his back as straight as human vertebrae allowed. The spell-threaded manacles sent a constant buzz through his mind and across his nerves. The attack was supposed to keep him from concentrating. Keep him from casting a spell.

To drive him mad, or even better, make him take his own life. The damned manacles were why Wu's master forced him to cast through such restraints decades ago.

Yet, when he tried to strengthen his own son and his stepson, Yu interfered. She accused him of torturing the boys. Despite their marriage, Yu listened to her old lover's prattling instead of her lawful husband.

Furthermore, Wu hadn't raised Chengwu to be a coward, but the boy didn't want the blood of patricide on his hands. He'd begged the yakshas of Balance to spare Wu, and the malevolent cunts had agreed to imprison him outside of the city proper.

Fools. They had no idea they put him within reach of his allies. There were no demon alarm spells in this underground cell.

Wu smiled to himself. The Assassins Guild believed the lies the demons told them. But the prophesies regarding Yu's sons were coming true, which meant if he could kill Po and any other claimants before the eastern or western saviors arrived, Wu could take the throne. From there, he could destroy the Temples.

How dare they consider him unacceptable! His generalized abilities were far more useful in the long term. He inhaled counting to five. No, he needed the Temples and the demons to destroy each other. With the game board swept clear, nothing could stop him from extending his influence throughout the continent. Jing would become a true empire under his control.

Wu's stomach growled. It was Bing's turn to deliver his one meal of the day. She should be here soon. His apprentice thought she had fooled him, but she wasn't as clever as she believed. The stink of demons permeated her glamours. However, she'd prove useful one last time.

He settled himself on the sleeping bench. With his legs crossed, his back straight, and his eyes closed, he meditated until he heard the keys rattle outside his cell door.

He opened his eyes as Bing toddled into his cell. As usual, she dropped her glamour of an aged servant as soon as the guards closed and relocked the door. She set the tray she carried on the table next to his sleeping bench before she raised her wards so the guards wouldn't overhear their conversation.

Chengwu's mistake was to provide guards who were resistant to magic. The opposing side of that coin? They couldn't detect magic either.

"It's been two weeks," Wu snarled. "Is the bastard dead yet?"

"The Assassins Guild team failed at the first caravanserai from Huang He." She sighed. "A Skoloti Thief priestess and the remnants of Chen's army foiled the attack."

"Chen's army?" Wu glared at her. "You told me the demons had destroyed Chen and his blasted forces."

She shrugged. "That's what His Grandness said."

"What else did His Grandness say?" Wu sneered.

"Eat your supper." She turned to leave.

No offer to free him like every other time. He stared at his bowl of rice with bits of dried fish and fruit. It didn't take a learned person to know the fruit hid the taste of southern blue, the Assassins Guild's favorite poison. His so-called allies now considered him a liability.

"Bing, wait."

Her fist raised to knock on the door, she paused and looked at him.

"I'm sorry for snapping at you." He choked out the words. "I'm angry at waiting for a year to obtain my revenge, and I'm angry I missed the opportunity to slit my own son's throat. I want Yu's bastard to taste my blade so badly I've forgotten who my true allies are."

"Your apology is accepted." She turned to leave again.

"Has Po returned to Chengzhou?"

Her shoulders sagged, and she faced him for the third time. "What is it you really want, Master Wu?"

"I need to kill the little bastard," he said. "I need to know he's dead before I die."

Her glance at his tray confirmed everything he suspected. He muttered the words to activate the hex he'd laid on her when she first warmed his bed. A woman as ambitious as Bing required safety measures.

"Walk to me," Wu commanded.

She strode stiffly across the chiseled stone floor, fighting the compulsion. He smiled at her struggle. It wouldn't have come to this if she hadn't decided to betray him.

"Eat my food."

Terror filled her eyes as she reached for the wooden spoon. Once again, she tried to fight his spell, but there was nothing she could do to stop herself from taking a bite.

On the third bite, she started shaking.

On the sixth bite, she shook so hard she dropped the spoon.

"Use your fingers and scoop the rice into your mouth," he said.

She dropped more on the floor than she placed in her mouth. It didn't matter. From the bright red tint in her fingertips as the blood vessels burst, the poison was taking affect. It didn't mean he wouldn't enjoy every moment of the traitorous bitch's death.

"Get on your hands and knees and lick up every morsel you dropped on the floor," he ordered.

Bing crouched like an animal and proceeded to obey him. When her vomiting started, he commanded her to eat that as well. She finally passed out, and her bowels loosened. He waited patiently until her labored breathing stopped. Her wards disappeared with her life, but they had disguised any noises she made with her dying.

Wu reached down and plucked two hair pins from her now mussed and filthy tresses. His old master's training kicked in. The spell-threaded manacles were no match for an experienced lockpick.

The relief from the constant buzzing in his mind almost made him cry out in joy. Somehow, he refrained.

Instead, he gathered Bing's corpse and laid it on his sleep bench. He laid his blanket over the body. The glamour he placed on Bing would fool anyone who might check on him before morning, though those random inspections had become rare since his son's death.

The feel of magic was the closest thing to ecstasy he'd experienced in over a year. With the second glamour completed, he picked up the tray from yesterday before he knocked on the door.

The four locks clicked open one by one. A guard opened the door enough to allow Wu to slip through. Not one of the famed imperial guards took a second glance at the old woman who toddled down the corridor.

This Skoloti Thief priestess couldn't possibly be the third of the trium-virate who were foretold to save the bastard and Jing from the demons. The high sister mentioned in the prophecy had already been killed. However, prophecies could twist in their meaning when anyone attempted to circumvent them. Wu simply couldn't take any chances. He would need to kill all three women and Yu's firstborn. First, he must sort through the remnants of his school to learn who was still loyal to him. And if no one was . . .

Well, sometimes, the only way to do things correctly was to do them himself.

CHAPTER 4

The rest of our journey to Chengzhou, while slower than we wished, was relatively uneventful, thank the Twelve. Reverend Father Biming seemed relieved to be given a task suited to his Temple's main duties, especially since it wasn't near his new empress or me. Rumor did the rest.

Once Thief spread word that their new emperor had returned to Jing, crowds of civilians lined the road the rest of the way to the capital. The throngs made all of the wardens and Imperial guards nervous, especially after the attacks on the Huang He docks and at the first caravanserai.

However, Po took my advice to heart. He made a point of speaking with every city and village's civilian, guild, and Temple leaders. Shi Hua spoke to as many commoners as she could as one of them. At one point, I feared Mateqai's heart would explode when a small child offered her new empress a bouquet of early spring flowers. However, Luc's former warden managed to keep his blades sheathed.

Each and every time, Po and Shi Hua told their stories of the Fall of Rambla and the Siege of Tandor as well as the demon attacks on Orrin. At the end of his tale, Po pointed out that only the quick actions of the Temples saved the city of Chengzhou, and subsequently Jing itself. He played on the people's sympathies by stating he lost his own family in the attack. And he would honor his brother's memory by continuing his commitment to all people of Jing and do his best to serve them. But it would be necessary for everyone, young and old, Temple and guild, noble and civilian alike, to work together.

If anyone had told me the decadent, selfish ambassador I first met nearly two years ago would become the epitome of an engaged, selfless ruler, I would have whacked that person with the flat of my blade. Luc seemed pleased with Po's new behavior, but I suspected his feelings were due to the fact Po no longer had the time or energy to chase my affections.

Not that I would ever have returned them. Or Shi Hua would tolerate such disrespect.

During our two weeks on the road, Jonata and Long Feather struck up friendships with the pair of Skoloti wardens accompanying Sister Darys. There were times when Yar had to translate Skoloti to Issuran and vice versa because neither side knew the Jing term for whatever they wished to convey.

In between our stops when she had to act as one of Shi Hua's guard, Sister Darys rode with Luc and me. Those were the only times she could push back her hood. According to Yar, her white hair was as much of an identifying marker as my red eyes. On a more positive note, she had started learning Issuran before she left Skoloti Territory and was thrilled to have someone to practice with.

We were three days from the Jing Capital before I finally asked her, "What made you want to learn our language?"

"It's . . . interesting intellectually," Sister Darys replied with her thick accent. "The Peaceful Sea and the Panthalassa Sea trade tongues are a patois of the coastal languages. Basically, an accidental dialect. However, Issuran is a deliberate blending of Chumash, Toscana, and Britannia speech."

I laughed. "I'm not sure it's as deliberate as you think. The Britons needed a home. The Chumash needed help rebuilding their territory. The Toscana wanted to make money off supplying all parties and rule over the survivors. It was necessary for everyone to understand each other."

"Yet, somehow it all works." She shook her head.

"Aren't the Skoloti made up of several different tribes from the Central Old Continent?" Luc asked.

"Yes." Danys smiled. "But that was prior to Balance's Revelation. If it weren't for the non-human invaders, we probably would have continued our separate ways, but like your Plains Nations, we joined together for survival. However, our languages descended from a mother tongue according to our Temples of Knowledge. Morphing them back together wasn't as difficult for our ancestors."

"Would you teach me your language, also?" I asked.

Are you sure you want to learn it?" Darys smiled. "It's nothing like yours."

"It can't be any worse than practicing Jing while being seasick for two months." I laughed.

"I've never been on a boat," she murmured.

"Not even a small craft to fish or travel on a river or lake?" I asked.

She shook her head. "I asked my novice brother about the oceans once. He said our seas are made of grass, not water."

"You spent a great amount of time in Huang He," Luc said. "You never took a river barge?"

"I admit I find anything beyond a stream to drink a bit unnerving," Darys admitted.

"My apologies, Sister," I said. "I've spent most of my life in Standora or Orrin. In port cities, it's hard to avoid the water."

"I suppose the Cradle's Great Desert would be just as unimaginable to all of us," she said.

"The closest I've come is the Valley of the Lost between Issura and Diné," I said. "But we travelled to Diné during the rainy season. The Valley of the Lost went from a sea of sand to a sea of mud to a sea of flowers in a matter of hours."

Darys laughed heartily at my description.

"It wasn't that amusing at the time," Luc grumbled. "We nearly lost Anthea and Sisquoc, a Wildling brother, in the flash flood one of the storms produced."

"Flash . . . flood?" Danys shook her head. "I do not understand. Like when a dam breaks and the water pours out?"

"Not quite," Luc said. "In the Valley of the Lost, Diné, or Cant, there's a relatively thin layer of sand and dirt over bedrock. On the rare occasions of rain, there are no plants to drink the water. No loam to absorb it."

"So, the rain rises where it lands?" Danys ventured. "As if filling a container?"

I laughed. "It does flow downhill. However, the water picks up everything on top of the bedrock. It becomes a slurry of mud and rocks. Nearly impossible to swim in, and immediately deadly if you hit a large rock."

"Or if a rock hits you," she added.

I nodded.

"And the water can undercut protruding rock," Luc added. "We found shelter on a high outcrop, but Anthea and Sisquoc were near the edge, keeping watch on the flood."

He deliberately allowed the long pause to drive Darys to distraction.

"What happened?" she blurted.

"The edge crumbled beneath us," I said. "Somehow, Sisquoc managed to toss me back so our wardens could catch me. He fell and was swept into the maelstrom." The old guilt hit me. The Wildling brother was so brave and decent, but he'd nearly lost his life many times in his attempts to protect me.

"Anthea managed to time freeze the maelstrom Sisquoc was dragged into," Luc continued. "One of the sisters with us is a mover. She and three others reached him before he was crushed or drowned, and they brought him back to our shelter. Other than a couple of broken ribs, cuts, and bruises, Thief blessed the brother."

Danys turned to me and blinked. "How big was this basin?"

I couldn't speak past my dry mouth.

"Roughly fifteen leagues in diameter," Luc said softly.

Danys shook her head as she stared at me. "No one from our Temple of Balance has that level of power."

"Some of your justices have the ability to foresee events." I couldn't stop the bitterness seeping into my tone. "I would give anything for that talent. Maybe then, I could save the people who keep sacrificing themselves for me."

I nudged my borrowed Temple mount, and the horse trotted away from Luc and Darys. I simply couldn't deal with my alleged heroics when I had to burn the bodies of so many of my friends because of my failures.

CHAPTER 5

Later that night at the next caravanserai, I supped by myself in one of the way station's many taverns. Well, as alone as I could be with so many travelers. This close to the capital, the place was packed despite being nearly ten times the size of the last two caravanserai at which we lodged. The only reason we had rooms here was due to Reverend Father Biming's vanguard. Ironically, most people lodging at this station were merchants hoping to sell their wares at the Spring Rituals festival and the celebration of the new emperor's coronation.

Long Feather and Jonata sat at a nearby table where they could watch me without them being in my line of sight. Yet, I couldn't avoid the familiarity of their spirits. My robes and badge kept the rest of the clientele away, though I could hear them murmuring about me. I still would have known I was the object of their discussions even if I hadn't learned Jing.

Sister Darys stalked up to my table and straddled the bench on the other side. Her wardens moved past us, no doubt joining my own guards at the table behind me.

"You can't continue blaming yourself for random misfortune," she boldly stated in Issuran.

I straightened. "You have no real knowledge about me. And you are stepping beyond your rank, Sister."

"Maybe I am," she replied. "However, I am not your enemy, Chief Justice. We have the same duty to perform—keep the Jing emperor alive long enough to reach Chengzhou."

"Go away."

"I see." She smiled and switched to Jing. "Do you truly believe that by driving away other people, your heart will not be broken by loss?"

However, I wasn't falling for her trap, and I refused to play her word games. "You are not from Child, and this is a public place," I snapped in Issuran.

She shook her head, but she resumed speaking in Issuran. "Maybe you should speak with one of Shang's people. You're not the only one who has lost comrades in this war, and I have no doubt I will lose people I care about before it's over."

I relaxed a bit. "So, you believe the demon war is not over?"

"Balance is noted for saying exactly what She means, Lady Justice." Darys shrugged. "According to Her Revelation at the Kemet capital, we have one more generation to go before we will defeat the demons."

It was my turn to test the Thief priestess. Using my eating sticks, I retrieved a vegetable from my bowl and held it up. "What is this?"

Darys frowned at my abrupt change of subject. "I don't know the Issuran word for it, but the Jing term is 'pak choi.' Our Temple of Knowledge says it's related to cabbage."

"Sister, do you think the other plants in the garden miss this particular pak choi?"

"I don't know." Her brows drew together.

"You seem to spend a great deal of time with Knowledge," I said. "Do they have any treatises on the emotions and intelligence of plants?"

"I've never searched for such information before." Her frown deepened, and she cocked her head. "What is the purpose of your question?"

"During our trip to Diné, Brother Sisquoc of Wildling and I discussed why the demons focus on humans and not any other life form in the World." I examined the leafy chunk of vegetable. "According to the Temples, all life is interconnected. If we have thoughts and feelings, and animals have similar thoughts and feelings according to the Wildlings' experiences, he conjectured that plants must as well."

"It makes sense," she murmured. "Don't justices pull the memories from stones and plants to learn of deeds around them?"

I nodded. "So, how could anything have a memory if it didn't also have thought?"

"By your logic, it cannot." Darys propped her elbows on the table. "Therefore, memories are thoughts we've recorded within our spirits. However, I still don't understand the purpose of your line of questioning."

"What's special about humans then?"

"Maybe it is the similarities between humans and the demons that attract them to us." She paused as the tavern girl asked for her choice in drink and whether the priestess wanted dinner.

Once the girl scurried toward the kitchen, Darys eyed me again. "There's also the fact they eat us and wear our skins as we would another animal's. Is this what concerns you? How closely the demons resemble us?"

"Yes," I said. "And our one fault is we do not regard each other with the same respect we should show to all living things. I believe they regard us with the same belief that we have for the animals and plants that nourish us. The only difference is we fight back."

She shook her head. "You are certainly not what I expected."

"What's that supposed to mean?" I glared at her.

"According to our own Reverend Mothers of Balance, the prophesized justice who can see would be the one who leads the final battle. I pictured you as a great hero. Someone of conviction. Not someone who doubts her purpose."

I froze. This was the first time I'd heard about the prophesy outside of Reverend Mother Alara. Maybe the old bat wasn't yanking my emotions around after all.

Darys frowned. "Have I offended you, Lady Justice?"

"May we continue this discussion in my quarters after you've finished your meal?" My tongue wanted to choke on my words. "This is not a conversation we should have in public."

"Of course." Darys inclined her head. "I beg your forgiveness. You are correct. I should not have mentioned such a subject in a public place."

"And I apologize for my behavior on the road," I said. "I had no right to inflict my ill temper upon you."

She smiled and nodded just as the tavern girl arrived with a full tray.

I finished my meal and sipped on another cup of Jing's cool light-tasting beer while Darys consumed her own meal. We continued to speak of the differences between the Skoloti tribes and Issura, and she taught me a few more words in her language.

When we finished, we left the tavern and headed toward our assigned suites. Our wardens prowled behind us. The crowd parted away from our path, but from the mix of fear and anger wafting from the people, it had more to do with what my Temple robes represented than the recent demon attack on their capital city.

I silently requested Luc, Po, and Shi Hua attend my discussion with Darys as we climbed the steps of the caravanserai. It was five stories tall, so the best rooms were on the top floor. This caravanserai had been built of stone, nearly a fortress in and of itself. Po said it acted as a warehouse for the goods flowing into and out of Chengzhou, but I had the impression commerce wasn't the building's original purpose.

When we reached the top floor, instead of mine and Luc's stateroom, we headed toward the suite used by the imperial couple. These days, the Jing guards bowed to us as befitting foreign dignitaries while Mateqai escorted us to Po and Shi Hua's private sitting room. I had mixed emotions concerning those who had accompanied us across the Peaceful Sea. I no longer viewed them by their rank, but rather honored comrades who survived that horrid voyage. However, it was necessary to adhere to the formalities, given our mission.

Inside the sitting room, Luc bowed before carefully lowering his body to a silk-covered cushion in front of the Jing emperor and his wife. Two other cushions lay on his right for me and Darys. Jing guards and our own wardens stood against the walls of the room.

Both Darys and I executed the appropriate bows for our ranks before I said, "With your permission, Your Majesty, I would like to ward the room."

Po nodded and fingered the gold beads on the left-side of his moustachio, an indication that he was worried about something. Shi Hua appeared exhausted, her normally bright smile a shadow of itself.

Darys sat on the far-right cushion while I circled the room and muttered the words for the warding spell. After I finished, I dropped to the cushion between Luc and Darys. I turned to her.

"Please tell us everything you know concerning your Reverend Mother of Balance's prophecy about the justice with sight."

Darys blinked. "You don't know?"

"The information has been withheld from me, and I have suspicions in regards to the reasons," I replied. "Nor has this knowledge been shared with the Temple of Light, according to the empress and High Brother Luc."

Darys remained silent for a long moment as she no doubt carefully considered her words. It was the first relatively normal Thief characteristic I'd seen her display since we left the coastal port of Huang He eleven days ago.

Finally, she nodded. "I will tell you about the prophesy on one condition—that you share with me whatever suspicions you have."

"We'll agree to your condition with one of our own," Shi Hua said. "You agree to be truthspelled."

Darys nodded again. "Considering your issues with your own Reverend Father of Thief, I understand your worries, and I agree to your terms, Your Majesty."

So, we weren't as subtle in regards to our collective change in opinion of Biming than I thought we had been. But then, I wasn't very forgiving when someone tries to kill me, especially when they use third parties.

I sucked in a deep breath at the warm tingle of Shi Hua's power, but Darys didn't seem a bit surprised it was the Jing empress who laid the truthspell on her.

"If you would start your questioning, Lady Justice," Po murmured.

Under our previous circumstances, I would have made a borderline rude reply to him about using me as bait. Now, all I felt from him was a gentle flow of trust. I was no longer an oddity he wished to seduce, but a useful ally. And from my discussion with Queen Teodora before we left Orrin, our liege regarded him in the same way.

I licked my lips, my mouth suddenly dry. It was one thing to have my suspicions. It was another to have them confirmed, which I had no doubt Darys was about to do.

"When did the Skoloti Reverend Mother of Balance have her premonition?" I murmured.

"Thirty-three winters ago."

Gorge rose in my throat at the proximity of my conception to the Reverend Mother's premonition.

"Can you give us the precise time of her prophecy?" Shi Hua asked.

"The Spring Rituals," Darys and I said at the same time.

Everyone, even our most trusted guards and wardens, stared at me. I cleared my throat.

"Did she see the manner in which a justice would gain sight?" Luc asked.

"If you don't mind, could I tell you the full story as I know it?" Darys smiled. "The tale will answer most of your questions. Then you can slice apart my recitation with your concerns."

I glanced at Po, waiting for his decision.

He nodded and said, "Please continue with your story, Sister Darys."

To my amazement, it was Mateqai who blurted, "Your Majesties, with all due respect, it would be best if Sister Darys were formally questioned." He glared at the Skoloti woman. "We had more than enough issues with Thief to warrant it."

CHAPTER 6

Luc sucked in a breath to reprimand Mateqai, but I silently said, *Don't, my love. He is no longer your warden.*

Thankfully, Luc relaxed a bit. However, Shi Hua turned to her captain of the empress's guard. Her expression was neutral, but her irritation grated along my psyche.

"Heed your place, Captain."

He dropped his gaze. "I beg forgiveness, my empress." But his own worry and suspicion were barely under control. A fact not lost on any of the clergy or the former priestess in the room, including Darys.

She raised her chin. "If it will ease your guards' fears, Your Majesty, I will submit to formal questioning. In making my suggestion, I did not wish to waste your valuable time."

Po stopped playing with the beads on his moustache. A whisper of his old, sly smile tilted his lips. "What say you, Lady Justice?"

I looked at the Skoloti priestess. Her skin didn't change from its warm yellow. I turned back to Po. "This isn't a formal investigation. Sister Darys voluntarily revealed her knowledge of her Reverend Mother of Balance's prophecy to me. While I trust Captain Mateqai's advice implicitly, I don't want to allow any prejudice I might have against two specific members of Thief to affect your nation's relations with the Skoloti tribes."

Po chuckled at my reference to Biming and Ogusuku, the Reverend Father of Ryukyu's Temple of Thief. My acknowledgement of Mateqai's concerns seemed to mollify the former warden. His skin color shifted from orange to gold.

Po inclined his head. "Tell us your story, Sister."

"As I said a moment ago, our Reverend Mother of Balance had her vision thirty-three years ago," Darys began. "At this time, she was technically a Temple novice." She glanced at me. "I don't know how such things are done in Issura, but for us, those novices, who are ready, take their final vows at the end of the Spring Rituals. Assignments are made so when the tribes split and go to their grazing lands or hunting grounds during the summer, they have sufficient clergy to care for the people until the Vintner's festival. The final vows happen during the last night of the Rituals.

While she was reciting her oath to Balance, she went into a trance and spoke in an odd voice."

Darys closed her eyes. "In thirty winters, the last demon attacks will start. A babe will be born, touched by Balance, but with a unique sight. She will lead the last battle because she can detect demons through their disguises. You will know her because her eyes will be the color of her birth mother's Temple."

Darys's eyelids fluttered open. "No one knew what to make of her words, though Balance clerks and Knowledge clergy had the presence of mind to record what she said. When she finished speaking, she collapsed to the ground, unconscious. After the healers roused her, she did not remember anything that had just happened.

"She recovered and took her vows that night, but she remained with the Reverend Mother of Balance instead of departing with the tribe she had been assigned to. Over the years, all Twelve of our Temples searched for signs of demon activity. The Reverend Mother of Balance at the time consulted all the records she had as well as those in the other eleven Temples. Justices queried their counterparts in neighboring territories. Other Balance Temples were contacted through distance speakers."

Darys chuckled. "It started a philosophical debate about whether a sighted justice was actually a justice. Others believed the blessed justice would develop a spell to pierce the demons' ability to shapeshift. It was all theory until word came from traders about Issura's Red Justice."

"Please do not call me that." My request was halfway between a snarl and a plea.

"No offense was intended, Lady Justice." Darys inclined her head by way of apology. "It is merely the description we received."

"It means something else in Issura," I muttered.

"Why is this prophecy such a secret?" Luc asked.

"It isn't." Darys's expression turned puzzled. "At least not among the Skoloti clergy. I cannot speak for other nations, but our Temple of Balance did send notice of the prophecy to their sister Temples in all the other lands."

"Your people are known for your oracles among your orders," Shi Hua said. "Isn't that correct?"

Darys nodded. "Yes, Your Majesty."

"Do the other nations' Temples often disregard the foresight of your fellow clergy?" Shi Hua asked.

Another chuckle from the Skoloti priestess. "I cannot speak on behalf of foreign Temples, Your Majesty."

"But your own people take these prophecies as truth, correct?" Shi Hua asked.

"We take any foresight quite seriously," Darys said. "However, understanding a prophecy isn't always as straight forward as we would wish. For instance, this divination did not specify how the justice obtains her method of detecting demons, nor did it delineate what is meant by 'sight'. Another factor, as the Chief Justice will tell you, relates to the future constantly moving because our decisions and actions change based on what we perceive. And that perception is not always accurate."

"This particular prophesy seems rather accurate." Po smiled. "It would explain the desperate attempts of the Assassins Guild and their partners to eliminate you, Anthea."

"Yes, it does," I replied dryly.

Darys's information troubled me greatly. None of my sisterhood back in Issura I'd spoken with in my careful inquiries had known about this prophecy, or rather did not admit to knowing it. Nor did I have sufficient reason to question them under a truthspell. Reverend Mother Alara had only mentioned it to me after I'd discovered the renegades had quietly taken over Orrin's Temple of Love, but she refused to answer any further queries I sent to the home Temple in Standora.

My birth mother's Temple. Love.

Their order's symbolic color was blood red.

Like my eyes.

At the time, I'd though my superior had been playing with me. Now, I wondered why she kept silent about this prophesy, especially after I had given myself my peculiar eyesight. Based on our past interactions, was she appalled I was the sighted justice?

That would have made sense under normal circumstances if I didn't suspect the traitor within Issura's Temple of Balance was Reverend Mother Alara herself.

"Is there anything else you wish to know?" Darys asked.

Everyone in the room watched for my reaction.

"May I ask a rather personal question, Sister?" I said.

"Of course." Her smile turned seductive. Luc's emotions prickled against my psyche.

"Do all with foresight have your color of hair?"

She laughed. "Those with the talent of actual precognition have silver hair, but not all of us with silver hair have true foresight. I'm afraid my abilities only extend to winning games of chance, which is why I was assigned to Thief. What else do you wish to know?"

"Nothing else at this time," I said. "You have given me much new information to consider. However, may I please speak with you again if I do formulate more questions?"

"Of course." She nodded.

"As for your request for information—" I began.

"You do not have to tell me, Lady Justice." Darys frowned. "I was not aware you have had previous troubles with the Assassins Guild."

"Do you withdraw your request because of your Temple's former association with the Assassins Guild?" I deliberately raised an eyebrow.

"No, I'm withdrawing my request because I understand your issue with Reverend Father Biming."

Part of me liked the Thief priestess, but she was one I'd need to keep an ear open for. Just like Biming. However, her insightfulness could be useful. Or very, very dangerous. I wish I knew for sure which way my instinct was pointing.

"Which issue is that?" I asked mildly.

She hesitated a moment, but her color did not change. "I learned from one of Duke Lixin's men the Ryukyuan Reverend Father of Thief tried to interfere with that kingdom's installation of their new Reverend Mother of Balance and to force you to stay in Ryukyu in his custody, not Balance's, because something that occurred during the attack on Naha. He also said Reverend Father Biming conspired with the Ryukyuan Reverend Father of Thief to accomplish such deeds."

"Which of the duke's men did you speak with, and what else did this guard convey to you?"

I recognized Po's cool tone. It was the same one he'd used with me after I'd discovered he'd tortured and executed an assassin within the walls of the Jing Embassy back in Orrin. I had been furious the man hadn't been properly questioned by a justice before being officially tried and convicted. However, an embassy was considered part of its nation's territory and I had no say in Po's disposition of the assassin. It angered me more Po had discovered the traitor thanks to the tracking spell I'd asked the Orrin Temple of Light to perform during our investigation into Sister Gretchen of Love's murder.

"It was Ma Li." Now, the Skoloti priestess's color did change to a dull orange. Was she embarrassed about gossiping? Or was she irritated that she wasted a good source of information? I couldn't tell. No emotion leaked from her shielded mind.

Po didn't bother to look at Huizhong who stood to the crown prince's right and behind his chair. "Captain?"

"Yes, my emperor!" The head of Po's personal guard stepped forward and executed a smart bow to his liege. He turned to me. "If you will, Lady Justice?"

I dissolved my wards with a murmured word, and Huizhong departed. I prayed to the Twelve his only task was to reprimand this unfortunate Ma Li.

"Is there anything else you wished to discuss, Chief Justice?" Po asked.

"No, Your Majesty," I shook my head. "I wanted to keep you and the empress apprised of any knowledge concerning demons since you were kind enough to warn me of the price the Assassins Guild had placed on my head." I deliberately didn't mention Shi Hua had an even bigger price on hers in front of Sister Darys, according to the information the former emperor Chengwu had forwarded to his brother. I was sure it had alarmed Chengwu to see Po's bodyguard, now wife, at the top of an Assassins Guild target list.

And it made me wonder if there had been a prophesy about Shi Hua as well.

CHAPTER 7

Three days later, the imperial procession entered the Jing capital. I tried not to gawk as if I were a child fresh from a tiny village, but it was impossible not to do so. The surrounding land, while not barren, was devoid of anything longer than tiny blades of grass. The lack of high vegetation made the three-story-high walls appear far taller. All minor buildings were three leagues from the stone base. The Jing people took the prohibitions concerning plant growth and out buildings near city walls far more seriously than we did in Issura, a subject I would need to bring up the next time I spoke with Duke White Eagle.

Chengzhou was much, much larger than Standora. As the city had grown over the centuries, a series of concentric walls had been built around the new stores and homes. Sister Yin Li had dropped back to ride with Luc and me as we approached the city's Eastern Gate. She pointed out the next wall under construction a half league from the gate in front of us. Men and women dug the deep pit needed to support the massive stone fortress that would eventually surround Chengzhou. I wondered if construction had started before Po's half-brother had been assassinated.

She didn't need to mention we avoided any delays with the bureaucracy while entering the city as part of the imperial party. For once on this blasted trip, Reverend Father Biming proved his worth.

Captain Huizhong and his men took point as we wove our way through the wide streets. Their announcement of the crown prince's presence was a contradiction. More people flooded the streets, but they kept well out of the imperial party's way. The people bowed deeply, and they did not rise until the last guard passed them.

In the meantime, Yin Li pointed out significant sites. I wasn't the only one enthralled by the art and architecture. The sister's son Yin Shang stared in wonder at the people and surrounding buildings. It struck me it had been nearly two years since he'd left Jing with his mother.

At approximately the same age I had been when I had been forced to leave Orrin.

While Yin Li identified specific monuments and dispensed stories about them, I looked at the boy on top of his shaggy pony. "How much do you remember of your birth city, Master Yin Shang?"

"Not much," he admitted shyly. "It's like coming to someplace new." He glanced at his mother and added softly, "I only remember I didn't want to leave Father when Mother was told to go to Issura." He looked up at me. "Do you think I had a premonition something bad would happen to Father?"

The child's insight took me by surprise. "I do not know. I've never had any experience with foresight. Have you spoken to your mother about this?"

He shook his head. "Uncle Po, er, the emperor said I should not say anything to Mother because it would trouble her. I don't want to hurt her in any way. He also said if I was ever in need of an honest answer, I should ask you."

I smiled at the boy, vaguely amused Po put that much trust in me. I knew he was quite fond of Yin Shang, and the soon-to-be-crowned emperor looked forward to having his own children. I didn't know if Shi Hua was aware she was with child yet, but I had learned my lesson about addressing such a matter before the mother-to-be or the potential father announced the coming babe. I had nearly destroyed my cordial relationship with the Duke of Orrin and Lady Katarina over her first pregnancy.

"And what did the emperor say when you asked him if you had foresight?" I asked.

The boy shrugged. "He said the Temples would determine my talents when I was a bit older."

"Do you wish to serve the Temples?"

Yin Shang glanced at his mother's back before he looked at me again. "Part of me wants to because Father and Mother serve." A mischievous grin spread across his face. "However, I learned a great deal while we were aboard the *Mars Tranquilus*. Perhaps I could serve the emperor by working on a ship."

"I think the emperor would gladly have you serve him in any capacity you both agree on."

My answer seemed to please the boy, and we both paid more attention to his mother's gracious discourse.

Our travel through the city wasn't as straightforward as it would have been in the cities of Issura. Whenever we reached an inner wall, we would have to traverse left or right to reach the actual gate. It was a maze that would have confounded even the builders of the Crimson Palace in Ryukyu. Both invaders and prisoners would have difficulty getting through the gate system even if they knew the city intimately. No doubt Chengzhou's architects planned for such things.

What surprised me most was the number of parks within each set of walls. They were as well kept as those in the Ryukyuan capital. The first flowers of spring blossomed in their beds, and brilliant yellow buds glowed at the tips of the small trees and bushes' green branches. It was a reminder of how close we were to the Spring Rituals.

What's wrong? Luc whispered in my mind.

Just my usual trepidation of the season, I replied.

At least we're not in Tandor this year.

His jibe didn't make me feel better. *You will still be expected to bed some of the local priestesses.*

He was silent for a long moment before he whispered, *After what Gerd did to you and Claudia, I doubt I would be able to perform for fear of some tragedy striking the woman.*

His concerns surprised me. *My birth mother is dead. She cannot touch either of us ever again.*

And I refuse to hurt you ever again.

I swallowed my bitterness at the strength of his declaration. Despite the months I spent under Child's care, the old emotions surged through me. I hoped I would have time to myself to meditate, but I doubted I would have such privacy before First Night.

Yin Li's running commentary slowed as we passed through the middle wall gate. This wall was much thicker than the last. At the third gate, I noticed the sentries on the parapets were no longer imperial troops, but Temple wardens and clergy. However, they were too high for me to clearly read their shoulder emblems.

"By the Twelve, how did the demons enter the city with this many priests and priestesses about?" I said in Issuran.

"There's usually not this many Conflict wardens and clergy guarding the inner walls," Yin Li replied in kind. "Nor as many soldiers manning the outer walls and patrolling the streets."

"Do you have civilian Peacekeepers?" Luc asked.

The priestess nodded solemnly. "The extra guards are a response to the winter attack. Especially with so many people flooding the city for the Spring Rituals."

Inside the third wall, large buildings clearly marked as guild houses interspersed with manors housing the noble class, the various philosophical schools, and high-class inns. Each structure was larger than Duke Marco's castle and the Orrin Government House put together. Small storefronts were housed in the corners of the guild buildings. From the quality of goods, they had been made by masters. The inns had similar corner shops where visitors to the inner city could purchase meals and drinks to eat on the street-side terraces.

As we passed these buildings on the way to the imperial palace, the quiet obeisance to Po continued. I watched facial features and colors of bodies as we passed. While the merchants, common tradespeople, and families had largely been relieved at their new emperor's return, the feelings had switched within the inner wall. Guild masters, their journeypeople, and staffs had mixed feelings, but nobles and the school staffs were perturbed though they did not openly express their hostility.

I could feel Luc watching through my eyes, silently comparing his impressions with mine.

This is not good, he said.

It's not as if we believed Po would be received with open arms by the nobility, I replied sourly.

Luc snorted. *Duke Lixin didn't sweeten the news either.*

I smiled at him. *Duke Lixin has no taste for more power. If it wasn't for his family, I think he'd be perfectly happy quietly farming in a small corner of Jing.*

Luc chuckled as the imperial procession swung south. At Yin Li's sharp glance, he quickly sobered.

I could smell the perfumed air before we reached the Temple District. As I expected, the next right turn opened onto the avenue of the Twelve. These Temples put the ones in the Ryukyuan capital of Naha to shame. Nor did they resemble the layered buildings in Huang He. Each of the Temples was an out-and-out fortress.

High walls surrounded each complex except for the main doors and the twelve steps leading to the entrance. The symbols of each Temple were inscribed with gold inlays on the lintel posts. Carved jade decorated the massive bronze doors of the main entrances. A palpable sense of worry emanated from the clergy, wardens, and staff as we passed. It was almost a relief compared to the animosity of the nobles.

"There's only one gate each for the two inner walls?" I quietly asked Yin Li.

Her slight nod was my only acknowledgement. She kept her eyes forward.

That must have been how the Temples and imperial guards kept the demons from spilling out to devour the civilians when they attacked the palace. Emperor Chengwu and his family were a high cost to pay for the rest of the nation. Did the people here even understand what had been done by the Reverend Mothers and Fathers to save their lives?

Even worse, did it matter if the nobles or school masters failed to acknowledge their new emperor?

CHAPTER 8

A huge square, easily a quarter league wide and long, stood between the Temples and grounds of the imperial palace itself. Bricks covered the entire ground space. Wooden poles stood around the edges of the square while some were embedded in the middle, marking off a smaller square.

Workers were already decorating the square for the Spring rituals. They ran ribbons from pole to pole, marking off sections. Yin Li said the tables and benches were transported by oxen and wagons from a nearby warehouse to the square.

"Is the middle section for dancing?" I quietly asked the Love priestess.

She smiled and nodded. "Knowledge will provide paper lanterns, which will be hung the night before the first day." She chuckled. "Unless the weather oracles predict rain. Then the Temple of Light will provide the lanterns."

I laughed in return. "Rain is one thing we rarely have to worry about in Issura. The winter storms are often long gone before the Rituals."

A waist-high wall separated the square from the imperial palace. No doubt, the vicinity of the Temples to the throne were part of what triggered the resentment of the schools of philosophy. I needed to research more Jing history. I had a strong feeling the schools existed before Balance's Revelation. If so, that would add to the masters' animosity.

We entered the palace grounds, and imperial guards lined the avenue. Like the majority of civilians, the guards exhibited an enormous sense of relief at the new emperor's return to Chengzhou.

The avenue itself was constructed of Toscana concrete. A great expense, but the material would last longer than cobblestone given the amount of traffic the palace normally might see. And the lane would definitely be crowded between the Spring Rituals and the upcoming coronation.

Huge troughs of soil held flowering plants, most of which were starting to bud under the balmy weather over the past four days. Statues were randomly placed on the lawn. Each art piece was surrounded by beds of plants or sand. In the sand beds, designs were drawn. I couldn't be sure if they were similar to Diné sand paintings because all sand looked the same to me. It was something I would have to ask Luc about later.

At the end of the quarter-league avenue, people I assumed were the

Dragon Palace staff lined up in neat rows at the ends of the wide steps up to the palace itself. Imperial guards kept a significant path in the middle of the stairs clear. The only people who weren't surrounded by the armed men and women were the handful of nobles and the many squires at the foot of the palace steps.

When we reached the end of the avenue, Po gave the signal to stop and dismount. I glanced behind us, half-expecting the heads of the Temples to have joined the procession, but no one was behind us except the escort loaned to us by Duke Lixin.

Once the riders stood on the pavement, the lead noble approached Po and bowed deeply. "Welcome home, Your Majesty."

"Rise, cousin." Po chuckled. "We'll have more than enough ceremony to stand on over the coming weeks and years."

"As you wish, Your Majesty." The noble straightened, a neutral expression on his face.

Po gestured Shi Hua to his side. "May I present my wife Bao Shi Hua? My love, this is my cousin, Duke Bao Mengchang, the Imperial Grand Chancellor."

I didn't miss the slight twitch of disapproval on the duke's lips when Po grasped Shi Hua's hand in his and led her to each noble present and introduced them to her. Mengchang may simply have conservative views. Or he could simply be biding his time. All of the Bao cousins with claims to the throne would be present for the coronation.

Or maybe Mengchang still thought Shi Hua was the concubine who'd accompanied Po to Issura nine years ago.

Gah! Now I was seeing plots where none might be. The events over the last two years had ruined whatever normality that had existed in my life. I glanced at Luc and amended my thoughts. We'd lost whatever stability we had the day Katarina came to me at the Seven Coins Inn.

Maybe there wasn't a plot, but Mengchang's disapproval increased when he noticed Captain Mateqai wasn't from Jing. And he was outright frowning deeply when Po instructed him to house Luc, me, and our wardens in the imperial family wing.

"The staff are still cleaning the family rooms in the emperor's wing," Mengchang said stiffly.

Po eyed his chancellor. "What are you proposing, my cousin? That we place the esteemed ambassadors from Issura in concubines' quarters?"

"They're Temple," Mengchang said. "I was not expecting clergy to reside in the palace, Your Majesty."

Well, I had to admit, if only to myself, Po had told us the truth about how his own people regarded him. If anything, he had undersold the problems he faced.

"The Issurans lost their southern border city of Tandor at this time last year," Po said coldly. "If it weren't for Chief Justice Anthea and High Brother Luc, Teodora of Issura would have lost her entire queendom. You will treat them with the esteem Queen Teodora holds them and the honor they have earned."

"Of course, Your Majesty." Mengchang bowed again. "I beg your forgiveness. No slight was intended. I shall double the housekeeping staff to make sure the rooms are ready for tonight."

"Also, Duke Lixin should be here in two days," Po added.

"We shall prepare for his arrival, Your Majesty." Another deep bow.

"Once my lady wife and I have refreshed ourselves from our long journey, please dine with us and our guests this evening."

"Yes, Your Majesty." Mengchang's annoyance lifted. Had he feared he would be dismissed due to Chengwu's assassination? Or worse, executed for failing to protect the previous emperor?

"Your Majesty, if I may be excused briefly," I said. "The high brother has had a proper audience with your Reverend Father of Light, but I must extend my own courtesies to your Reverend Mother of Balance."

Po inclined his head. "Of course, Chief Justice. Dinner shall commence a candlemark after First Evening."

I bowed. "Thank you, Your Majesty." This time, I had to bite my tongue to keep from making any flippant remarks concerning the imperial couple staying out of trouble while I was gone. As much as I worried about their safety and Luc's, etiquette needed to be observed.

And it gave me a chance to escape Sister Darys's watchful eyes.

CHAPTER 9

I could feel unseen eyes watching me while Long Feather, Jonata and I retraced our path back to the Jing home Temple of Balance. Hopefully, I would be able to meet with Justice Mei Wen as well, if only to reassure Shi Hua her friend had recovered from the injuries the young priestess had received during the demon attack on the city last winter.

When we reached the Temple of Balance, the wardens on guard at the main entrance treated us courteously. One of them raised two fingers to his mouth and blew a piercing whistle that would surely have deafened me if I stood right next to him.

A squire burst through the left door and raced down the steps to take the reins of our horses. She had to be three or four winters older than my own squire Nathan. Once again, I bit my tongue to keep from insulting the child, but she handled all three steeds with aplomb as they disappeared down the street between Balance and Knowledge.

Something must have shown on my face however. The warden with the piercing whistle said, "Do not worry, Lady Justice, Squire Yang has a talent with all animals. Your horses will be well cared for."

I smiled and inclined my head. "If it were my own Nassa, I would not be as concerned. However, the Reverend Mother of Balance in Huang He was gracious enough to allow me to borrow the mares from her Temple's stable for the journey to Chengwu. I pray the Twelve will allow me to return the horses to her in the same, if not better, health than when I left."

The warden shrugged. "Balance in all things. Ours is not to reason why any of the Twelve do as They do, Lady Justice." He gestured for me and my party to follow him up the steps.

As we stepped through the main doors, the first sense of familiarity I'd felt in nearly three months enveloped me. Hallways led left and right from the foyer. Through the second set of doors, the statue of Balance stood on Her dais on the opposite side of the courtroom. Her hood hid Her features from view, and She clasped Her hands in front of Her, holding a non-existent sword.

A podium rested in front of the statue of Balance. High windows illuminated the court for those with normal sight. The gallery was larger than the one in the courtroom in Standora, as was the defendants' box. But everything else was so similar that for a moment, homesickness nearly drowned me.

"Greetings, sister." The justice, who entered the courtroom from the door to the back hallway and the clerks' offices, spoke Issuran. A warden guided her to me.

"Greetings to you," I said in Jing. My wardens and I bowed even though she couldn't see our motions. The Reverend Mother's own staff would inform her if we were disrespectful in any way. "I am Chief Justice Anthea, the seat of the Duchy of Orrin in the Queendom of Issura. I have come to pay my respects to your Reverend Mother."

The justice pushed back her hood and smiled. The only hair on her head were her brows and lashes. Yet, there was a sense of familiarity about her.

"It's a pleasure to finally meet you in person, Chief Justice Anthea. I am Justice—"

"Mei Wen?" I blurted.

Her smile turned into a full-on grin. "Yes."

I forgot all etiquette and pulled her into a tight hug. "Shi Hua has been so worried about you! So have I and the crown prince!"

She laughed. "It was a close thing. If it weren't for Warden Yichen here, the demons would have surely killed me."

"Thank you, Warden Yichen." I bowed deeply to the warden. "Not only from myself, but from Crown Prince Po and Lady Shi Hua as well."

His cheeks glowed red at my sincere gratitude. "I serve the Temple of Balance to the best of my ability." He wrapped Mei Wen's right hand around his left elbow once again.

"If you and your wardens will follow us," Mei Wen said. "Our Reverend Mother is looking forward to meeting you as well."

The Chengzhou home Temple of Balance was indeed much larger than Issura's home Temple back in Standora. However, the general layout was much the same. The justice and staff offices were directly behind the courtroom. A single warden was stationed at several the doors we passed. However, Mei Wen and Yichen led us past the business area and to the personal quarters. Two wardens stood guard at a single door.

"Chief Justice Anthea of Issura to see Reverend Mother Xiang," Mei Wen announced in her crystal bell voice.

Both wardens at the door nodded, and the one on the right opened the door and repeated her statement.

"Come in, come in," said a woman. Her melodious tone made it difficult to determine her age.

Mei Wen and Yichen led the way inside. My wardens and I followed.

And it struck me that I'd never seen Reverend Mother Alara's personal receiving room.

A woman in clerical robes sat beside a huge fireplace. A female warden with the badge of chief stood behind the beautifully carved wood chair and slightly to the left. What struck me was the Reverend Mother was as bald as Mei Wen. I needed to ask Yin Li about the style. Last thing I needed was to stumble over a cultural issue on this mission.

The Reverend Mother rose, and both she and her chief warden bowed. "A pleasure to meet you, Chief Justice Anthea. Justice Mei Wen has spoken highly of you." When the Reverend Mother straightened, a bit of a smile tilted her mouth. "After assisting the Lady Shi Hua with her marriage trousseau, I hope you would allow our Temple to reimburse you."

I bowed in return though she couldn't see my gesture. "I appreciate your offer, Reverend Mother, but the trousseau was my wedding gift to Lady Shi Hua. No recompense is necessary."

The Reverend Mother's smile brightened. "I shall send for some tea. Would one of your wardens care to accompany my squire to the kitchen?"

Safety warred with etiquette in my mind, and I hesitated.

"My dear, you would not offend me by being cautious," Reverend Mother said gently. "Justice Mei Wen has made me aware of the issues in Issura." She sighed. "And frankly we've had our own share of problems here in Jing. If it weren't for you, Crown Prince Po would not have discovered the complicity of the School of Sorcery with the demons and Assassins Guild. Jing owes you a great debt."

"I come to serve," I said. "There is no debt, Reverend Mother. I have come to regard the Lady Shi Hua as family. All I ask is that you allow Justice Mei Wen to visit your future empress as much as her duties allow. The lady will need a confidante in her new role much as I did when I was assigned to the Balance seat in Orrin."

Mei Wen emitted a slight gasp of surprise.

However, Reverend Mother Xiang chuckled. "Fumiko didn't overestimate your shrewdness."

I quelled my shock. "You have spoken with her?"

"Don't dissemble with me, young lady." The Reverend Mother settled back in her chair. "She followed through with her complaint against Reverend Father Ogusuku. I would like to hear your side of the tale. To my knowledge, no human who entered a demon portal has ever returned from one."

"Warden Long Feather, would you please accompany Warden Yichen to fetch the Reverend Mother's tea?" I said.

"Yes, m'lady."

"Please sit, my dear." The Reverend Mother gestured in the direction of another carved chair across from her. From the position, the sharp white light of the fireplace made me squint, but I didn't dare refuse.

While we waited for our refreshments, I told Reverend Mother Xiang of my strange adventures. She didn't truthspell me, but her questions were rather thorough. And the conversation lasted through two pots of tea and a platter of almond-flavored short bread cookies.

I didn't even register the temple bells until Jonata murmured, "I beg your pardon, Chief Justice, but it's First Evening."

"I apologize, my dear," the Reverend Mother exclaimed. "Please stay for the evening meal. I still have so many questions to ask you."

"I'm afraid I cannot, Reverend Mother." I rose from the chair. "The crown prince has requested my presence at the palace. I enjoyed our conversation. I hope we can speak again."

"We will, my dear." She smiled. "I formally invite you to the evening meal tomorrow night. It will be our last chance before the Spring Rituals begin."

I bowed to her. "I accept your gracious offer, Reverend Mother."

The young squire waited with our horses at the bottom of the steps when we exited the main doors of the Temple.

I bowed to the girl. "Thank you for your assistance, Squire Yang."

Her face brightened to a lovely orange, and she bowed in return. "I am here to serve, Chief Justice."

As we rode back to the palace, I sense Long Feather holding in a round of laughter. I turned to him. "What is so funny, Warden?"

"I merely imagined the chief warden and Sivan's pleasure upon hearing my report when we return home."

"Your report?" I ground out.

"You remembered a squire's name and addressed them as such." He shrugged.

Jonata made an odd sound in her throat before she added, "I believe Little Bear's exact words were 'Do whatever you must to prevent the chief justice from starting a war with Jing. We have enough problems with the demons."

Even I had to laugh along with my wardens as our horses trotted down the Avenue of the Temples to the palace.

CHAPTER 10

My wardens and I barely had time to sponge off the road grime and dress appropriately for a state dinner. It was all my fault, and I apologized to them repeatedly.

And repeated the apology to Luc in silent speech while a palace steward escorted us to the dining room.

My fellow priest and his warden Yar had waited for us outside of our shared suite when we return from the Chengzhou Temple of Balance. When I and my wardens exited the suite once we'd changed our clothes, the palace steward stood nearby. His expression remained serene, but the power of his internal seething slammed into my mental shields.

While we followed him, I said yet again to Luc, *I'm terribly sorry for my tardiness.*

What was so blasted important you would risk embarrassing or insult-ing Quan?" Luc wouldn't look at me. He stared straight ahead, swinging on his specially designed crutches at a rapid pace.

The same pace as the palace steward's.

Reverend Mother Xiang asked for my testimony regarding the complaint Reverend Mother Fumiko filed.

Luc let out a stream of invectives in several different languages that would have made the crew of the *Mars Tranquilus* blush. Thankfully, my love didn't speak the words aloud.

Is she planning to bring formal charges against you?

No. From the murmuring voices ahead, we must be approaching our destination. *She wanted to know if Reverend Mother Fumiko exaggerated Ogusuku's behavior and actions.*

Did she question you under a truthspell?

I glanced at Luc. *No. But she wanted to know if I wished to file a charge of slander against Ogusuku and Biming.*

What did you say to her?

I told her if Ogusuku or Biming insult me when I'm not charged with escorting the Jing crown prince home for his coronation, I would consider her suggestion.

Luc made an odd sound deep in his chest as he tried to contain his physical laughter.

"Are you all right, High Brother?" Yar murmured.

Luc cleared his throat. "Just a bit of a digestive issue. Something from our last caravanserai stop didn't agree with me."

"You've probably burned away all of your digestive tissues with Cantan sauce," I said.

"Or else my sauce coated my stomach so nothing bothered me." He shot me a wicked grin. "It's been three weeks since I ran out."

The steward paused midstride and whirled to face us. "Is everything all right, Chief Justice?"

I realized we'd been speaking in Issuran, which was incredibly rude of us. I inclined my head to the steward. "We beg your forgiveness," I said in Jing. "The high brother has pointed out I should have been more attentive to the time. Your Reverend Mother of Balance had some concerns that needed to be addressed. No insult was meant to you, your liege, or your Temples."

His serene expression didn't change, but his mood lightened. I realized in all of my apologies in the last few moments I'd neglected one.

The steward nodded in return. "Etiquette may be different in your queendom than it is in our empire, but one does not keep a higher rank waiting at his own table."

"I will not forget, good sir."

He sniffed, pivoted, and continued toward the sounds of conversation. My party followed him. For once, Luc didn't make a witty aside at my expense. Neither did my wardens. I would probably pay for my moment of grace later, but for now, I accepted the quiet.

We entered a large room that would have made Queen Teodora's throne room appear provincial. The steward made no grand pronouncements of our titles upon our appearance. However, we drew the attention of the entire crowd.

A wave of curiosity from them flowed over me. Neither Luc nor I wore our clerical robes. However, our formal wear did display our Temple affiliation. Gold beads on the left chest of Luc's deerskin vest outlined the flame of Light while the silver broaches that pinned the shoulders of my dress in place formed Balance's scales. My deal with the silversmith Govind had paid off handsomely with the accessories he'd crafted for me.

Duke Mengchang approached us and bowed deeply. "Chief Justice Anthea, High Brother Luc. May I introduce you to the rest of the guests?"

I bowed in return. "We would be honored, Your Grace."

"We appreciate your hospitality." Luc bowed as well.

Mengchang led us through the crowd. Everyone was perfectly polite. Almost too polite. Now that their curiosity about our identities was satiated, a general sense of unease filled the room. While Po hadn't been formally exiled to Issura by his half-brother, he'd been gone long enough his subjects no longer viewed him as Jing. Emperor Chengwu's attempt to protect his half-brother had backfired spectacularly with the former's assassination.

I could pick out suspicion and worry as the primary emotions swirling around us, some of which was aimed specifically at our party. There were occasional flashes of shock from the other guests that Luc and I were fairly proficient in their language. But the majority of feelings were concerns over the demon attack within the walls of Chengzhou.

For once, the appearance of my eyes took a back seat in the pieces of gossip I could pick out.

Considering the majority of people were capital bureaucrats, their basic dread over the new emperor made sense. Humans loathed change when it affected their livelihood. With the switch in regimes, they feared for their positions.

Everything was politely pleasant until Mengchang led us to the heads of the various schools of philosophy. We were met with stiff postures and cold attitudes, which barely stayed on the correct side of etiquette.

Were they still upset over the demise of the School of Sorcery? The idiots from that particular center had been consorting with demons. They'd even managed to get a demon inside the city walls of Orrin without setting off the Temples' alarms.

I think it's time to cast our line into the water, I silently said to Luc.

He chuckled in the back of my mind. *Be careful. You might accidently hook a sea wolf.*

"Chief Justice, High Brother, this is Master Ma of the School of the Phoenix and the Dragon," Mengchang announced.

I forced a brilliant smile and bowed. "It is such a pleasure to meet you, Master Ma. Master Quan spoke quite highly of you during my visits with him."

My pronouncement took all the philosophical school dignitaries by surprise, including Master Ma, whose beaded moustache ends swayed with the twitch of his lips. "He was one of our most learned members and a dear friend. Do you visit with him often?"

"As much as I could for the short time he spent in our city of Orrin." I let my smile drop. "However, I fear I bring sad tidings. Death embraced Master Quan during our voyage to Jing."

Ma's eyes closed, and grief spilled from his psyche. He swallowed hard before he opened his eyes again. "Your news grieves me, but it is not unexpected."

"The Child's Curse is a terrible affliction," another master I hadn't been introduced to yet muttered.

"The Child's Curse?" I affected a confused manner.

"Yes," Master Bolin of the School of Nature said. "Master Quan's decline showed all the classic symptoms of the condition."

"He didn't have the Child's Curse." I frowned. "Master Quan was murdered."

CHAPTER 11

A member of the imperial household banged a gong with a huge hammer before anyone from the schools of philosophy could make a comment or ask a question about Master Quan's demise. The guests immediately quieted before the last echoes of the instrument died.

"His Imperial Highness, Crown Prince Po and his wife Lady Shi Hua invite you to join them for the evening meal!" the household staff member cried out.

The walls next us slid apart to reveal a larger, ornate dining room. The walls inside were covered in lacquered panels. Swatches of silk hung at intervals. Imperial guards stood at every other painted section.

Po and Shi Hua were already seated at the head of a series of humungous wooden tables arranged in a narrow U. Captains Huizhong and Mateqai stood at attention behind their charges. The arrangement was reminiscent of a Temple convocation on a much larger scale. Except I had no clue of where to sit since Luc and I were the only clergy present.

Follow Duke Mengchang, Shi Hua whispered silently inside my mind.

Thank you, my lady, I responded as the duke subtly gestured for us to follow him.

Stop being so formal, Anthea, she chided. *It's silent speech.*

Except thoughts can become deeds, I responded. *I can't make a mistake while in Jing.*

The empress-to-be giggled silently, her mental voice girlish in nature. Deep down, I pitied the young woman. She would have been an excellent leader of a Temple of Light in any place in the world.

She would have been an excellent leader anywhere.

Was that why the Twelve had seen fit to condemn her to a throne in the middle of the fight to save the human race from extinction?

And then it registered where the duke was leading us.

He stopped at the bend to the left of Shi Hua and bowed to us. "High Brother." He gestured at the chair closest to Shi Hua. "Chief Justice." He indicated the chair to Luc's left.

A glance at the other dinner guests hinted that we should remain standing. Yin Li had taught us a bit about Jing etiquette during our voyage across the Peaceful Sea, but we didn't have much chance to practice the formalities on the journey from the coast to the capital. I was grateful for the pointers in the middle of the welcome dinner.

Once all the guests were in their places, Po rose to his feet. "Thank you for coming, my friends. Please be seated."

No one moved until he lowered himself to his throne-like chair. Then as one the rest of the guests sat. Luc handed his crutches to Warden Yar. Much attention was on him with a whisper of surprise emanating from those people who hadn't met him yet as he maneuvered in front of his assigned chair and sat.

I didn't have to look behind me to feel our wardens take places between the imperial guards behind us. We weren't the only ones with security personnel, but there was only one guard for each noble and their family. From Yin Li's lessons, this was highly unusual.

What was Po's purpose in allowing his nobles to bring guards to his table? To reassure them? Or to test the noble's loyalty by seeing if they would use their own people against him?

Po struck a smaller gold gong next to him. On that cue, servants paraded into the dining room with huge steaming pots. They ladled what smelled like a savory soup into the bowls in front of the guests.

I surreptitiously watched the other guests. As I'd hoped, Master Ma and those who had been within hearing range of my revelation concerning Master Quan's death passed along the tidbit to the other diners. Many of the Jing nobles and sorcerers glanced at me. Some with speculative expressions. Others with worry. But a token few eyed me with suspicion.

I think your plan is working too well. Luc pretended to focus on his soup.

I'm not trying to kill two geese with a single sling stone, I chided. *But I do believe the murders of Master Quan and Emperor Chengzhou are connected.*

That's assuming Po is correct the School of Sorcery was behind his father's condition. The Healers Guild and High Sister Mya could only say it was a spell that killed him. Luc turned to Shi Hua and answered her question. "I believe this is the best meal I've eaten since we left Orrin."

"What do you think of our cuisine, Lady Justice," the man seated to my left asked in careful and heavily accented Issuran.

"Thank you for the effort to learn my language . . ." I examined him as I smiled. I hadn't been introduced to him by Duke Mengchang. Like most

Jing men, he wore his hair in a top knot with jewels dangling from the tips of his moustache.

"Lord Jia Hao." He inclined his head.

I switched to the Jing tongue. "A pleasure to meet you, my lord. If you don't mind, may we please use your own language for this dinner. I do not wish to disrespect the crown prince."

Jia Hao nodded politely. "As you wish, Lady Justice."

"And to answer your initial question, I enjoy trying new delicacies." I dipped the ceramic spoon into the hot soup and tasted the broth and meat. "This is delicious. What is it? I don't recognize the meat."

"Turtle soup." He ate a spoonful from his own bowl. "It's considered good luck." He leaned closer. "The palace cook will probably serve swallow's nest soup for the coronation. A very rare delicacy that's only made during the Spring Rituals." He smiled. "Which is why most heirs to the throne schedule their coronations for this time of year."

"I don't think he chose this time of year on purpose," I murmured.

"No, he didn't." Jia Hao stared at his bowl. "That's one thing the crown prince and I have in common."

A hint of grief leaked from the lord. I hesitated a moment before I said, "He never believed he'd be in this position with the births of his nephews."

"And I never believed my sister would die on the same day as her husband and children," he said sadly.

Air caught in my lungs, but I forced out the words. "Your sister was the former empress?"

"Yes." Jia Hao met my horrified stare with his own glare. "And I'll do anything to make her murderers pay."

Chapter 12

The rest of the meal passed far more sociably after Lord Jia Hao's pronouncement. He quickly changed the subject to our sea voyage from Issura during the late winter. I kept him entertained with some of the more amusing aspects of the trip, such as Yin Shang's fascination with sailing.

I had a strong suspicion Po and Shi Hua had Duke Mengchang sit Jia Hao next to me to analyze any potential trouble from him. However, the young lord only exuded an expected level of grief at his family loss despite his pleasant demeanor after his declaration.

He explained each of the dishes to me and how to eat them properly. The foods were more exquisite than the simple fare at the caravanserai and definitely more flavorful than the dried and salted rations during our sea voyage.

"What do you miss in Orrin at this time of year?" he asked.

"I—don't know." I chuckled. "I was on circuit for the first ten years after my ordination. My partner and I usually spent the Spring Rituals in one of the small mountain villages on our route." I left out the part where I deliberately planned to avoid Orrin and Nastine during the holidays. "And last year, we were trapped in Tandor during the siege. I and the other Orrin seats spent most of the Ritual week arranging for housing for the Tandoran refugees."

"If I may ask . . ." Jia Hao started.

I nodded. "Please feel free to inquire about anything."

Jia Hao lowered his voice. "What is it like? Actually battling a demon, I mean."

"Difficult." I shook my head as I sought the best words in his language. "Even with magic. They are faster than a Gray Mountain panther. Stronger than the white bears of the northern ice fields." A vision of Warden Tyra protecting me when the demons breached the city. High Sister Beatrice giving her life to hold the Death spells to destroy the demons. My own grandfather. All of those memories stabbed me with old grief. "You're not the only one who has lost people to them. If there's anything I miss at home, it's the people I've lost to this war."

Beneath the table, Luc squeezed my thigh in reassurance. Of course, he felt my pain.

"I apologize, Lady Justice," Lord Jia Hao murmured. "I did not mean to cause you distress."

"You didn't, my lord." I forced a smile. "It's the demons who have. Therefore, I understand your feelings regarding your own losses."

He nodded and dropped the subject as the servants laid bowls containing the last course of the state dinner before us.

We had returned to our suite long enough for Warden Jonata to light the kindling in the fireplace against the chill night when there was a knock on the suite door. Warden Long Feather answered, and the imperial guard announced Duke Mengchang.

"Please forgive the late hour." He bowed and straightened. From his coloring, his news bothered him. "The crown prince and his lady wife request the presence of Chief Justice Anthea and High Brother Luc to accompany them in breaking their fast and during their inspection of the palace household afterward tomorrow morning."

Luc and I exchanged looks. We didn't need silent speech to know why the duke was miffed or Po's reasons for wanting us with him.

"Unless you are pressed for time, Your Grace, would you like to join us for a small glass of Pana wine?" I asked.

My invitation startled him. "You have Pana wine?"

"It's our private supply." Luc inclined his head. "We'd be honored to entertain a noble the crown prince holds in such high esteem."

Mengchang's obvious desire for a portion of the prized wine and Luc's flattery mollified the duke's hurt feelings. "I would be honored to join you."

Warden Yar retrieved one of our last two bottles. While he poured the wine, Luc and I sat with Mengchang before the fire. Thankfully, Long Feather had already positioned my chair so I wouldn't squint at the brightness of the fire due to my odd sight. Few outside of my Temple household knew my peculiar vision was affected by heat.

"Did the crown prince explain why he wished us to accompany him and Lady Shi Hua tomorrow?" I asked.

"Yes," the duke replied stiffly. "Is it true you can see demons no matter what form they take?"

I nodded, but I wasn't about to list the exception to my odd sight. "But that's probably not his only reason. Do you know what a skinwalker is?"

"A skinwalker is a human sorcerer dealing in demon magic," he said.

"I can also see them as well." I accepted the goblet Yar handed to me. "Thank you, Warden." I faced Mengchang again. "In some ways, they're far more dangerous. Demons are simply hungry. Skinwalkers combine the worst attributes of human and demon."

"I don't remember that item of information during my childhood lessons." He sipped the Pana red. "I wish we had the soil to produce such wine."

"You know your horticulture?" Luc said.

Mengchang nodded. "My duchy brews a hearty beer and plum wine. However, I promise not to bore you with the details. My eldest daughter manages our family interests while I serve the emperor."

Again, I braced myself as I endured Mengchang's grief. It relieved me to know it was honest grief for a family member and not fear at losing his position.

"I hope you aren't planning to leave the capital after the coronation ceremony," I said.

He blinked, and surprise muted his pain. "That is not my decision to make, Chief Justice."

"Nor is it mine, Your Grace," I replied gently. "However, the crown prince needs people he can trust to assist him in his service to Jing."

His eyes narrowed. "Is this the true reason you invited me for a cup of your wine? To test my loyalty? Did you already lay a truthspell on me?"

"The answer is no to all of your questions," I said. "The crown prince was trapped with the high brother and me in Tandor. He knows firsthand the speed and destructive force even a small division of demons can inflict. He and his guards were instrumental in the plan to evacuate the city. Only by Thief's grace did we save as many citizens as we did."

Mengchang's chin lifted. "I already know the ferocity of our foes. And I know my failures very well."

"Someone within the palace let those demons in," I said softly. "Neither the Lady Shi Hua or I believe it is you, but we ask your assistance in investigating the matter."

"The crown prince rules here," Mengchang snapped. "Not the Temples."

"And the nobles and clergy working together are the only reason we didn't lose our entire queendom," I replied. "Crown Prince Po hopes to unite all the factions of Jing in order to do the same."

The tension eased from the duke's shoulders. "I will consider your words, Chief Justice." He swallowed the rest of his wine before he rose. "However, I reserve the right to give my answer to my liege."

"Of course." I inclined my head.

"Good night, Chief Justice, High Brother."

"Good night, Your Grace," Luc and I said in unison.

Once the duke departed, Luc laid a ward on the receiving room of our suite. "Opinions?"

"The duke hasn't discovered how the demons entered the palace, and he's worried he will be blamed for Emperor Chengwu's death," Jonata said.

"The chief justice's compassion is improving," Long Feather volunteered.

"Tomorrow, you and the chief justice will need to address the crown prince's favoritism toward you, High Brother. It will not be seen gracefully by any Jing citizen." Yar rarely said anything, but when he did, I listened.

And the warden was totally correct in his analysis.

Luc nodded. "That was one of my concerns as well." He eyed me. "What are your thoughts on the matter, m'lady?"

I sighed. "I have more fun playing Mill than I do with these political games. But I share Yar's concerns. I'm praying to the Twelve our esteemed crown prince isn't setting us up to take the fall for the loss of his brother."

Until that moment, I hadn't realized my internal concern. The fact that none of my companions disputed my point of view compounded my worries.

CHAPTER 13

A year and a half ago, I didn't trust the former Jing ambassador by even a fingertip. The Siege of Tandor had changed our relationship, but had he counted on our nation's mutual needs in order to eliminate two of the few clergy Queen Teodora trusted? Part of me wished I had my own distance speaker in order to ask the queen for more information.

Jonata took the night watch despite being on horseback since dawn yesterday and woke us in plenty of time before we had to meet the royal couple for the morning meal. I didn't like leaving her in our suite alone, but the poor woman needed the sleep. She asked me to put a protective charm on her nose ring before we departed. I also warded her sleeping chamber before we left as an extra precaution.

The same steward who guided us to last night's banquet led us to a different section of the palace. From the number of imperial guards, this was a section foreigners wouldn't normally be allowed.

We followed him to a shaded outdoor patio. It reminded me of the garden gazebo at the Jing Embassy back in Orrin. The only difference was the types of plants. Plum trees were starting to bloom, lending a delicious scent to the morning air. While the slight breeze was cool, it had a hint of a warmer day to come.

Like at the banquet, Po and Shi Hua were already seated, nor did they rise. Huizhong and Mateqai stood behind their respective charges.

The steward bade us to stop. The imperial guards on the patio checked Luc and I for weapons.

I was loathe to leave our swords and knives with Jonata. I had to remind myself this was a diplomatic assignment. However, the demons had already breached the palace once to the former emperor's detriment. I couldn't fault the guards for trying to keep the new emperor alive.

But were we going to pay for the imperial guards' caution with our own lives?

The guards checked Long Feather and Yar's weapons before they instructed our wardens to remain at least fifty paces from the edge of the patio.

"And how are you and we supposed to protect our charges if we are all standing that far away?" Yar protested.

Captain Huizhong stalked up to us. The imperial guards snapped to attention.

"The crown prince wishes the two wardens to accompany his guests," Huizhong said.

"But Captain, we cannot allow weapons near the prince and his lady," the lieutenant complained.

"Use some of Balance's logic," Huizhong said. "If Wardens Long Feather or Yar wished to harm Crown Prince Po or Lady Shi Hua, they could have more easily done so during our voyage home and dumped their bodies overboard."

The guards nervously eyed Luc, me, and our wardens. I chewed on the tip of my tongue to keep from making a snide comment that steel wasn't the only way to kill a human. I didn't count on my love to do something worse.

"If we raise a hand against the crown prince, you would be well within your rights to kill us and collect the bounty on the chief justice," Luc said. "The problem will be collecting the reward from the Assassins Guild or the demons."

Huizhong chuckled. "Well, Lieutenant, which side do you choose? Though I will point out from experience, the Assassins Guild, the demons, and their renegade allies have tried more times than I have fingers and toes to kill Chief Justice Anthea."

The poor lieutenant looked and felt thoroughly confused. "B-but she's unarmed?"

"And that's when she's the most dangerous," Huizhong murmured.

The lieutenant turned to me, his skin gleaming a brilliant reddish orange beneath his helmet. A yellow bead of perspiration trickled from his forehead to his nose. He executed a formal bow. The rest of the nearby imperial guards followed suit.

"I beg your forgiveness, Lady Justice," he said in a conciliatory tone. "Our new emperor chooses his allies well."

"Apology accepted." I bowed in return. "I have no taste for killing simply for the sake of killing."

Huizhong gestured for us to accompany him.

As we followed his brisk stride across the patio, I silently asked, *Are you trying to get me killed, Captain?*

Not at all, Lady Justice. Huizhong grinned. *I need the people under my command alive to fight the demons, not stupidly throwing away their lives attempting to kill you.*

As irritated as I was with him, I had to laugh along with Po's captain.

Both Po and Shi Hua were also smiling when we greeted them. "Are you upsetting my guards, Chief Justice?" he teased.

"It wasn't me," I said as I took my seat. "I'm afraid it was the high brother and Captain Huizhong who used me as a cudgel to knock some sense into your guards."

"I sincerely doubt either man threatened the security," Shi Hua murmured as she poured tea for us. She glanced at Mateqai with a mischievous expression. "And do not worry, my captain tested all the food and drink."

Luc raised his right eyebrow. "That's a good way to lose your captain of the empress's guard."

Po handed the platter of sausages to me. The grilled meats smelled of cinnamon, cloves, and . . . licorice? I must have made an expression at the odd mix because he just had to make a comment.

"Really, Chief Justice?" His lips twitched, which sent the gold beads at the ends of his moustache swinging. "I've been eating Issuran fare for eight years, and you dare to turn up your nose at my culture's cuisine?"

"Considering Issuran cooking is an amalgam of several different cultures. I was surprised to smell something familiar." I placed two of the sausages on my plate before passing them to Luc. "However, I don't believe we've used Briton licorice to flavor our meats."

"It's anise," Shi Hua said. "The taste is similar to Briton licorice, but anise is originally from Kemet."

If I thought last night's banquet was delicious, the simple fare of sausage, rice, and stewed dried fruit was even more delightful. To my surprise, Po spooned portions into bowls for the four men guarding us.

"My personal thanks to you, Captains and Wardens, for returning my lady wife and me home safely." Po sat, and Huizhong raised his bowl.

Those actions were the only reason the crossbow bolt that whizzed over my head didn't kill either man.

CHAPTER 14

✦

I automatically froze time in the courtyard. Huizhong's wooden bowl with the crossbow bolt sticking out of it hung in midair, as did the bowls of Mateqai, Yar, and Long Feather. Shi Hua crouched, no doubt planning to leap on her husband to protect him. The slight tingle of Light magic and position of Luc's hands meant he'd started to raise wards about the platform.

The rest of the guards in the courtyard showed no sign of motion in progress. Only the lieutenant, who Huizhong had gently reprimanded only moments ago, had any realization of the danger from the widening of his eyes as he looked at his captain.

I rose to my feet and examined our surroundings.

There. On a second-floor balcony directly across from Po. The shooter crouched behind the stone balustrade. The crossbow in the masked assailant's hand was already cocked for a second shot at the crown prince.

I'd gotten more proficient with time freeze spells thanks to the continued attempts on my life and those around me, but I couldn't hold it long enough to find my way through the palace to the assassin. Not to mention explaining my actions to the imperial guards inside who weren't frozen.

Even if I borrowed one of Long Feather's throwing knives, I couldn't be guaranteed to hit the assassin at this distance. I looked around wildly. An imperial archer stood next to one of the nearby dragon statues.

I raced over to him and somehow managed to remove her bow and quiver from her stiff body without knocking her over. I ran back to the shaded patio. Both Shi Hua and Luc were better shots than me. After a moment of indecision, I pulled the empress-to-be upright before I concentrated and carefully excised her from my time-freeze spell.

"Wh-what?" Shi Hua looked wildly around her. "An assassin—"

"Is frozen in my spell." I pointed toward the figure peeking through the stone rails. "Can you hit them from here?"

"Hold your spell as long as you can. I have a better idea." She took the bow and quiver from me. From the look on her face, I almost pitied the assassin's fate. "Take care of our men."

While Shi Hua ran across the court, I lowered Po to the wooden platform on which we dined as gently as possible. Unfortunately, the men's mass was still the same whether time was moving or not.

I tipped Luc off his chair and shoved him under the table. I lined Yar and Long Feather along the bottom support beams. By the time I reached for Mateqai, Shi Hua had removed her silk overtunic and skirt and was climbing the stone wall up to the balcony.

When I placed Huizhong's bowl on the table, I sniffed the bolt. Bitter almonds. Poison. I sighed. Thief was definitely watching out for the crown prince, his captain, and me this morning.

The physical exertion coupled with the mental effort to hold the spell ground against my overnight rest. I dropped next to Po's captain of the guard. Sweat poured down my face and torso. I didn't have the energy to check on my friend.

"Shi Hua, I can't hold this much longer!"

"I've got her! Release your spell!"

The relief at releasing the spell was so marvelous I fell over and lay beside Luc. Shouting erupted from the imperial guards. A higher-pitched shriek silenced everyone before the laughter started.

Luc blinked. "What am I doing on the floor?"

Behind me, someone poked me in the back. "Anthea, what is going on?"

"None of you get up until the lieutenant says it's all clear," I ordered.

As I finished my statement, the lieutenant crouched next to us, a wide smile on his face. "I believe it's now safe for you, Your Highness, Captain Huizhong, Honored Guest."

"Long Feather!" Po barked.

My own warden assisted me to my feet while Yar did the same for Luc. When I got a look at what Shi Hua had done, I burst out laughing as well.

The empress-to-be had stripped the assassin, who turned out to be female, and used a rope to hang our assailant upside down from the balcony. I followed Po as he stalked over to the assassin. Meanwhile, his wife emerged from the shrubbery to the right of the balcony.

She dropped the assassin's clothing and accoutrements on the lawn at his feet. "No, identifying papers or other marks on her, my husband. However, she carries a vile of southern blue and her bolts have been dipped in it. I also removed her false tooth." She reached into a pocket sewn into her undertrousers and produced a small-bag stained with pink blood.

"Why don't you dress for our guests, my love?" He smiled at her before he turned to Huizhong. "Send one of your men to the Temple of Balance with my regards to Reverend Mother Xiang. Tell her we have a case of attempted murder here at the palace."

Po eyed the assassin still hanging upside down though she'd stopped her insane shrieking. "In the meantime, let us turn our unwanted guest upright. The Reverend Mother won't be able to question her if she dies of a brainstorm.

Less than half a candlemark later, Reverend Mother Xiang arrived. To my surprise, Justice Mei Wen and another justice I hadn't met along with Reverend Father Jin of Light and two of his priests accompanied the Reverend Mother along with full squads of Balance and Light wardens.

After the demon attack near the beginning of winter, I couldn't blame Xiang for coming fully armed as if she were on a bear hunt. The Balance and Light clergy quickly separated everyone in the courtyard and began questioning us.

The junior Balance priestess who had accompanied the Reverend Mother and Mei Wen introduced herself to me as Justice Aihan. I sat patiently while Brother Bolin laid the double spell to prevent a witness from lying. I had to say Justice Aihan was quite efficient and thorough in her questioning. And Balance bless her, she didn't step into any diplomatic issues by making the wrong inquiry.

Once she was finished and Brother Bolin dissolved the truthspell, Aihan said, "May I ask a personal question?"

I resisted the urge to smile as she rubbed her swollen belly. She may not be able to see my face, but Bolin could, and it was very obvious from his solicitous behavior toward her that he was the father of her babe. "I'll answer it if I can."

"Or if it doesn't violate any previous sworn oaths," Aihan added.

I did laugh at that comment. "Of course."

"How did you stop time in that large of space for such a relatively long period?"

"Too much practice, I fear." I sighed. "And too much desperation on my part."

"I do not understand, Chief Justice," she murmured.

My stomach rumbled, and a wave of nausea had me bent over double.

"Chief Justice, are you—" Bolin stepped closer to assist me.

I waved him off. "I expended too much energy on an empty stomach this morning, Brother."

Aihan held up her hand. "Warden Chao Xing, please fetch some tea and rice for the chief justice."

The nausea passed on the promise of some food, and I straightened. "My apologies, Justice Aihan, Brother Bolin."

Bolin chuckled. "There's nothing to apologize for Chief Justice. Nearly every priestess of child-bearing years has endured pregnancy sickness since the order to increase breeding was issued last year."

"I wish that was my case as well." I'm sure my own grin was rueful. "Alas, my issues are more mundane. To answer your original question, Justice Aihan, I've been in too many situations where the skinwalker and demon numbers were overwhelming. I've had to stretch myself and my abilities."

"Our Reverend Mother insisted that all of us at Balance read Chief Justice Elizabeth's account of the takeover of Tandor and the subsequent siege." Aihan tilted her head to the right as she considered her next question. "May I request the Reverend Mother's permission for you to teach those justices currently in Chengzhou some of your techniques? When you have some free moments, of course," she added hastily.

"I would be honored to share my knowledge with you and your sisters." I inclined my head though she couldn't see me. Or perhaps she viewed the world through Bolin's eyes or her wardens' as I sometimes did with Luc and our wardens.

Warden Chao Xing reentered the room carrying a tray with a hot tea pot and bowl. My stomach rumbled again when the steam carried the scent of freshly cooked rice.

"Is there anything else you need from me, Lady Justice?" I asked.

"No." Aihan inclined her head. "You have our gratitude for your cooperation, Chief Justice."

I rose. "I'll take that tray if you don't mind, Warden."

Chao Xing blushed as she reluctantly handed it to me. "Do you need any assistance, m'lady?"

I laughed. "The rumors are true, Warden. I can see. However, I'm starving, and the justice and brother have more people to question. Good day, everyone."

The members of the Jing Temples really needed to accept my presence instead of gawking at me. I had been on circuit for ten years, and most villagers never became accustomed to my red eyes, but my lack of a warden to guide me was a totally different situation. Or rather, that was the tiny lie I told myself.

I strode out of the room and into warm sunshine. Imperial guards milled around the grounds as if unsure what to do. One squad of Balance and Light wardens watched our assassin as she swung from the balcony. Her torso had been raised to be level with her ankles so the blood wouldn't pool in her skull and cause a brainstorm. The swaying of her body was caused by her testing her restraints. At least, she was silent now.

Personally, I would have ordered her to be placed in spell-threaded shackles and locked in the Balance gaol. But I had no true jurisdiction in Jing. I prayed to the Twelve the Temple leaders listened to both Po and Shi Hua and heeded their advice.

I claimed a decorative bench and set the tray beside me. The sun quickly heated my robes while I nibbled on the sweetened rice and sipped tea. I pushed back my hood and closed my eyes, enjoying the moment of respite.

"Would you like to try some sausages?"

I opened my eyes, made a face at the emperor-to-be, and switched to Issuran. "I truly hope you're not making an improper suggestion, Your Majesty."

"Me?" he answered in kind. "Never. I don't wish either you or my wife to practice your blade work upon my person." He grinned and sat on the other side of my tray before he handed me the dish of sausages.

As I examined them, I noticed bits were missing from each link.

"Do not fear, m'lady," he said. "Lady Shi Hua sent her captain to fetch freshly cooked sausages, and he tested them for you."

I laughed. "Captain Mateqai is going to gain a large belly at the rate he's tasting everyone's food."

Po exhaled gustily. "He won't be at the rate the assassins are coming after the entire Bao line."

A shiver ran through me. "What happened?"

"A messenger arrived while you were being questioned," he said softly.

He stared at the woman hanging from his palace's balcony. "Duke Lixin was assassinated on his way here."

"Poison?"

Po nodded.

No wonder he went along with my switch to the Issuran language. This news cast more of a pall over the morning.

"His wife and children?"

"Alive. They are continuing on their way here once his ashes have cooled. The duchess will, of course, petition to be her eldest's regent."

I grimaced at the thought of the flighty Duchess Jia managing her husband's holdings. That assumed we'd all survive through the Spring Rituals and the coronation. For an instant, I almost suggested we head back to Huang He, board the *Mars Tranquilus*, and return to Orrin. But neither of us would do so. Duty was too ingrained in our being.

"I didn't take any of this seriously until this morning." His voice held a bittersweet note.

"This? What else happened?" I took a bite of sausage. It's spicy-sweet flavor matched our moods.

"My new role as emperor." He stared turn to me. "Shi Hua told me she's pregnant."

"Congratulations," I replied.

He turned to face me with a sly smile. "When did she start showing to your sight?"

I chuckled. "Right before we docked at Huang He."

His sly smile turned into a full-on grin. "Good to know you learned not to announce the news before the mother tells the father."

I smiled in return. "I may be slow, but I eventually learn my lessons." I nibbled a bit more sausage before I said, "Did she tell you before or after she insisted on being present at our potential assassin's interrogation?"

"She told me last night, which is why you and the high brother were invited to break your fast with us."

One of the imperial guards shouted in alarm. Po and I both turned our attention to the group guarding our potential assassin in time to watch her drop to the stone beneath her.

CHAPTER 15

I dropped the sausage bowl and raced over to the wardens surrounding the prone woman. She stared blankly at the sky, a crossbow bolt sticking out of her chest. Blood pooled about her head where it smashed against the flagstone. I looked up at the surrounding walls. A second bolt still quivered where it struck a trellis with a vine I couldn't identify. That would have been the bolt that slice through the ropes holding the assassin. Between the two projectiles, I stared at the roof lines and calculated angles in my head.

"The bolts came from the west roof," I shouted in Jing. "Shut down the main entrance to the palace grounds. The second assassin is still in the complex!"

No one moved until Po roared, "Do as she said! NOW!"

All of the wardens but one scrambled towards the west side of the courtyard. The lieutenant who'd thrown a fuss about Yar and Long Feather's weapons glanced as Captain Huizhong.

"Do as the emperor said," he snapped. "Shut down the palace entrance."

Half of the imperial guards took off for the main entrance with the lieutenant leading the charge.

Po turned to me and switched back to Issuran. "While I appreciate your wisdom and your strategic acumen, you do not have jurisdiction here, Anthea."

A few choice Cantan slurs Luc had taught me over the years flew through my mind. But spouting them at a foreign leader, no matter our personal relationship, would not help the situation. I simply hated it when Po was right about something. And in this case, he was totally correct.

I bowed my head, mainly so he couldn't see my expression. "I beg your forgiveness, Your Highness. It shall not happen again."

"Good," he muttered.

When I straightened, the one remaining Balance warden approached me and bowed. "Forgive the intrusion, my prince, but I have been commanded to watch out for Chief Justice Anthea until her own warden returns from their questioning."

At the same moment, I felt someone strike the ward I'd placed on Jonata's sleeping chamber. *Warden, are you all right?*

Let me out, m'lady, she replied. *One of the stewards and two maids are here. Something about an assassination attempt.*

Everyone is fine except the assassin herself. I closed my eyes and murmured the spell to release Jonata from the chamber. I hadn't meant to trap her. My second mistake of the morning. *Tell the steward to guide you to the private courtyard where Crown Prince Po planned to break his fast.*

At her silent acknowledgement, I turned to the Jing warden. "I appreciate your offer. However, Warden Jonata is on her way down from our suite. She wasn't here when the incident occurred."

"Very well, Lady Justice." The Jing warden nodded sharply. "I will leave when she arrives."

"Was Jonata awake all night?" Po snapped.

I should have known he would have deduced the reason she wasn't with me this morning, but there was a limit to my patience with diplomatic dung. I glared at him. "Your Highness, after everything that's happened since your family's deaths, do you really believe either my wardens or your guards will take any chances with our safety?"

He leaned away from the vehemence in my voice, but his skin quickly shifted from yellow to orange, and irritation flowed from him. "Mind your tone, Chief Justice."

"I will when you stop criticizing my wardens for performing their jobs," I spat.

Stop! Both of you!

Po and I jumped at Shi Hua's silent reprimand.

We have enough problems without you two adding to the pile.

Yes, my love, Po replied.

Anthea? Shi Hua said in a warning tone.

We will behave, I replied.

"Talk to Reverend Mother Xiang and Reverend Father Jin," I said aloud as softly as I could. "They will help you question the palace staff. I want to offer my services, but you don't need accusations of requiring foreign aid to take the throne."

"Understood, Lady Justice." Po's smirk was back. He strode over to Huizhong to discuss—whatever they needed to discuss.

"You understand the blade edge the prince stands on," the Jing warden murmured.

I turned to her. "How bad are the whispers among the nobles?"

"It's not just the nobles," she said. "The other philosophical schools still don't believe the School of Sorcery dealt in demon magic."

"Is that why they were at last night's banquet?"

She nodded. "Unfortunately, the argument between Reverend Father Biming and the prince over the prince's lady wife is being used against the Temples."

I shook my head in disgust. "So, everyone holds the prince's minor Thief talent against him, but they're angered he married a woman with Light talent?"

A slight smile tilted the corners of the warden's mouth. "Illogical, isn't it?"

I snorted in disgust, but said nothing. The Cantan obscenities were still on the tip of my tongue. Had Reverend Father Biming spread the rumor of his and Po's split over Shi Hua? Or was someone else using their feud to further isolate the Temples from the rest of the Jing population? The Jing leaders were playing far too many games at a time when their unity was the only way to ensure their survival and that of the human race.

For the first time in my life, I found myself wishing I had a better relationship with Reverend Mother Alara. Or that High Brother Kam were still alive. I could use some excellent advice in this moment.

Luc and I weren't scheduled to speak with Duke White Eagle and the queen's new distance speaker Lord Ayatulutul until tomorrow night. And I wasn't sure if we'd survive until then.

CHAPTER 16

As a precaution, Captain Huizhong politely requested the entire Issuran party to remain in our suite while the palace was searched and the staff were questioned. I couldn't argue with his precautions. I would have insisted on doing the same with the Jing diplomats if our positions were reversed. It still rankled that I was not included in the investigation.

Unfortunately, it also meant the five of us drove each other mad as the morning and then the afternoon wore on. I discovered Yar liked to practice knife throwing when he was under duress, which interfered with my pacing. Luc, who was trying to read, threatened to throw us both off our suite's balcony. The meditating Long Feather volunteered his services to Luc when there was a knock on our main door.

The three wardens immediately drew their swords, even Jonata, who had been catnapping the afternoon away.

At Yar's nod, Long Feather approached the door and unlocked it. "Yes?"

"Sister Darys of the Skoloti Tribes wishes to speak with Chief Justice Anthea," the imperial guard outside our suite announced.

Long Feather looked at me, and I nodded.

"Please enter, Sister." Long Feather stepped back.

Darys entered with two of her own wardens. She inclined her head. "Thank you for seeing me, Chief Justice."

As soon as Long Feather shut the door, she dropped the polite pretense. "Chief Justice, would you mind warding the room while we speak?"

"Not at all. Please have a seat, Sister." I gestured at the free chair beside Luc.

She lowered herself onto the chair's cushion while I circled the room and cast my warding spell. I was curious about what she didn't want the Jing guards to know. But I also noticed her wardens and ours eyeing each other with suspicion. When I finished, I said, "Sheathe your swords, Wardens."

Our trio reluctantly did so. My order relieved the Thief wardens accompanying Darys to the point they removed their hands from their own blade hilts, but the wardens' unspoken truce didn't settle my own nerves. However, more bloodshed would not make my day any better.

I sat down in the chair across from Darys and Luc and waited for her to speak.

"Please tell me no one was harmed in this morning's attempt on Crown Prince Po," she practically pleaded with me.

"Only the assassin herself." I smirked. "While Lady Shi Hua was careful in the woman's apprehension, someone considered our prisoner a liability and shot her with a crossbow from the roof. That's the reason for the current commotion."

Darys relaxed in her chair. "Thank the Twelve, the prince was uninjured. We were hearing all kinds of rumors from the staff."

"Gossip seems to be a major occupation in Jing," Luc said sourly.

"Far more than it should," Darys agreed. "What do either of you know about these schools of philosophy?"

"You mean there's something Thief doesn't know?" I teased.

"There are things we all need to find out, and there are things I need to share with you," she replied evenly. "Is it true Emperor Chengwu imprisoned his father rather than see him executed for treason along with the rest of the School of Sorcery?"

"That is our understanding," Luc said. "Why?"

"Could Master Wu be retaliating against the Bao line for his imprisonment?" she asked.

Luc and I exchanged glances before I said, "What makes you think the master is behind the death of Duke Lixin and the attacks against Crown Prince Po?"

"Duke Lixin is dead?" The three Skoloti women appeared shocked at the news.

"Unfortunately." I shrugged. "His murder could be due to his support of the crown prince. Various factions have been trying to eliminate Crown Prince Po since Emperor Chengwu's birth."

"I was only aware of Prince Pu's death," Darys stammered.

Luc and I exchanged looks again, but we didn't need silent speech to share our mutual shock.

I turned back to Darys and cleared my throat. "Does the crown prince know about his cousin Pu's death?"

Darys looked over her right shoulder at her warden. "Antiope?"

Warden Antiope's face and hands shifted from gold to orange, but it was embarrassment that prickled against my shields. "This morning, I went out into the city to buy jade for my younger sister who is a jeweler. I saw Jing bureaucrats raising second white flags. When I asked who had passed, I was told either Prince Pu had died or to mind my own business."

"This news concerning Duke Lixin's fate disturbs me," Darys said. "I fear it will be used against the crown prince."

"He is not a stupid man," Luc said.

I scowled. "And he definitely knows better than to assassinate his rivals for the throne so openly."

"The demons need the renegades to make inroads in the various centers of human authority in order to bring them down." Darys rubbed her palms together, and I had a glimpse of greenish-yellow sweat on them. What was she so nervous about? "If the School of Sorcery was demon dealing—"

"They were," Luc and I said in disgusted unison.

"I must ask your evidence." Again, her expression was more of a pleading one than demanding.

"Somehow, Master Wu or one of his associates had Arturo, the former captain of an Issuran ship the *Mars Tranquilus*, bring a demon egg to the Jing embassy in the city of Orrin the week before the Day of Death nearly eighteen months ago." A shudder ran through me at the memory of the captain's body, literally frozen in his cabin despite the fair autumn weather. "During our investigation into Captain Arturo's death, we discovered the crown prince's staff sorcerer had a demon with him inside the embassy. The sorcerer also used the egg in an attempt to kill Lady Shi Hua. Unfortunately, we never discovered if Arturo himself was a renegade or was tricked, but the rest of the crew of the *Mars Tranquilus* were cleared of any wrongdoing."

Darys's exhalation whistled her dismay. Even her wardens appeared appalled at my revelation.

"Even worse, Reverend Father Biming chased a part of a cache of demon eggs from the School of Sorcery to the Northern Long Continent a few weeks later," Luc added. "Those were hatched right across the Issuran border. That's how we and Cant lost the cities of Tandor and Rambla. I'm sure High Brother Shang told you what happened with the remainder of the cache from the School of Sorcery."

Darys nodded. "It was only a small force of demons chasing him and what remained of the Jing Conflict army. Our clergy and warrior destroyed the demons. Our own search parties found very little trace of the invaders though the tracks of the Jing survivors were obvious."

"How far did your Wildlings backtrack the path of the remaining Conflict party and the demons?" I asked.

She pursed her lips for a moment. "I lied to the crown prince because I didn't want to start a war between the Skoloti and the Jing. I apologize for lying to you in the process, Chief Justice, High Brother."

"Leave aside our national leaders' idiocy for the moment," Luc said. "How far did you backtrack?"

"We followed the scents and trails to where High Brother Shang said Reverend Father Chen made his last stand."

I didn't blame the Skoloti Temples for entering Jing territory to investigate. For all they knew, the entire Jing nation could have been destroyed. But my empathy for the breach would not calm some of Po's retainers, which was another reason Reverend Father Feng remained silent about the matter.

Anxiety flowed from Darys. Whether it was concern about our reactions or fear that we would inform Po, I couldn't tell.

She swallowed hard before she continued her story. "From what we could piece together, the demons who weren't killed in Chen's boobytrap split up. Half headed north into the Xiongnu Confederation. The other half headed southeast to Chengzhou. We also split our forces to follow each path." She bowed her head for a moment. "We were less than an hour too late to stop the attack on the city. However, in hindsight, the demons sent to Chengzhou were a decoy for whatever was happening within the city's innermost wall."

Luc and I exchanged looks. The slightest tilt of his head said he believed her. However, I didn't like her efforts to evade a truthspell and proper questioning. Mateqai had been correct not to trust her all along.

"Damn Thief and all his minions," I snapped before I rose to pace once again. "Your games are going to kill the entire human race."

"And from the color of your eyes, have you never played loosely with the rules of conduct, Chief Justice?" Darys's rhetorical question lay on the edge of taunting.

"My childish fantasy of escaping the Temple of Balance doesn't address your true reason for wanting this audience," I bit back.

"You're right." She inclined her head once again. "My apologies. I have my own issues with authority."

"So do quite a few of your fellow Thief clergy," Luc commented. "Please tell us why are you are here."

"Because I questioned the wisdom of revealing the rest of the prophecy to the chief justice in front of the crown prince and his wife or in front of Captain Mateqai." Worry poured from Darys again. "He appears to be from the Long Continents. What do you know about him?"

"He's a former warden from the Orrin Temple of Light, he's served all of the clergy at my Temple beyond any normal calling, and I trust him implicitly, as does Lady Shi Hua," Luc said. "Otherwise, I would not have granted him permission to leave the Temple, nor would Lady Shi Hua have accepted him as the captain of her personal guard."

Darys frowned. "Does he love her?"

"Why does everyone assume Mateqai's carnal desires have anything to do with Shi Hua?" I asked. "No, he does not lust after the lady. He respects her, and he understands the precariousness of her leaving the Temple of Light to serve her emperor and her people. That is all."

"No, let's tell her the full truth." Luc flushed orange. "I am not proud of this. Mateqai was the only member of my Temple to treat the lady with the respect due her previous station as a priestess of Light, and I include myself in that failure."

"I'm sorry if I caused offense to you, High Brother," Darys replied. "Lady Shi Hua and the chief justice's safety is of paramount concern to me. You see, the reason we three are at the top of the Assassins Guild's list of targets is due to a major prophecy. Apparently, we three will ensure the crown prince takes the throne of Jing."

I stared at Sister Darys. "What are you talking about?"

Shi Hua had shown me the Assassins Guild list. There had been a Skoloti priestess among the prospective targets, but her name wasn't Darys. The poor woman had been marked as a contract completed.

The Thief Priestess swallowed hard. "Have you seen the list?"

"Yes." My fingers flexed, a time freeze spell ready to be launched.

"I'm High Sister Zhanna." She made an odd sound, like she swallowed the grief emanating from her. "Sister Darys was my twin by blood."

CHAPTER 17

By the Twelve, that was most certainly not the answer I expected.

"Why the falsehood?" Luc snapped.

Our three wardens drew their swords, which prompted the Skoloti to produce their own blades.

Darys, or rather Zhanna, sagged in her chair. "With the prophecy, my sister and I often switched places at our Reverend Mother's command. The Assassins Guild thought she was me when they beat her and slit her throat."

"You lie," Jonata hissed.

"Warden, stand down!" I barked at her. My gaze swept over the other four wardens. "All of you sheath your weapons before I really get irritated. And as hungry as I am, it won't be pleasant."

"I beg your forgiveness, Chief Justice," Jonata sheepishly murmured as she slid her weapon into her scabbard. Long Feather and Yar followed suit as did the Skoloti wardens.

I watched Zhanna. "You realize you're forcing me to truthspell you."

She nodded wearily. "Do what you have to, Chief Justice."

I started to cast the spell when Luc placed his hand on my arm.

"Let me."

I looked at him, and he shrugged.

"This room isn't an Issuran embassy." A wry smile crossed his face. "I can't let you . . . accidentally kill her with your truthspell. You being arrested for murder in a place we do not have jurisdiction would most certainly violate the queen's orders not to cause a diplomatic incident in Jing, even with the high sister's permission to do so."

That didn't soothe Zhanna's wardens one bit, but it did draw chuckles from our own wardens.

"I agreed to being truthspelled by Chief Justice Anthea," the Thief priestess protested.

I laughed bitterly. "High Brother Luc is actually trying to save your life. A renegade did expire under my truthspell the winter before last."

Zhanna blinked. "Then he shouldn't have worked so hard to avoid your questions, m'lady. I withdraw my statement. You must do whatever you need to ensure the crown prince's safety."

At my nod, Luc performed the two spells, the first to ensure she could not block the truthspell and the second the truthspell itself.

Once Luc's magic settled over the Thief priestess, my old habits reasserted themselves. I quickly ran through the establishing questions of her identity and rank. She confirmed she was High Sister Zhanna, not Sister Darys. Tears ran down her cheeks while she answered my queries about her twin and the incident which ended the young priestess's life. The facts she told us concerning the prophecy had been accurate, assuming she hadn't found a way to circumvent a truthspell.

"Why didn't you tell us about your relationship with this prophecy earlier?" Luc demanded.

"The problem with prophecies is knowing the terms can change the outcome, High Brother," Jonata said.

"To answer High Brother Luc's last question, I couldn't reveal I was still alive unless I was forced to, and none of you asked the right questions during your first interrogation of me at the caravanserai." Zhanna sighed in relief as her discomfort from the spell eased from Jonata's unintentional delay, and she bowed her head. "Your warden is correct, Chief Justice. My own Reverend Mother and the Skoloti Reverend Mother of Balance feared informing me of the entire prophecy. However, our Reverend Father of Knowledge insisted I and my party be forewarned since we were selected to escort the remaining Conflict warriors back to Jing. That was when I learned I had been the real target of my sister's assailants."

"The future is always in motion," I murmured.

Zhanna lifted her head. "And knowledge is the only true power."

"What is the rest of this prophecy?" Luc demanded.

Reverend Mother Alara teased me with an alleged prophecy about me nearly two years ago. Could Zhanna be doing the same? At her hesitation to Luc's question, I murmured, "Withdraw your question. Maybe it's best we do not know."

"And maybe we should." Luc stared at me. "Especially if it has anything to do with the assassination of Prince Pu and Duke Lixin. Do you really believe Quan Po is stupid enough to eliminate his rivals to the throne? It will only arouse resentment among the nobility."

"The other dukes with possible claims to the throne will be the next targets of the renegades," Long Feather said. "If this were Orrin, we'd know who we can trust to protect them."

"But this is not Orrin," Yar snapped. "We would be accused of interfering with Jing's independent rule."

Zhanna whimpered and clutched her midsection. "For the love of the Twelve, let me answer the question!"

"I apologize," Yar murmured.

Zhanna cried out, and her words tumbled out so fast that they were barely understandable with her accent. "The rest says one woman from the east, one from the west, and one from Jing itself would ensure the ascension of the eldest son to the Dragon Throne, and thereby the safety of the empire."

Warden Antiope knelt next to her charge and yelled in Jing. "Stop doing that to her! You're being cruel for the sake of cruelty itself!"

I gave Luc and Yar a disgusted look as I said in the same language. "And you were worried about me torturing the poor woman."

Luc blushed a dark orange. His shame whispered through my mind. "My apologies, High Sister."

"Mine as well," Yar murmured.

"I'm fine." Zhanna waved off her warden and straightened in her chair.

Luc eyed me, and I shook my head. I couldn't think of any other questions to ask the Thief priestess. He dispersed his truthspell.

"High Sister Zhanna's information doesn't solve our immediate problem regarding the Bao family," I said. "How do we protect them without jurisdiction here?"

"Regardless of possible interference by you Issurans or my Skoloti, I wouldn't trust many in Jing beyond High Brother Shang and his survivors," Zhanna said.

"Maybe it's time we get some help from the Jing Temples," Luc mused. "Other than Biming's stunt in Ryukyu, I have no problem with Reverend Father Jin. What's your opinion of the Reverend Mother of Balance?"

I smiled. "Let me give you a further evaluation after my dinner with her tonight. However, I believe we have one ally in Balance."

"What would be our next step?" Zhanna asked.

"Give me a moment," I said and closed my eyes to concentrate. *Shi Hua? Are you busy?*

Only getting fitted for another damn mourning dress, the empress-to-be grumbled. *I didn't realize how much I enjoyed wearing a Temple uniform until now.*

You wore dresses while you were Po's bodyguard, I teased.

That was a part I played, she snapped. *What to you need?*

Is Yin Li still within the palace? I asked.

As far as the staff are concerned, she's officially one of my attending ladies as my kinswoman. Shi Hua's mental tone changed to one of concern. *We just learned Prince Pu—*

Is dead, I interjected. *We know.*

Her sigh felt like a warm spring wind through my mind. *I should have known you would find out before either Po or I had a chance to tell you.*

Sister Darys has some additional information I think the crown prince needs to know. I hated not telling her the full truth about the Skoloti priestess, but it would have to wait.

Does this have anything to do with Lixin and Pu's deaths? Concern flavored Shi Hua's mental voice.

Yes, I said before I laid out Zhanna's worries though I didn't tell Shi Hua of the rest of the prophecy. Somehow, it didn't seem right to lay that burden on her slim shoulders. She had more than enough to deal with in the preparations for her husband's coronation.

And we have the same fears as you do about the lives of his remaining cousins. One moment. She withdrew from my mind.

"Well?" Luc asked impatiently.

I held up my right index finger. He grunted, but his annoyance was more that I spoke with Shi Hua privately. None of us needed Zhanna poking through our psyches if I opened the link further than necessary.

After a long moment, Shi Hua said, *Yin Li and Shang are on their way to your suite.*

Yar was correct. A little diplomacy was necessary in this situation. *Do you or Po have a problem with us taking the lead in this matter?*

No, we don't. Shi Hua hesitated a moment before she added, *If you do not mind, I will send Mengchang to your suite as well. He needs to be included.*

I stifled my groan, both mentally and physically. *That may pose a problem. I fear in my efforts to cultivate the duke's alliance I may have offended him.*

Then I suggest you fix it, Anthea. She abruptly withdrew from my mind.

I don't know what I was expecting from her. We were no longer fellow clergy. Things between us had changed when she left the Temple of Light to marry Po. She followed her duty to her nation, but was she having second thoughts about her decision? If she were, there was nothing either of us could do to change her circumstances.

I blinked. Everyone stared at me with concern.

"Lady Shi Hua is sending Yin Li and Shang to our suite along with Duke Mengchang," I reported.

Even Zhanna and her wardens winced at my announcement.

"I take it you heard about my talk with Duke Mengchang," I said sourly.

The Thief priestess grimaced. "Again, the palace staff is worse than the fishwives along the Sea of Zalpa when it comes to spreading rumors. This is an opportunity for you to repair the duke's apprehensions regarding your influence over his emperor."

"Guarding him from harm will do much to ameliorate the duke's envy of your relationship with the crown prince," Yar said. "And please remind him we will leave soon after the coronation."

"We will need refreshments if we will be entertaining Jing dignitaries," Long Feather said.

"Then you will be in charge of food and tea." I smiled. "Besides I'm so hungry from missing the midday meal, I could eat one of those giant, gray, long-nosed creatures we saw passing the Chengzhou market yesterday."

By the time Long Feather arranged for the tea and food to be sent to our suite and obtained extra chairs for our guests, Duke Mengchang arrived with High Brother Shang and Sister Yin Li.

"What is this about?" the noble demanded. "You may have different customs in Issura, and your nobles will jump at your commands, but this is Jing—"

"One moment, Your Grace," I said and re-established my wards once the maids left our receiving room.

"Your life is in danger, my lord," Shang said sternly. "Two of your cousins have been assassinated within the last day besides this morning's attempt on Crown Prince Po's life. You and the rest of your kinsmen with a possible claim to the Dragon Throne will be targeted as well if we don't take immediately action."

Blood drained from Mengchang's face, turning his skin a sickly yellowish-green. "Crown Prince Po would have informed me—"

"Our new emperor trusts you," Yin Li said. "And as of this moment, you know as much as the rest of us in this room, which is why he ordered us to include you in our discussion of how to protect you and the remaining Bao claimants to the throne."

"I do not wish the throne," the duke protested. "I had more of a taste between the emperor's death and the crown prince's return, and I do not find the flavor one to my liking. I will serve in whatever capacity the crown prince desires, but I will not raise a hand against him."

"However, someone is doing their damnedest to set Bao against Bao," I said. "They did similar things in Issura between the various Temples. It's part of the reason we lost Tandor."

The duke frowned. "My first inclination would be to send the imperial guard to escort the remaining Bao nobles to Chengzhou, but they would assume it would be the crown prince's effort to eliminate his rivals."

"Which is truly the last thing he wants," Luc said.

"Would they trust their priestesses?" Yin Li asked. "Especially their Love and Mother priestesses?"

Mengchang grunted and played with the jeweled beads at the end of his chin-length mustachios. The unconscious gesture was so much like Po's I had to bite the tip of my tongue to keep from laughing.

"I beg your pardon, Chief Justice, High Brother—" The duke paused and glanced at Yin Li, choosing his next words carefully. "I realize the Lady Shi Hua wants her aunt close by for assistance, but the young woman has a peasant's view of the world."

"Really?" I said. "The majority of non-affiliated people I've met in Jing don't have a very high opinion of the Temples. Also, aren't you concerned about your family? At this point, I trust very few people in Jing, but the lady wife of the crown prince is one of the few. The imperial couple are both highly concerned about their subjects' safety, whether they are family or not."

"I cannot and will not take responsibility for those cousins who believe they deserve the throne," he spat. "I do not wish the throne. I will not claim it even if I am the last Bao alive."

"What about your children?" I said softly.

His skin cooled to a pale green as the implications of my words settled in his spirit. "Are you threatening my sons and daughters, Chief Justice?"

"No, I want to keep them alive. I view Lady Shi Hua as a blood sister.

Therefore, you and I are family. In Issuran society, children are treasured. I have no wish to see my cousins by marriage harmed, and that includes you, your wife, and your children. I understand why you do not want the Dragon Throne, but our joint enemies will still view you and your children as a threat."

He watched me, trying to determine whether I was mocking him. Finally, he set aside his tea cup. "There were times as a child I wished for Temple abilities."

"Like truthspelling?" Shang asked.

The duke nodded. "It would make some of my duties easier."

The Conflict priest looked at the duke long and hard. "Would you be willing to be truthspelled in return?"

Mengchang glanced at Zhanna, Luc, and me before he frowned. I could feel Luc's laughter in my head. I didn't need to Hear the duke's thoughts to know what he was about to ask.

"I do not wish to insult any from the Temples, but I would prefer a member of the Jing clergy to protect both me and the crown prince," Mengchang said.

Yin Li turned to me. "Shang and I have our instructions, Chief Justice, but the crown prince informed us you should have the final say. He said you have an uncanny ability to ferret out the truth even without a truthspell."

"Duke Mengchang, may I present Sister Yin Li of the Jing Temple of Love and High Brother Shang of the Jing Temple of Conflict," I said.

Mengchang's lower jaw dropped. I was rather glad he'd set aside the palace's fine ceramic cup before we decided to include him in our plans.

"I don't understand," he stammered.

"I was trained to be Emperor Chengwu's personal bodyguard from the moment I became a novice," Yin Li said. "However, he deemed my presence necessary to guard his brother in Issura after multiple attempts on Crown Prince Po's life. High Brother Shang was Reverend Father Chen's personal assistant until the head of Conflict's untimely demise."

"B-but the Reverend Father's army disappeared nearly a year ago. Surely, you—" Mengchang stared at Shang as if he were one of the dead raised by our enemies.

"The demons laid a trap for us in the desert." Poor Shang's voice was hard, unemotional. Nothing seeped from his psyche. "The Reverend

Father ordered a handful of us who could still move to flee to Skoloti Territory to ensure the alarm was sounded. Unfortunately, we were not successful."

I hadn't dared to ask, but I hoped he and the other Jing survivors had received additional help from Jing's Temple of Child. I had no reason to question the Skoloti tribes' aid to Shang and his comrades, but sometimes, mental damage needed to be addressed by a person with knowledge of the injured's culture.

"The Temples would quietly send clergy we trust to guard your royal cousins and their families," Yin Li said. "Chief Justice Anthea and High Brother Shang will coordinate our efforts outside of the capital while Sister Darys and High Brother Luc will assist you and me with a more thorough examination of the palace staff."

Mengchang grimaced. "You heard about our lack of success in regards to learning the identity of this morning's assassin or finding her killer."

"Yes." I tilted my head and regarded him. He seemed more embarrassed than angry. "The gossip within the palace is the first thing we need to address. There's always a certain amount of chatter, but the rampant rumor-mongering is going to get a lot of innocent people killed if the staff isn't more careful."

"And how do you plan to curb the prattle, Lady Justice?" he said with a wry smile. "My threats and punishments do little to stop the staff gossiping."

I smiled. "Use me as your whip, Your Grace. Surely, rumors of the Red Justice from Issura have been floating around Chengzhou long before our arrival yesterday. Add in the tale that I'm the only one to return from a demon portal. My simple presence in Chengzhou should provide you with the appropriate incentive for your people to cooperate."

I held my breath, hoping the duke would take my hint.

And not arrest me for threatening the people under his control.

CHAPTER 18

Duke Mengchang stared at me for a long moment before he broke out in raucous laughter. Maybe there was some hope in winning him over after all.

"A-aren't you going to coordinate protection for my cousins, Lady Justice?" Mengchang swiped away his tears with a silk handkerchief he produced from inside his coat.

"Hold me in reserve." I gestured at Luc. "The high brother is much more adept with a truthspell than I am. But if the staff refuses to cooperate with you and the high brother, you use me to threaten them."

"And I can guarantee the chief justice's ability with a truthspell will make anyone prefer to be lashed instead of questioned," Luc added.

"I doubt that," Zhanna muttered sarcastically.

I ignored the Skoloti priestess and leaned closer to Luc. "I think my eye color will do more to convince the staff to cooperate than my lack of finesse with a truthspell."

Yin Li and Zhanna laughed. My jest even drew the slightest smile from Shang.

Mengchang turned to Yin Li. "Should I assume the Temples quietly placed you and High Brother Shang in the palace for their own reasons? Quite honestly, I am relieved nothing had happened to you since I had not seen you, Sister."

"It's not like you could ask," Yin Li said.

Mengchang's face glowed a brilliant orange. "I know it wasn't my place, but I did inquire about you. The empress told me you had packed and left before she added that I needed to mind my own responsibilities."

"Her Imperial Highness was covering for me," Yin Li said. "As I said, with the circumstances in Issura, the emperor feared for his brother's safety." She sighed. "And frankly, the renegades would have had to kill me if I were in the palace before they could strike at Emperor Chengwu. Indirectly, he saved my life. I owe the crown prince more than mere fealty."

Mengchang nodded. "I understand why he sent you to Issura. It was about the same time as the raids on the School of Sorcery. He truly believed he'd dealt with the problem in Jing." He turned back to me. "I saw the list found within the school's manor house. It matched a list the Temple of Thief found on a dead renegade three years ago."

"What list?" Shang asked.

"A list of Assassins Guild targets," I said to the Conflict priest. "Lady Shi Hua, Sister Darys's twin who is also a Thief priestess, and my name are on the top of the two lists recovered." I eyed the duke. "Do you know why the Assassins Guild wish us dead most of all?"

"Emperor Chengwu wouldn't tell me." Mengchang stared at his clasped hands for a moment before he met my gaze again. "Given that his brother has married the lady, and you and Sister Darys are here for the coronation, I assume it has something to do with Crown Prince Po."

"There's a prophesy making the rounds," I said. "The three of us are supposed to ensure the crown prince is coronated. For some reason, the Twelve deem him essential to our survival against the demons. The Assassins Guild and the renegades are taking this prophecy even more seriously than the Temples are. That's all we know at the moment."

Duke Mengchang looked at Zhanna. "Why isn't your sister here?"

"She was assassinated shortly before your emperor." Zhanna didn't bother to clarify it was Darys who had been killed. Neither did the rest of us. Po may trust his cousin, but if Luc or I couldn't truthspell him, it was best to keep him partially in the dark.

"Based on the terms, the prophecy only mentions a priestess from the west," I said. "Unfortunately, it was more descriptive of Lady Shi Hua and me."

Mengchang finally relaxed. "So, this morning's incident could have just as easily been about you, not the crown prince."

"We believe the crown prince was the target," Luc said. "Anthea didn't change her position once she was seated. Given the flight path of the bolt, if the prince had stood for a moment longer, the assassin would have killed him. And would have killed Captain Huizong if he hadn't lifted his bowl at the same moment."

The duke nodded. "Therefore, the renegades are going after the crown prince directly since Sister Darys could possibly replace her sister and still meet the terms of the prophecy." He exhaled gustily. "I assume no one outside of this room is to know Yin Li and Shang's affiliation either."

"No," Yin Li answered. "The fewer people who know our true ranks gives us a chance to help you ferret out any renegades still within the palace. And as far as you know, Sister Darys is still a member of the empress's guard. For now."

Mengchang stood. "Very well then. Do you need anything else from me, Lady Justice?"

I rose as well. "No, Your Grace. I have been invited to the Temple of Balance for this evening's meal. A totally normal action for a Reverend Mother to tend to a visiting justice from another nation."

The duke nodded again. "Shall we get started, High Brother? Our own Temple of Light is sending over a Brother Jian to assist us. Do you have any objection to him accompanying us?"

"None at all." Luc grinned. "He's a very capable young man. He was aboard one of the Jing ships that saved the *Mars Tranquilus* from skin-walkers on our voyage here."

The duke grunted again. Apparently, the noncommittal sound indicated while he didn't agree, he wouldn't make a fuss about our plans. I hoped Shi Hua had truthspelled Mengchang. Luc nor I couldn't. At least, not without starting a major diplomatic incident.

The very thing Queen Teodora wanted to avoid. She should have sent one of her many, more experienced nobles. However, she sent Luc and me to Jing instead because our combined talents made us more difficult to kill.

Unless Reverend Mother Alara had told her about the second prophecy. But I couldn't see Alara pushing the queen to send me abroad, much less out of her control. Crown Princess Chiara and Duke White Eagle were the ones championing me for diplomatic duties. Did they know about the second prophecy? If Duke White Eagle did, he wouldn't have told me for fear of me making the wrong choices.

Balance help me, the conjectures of time theory gave me an aching head.

Yar handed Luc's specialized crutches to him. He rose and winked at me as he swung past. However, Yar glared at Jonata and Long Feather as if to say, "You'd better do your jobs because I won't be here to save you or your seat."

I dissolved the wards, and everyone left except my own wardens.

"May I make a suggestion, m'lady?" Long Feather murmured in Issuran.

"Of course," I returned in kind.

Jonata paused in collecting and neatly stacking our used plates and cups.

"We need to discover where Emperor Chengwu's father is being kept and whether he is still there."

I looked at Jonata. "Do you agree, Warden?"

"Yes, m'lady," she said. "Warden Yar agrees with our concern."

"What concern?" My gut ached like it had the first week of our sea voyage to Jing.

"That this morning's attempt on the crown prince was ordered by Master Wu of the former School of Sorcery, not the renegades."

Maybe I'd trained my wardens too well in analyzing evidence for themselves. But I shared the very same suspicion. Emperor Chengwu had admitted to Crown Prince Po a few members of the school had escaped despite the Temples and the Imperial army's best efforts.

I nodded. "I planned to broach the subject with Reverend Mother Xiang this evening. Anything else you've noticed?"

Again, my wardens exchanged looks, but this time, Jonata spoke, "Did Lady Shi Hua truthspell Duke Mengchang?"

"I don't know." I sighed. "Our attempt to have a private conference over breaking our fast was spoiled by a crossbow bolt."

"Maybe that was the true purpose of this morning's incident," Jonata lowered her voice though we still spoke in Issuran, though a guard who knew our language could easily be stationed outside our suite's door. "The Jing are rather suspicious of outsiders. If a foreigner were a regular source of advice for the crown prince, our opposition would want to take that source from him. If they can't do that, they would twist the truth so no one in Jing believes you. They cannot kill you since your death would arouse further suspicion, but if Duke Mengchang knows about this prophecy of the Skoloti . . ."

I didn't like the fact both of my wardens had come to the same possibility I had. Mengchang would be in a perfect position to thwart Po's allies.

CHAPTER 19

For the second afternoon in a row, I found myself and my wardens riding down Chengzhou's main boulevard between the imperial palace and the Temples. We could have walked. I would have enjoyed a stroll to explore the city. Alas, it was not to be between my wardens and the imperial guards with assassins running loose in the city. I would have preferred the Twelve grant us more than one night's small measure of rest before more chaos descended upon our heads.

Jonata and Long Feather's insistence on riding to Balance seemed prophetically prudent. This time, the citizens of Jing openly stared at us. Murmurs and whispers followed us all the way down the Temple boulevard. Being the object of fear and curiosity reminded me too much of my first months as the new seat of Orrin's Temple of Balance.

High Sister Zhanna, or rather Sister Darys since saying the wrong name could be disastrous, was correct. Gossip seemed to be the main occupation of the Jing denizens. However, I couldn't blame the general population of the empire when they were only three months past a major demon attack along with today's attempt on their soon-to-be emperor.

Change was frightening to humans. Major changes were the most frightening of all. And for the first time, I truly understood the real challenges Crown Prince Po faced. He could survive the demons and renegades, but if he didn't earn the respect of his people, his reign was doomed.

When we arrived at the Temple of Balance, two different wardens stood sentinel before the main doors, but one of them whistled as the previous warden had done during our last visit. Squire Yang exited the Temple's main doors and scampered down the steps.

"Greetings, Squire Yang. It's a pleasure to hear you again." I dismounted with some stiffness. One day's rest did nothing to alleviate our road journey over the last fortnight. I really must ride Nassa more when we returned to Issura.

If we returned to Issura.

Yang smiled brightly and bowed before she accepted my reins. "We come to serve, Lady Justice." She quickly collected Jonata and Long Feather's borrowed mares, and led the horses down the alley to Balance's stables.

When we entered the Temple, our escort awaited us. Justice Mei Wen's face glowed a brilliant yellow. "Welcome, Chief Justice Anthea. Wardens." She and Warden Yichen bowed to us, and we returned the gesture. "After we heard of this morning's chaos during the crown prince's morning repast, we feared you might be reticent to join us for the evening meal," she continued.

"One does not turn down a Reverend Mother's invitation two nights in a row, Lady Justice," I responded. "Not even I'm that stubborn or stupid."

Mei Wen's giggles reminded me of just how young both she and Shi Hua were. Warden Yichen released his charge so I could embrace her. Since she was Lady Shi Hua's primary contact and one of her closest friends in Jing, I considered Mei Wen as much a sister beyond our shared Temple affiliation.

"Are they feeding you enough at the palace? I warned . . . ur, informed Duke Mengchang of your appetite before your arrival to Jing." She chuckled to hide her discomfort as I released her.

I wish I could give her more support in her grief. I had no doubt she had been about to say, "my emperor" out of years of habit.

"Luckily, the city of Orrin's primary craft is fishing," I replied. "The crew of the *Mars Tranquilus* kept me well fed so I didn't consume all their stores before we were halfway across the Peaceful Sea."

Everyone laughed at my jest before Warden Yichen wrapped Mei Wen's left hand around his right elbow. Instead of heading toward the private rooms, the pair strode in a different direction.

I'd never been in certain sections of the Issuran home Temple in Standora, but I knew the area Mei Wen and Yichen led us toward was used for records storage and if necessary, Temple leaders' convocations. The memory of my time in the Issuran capital sent a shiver down my backbone. When I was fifteen winters, Reverend Mother Alara and the queendom's chief justices had convened over giving myself sight. I was sure I would be executed, but the senior members of Balance settled on a lashing. I still bore the scars on my back.

But a greater surprise greeted me when I walked into the convocation room. It was filled with all of Jing's Reverend Mothers and Fathers seated at the huge table.

Including Reverend Father Biming.

I gritted my teeth in my effort to clamp down on my emotions. Our gazes met, and he inclined his head.

"Don't you have something to say to Chief Justice Anthea, Biming?" Reverend Father Jin of Light prodded the leader of Jing's Temple of Thief with his elbow.

Biming rose to his feet, and the gathering abruptly became silent. "Chief Justice Anthea, I sincerely apologize for my role in the charges brought by Reverend Father Ogusuku after the demon attack on Naha. I made assumptions about you without investigating the matter thoroughly. For my rashness, I am truly sorry."

I cocked my head and regarded him. His skin color grew warmer from his embarrassment of having to extend his admission in front of the peers of his nation to someone of a lower rank, but I couldn't detect any obvious deception on his part. A demon wearing a human skin wouldn't have been chagrinned under the circumstances. Maybe I also needed to make amends.

"On behalf of the citizens of Tandor whose lives you saved last spring, I accept your apology, Reverend Father." I executed an appropriate bow.

My actions abruptly eased the small amount of tension I hadn't realized existed until it was gone. Mei Wen's relief was far more palpable.

"Chief Justice Anthea, please be seated." A wry smile tilted Reverend Mother Xiang's mouth. "We will eat first before we discuss the needs of our new emperor and our nation."

Warden Yichen assisted Mei Wen to sit in one of the two free chairs between the heads of the Temples of Death and Vintner. I settled into the chair to her left. A case of uneasiness washed through me. I never expected to have the attention of all twelve religious leaders in Issura, much less here in a foreign land.

To my further amazement, Reverend Mother Xiang did not dismiss any of the wardens present. She made the formal introductions of her counterparts I had not met yet while her staff served the first course, a selection of fresh first of the season greens splashed with a spiced vinegar and oil sauce. Long Feather insisted on tasting everything before he'd allow me to take a bite.

Only the Balance chief warden took any offense, but the Reverend Mother quickly told her to stand down.

"The chief justice's wardens have kept her alive for this long by not taking any chances," Biming added. "That in turn has saved the lives of Crown Prince Po and Shi—" He cleared his throat to cover his slip. "Lady Shi Hua many times over. For that, we of Jing owe her a debt."

Was that part of his issue with me? Shi Hua had been his protégé in protecting the imperial family. Did he still regard her as a child, instead of the woman she'd become? I knew he had no sexual interest in her, but that doesn't mean jealousy over my relationship with her wasn't behind his recent actions.

Mei Wen laid her left hand on my thigh. *If you wish to speak to Reverend Father Biming privately, I'll arrange for a conference room for you.*

Are we that obvious? I asked.

I've come to know you both over the last two years. She removed her hand and said no more silently or otherwise as the informal convocation discussed methods of protecting Po's kin from the rogue factions' efforts to start a civil war in Jing.

CHAPTER 20

After most of the guests departed the Temple of Balance, Reverend Mother Xiang quietly bade me and Reverend Father Biming to remain behind. Her chief warden led the two of us and our own wardens to a small sitting room. Surprisingly, Biming joined in my decision for our guards to wait outside for a few moments.

After he closed the doors on our parties and warded the room to keep our conversation private, I said, "I am surprised you don't want your wardens present, Reverend Father. I recall threatening you the last time we spoke."

He chuckled softly. "I don't wish for my people to pay for my foolish choices with their life's blood, Lady Justice." He sobered. "I am sorry I allowed myself to be taken in by Ogusuku's machinations. Xiang has chastised me thoroughly for my part in what happened in Ryukyu. And she reminded me . . ."

When I was sure he wouldn't say more, I prompted, "You mean the Skoloti prophecy?"

His eyes widened. "You know about that?"

"Reverend Mother Alara of Issura was the first one to mention such a prediction to me." I shrugged. "If the rogues also believe it, it would explain the spate of attempts on my life after I was sentenced to the seat of Orrin." There was no reason to act coy about the actual events. I had no doubt that Po or Shi Hua had informed him of the incident that left me the seat of Balance in my birth city.

He drew in a deep breath and released it. "Do you believe in such things as prophecies?"

I shrugged again. "I do not pretend to know what the Twelve intend by such things. I've never had a direct experience with foresight. However, if I can rewind time to examine a specific incident, then it makes sense to be able to jump forward to see possible future events." I smiled. "And if my experiences after I fell through the demon portal are any indication, time can also move side to side as well."

He smiled in return. "You have given me a great many concepts to ponder, Anthea."

"May I ask you a personal question, Reverend Father?"

"That depends."

"Why are you jealous of my relationship with Shi Hua?"

He held up his hands. "I am not attracted to another man's wife."

"I unfortunately know more about the crown prince and his associations than I truly care to or even want to know," I said dryly. "I have no intentions of interfering with Jing internal politics either. I am merely fond of her, and . . . she's the closest thing I've ever had to family since my birth father and a majority of my half-siblings are Diné. I know she regards you as such as well. Or she did. I do not wish to see your bond with her be ruined for anything, perceived or real, due to me."

My stinging eyes took me by surprise. I'd never been this emotionally honest with anyone beyond Luc and High Sister Mya.

"Any breaking of my bond with Shi Hua is due to my own insecurities." He stared at the floor. "She is the closest thing I will ever have to a daughter."

Compassion filled me. "You need to tell her that. She fears you hate her for accepting Po's proposal and that you plan to use her to manipulate Po."

"I-I need to rectify her impression."

I realized Biming was staring at the floor so I would not see his own tears. A weak chuckle rumbled from his chest. "Po needs someone he trusts to give him an heir, and that most certainly won't be me."

"Then, can we agree that we will work together for our friends' and humanity's best interests?" I asked.

He surreptitiously wiped his face before he raised his head. "That is something we can definitely agree on." Again, a wry smile crossed his features. "We might want to let our respective wardens know we're not killing each other in here. Not even my wards are blocking their anxiousness."

He dropped them, and I strode over to the door and opened it. Reverend Mother Xiang stood before the entry with an amused smile. However, she leaned on a cane. The wooden head had been carved into an ornate dragon with jade beads for its eyes.

"I don't smell any blood," she commented. "Are both Biming and Anthea intact, Chief Warden?"

"Yes, m'lady," she barked before she stepped forward and poked her head past me to examine the interior. "And none of the furnishings are broken or torn."

"Well, Imp, I'm pleased you minded your manners for once," Xiang said.

Biming inclined his head. "My sentence to learn proper etiquette was quite useful, Reverend Mother."

Xiang snorted. "Useful in seducing the imperial princes maybe."

I slowly pivoted and stared at Biming. "Sentenced?"

"You weren't the only one who couldn't stay out of trouble as a novice, Anthea," Xiang said dryly. "Why Thief voted Imp as their Reverend Father is beyond my comprehension."

"I'm more concerned about Reverend Father Ogusuku," I murmured.

"Inside." The Reverend Mother flicked her fingers in the direction of the sitting room. "I'm not discussing this in an open corridor."

Her proclamation sent a chill up my backbones. It meant she was also concerned about spies within her own Temple.

I stepped back, and the Reverend Mother limped into the room on her chief warden's arm. She was followed by Justice Mei Wen, Yichen, my wardens, and finally Biming's escort. Once we were seated, Reverend Mother Xiang bade Mei Wen to ward the room.

"All the home Temples of Balance have been in close contact concerning the battle in Naha and its aftermath." Xiang stretched out her right leg. "And stop staring at me, Anthea. I fell off a horse when I was a novice and broke my knee bone. On a positive note, it allows me to predict rain or snow with an accuracy to rival a weather oracle."

Everyone in the room, including the wardens, chuckled at the Reverend Mother's dry humor.

"Forgive me, Reverend Mother." I inclined my head. "At the rate my friends and colleagues acquire injuries around me, I fear for your well-being."

Xiang sighed. "The price on your head is the reason Alara acceded to your queen's request for you and High Brother Luc to accompany the crown prince. She—"

"Knows about the prophecy," I interjected. "She was the one who first told me about it two winters ago, but only a part of it. She—"

"Is struggling with several problems at once in Issura," Reverend Mother Xiang stated with finality. "As much as we wish to be forthcoming with the clergy who report to us, it is not always safe to do so."

I bowed my head at her mild chastisement. She was correct, of course.

Even I knew we had at least one spy within the Issuran home Temple of Balance. Plus, there had been several infiltrations by rogues into the Temple of Light. One of them was at fault for Luc's loss of his left foot.

"I beg your forgiveness for speaking out of turn, Reverend Mother," I murmured.

"No apology is needed where no offense occurred." She gripped her cane the same way I played with my dagger hilt when I was bothered by a particularly vexing puzzle. "Have you two found a common ground?"

"Yes," both Biming and I said at the same time.

"Good." She tapped her cane against the bare wooden floor. "From your buzzing like a blooming plum tree full of bees, tell us your theory, Chief Justice."

"First, I have two questions. Where is Emperor Chengwu's father Wu Sunshu imprisoned, and has anyone verified he is still there since the crown prince arrived in Chengzhou?"

CHAPTER 21

As much as it pricked Wu's pride, he found it quite easy to blend in with the servants of a textile merchant as they entered the gates of Chengzhou shortly before First Evening. Garlands of flowers from the imperial greenhouses decorated the streets. Banners in imperial red hung from windows. The characters on the banners, drawn with yellow paint seeded with gold flakes, gleamed beneath the last rays of the sun.

Everything had been cleaned in preparation for the Spring Rituals. The streets. The shops. Even the peasants had swept their hovels and wiped down their windows. Vendors sold potions to increase virility and fertility in advance of the festivities. Others sold charms to farmers to increase their herds and flocks. And everywhere, the people spoke of the Issuran Red Justice who had escorted the crown prince back to Jing, as well as his new wife, a farmgirl whose only link to respectability was that she had been an ordained Light priestess.

Wu cursed silently. Two out of the three women who were foretold to place that common bastard on the throne were in the city. He needed to contact the remaining handful of his students from the School of Sorcery. Their assistance was necessary to eliminate at least one of those common-born whores before the end of the Spring Rituals.

A Conflict priest and a squad of wardens approached the merchant. Wu forced himself not to tense as the wardens spread out to examine the wagons and the merchant's servants. Instead, he gazed around as if this were his first visit to the capital as one of the wardens approached him.

"Name?"

"What?" He pretended to force himself to focus on the Conflict warden.

"Your name," the man prompted.

"Li Po." A nice, common name. Just like the bastard.

"Place of birth."

"The village of Shanmen."

"How many winters have you seen?"

"Forty."

"Thank you, Citizen Li." The warden smiled at Wu. "May Love grant blessings upon you and yours." The warden leaned closer. "Steer clear of Thief so He doesn't take all your earnings for the holiday." The warden winked before he moved on to the next wagon.

Wu managed to smile and nod like an imbecile. As if he ever trusted any of the Temples.

Nearby, a woman with a measure of fire talent entertained a mixed group of citizens. Wu sauntered over and blended with the crowd watching the artist. The darkening sky and the fire talent's creations created sufficient shadows to escape the watchful eyes of the peacekeepers, soldiers, and wardens. Within a moment, he was in the alley and headed toward his school's last remaining safe house according to the departed Bing.

"Wu Sunshu?" A startled expression crossed Reverend Mother Xiang's features at my question. Heat drained from Reverend Father Biming until his exposed skin turned a dull greenish-yellow.

"There is no method for him to escape," the Balance chief warden stated firmly.

"There are always ways to escape." Biming murmured. "He's being held in a prison outside of the city. No one outside of Xiang and myself know where he is except the dozen soldiers who guard him and the seven women who take care of the needs of both the prisoner and the soldiers. Those seventeen are all impervious to magic."

Humans who were impervious to any talent were even more rare than healers, distance speakers, and justices.

However, it merely meant no magic could be used upon their minds and bodies. It didn't stop a user from tricking an impervious human.

Biming must have read my expression. He sighed. "Please don't think us idiots, Chief Justice."

"Whatever do you mean, Reverend Father?" I replied innocently.

"We hoped to draw out any of Wu's remaining allies," Reverend Mother Xiang said. "Random checks are made by either Biming or myself. And the sarcasm is unnecessary, young lady."

"No mockery was intended, Reverend Mother." I sipped my tea. "However, I have noticed neither of you have answered my initial question."

"I visited the prison three days ago," she said.

"And you know where I've been for the last month," Biming pointed out.

"This is about more than Wu's treason, isn't it?" the Reverend Mother asked.

"Yes," I replied. "He is our chief suspect in the murder of Master Quan of the School of the Phoenix and the Dragon."

CHAPTER 22

Wu pulled the glamour of the old woman over his true form as he approached the last refuge for the School of Sorcery. The house appeared dark and foreboding. An abandoned hulk rotting where it squatted. If anyone approached, a low-level spell would cause rising anxiety the closer an intruder came to the gates or surrounding wall. The spell worked on animal pests as well as human ones.

The city bureaucrats didn't care or interfere with the alleged derelict as long as the taxes were paid. Nor was it a neighborhood where anyone cared about the appearance of their neighbors' homes. The decrepits living in this slum believed the place had been looted long ago and left it alone.

The tingle of the illusion spell caressed his skin as he passed through the front gate. The real grounds didn't look much better than the glamour. Overgrown weeds clogged the flower beds. Tufts of grass thrust up between the bricks that formed the paths. While he couldn't detect any power on the grounds, the manse itself practically reeked with it. However, there was no sense in acting foolishly. Wu worked his way through the unkempt gardens to the back of the manse, his senses alert for any magical trap.

When he reached the back entrance, he knocked the specific signal on the door. The blue lacquer on the wood was peeling away for real here. He knocked again, this time releasing pulses of magic in the same pattern.

No answer at all.

He strode back to the front and performed a different set of knocking and magical signals. Still, no answer. Anyone from the School of Sorcery would have recognized both valid codes. Someone should be guarding both entrances, but bursting into the building would not be smart. Especially if his students had added additional protective spells after the raids by the damn Temples last year.

And if no one were here, if his surviving students had to evacuate, they would have left a message. The only way to find out would be to risk going inside.

He concentrated and murmured the spell to deactivate the normal protective charms. A layer of magic faded from his awareness, and he opened the door.

An atrocious sickly-sweet odor assaulted his nose. Had someone performed a sacrificial spell and not cleaned up after themselves? How careless!

Wu stepped inside, closed the door, and sniffed again. The putrid smell wafted from the direction of the staircase. He created a light ball just large enough he could see without tripping over furniture. The glamour over the grounds would prevent someone outside of the property to see the glow.

The wooden floor boards and stairs creaked despite his careful steps. When he reached the second floor, the odor was more intense to his right. He strode in that direction, checking each room as he went.

Had the rest of his students been idiotic enough to mess with demon magic as Bing had been? Had something they tried backfired on them? He had taught them better than to work demon magic. The damned creatures were only useful for getting rid of the Temples. No more, no less.

At the last door on the left, the odor turned nearly unbearable. He entered the room. Inside his own backup study, four skinned bodies haphazardly sprawled on the expensive Madan rug in the middle of the room.

The oddest part was the lack of blood.

Reverend Mother Xiang's mouth pursed before she said, "It was my understanding Master Quan was afflicted with the Child's Curse. That was the reason he left his school to see his son one more time before he forgot him."

"Our best healers and Orrin's High Sister Mya of Child examined him thoroughly and multiple times," I replied. "There was a subtle spell upon Master Quan that only Mya and Master Bly, our most sensitive healer, could detect. It mimicked the Child's Curse. Despite the ladies' best efforts and research, they could not save him."

The Reverend Mother scowled. "Are you sure this isn't a political demon hunt by our soon-to-be Emperor?"

I sighed. "I do wish I could blame my theory on such a common reason. However, the spell was laid upon him before he reached Issura. Based on Crown Prince Po's testimony, Emperor Chengwu consulted about the matter with Reverend Father Runchu of Child."

Biming nodded. "The emperor also consulted with Master Healer Zhi and Reverend Mother Xiao Mei of Knowledge. None of us could discover how this spell worked. I was the one who recommended that Master Quan spend his final months with his son."

"You know about this assault?" Xiang stared in Biming's direction as if she could actually see him.

"Yes, I did," he answered in a neutral tone.

"And did the School of the Phoenix and the Dragon know about this amateurish investigation?" Xiang snapped.

"Yes, their elders did." Biming didn't look the least bit contrite. "There was no point in spreading the news. To do so would have stoked further fear and mistrust of the Temples."

"Bah!" Reverend Mother Xiang waved her free hand. "The renegades and sorcerers' whisper campaigns have already done that. Now, the rest of us are at risk from the subtle spell worked on Master Quan."

She turned back toward my general direction. "We need to check on Wu. And Anthea, you have my permission to question him. It is no secret he resented Quan for his closer relationship with the empress."

"But what is the legal basis for allowing an Issuran to question him?" Biming protested. "As unfortunate as the case may be, he is still a Jing citizen."

The Reverend Mother snorted. "Would you like to educate our dear Reverend Father of Thief concerning the finer points of jurisdiction, Anthea? Because my first inclination is to have my chief warden hold him down while I beat him with my cane."

Somehow, I resisted the urge to laugh at the picture the Reverend Mother painted. Biming turned to me expectantly.

"In the case of assault, jurisdiction is with the closest Temple of Balance," I said. "However, if death from the initial assault occurs in a different Temple of Balance's jurisdiction, that Temple has the primary responsibility to try the case. However, the justice with jurisdiction of the death can call on other justices for assistance. Since we cannot pinpoint exactly where and when the assault took place, the justice with jurisdiction would be required to seek assistance from the Reverend Mother of the nation where the assault is presumed to have happened."

Xiang used her cane to assist her in rising from her chair. "Which means, my darling Imp, we need to check on our imperial traitor and allow Chief Justice Anthea to question him. Do you have any additional plans tonight, Anthea?"

"No, Reverend Mother, none at all." And I had to admit to myself, I looked forward to meeting the idiot who foolishly unleashed horrors on Cant and Issura a year ago.

CHAPTER 23

The sun had set long before we struck out for Wu Sunshu's private detention cell. However, my peculiar eyesight allowed me to examine the site more thoroughly than my wardens could. From the exterior, the prison appeared to be another rolling hill among many a few leagues outside of Chengzhou. The guards' houses sat at the base of the hill, and a series of bushes disguised the entrance into the hill itself.

But instead of questioning the disgraced schoolmaster, I stared at the corpse of a woman lying on the makeshift bed in Wu Sunshu's cell. I couldn't call the locked room beneath the hill a gaol or a prison since he'd been the only person kept here. While I tried to summon the calmness to weave a rewind spell, Biming yelled imprecations at the guards and their support staff out in the tunnel.

A sharp buzz against my mental shields as I stepped closer to the corpse alerted me to our first clue.

"Do you feel the odd power emanating from the corpse?" I asked Reverend Mother Xiang.

"Demon magic," she spat.

"But she's not a skinwalker," I mused. "Not yet, anyway. There's the possibility her teacher is within the city."

"Conjecture, Chief Justice," the Reverend Mother gently chided.

"Do I believe this woman is related to this morning's attempt on the crown prince?" I chuckled. "Not necessarily. But her presence raises the question of why a potential skinwalker trainee, and therefore the demons, want Wu dead."

"More conjecture, Chief Justice," the Reverend Mother pointed out.

I crouched next to the bed and ran a hand over the chains lying on the chiseled stone floor. The power-damping spells sizzled against my touch, an indication they were still active. However, there were two hairpins lying on the floor besides the empty manacles.

"It appears the locks of the spelled manacles may have been picked." I chuckled. "Maybe Crown Prince Po isn't the only one in the imperial family with some Thief talent."

Finally, Biming's shouting had died down out in the corridor.

"I should have brought a Light priest with us," Reverend Mother Xiang muttered.

"I don't think any of the staff aided Wu in his escape, except maybe our friend here indirectly." I sniffed the body. Vomit, feces, and the beginnings of decay were the only odors I could detect. "Jonata!"

"Yes, m'lady." She stepped into the cell with us, making the space feel even smaller.

I rose and stepped away from the bed. "Describe the corpse to the Reverend Mother and me, please."

My warden stepped next to the dead woman. In a smooth motion, she drew her dagger and carefully lifted the blanket from the body "A woman with straight black hair though it is currently mussed. An extra skinfold on the upper eyelid. Her skin coloring is consistent with someone whose ancestors came from the eastern Old Continent."

Her breath hissed from between her teeth. "The corpse's fingertips and toes are a bright red. Possible indication of southern blue poisoning. Unfortunately, I cannot smell bitter almonds. The woman has been dead for too long."

Jonata donned her gloves and used a section of blanket to test the movement of the corpse's finger joints. "Rigor mortis has come and gone. I cannot see any insect activity on the surface. Do you wish to—"

Old habits inserted themselves with the presence of a corpse despite being three months away from home. I nearly agreed with her in fetching one of our healing masters in Orrin, even as she started to ask.

Unfortunately, Reverend Mother Xiang missed nothing. "What is your unspoken command, Chief Justice?"

"I do not wish to offend you, Reverend Mother," I murmured. "As both you and the crown prince have pointed out, I do not have jurisdiction in Jing other than to search for my lead suspect in Master Quan's murder."

"She was about to send Warden Jonata for Master Healers Bly or Aaron, but she remembered she wasn't in Orrin." Biming chuckled.

Looking behind me, I realized the head of Jing's Thief temple and nearly all the wardens we had brought with us were crowded in the cell's doorway to watch us.

"Biming, send one of your wardens to Master Zhi." Reverend Mother Xiang frowned. "They'll be circumspect enough to not attract undue attention."

Her request startled me. The Reverend Mother must have felt my surprise. She turned in my direction and smirked.

"I do listen to the reports from Lady Shi Hua. Especially her descriptions of your investigative techniques. We have implemented some of them."

"Forgive me, Reverend Mother." I bowed to her. "I am used to being doubted by the seats in Issura."

Biming snorted. "And those who doubted you are no longer seats in Orrin."

I sighed. "No, those who committed crimes have been removed as they should be. There are still those clergy who do not agree with my methods."

"New ideas are often questioned by those who do not yet understand," Xiang murmured. "While we wait for Master Healer Zhi, Biming and I will formally question the guards and householders. May I borrow Warden Jonata for a moment?"

"Of course, Reverend Mother." I bowed again.

"Please try not to get yourself killed while I'm gone," Jonata said in Issuran.

The Reverend Mother burst out laughing, but she resorted to the Jing language. "Do you always speak with such impertinence to your superiors, Warden?"

"Only to Chief Justice Anthea, Reverend Mother." Jonata switched back to the Jing tongue. Her expression was perturbed at best. "We must remind her as one would a toddler. The wardens stationed at Balance in Orrin believe the Twelve themselves must work constantly to protect the chief justice from her own curiosity and sense of integrity because we surely cannot succeed on our own."

That resulted in another round of laughter from the Reverend Mother. From the shock emanating from the Jing wardens, her display of humor was not a regular occurrence.

Once Jonata guided the Reverend Mother from the cell and the Jing personnel dispersed to formally question the prison's staff, Long Feather stepped into the cell.

"Instructions, m'lady?" he said in Issuran.

"There's nothing we can do for the moment," I said in the same language. "Unfortunately, we are in a foreign land. I am . . . disappointed Wu was not here. I hoped to find a way to protect all citizens from this spell that mimics the Child's Curse."

Before we left the city, the heads of the Twelve Temples had issued the orders for clergy and wardens to meet the incoming members of the Bao line as extra protection. Now, we learned Emperor Chengwu's father had escaped. Only the Twelve knew if one or more demons were running around the Jing capital. There were simply too many possibilities and directions for trouble to come from.

Worst of all, I couldn't do anything to change our circumstances besides pray to the Twelve that Po's coronation would go smoothly.

CHAPTER 24

Wu dropped his glamour and raced down to the basement of the manse. Beneath the stairway, he pried loose a section of stones with a hammer and chisel. Inside were his pack and a stash of gold and silver coins.

He quickly changed into a set of civilian clothing. His formal School of Sorcery robes would have to be left behind as would a majority of the weapons. The school robes would be an invitation to any warden or Imperial soldier to execute him. Anyone less than noble and Temple ranks would not be allowed to carry weapons beyond a personal dagger during the Spring Rituals. And none at all during the coronation.

Not that he needed conventional weapons.

The acrid odor of smoke filtered through the air from the fire he'd set up on the second story. Not even he was foolish enough to leave corpses lying around where a demon could find and use them, though likely the demons or their lackeys were responsible for what had been done to his students.

He crossed to a cupboard and shoved dried meats and vegetables, hard cheeses, and a small sack of rice into his pack along with flint and steel, a tiny cook pot, and eating sticks.

Heat emanated from the ceiling. Time to leave.

Wu strode to the opposite side of the basement and yanked open a pantry door. The Temples weren't the only ones with a tunnel system in Chengzhou.

He shoved the shelves until they rolled backward with a loud squeal. No one had been lubricating the wheels or their rails while he was imprisoned. The failure to maintain the manse didn't matter. His surviving students had already paid for their stupidity with their lives. And if Bing had succeeded in killing him, she would be lying upstairs skinned as well.

Unfortunately, the missing skins meant four demons were running around the city disguised as his former students. Well, he would hunt them down.

After he dealt with his late wife's bastard.

Reverend Mother Xiang questioned the soldiers and staff charged with guarding Wu Sunshu. None of them were directly involved in the prisoner's escape, but the four guards on duty said the woman who arrived with Wu's meal was the mother of the officer in charge of the facility. Under truthspell, she admitted to falling asleep before delivering the tray. When she awoke, she saw the dishes from the previous day next to the wash basin and had assumed one of the other women had delivered the food to the prisoner.

The elderly woman took the blame, totally expecting to be executed.

However, the Reverend Mother rewound the time in the building that served as the small units' dining hall. One of the other six women had brought the elderly woman tea. Jonata recognized the effects of a tiny dose of soma tears.

The Reverend Mother subsequently rewound time at the laundry room, and discovered the other six women were collectively cleaning clothes at the same time the elderly woman had been served the drugged tea.

"Chief Justice Anthea, may I please impose on you to cast the rewind spell in Wu's cell?" Reverend Mother Xiang asked.

"Yes, Reverend Mother." I didn't need to question why. I knew from experience how exhausting two back-to-back rewind spells could be. My spell confirmed that the woman on Wu's pallet had used a glamour to disguise herself. From his behavior, Wu deduced she planned to poison him. The most horrifying part hadn't been the spell he used to force her to eat the food laced with southern blue, but that he managed to cast it through his magic-dampening shackles.

No one said a word during or after Jonata's recitation of the facts. Except for Reverend Father Biming's praise that no one from Light could have done a better job than my warden had.

We remained silent until Master Zhi arrived shortly after my rewind of Wu's cell. I was struck by her mannerisms. She simply didn't put up with nonsense from anyone. Not even the heads of her nation's Temples.

"Everyone, clear out of the cell!" she ordered. "Except you, Chief Justice."

"I won't leave my justice alone—" Long Feather started to protest.

"Have her truthspell me if you think I'm a renegade," the master healer shot back. "Otherwise, let me and the chief justice get to work." She hung an additional paper lantern lit by Knowledge magic with a piece of string through one of the metal hoops holding the shackles and tied it in place.

"I've already truthspelled her, Warden," Reverend Mother Xiang said.

Satisfied that matter was put to rest, Master Zhi turned to me. "Is it true you can see, Anthea?"

For some reason, the healer throwing away all decorum and rank made me feel better about her assisting in this investigation.

"Yes, I can."

"But I've heard you see differently than most sighted people do?"

"Yes," I said. "I had no real reference when I tried to give myself sight through a healing spell."

Zhi sighed. "The damn Temples and the philosophy schools think magic can solve anything. Tell me how you see our decedent."

I didn't have to look at the cell doorway to know everyone hung on our words. I inhaled deeply and turned to our victim.

"She simply looks like a corpse," I began. "Her chest does not rise. I cannot see fine details of the skin, but she appears much younger than the elderly woman the guards described who brought the prisoner his meal and left."

"How did you know to ask about southern blue?"

"It's been used by the renegades far too often on cases I've adjudicated in Orrin. Plus, a majority of renegades we have apprehended or attempted to apprehend have fake teeth with southern blue inside them."

Zhi snorted. "Suicide instead of capture, eh?"

"Suicide does prevent those of us with talent from truthspelling the captives," I said dryly.

"What color is the corpse's skin, other than the fingers and toes?"

For an instant, I considered lying, but I couldn't alienate Xiang or Biming. "To me, she appears dull blueish-gray."

Zhi chuckled. "Sounds to me like your eyes work just fine."

Was that how the skin of a corpse looked to those with normal sight? Over the years, I hadn't asked Luc, much less the staff at the Temple of Balance. And given how many times my wardens had disgorged the contents of their stomachs, I wasn't sure I wanted to see the corpses as they did.

Though in a few cases, the smell was enough to disturb my own appetite.

"The Reverend Mother said you both detected demon magic," Zhi said as she knelt to take samples of waste material on the blanket.

"Yes, we did."

Zhi paused in pulling on protective gloves and looked up at me. "Can you tell the difference between a caster and one whom the magic has acted on?"

"Yes."

"And?"

"The dead woman has used at least one demon spell, but has not cast enough demon magic to become a skinwalker," I answered.

"Do you know how many spells it takes before a human is so corrupted?" Zhi asked.

The curiosity of those standing at the doorframe felt like a giant boulder sitting on my head.

"I'm not sure if it's a specific number as much as the intent of the caster," I said. "In the six months between her initial arrest for demon dealing and her death, Gerd, formerly the High Sister of Love in Orrin, became a skinwalker. In her case, she wished to murder me for discovering she dealt in demon artifacts." A shiver ran through me at how close she came to killing everyone in the city using the death of Sister Claudia's unborn babe.

Zhi grunted. She reminded me of Magistrate DiCook back home. He often grunted when he agreed or understood what I was attempting to convey.

"With your permission and the Reverend Mother's, may I bring in my journeyperson?" Zhi asked. "It will speed my work in collecting samples, and I will have answers for you both much sooner."

"Of course," I said.

"Whatever you need, Master Healer," Reverend Mother Xiang said.

I stepped out of the cell while the master healer's journeyperson, a *berda*, worked quickly and efficiently. But I had to give them credit, they merely glanced at me out of curiosity, not fear or distaste like so many others.

"What!" Biming's exclamation drew everyone's attention, but he wasn't talking to anyone present in the tiny corridor. His attention had the far away quality of someone distance speaking.

He shook himself before he turned to the Reverend Mother. "Xiang, we need to get back to Chengzhou. There's a huge fire in one of the outer sections of the city."

Twelve take the renegades! I knew I shouldn't leap to any conclusions, but they obviously weren't going to give any of us a moment of rest before Po's coronation.

CHAPTER 25

We rode at a steady canter back to the Jing capital. However, we all could smell the smoke within a few leagues of the city, and even I could see the glow of the heated air over Chengzhou long before the walls came into sight.

The tingle of magic penetrated my clothing and brushed against my skin. From this distance, a great many talents had to be working in tandem to quench the blaze for me to feel their work.

A chill ran up my spine, a counterpoint to the warm caress of power. After kidnapping the pregnant Sister Claudia of Love, the renegades in my birth mother Gerd's company had burned a warehouse at Orrin's docks to simulate the priestess's death when we used a tracking spell to find her. They used the confusion of that same massive fire to abduct High Brother Luc as well.

"Reverend Mother?" I called.

Speak silently, the leader of the Jing Temple of Balance commanded. *Save your breath for whatever awaits us within Chengwu.*

I quickly related the events of last summer's fire in Orrin. Reverend Mother Xiang's concern mixed with my own.

She withdrew from my mind momentarily, but I caught a whisper of Mei Wen's essence. The junior justice allegedly wasn't a distance speaker, but it indicated the young woman's power that she could speak silently to someone leagues away.

Mei Wen is spreading the word the blaze may be a diversion, the Reverend Mother said. "Biming!"

Jing's Reverend Father of Thief glanced over his shoulder at us. I couldn't Hear his silent speech except as an echo in Xiang's mind. Quicksilvers like Biming were practically invisible to anyone with talents unless they deliberately opened their spirit to another. It was one of the reasons Thief recruited as many quicksilvers as they could find. Who else could spy on demons and renegades without being detected?

You Thieves should go on ahead, the Reverend Mother said. *The fire could mask another demon attack.*

No! I said at nearly the same moment as Biming.

A spy may have noticed us leaving Chengzhou, he said.

And they may have set a trap for us along the road, expecting just such a measure, I added. *You've warned your Temple. They will pass the word to the rest.*

You are both correct, Reverend Mother Xiang grudgingly admitted. *The idea of demons inside Balance again—*

I've been in your position, Reverend Mother, I said. *You have to trust that you've trained your order to do their duties. And none of you would have survived last winter's attack if you hadn't trained them correctly.*

Your wisdom does our order great honor, she replied.

No one else spoke, silently or otherwise. Only the clopping of hooves and the harsh breathing of both horses and humans filled my ears.

The silence around us bothered me. On our ride to Wu's prison, we heard nocturnal animals and birds rustling in the orchards as we passed. We even passed a handful of travelers, who couldn't afford the rates of the closest caravanserai. They conversed and laughed while they camped along the imperial road, and they had returned the wardens' hails.

At this time of year in Issura, farmers would be out tending flocks and herds as the livestock gave birth. We'd seen the same among the Jing farmers as we journeyed from the coast to Chengzhou.

But now, I heard nothing.

Yes, the quiet bothered me quite deeply.

Jonata, Long Feather, do you hear anything beyond our group? I asked silently.

No, Chief Justice, Jonata answered. *The silence disturbs me. The Jing farms we passed on the way to Chengzhou had herdspeople tending their animals closely since it's birthing season even here.*

I agree, Long Feather said. *There's no indication of nocturnal animals either.*

The feeling of unease grew stronger in the back of my mind. I scanned the area ahead but only the wardens who rode point stood out. I glanced behind us and my heart nearly seized at the gray-green figure stepping out from behind a plum tree. It was followed by the whisper of demon magic.

"Skinwalkers!" I shouted.

Balance help me, I hated when my unconscious suspicions were correct. My wardens drew their swords even as I did.

A shriek from the head of our group drew my attention as the Jing contingents produced their own weapons. I watched in horror as a demon jumped out of the hedges on the west side of the road. It quickly dispatched the steed of the Balance point rider, and the warden tumbled to the cobblestones and lay still. The horse's bright pink blood spurted from the torn blood vessels in what was left of its neck.

"Demons!" The warning cry from the Thief point rider was too late for her counterpart, but it allowed Biming the opportunity to throw a ward about her.

Just in time, too. The demon ignored the fallen Balance warden and sprang for the Thief warden. It scrabbled for purchase on the invisible shield, which gave the junior priest with Thief a chance to shoot the demon with a magic-enhanced crossbow bolt.

"How many, Anthea?" the Reverend Mother shouted.

"Three, no four demons alive," I reported as the last one dropped from the trees on our left. I glanced behind us. "A dozen skinwalkers closing in from the rear. Wardens! Circle around the clergy and healers!"

I was shocked that the Jing and the Issuran wardens all obeyed me.

And even more shocked when the lead skinwalker held up his right fist and shouted something in demon language. And the cursed beasts backed away from the surviving point rider.

"Give us Wu Sunshu!" the lead skinwalker shouted in the Jing language.

What in the Twelve was he blathering about? Surely, they had helped the sorcerer escape.

Hadn't they? Or had Wu's attempted assassination been ordered by our foes and he took advantage of his assassin's presence?

"Why?" I demanded.

"Give him to us, and we will allow you and your companions to go free," he said.

I laughed as if he told the funniest joke known to humans. "You shouldn't have killed one of us if that were the deal you wanted to make."

Why would they want the traitor? the Reverend Mother whispered in my mind.

Good question. I could feel Biming listening to our conversation. However, he didn't offer a comment.

"You still haven't told me why you want him," I said aloud to the skinwalker. "He would not make a good suit for you or the demons. He's too well known in Jing, and the new emperor has no reason to spare his life."

The skinwalker laughed. "My compatriots want the rest of their children back."

My breath momentarily caught in my lungs. They didn't know what had happened to the rest of the demon eggs that had been sent to the Northen Long Continent.

Or had there been a third cache none of us knew about?

Reverend Mother, I do not wish to negotiate on your behalf, I said.

Continue, Anthea, Biming said through Reverend Mother Xiang. *You are asking the same questions we would.*

Behind his words, I could feel the Reverend Mother's agreement.

"Do you mean the demon eggs you gave to the School of Sorcery for distribution?" I asked.

"Of course." The skinwalker's smile resembled a bizarre death rictus.

"You already know they were hatched to destroy one of the imperial armies and snuck inside the capital to assassinate Emperor Chengwu," I said. "Why do you play with us?"

"We know the dead emperor's warriors seized some of the eggs." The skinwalker inclined his head toward the demons behind. "My compatriots simply want their remaining siblings back, and for that, we want Wu."

How can they not know the eggs that were seized were already destroyed? the Reverend Mother said.

They know, Biming answered.

The Reverend Father of Thief was right. Emperor Chengwu's people hadn't discovered all the eggs the idiot demons had given to the equally idiotic sorcerer. No doubt Wu kept some back as insurance against both sides in this war. So, what game was the sorcerer playing?

"We would have to return to Chengzhou and retrieve the seized eggs for you," I said.

The skinwalker laughed again. "Don't play with us, Red Justice. As I said, we want Wu. He betrayed us as well as your kind. Don't you want to see him suffer for the harm he caused you? For what he made you do to your mother?"

It was my turn to laugh. "The woman who bore me needed no assistance, much less coercion, to walk your path. But what do we get in return for delivering Wu and the remaining eggs?"

"Only one of you is necessary to ride back to the city." The skinwalker's threat hung in the air.

"The one person you allow to leave has no reason to believe you will return the hostages," I said.

"Then there's no need to keep any of you." The skinwalker sneered.

Biming, Xiang, I'll take care of the demons, I said silently. *Gather your people. My wardens and I will cover your retreat to Chengzhou.* Static tingled along my fingers and up my arms beneath my gloves and sleeves. I wouldn't be able to hold back this strange new lightning ability for long.

Anthea, don't be ridiculous—

Biming, your people need you and Xiang. Go!

There's no reason to sacrifice yourself, Anthea! she cried silently.

I don't intend to, Reverend Mother. We're getting out of this together. I nudged my left knee against the ribs of my horse. A Temple-trained steed, she obeyed and whirled to face the demons. I stood in my stirrups and took aim at the four demons. Lightning flew from my fingertips.

CHAPTER 26

Before the demons could change shape or sink into the soil, my lightning fried them into ash. A wave of dizziness struck me as I sat and nudged my horse to face the direction back to Wu's former prison. Biming and Xiang must have silently communicated with their own people. The Jing wardens launched a barrage of arrows and crossbow bolts at the skinwalkers.

"Get to safety!" I roared.

This time, none of the Jing listened to me. Instead, they formed ranks around me and my two wardens. The expressions of the Jing were quite serious compared to Jonata's wild grin.

"You don't get your wish today, Chief Justice!" She cackled. My own magic caressed my skin as she took aim and fired one of her Balance-charged arrows at the skinwalker shielding her companions.

The steel head didn't touch the skinwalker, but the spell on the arrow destroyed her shield and knocked her flat on her back. Another skinwalker screeched when a crossbow bolt penetrated a nearby hedge.

I shot a bolt of lightning at the same hedge. Two more screams filled the air from that direction while the surviving branches of the hedge caught fire.

Raw power filled the air as a Balance ward snapped up in time to intercept a series of three demon-magic spells.

Reverend Mother Xiang smiled as fiercely as Jonata. "Take them out, Anthea!"

Another round of arrows and bolts flew from human bows and crossbows. The surviving skinwalkers scattered. Some ran into the woods on the eastern side of the road. The rest of them dove into the hedges on the western side.

Once again, I stood in my stirrups. The surviving skinwalkers must have believed I couldn't see them. Maybe the rumors flooding the world only mentioned I could see demons. If that was the case, I couldn't let these skinwalkers escape.

Power thrummed deep from within the earth, the odd feeling of heat and static. I aimed that energy at the gray-green figures slipping between the gold awakening trees. Blue-white lightning rent the very air.

No screams filled the night this time, but a falling tree crushed one of the skinwalkers, which made up for the lack of shrieking. Lightning incinerated the other two who dodged the trunk.

I climbed down from my borrowed horse and gestured for Long Feather to accompany me to a nearby tree on the hedge-side of the road. Even though I was tall for a woman, the closest climbing branch was just out of my reach.

No words were needed. Long Feather bent his knees and clasped his gloved hands together, palms up. I stepped onto his hands and he boosted me high enough for me to grab the branch. He ducked out of the way as I swung to loop my leg over the limb. Once seated in the tree, I could easily see the four skinwalkers running through the freshly plowed field.

Biming, his fellow priest, and a pair of their wardens slipped through the holes in the hedges the skinwalkers had made. Each man from Thief now carried a spear as they raced silently after our foes.

Spears? Where in the Twelve had the spears come from? However, each weapon had the same soft cat's paw feeling of Thief magic.

No, not just spears. The spears were held within throwing tubes that some nations of the Cradle used to increase their range.

Maybe I could assist them. I concentrated on the rows of sprouting plants and used them as markers. My time freeze spell sprang to life. The skinwalkers paused in mid-stride. The Thief personnel halted, totally confused.

In the back of my mind, the Reverend Mother told Biming what I did. She ordered them to get closer and throw their Balance-damned spears before my spell slipped.

My entire body shook in my efforts to hold time around the skinwalkers. I felt more than saw Jonata climbed the tree where I perched. Behind me, she straddled the branch and hugged me to prevent me from falling at the strain of clinging to the time around the skinwalkers.

The Thief personnel launched their spears, and I dropped the time freeze. Biming and his people's aims were true. The spearheads pierced each of the skinwalkers, and they tumbled across the field, crushing the new plants with their corpses.

I sagged against Jonata. Part of me wondered if I could make it back to the palace in my exhaustion.

"We'll sit here for a moment, m'lady," she whispered in my ear. "Long Feather and I would be terribly embarrassed if we accidentally dropped you on your head getting you out of the tree."

I couldn't stop the loud laughter that erupted from my throat.

CHAPTER 27

Finally, I felt strong enough to climb down from the plum tree. Granted, I needed Jonata and Long Feather's assistance, but they didn't have to haul my dead weight back to my borrowed horse.

The Jing Thief wardens collected most of the corpses. However, they didn't have any axes to remove the body crushed under the tree. Master Zhi produced two bone saws, and she and her journeyperson cut off any part they could reach.

The Jing Balance wardens moved among the dead on the road and cut off the heads. The healers made room on their wagon to carry the corpses back to Chengzhou. Perhaps we would return in time to throw the dead skinwalkers inside the burning buildings. They didn't need the formal prayers of Death. The skinwalkers had already betrayed the Twelve by wallowing in demon magic.

However, they carefully wrapped their dead comrade in his own robes, and tied him to a fellow warden's saddle. Another innocent in the long list of those who died around me in this mad war.

Reverend Mother Xiang nudged her horse closer to me. "The lightning is an interesting talent, Chief Justice." Her unspoken question hung in the cool night air.

"Yes," I answered. "May we please discuss my unusual predilections tomorrow? We need to get back to Chengzhou and inform the crown prince and the rest of the Temples of Wu's escape."

She sighed. "Yes, we do. Not to mention we have demons and their allies roving so close to the capital during the Spring Rituals."

I said nothing more. I hated the rituals, mainly because I was a product of them, not from a loving couple, but two people who were nearly children themselves and barely knew what they wanted or would become.

But last year, I realized how much everyone else needed the release of emotions and, more importantly, the symbol of hope. That everything would keep on going no matter what.

The demons didn't just want to prevent a stable Jing. They wanted to destroy the people's spirits. Crush their hopes. It reminded me of how livestock didn't fight back.

And frankly, I wasn't sure how I would hold on to my own hope with all the death surrounding me.

Crawling through the sewers of Chengzhou wasn't Wu's first choice, but if his son followed imperial family precedent, he would have sealed any palace escape routes Wu had known about after he had been sentenced for treason. However, Wu had created his own plan shortly before Yu's death. Just in case Po ceased the throne from Chengwu.

His gut instinct not to tell his own son of his plan had been accurate, but not for the reason he expected. If anyone would have asked him at Chengwu's birth, he never thought his own son would let the Temples try and convict him. But he watched Chengwu grow soft like Yu. Softness would not save the empire from destruction.

Wu needed the demons to make Jing strong so that when the thousand-year war was over, the empire could rule over the entire world.

Magic caressed the earth and terra cotta pipes around him. Both citizens and Temples were fighting the fire he'd started. Even he had been surprised at how fast the conflagration had spread to the surrounding buildings. From the heat that penetrated the sewers, he was guaranteed the blaze had eliminated the corpses of his students.

It seemed like hours later before he reached the magically sealed steel door above his head. With the magic permeating the city as talents battled the fire, no one would feel the minor works he needed. He murmured his counterspell and pushed the door upward. The hinges squeaked loudly.

He paused and waited to see if anyone responded to the noise. However, no one came. He breathed the putrid air in relief, climbed out of the sewer, and lit a tiny light ball to find his way.

This was the lowest level of the palace. The staff only came down here when there was a problem with waste blocking the sewer exits. Otherwise, no one entered this section of their own volition. The smell made the petty commoners lose the contents of their stomachs.

Wu strode in the direction of his access to the palace. There was a private room in the harem wing that had been sealed off from the rest of the palace centuries ago.

According to the gossip he'd overheard from the staff, one of the earliest emperors had bricked his cheating concubine in her quarters to slowly starve to death. The ghost of the concubine allegedly haunted the harem quarters and appeared to those concubines who were about to be killed for displeasing their emperors or empresses.

Oddly, the staff had been correct in the first part of their rumor. When Wu found the room, a mummified corpse lay on the bed. He chopped up the body and flushed the bits down the sewer before he turned the room into his own fortress.

When he reached the appropriate wall, he shed his clothing. It would have to be disposed of, but first, he needed to bathe, eat and rest. He murmured the appropriate spell. The bricks folded back upon themselves, and he entered the room.

Other than a little dust, the room was exactly how he left it a little over a year ago. He placed the light ball in an alabaster receptacle on the writing table before he turned and folded the bricks back into place.

Inside the bathing area, he found the flint and steel next to the oil lamp. He struck a spark to light the lamp. The flame flickered and smoked from the dust for a moment. Once the lamp burned bright and steady, he twisted the knobs to fill the tub with water. The spout chugged, gurgled, and spat. Residue clouded the water, but after a few moments it ran clear.

Wu plugged the drain with a piece of cork and climbed into the tub. The water immediately clouded as he sluiced off a year's worth of dirt and the recent sewage from his skin. It may take a couple of baths to feel totally clean again, but he had the time. No sense rushing into any action.

No, he'd take the time to spy on Yu's bastard and discover the best way to eliminate the thorn in his side once and for all. Then he'd impregnate the peasant girl who overreached her position before he claimed the Dragon Throne as the savior of Jing.

CHAPTER 28

When we reached Chengzhou's northern gates, I feared for a moment the guards would not let us in. I couldn't fault them. After all, Reverend Father Biming and Reverend Mother Xiang had warned the city the fire might be a distraction from additional demon attacks.

Thankfully, a Wildling sister was on duty at the gate. She turned into a beautiful large tiger, like Shi Hua's friend Fa. The sister took her time sniffing each one of us and our horses before she shifted back to human form and bowed to the Temple leaders.

She straightened. "Forgive me for taking so long, Reverend Mother. The odor of demons—"

"Clings to us like Death's shroud," Reverend Mother Xiang replied. "I don't fault you, Sister. Your care and that of the rest the guards is necessary in these trying times."

The wildling bowed again before she ordered the portcullis raised to allow us through.

Smoke lingered heavily in the air, obscuring even my unusual eyesight. However, we headed for the center of the city instead of the direction of the heat sitting over the west side of Chengzhou. But I held my tongue about assisting in fighting the blaze. I'd already pushed my luck in dealing with the leaders of Jing over other issues.

Plus, I wouldn't be much help. I barely had the fortitude to remain upright on my borrowed horse.

The Reverend Mother chuckled. "I can hear your unspoken question, my curious one. The fire is contained. Justice Mei Wen says it's a matter of time before the flames are totally extinguished."

I sighed. "Forgive me, Reverend Mother. I did not intend to insinuate, even silently, that the leaders of Chengzhou couldn't perform their duties."

"I realize you enjoy being in the center of all the action, but you can relax in this matter," she said. "I promise to inform you once we have more information concerning a certain someone's escape."

"Thank you, Reverend Mother."

The healers and the Thief personnel stopped at the Temple of Death to dispose of the skinwalker corpses and ensure the body of their fallen

Balance warden received the appropriate respect. The Reverend Mother and her wardens escorted me and mine directly to the palace. I thanked her again for dinner.

She laughed loud enough she startled the imperial guards. "I hope our next dinner together will be much more boring, my curious one."

After the squires took our horses, Jonata whispered in Diné, "I think the Reverend Mother of Jing has taken a liking to you."

"Everyone loves the chief justice when she saves their asses," Long Feather added in the same tongue. "Let's see what tomorrow brings."

I had to laugh. "Can we please get some rest this night before you two add more to my plate?"

"Of course, Lady Justice," Jonata murmured. But the three of us were so tired, we giggled as the imperial guards escorted us to our quarters.

I took a long bath to rinse the smell of the dead and the smoke from my skin and hair. When I stepped from the bath, the bells of the Temples rang Second Night. Despite my exhaustion, I wasn't sure I'd be able to sleep this night. Too many questions whirled through my head.

After donning a robe, wrapping my hair in a towel, and grabbing the bottle of ojon oil, I stepped into our bed chamber to find Luc reading by the fire. In all the excitement, I hadn't realized how much the night had cooled. It was still technically winter after all.

At least until the middle of the coming week. I had hoped to have one Rest Day to relax on this blasted journey that didn't involve being severely injured and in pain. But this Rest Day had been fuller than any other during this mission.

Luc looked up from the tome he read and smiled. "I hear you had some excitement after your dinner at the Temple of Balance."

"I hear you had some excitement in the city as well." I retrieved my comb from my pack. Things had been so insane I hadn't unpacked any of my belongings yet. Perhaps I should have done that instead of pacing in our suite's common room earlier today.

"Don't worry. I wasn't involved." He marked his page and set aside the book, but not before I noticed it was written in the Peaceful Sea trading language. Interesting. The written version of the patois was rarely used except for shipping contracts and bills of lading. He hooked his right foot around the padded stool he'd been using for his legs and pulled it closer to his chair.

"Is that because Yar threatened to tie you up if you tried to leave the palace," I teased.

Luc laughed and took my comb from my outstretched hand. "Actually, it was the current captain of the empress's guard."

I laughed as well as I handed him the bottle. "No doubt, he was ordered by his mistress. Mateqai and Shi Hua both know you too well." However, I quickly sobered. "What did Mateqai tell you?"

"Not Mateqai. Shi Hua." Luc opened the bottle and sniffed the contents. "Ojon oil? Should I have Long Feather taste it?"

"No, Jonata already tested it for poisons." I sat on the stool and looked over my shoulder at my love. "And you're avoiding my question. What did Shi Hua tell you?"

Luc snorted as he unwound my towel. "That Wu Sunshu has escaped, and you ran into some demons and skinwalkers on the way back to the city. Captain Huizhong has already doubled the guards around the crown prince. Mateqai had Lady Shi Hua move to separate quarters as a precaution. One of the Skoloti guards is staying in her bedchamber."

I sighed. "As if poor Po doesn't have enough problems."

"Poor Po, my ass," Luc snapped, but he was gentle while he worked the oil through my tresses.

"What is your problem with him now?" I asked in a quiet voice.

He paused his motions for a moment. "It's not him exactly. I . . . don't like the fact that you put your life at risk for a people that would just as soon kill you because you are Temple."

"And these people deserved to be fed to demons because of the idiotic power struggles by their own leaders?"

He exhaled and started combing my hair. "You're right. They don't." After a long moment, he added, "It's been a long time since I've helped you with your hair."

"Nearly two years," I murmured.

"Maybe I should have run away to Cant with you while we had the chance." He hugged me from behind.

"We've long since passed that particular fork in the road, my beloved." I patted his hands. "All we can do is continue forward."

I deliberately changed the subject. "I'm sorry to have missed our conference with Duke White Eagle and Lord Ayatulutul. How are things back home?"

"Allegedly uneventful compared to here, but the duke was . . . rather distracted during our short talk."

"What do you mean?"

Luc paused again and I looked over my shoulder at him.

"It's nothing to do with Issura, and I didn't want to ask him a personal question with a third party involved in our conversation. Nor did I tell him about Wu's escape and your encounter on the way back to Chengzhou. Not until I had more information."

I chuckled. "By our next Rest Day communication, Po will be coronated or dead. I doubt the missing aspects of your report will matter by then."

"True." He continued combing my hair, working the oil through my tresses and allowing the fire to dry it.

After the task was complete, I rose, shed my robe, and donned my night shift. He banked the fire before he shed his own clothing and joined me in bed. We didn't speak another word. There was nothing else to say, except to rehash the same worries and concerns. But holding each other kept the fears at bay long enough for us both to fall asleep.

CHAPTER 29

The peals of the Temple bells woke me. I listened to the pattern. Third Morning, already?

I rolled over and patted the bedding, but Luc had been long gone from the chill of the material. I sat and looked around. My spare uniform was laid out on one of the padded chairs.

I rose and quickly dressed before I poked my head through the door. Only Long Feather sat in the common room. He looked up from his Leaf cards.

"Good morn, m'lady." His smile was brilliant. "Do you need assistance with your hair?"

"Yes." I frowned. "Where's everyone else?"

"The high brother is assisting Duke Mengchang with his questioning of the palace staff. Warden Yar is with him. Warden Jonata is still sleeping."

"Who was up all night on sentry duty?" I asked.

"Warden Yar and I split the night watch since Jonata took last night," Long Feather said. "You and she needed the sleep after our extracurricular fun yesterday."

My still awaking mind finally noticed his own tresses. Instead of leaving them loose or tying them back with a thong, they were wrapped in a Diné warrior's knot.

"Why did you bind up your hair?"

A wry smile crossed his face. "It was still damp after I bathed this morning. Jonata wrapped it for me so the moisture didn't ruin the leather of my jerkin before she went back to bed." He shrugged. "A precaution since we can't anticipate where the next emergency may come from. I hope we didn't offend you."

I laughed. "No, you didn't. My blood may be three-quarters Diné, but I'm Issuran through and through. However, could you do the same for my own tresses? You wardens are not the only one anticipating the next alarm. It would be much faster than braiding my hair."

"Of course, m'lady." He nodded and rose. "Also, you and the high brother have been invited to dine with the crown prince and his lady wife at the midday meal."

I retrieved my comb and the appropriate ties from my bags. I check the bathing room. Sure enough, my dirty uniform was missing.

When I return to the common room, I asked, "Where is my filthy uniform?"

"One of the Justices and her wardens came to the palace while you were still asleep." He accepted my comb and ties before he gestured for me to take the chair he'd vacated. "They took our dirty uniforms for cleaning. When they return them tonight, they will bring additional uniforms for us, courtesy of the Reverend Mother."

I opened my mouth, but he held up his hand holding my comb.

"Do not fear. High Brother Luc truthspelled them to confirm their identities. The Reverend Father of Light is providing the same uniforms for the high brother and Warden Yar."

"It's still terribly generous of them," I murmured as I sat in the chair.

"As I said last night, everyone loves you when you save their asses." He placed the ties on the table.

His sharp tone was unlike his normally jovial disposition. I looked over my shoulder at him.

"Is there a problem you wish to discuss, Long Feather?" I kept my voice gentle. I didn't want him to think this was a reprimand.

Orange bloomed in his cheeks, and he dropped his gaze to the carpeted floor. "I beg forgiveness, m'lady. I was out of line."

I turned in the seat to really look at him. "I want you to be honest with me. I trust your instincts. If there's something bothering you . . ."

"It's personal, m'lady." He pursed his lips.

"Then this will remain between us." I grasped his free hand. "I depend on you to watch my back. I hope you know I will always do the same for you."

He blew out a deep, resigned breath. "I am frustrated on your behalf. I see you sacrifice everything for people. In Issura. In Diné. In Jing. When times are stable, they treat you like manure. But the instant a demon or a skinwalker shows, they are pleading with you to save them."

I chuckled. "I don't recall much pleading from the general populace."

"And last night, Jing would have lost two Temple leaders if it weren't for you," Long Feather spat.

"And Reverend Mother Xiang is showing her appreciation by providing us with things we need." I squeezed his hand. "However, I understand your feelings. I have the same ones occasionally. But I also have my duties, as a justice and as a priestess. I hope you don't resent me because I feel the sacrifices you and all of my wardens make, and I wish to Balance that you didn't have to make them."

He squeezed my hand in return. "None of us resent you, m'lady. I just wish everyone else in the world could see you as we do."

My eyes stung at the love and loyalty in his voice. "Thank you for trusting me with your emotions." I wiped away the tears that escaped down my cheeks. "However, let's deal with today before we deal with tomorrow."

He nodded. "Of course."

As he combed out the few tangles from me tossing in my sleep, I wondered why Balance blessed me with such a wonderful squad of wardens. I surely didn't deserve them or the sacrifices they made on my behalf.

After the best night's sleep Wu had in over a year, he explored the palace's secret passages with a shielded conventional lamp. As he suspected, his son had sealed off those emergency exits Wu had known about. However, several of the spy passages were still accessible, though none anywhere near the imperial family's quarters.

He resigned himself to listening to the palace staff's gossip, hoping for a scrap of real information. What he hadn't expected was to hear the Issuran Light priest question the staff about their loyalties and any knowledge of an assassin who had infiltrated the palace.

Wu leaned back against the stone wall in the cramped passage. So, his former allies tried to kill the bastard again and failed. Again. Was Po more skilled in his Thief magic than he let on? No one should have that much luck in escaping death.

Or had Yu known about the bastard's skill and hidden it from the Temples so they wouldn't claim the boy?

No. His dead wife had no method to shield the bastard. She could barely light a fire with her own abilities. Po marrying a Light priestess was the only damn thing the boy had done that made sense.

Wu smiled to himself. The renegades shouldn't have tried to kill him. He would have been happy to show them alternate routes into the palace besides the one path he'd handed to them. Maybe the demons and renegades weren't as fearsome as everyone else believed. They made so many mistakes.

His ears pricked when two of the kitchen workers started whispering about the Red Justice. That she'd killed a dozen demons last night and saved Biming and Xiang.

Wu frowned as the rumors turned to the tale she had returned from a demon passage. That perhaps she was a demon herself. How else could she fight demons so fiercely? What if she defeated the demons only to take over the world?

The palace staff tended to exaggerate, but he needed to do some research. This Issuran priestess could be more of a problem than he originally suspected.

CHAPTER 30

Jonata woke before I needed to leave for our meeting with the imperial couple. She grinned when she saw how Long Feather had styled my hair to match his, and she did the same.

The crown prince held our midday meal in the emperor's private dining room. In addition to the Issuran party, our false Sister Darys and Duke Mengchang were included. The shutters were closed against the bright spring sunshine and fresh air. Shi Hua took the precaution of warding the room once the imperial guards and our wardens were satisfied our food was not poisoned.

"The entire staff has been questioned, Your Highness," Mengchang reported. "I extend my thanks to High Brother Luc and Warden Yar for their assistance. The high brother and Brother Jian made quite a team." He turned to me with a smirk that reminded me of Po's expression. "And you were quite correct, Chief Justice. When given the choice between being interrogated by High Brother Luc or you, the staff overwhelming chose the high brother."

Everyone around the table laughed.

"Reverend Father Biming says you and he have mended your relationship. Is this true, Chief Justice?" Amusement tilted the corners of the crown prince's mouth as he watched me.

I nodded. "We both understand our mutual objectives must take precedence over any personal disagreements."

"And saving his ass last night had nothing to do with it?" Po teased.

"We spoke honestly with each other prior to the demon attack," I said. "In fact, that honest discussion was the reason we were outside of the city after dark to check on Wu."

"Unfortunately, the Wildling and Thief Temples had no success in tracking our escaped prisoner." Shi Hua sighed. "Too many other scents obscured Wu's with citizens coming into the city for the Spring Rituals and demons running around the countryside."

She turned to me. "I know you are supposed to be our coordinator with the Temples, Anthea, but Mei Wen has been reporting to me while you caught up on your sleep this morning."

"It is not a problem, m'lady," I murmured. "I appreciate the extra rest."

Shi Hua frowned. "It's just us. Can we please not stand on ceremony right now?"

"I apologize. I just—" I shrugged as I searched for the right words. "I don't want my tongue to slip in public. I am supposed to be Issura's ambassador at the moment, not your friend. The last thing I want or you need is for me to treat our relationship in a casual manner."

She nodded, but her sadness at her realization in the changes of our statuses mixed with my own.

Po cleared his throat. "You were instrumental in getting the Temples off their collective asses, Chief Justice—"

"Your Highness, please stop there." I held up my right palm to emphasize my words. "The Temples in Jing have had to dance around the nobility and the schools of sorcery. And even though you married a woman who left her Temple for you, they weren't sure of your feelings or your intentions towards them. You have been gone for the last eight winters."

He nodded. "Your advice is welcome, m'lady. I have become used to the initiative of Orrin's Temple seats over the last few years. For that alone, I appreciate your efforts as well as those of High Brother Luc and Sister Darys."

He nodded to the other two clergy members before his attention returned to me. "Since we don't have enough distance speakers, each team of clergy and wardens guarding the members of the Bao family have been reporting to Lady Shi Hua as well."

Mengchang blinked. "Th-the lady is a distance speaker?"

Shi Hua looked at her husband. "Did you forget to inform the duke of an important matter, my love?"

Po chuckled. "My apologies, cousin. We've had to keep the secret of my lady wife's ability for so long it has become second nature. I did not intend to keep you in the dark."

The duke inclined his head. "No apology is necessary, Your Highness. Your brother had informed me he sent a distance speaker with you to Issura, but I had not known who it was. The late emperor hid the distance speaker's identity as a precaution. It never occurred to me it was Lady Shi Hua." Mengchang turned and inclined his head to her. "Forgive an old man his presumptions, my lady."

"You have offered no offense, Your Grace," Shi Hua said. "It says more about the situation in Jing that we cannot be honest with our own allies at times."

"Unfortunate, but true." The duke smiled. "The fact that you and the crown prince include me in your inner circle means more to me than you'll ever know."

"Cousin, do you know of any other private accesses to the palace I am unaware of?" Po played with the gold beads on his left mustachio. I really needed to speak with him about his unconscious gesture. The habit could be detrimental to him in the future.

Mengchang shook his head. "The only ones I knew about were the same ones Wu knew of. Upon his sentencing, the emperor—that is, your brother ordered me to brick them up, so if Wu revealed them, no one could gain access."

"That doesn't mean Wu didn't make alternate arrangements when he decided to demon deal," I murmured.

"That was my fear as well, Lady Justice." The duke frowned. "My fears doubled with the assassination of the imperial family." He hesitated for a moment. "Reverend Mother Xiao Mei of Knowledge has been privately assisting me in going through the records for any other egress into the palace."

"If I may speak, Chief Justice," Jonata piped up from behind me.

I turned to her and nodded. "Of course, Warden."

"I've assisted in research within the Orrin Temple of Knowledge, Your Grace," she said. "With the chief justice's permission, I would like to offer my services."

Duke Mengchang frowned and looked at the crown prince. "Is this acceptable to you, Your Highness?"

Po chuckled. "In case you haven't noticed, the chief justice of Orrin likes to train her people in other Temples' responsibilities. I can say Warden Jonata is telling you truly that she has served as Balance's researcher when one of their clerks was attending to other duties. She may also catch things because she is not Jing."

The duke nodded. "Your help would be appreciated if Chief Justice Anthea can spare you."

I nodded. "Of course, Warden Jonata can assist you. The more fingers to read the books and scrolls, the faster your task can be accomplished."

"You speak the Jing language well enough, Warden, but can you read it?" False Darys asked Jonata. "It is for most of us who aren't from the empire."

"I'm still learning." Jonata smiled. "I may have to ask about characters I do not know."

"My warden is being overly modest, Sister." I smiled at Jonata. "She spoke six languages and reads in all of them before she picked up Jing on our voyage here."

Jonata's face glowed a bright yellow.

False Darys chuckled. "You have a knack for picking people with non-magical talents."

"No, I don't." I laughed as well. "Balance has blessed me with competent staff. I merely give them their lead, and not one of them has disappointed me."

Jonata's cheeks flushed from brilliant yellow to orange. "You are too kind, Chief Justice."

Luc burst out laughing. "You know damn well she's not, Warden,"

Everyone in the room chuckled at Jonata's surface discomfiture. But her pleasure at my confidence in her, and Luc's teasing of me, overrode her embarrassment.

With all of us working together, maybe, just maybe, we could get through the week with everyone still alive.

CHAPTER 31

Two squires from Balance arrived at the palace shortly after we returned to our suite from our meeting with the imperial couple. They carried one new uniform each for me and my wardens and our cleaned clothing, and they collected our soiled uniforms for the launderers.

Later in the afternoon and well into the evening, the palace grew busier as members of the nobility arrived. A strange mix of anticipation and somberness formed the emotions battering my mental shields. I couldn't imagine how High Sister Mya, much less other clergy from Child, survived the normal progression of the Spring Rituals with their sanity intact.

However, every set of travelers retired to their suites without more than the usual fussing at the servants. Duke Mengchang was kind enough to send us a message that the rest of the Bao extended family had arrived intact, except for Duke Zixin and his party. Apparently, they had been delayed for a day, though Mengchang didn't say why. I prayed Zixin and his people were alive and well, and that this wasn't a deliberate slight aimed at Po. However, there was nothing I could do no matter which was the case for the delay.

Our small party from Issura dined in our suite. The fare was light with breads, cheese, dried fruits, and nuts. With the Spring Rituals starting tomorrow morning, the palace kitchens were busy preparing the feast for the opening day.

When we finished our meal and sipped plum wine, our wardens exchanged glances before Long Feather cleared his throat.

"Spit out whatever the three of you are thinking," Luc said dryly.

"Do you have a particular schedule for us in mind for the week?" he said.

Luc and I exchanged looks before I turned back to my warden. "What do you mean by a schedule? Steward Chin delivered the week's schedule of events we're expected—"

"No." Yar shook his head. "He means a particular schedule for us wardens during the non-official events."

My face grew warm as I realized what they were asking.

Luc chuckled. "The chief justice and I apologize for our miscommunication and lack of foresight. We're used to the chief wardens looking out for the rest of you during the Spring Rituals."

"Both the Jing Balance and Light chief wardens have said they'd be happy to cover our duties if we want to join the festivities," Jonata murmured. "Mateqai also had a private word with Yar. Plus, the Skoloti wardens said they would exchange duties in regard to our respective charges. Apparently, Sister Darys trusts us. However, we won't do anything without your approval, Chief Justice, High Brother."

"I-I beg your forgiveness, Wardens," I choked out. "I've been so consumed with the current matters—"

"We know, m'lady," Long Feather interjected. "Nor do we blame you. We had not expected to be involved in the festivities . . ."

"I hear the 'but' in your words," Luc teased.

"We actually want to do some investigating on our own," Yar stated brusquely. "We're not simply shirking our duties to either of you given the current circumstances in Chengzhou. Even though we're foreigners here, we may be able to extract more information if we attend the festivities as civilians."

"But we won't leave you with wardens you are uncomfortable with either," Jonata blurted. "Your safety is paramount."

"What do you suspect that you wish to investigate, Yar?" I asked.

"The fire on the west side of the city." A fierce expression took over his face. "One of the Love wardens said it appeared to be deliberately set in what most who live in that section believed to be an abandoned house."

"And how would a Love warden know this?" I asked.

"Messages are being passed through a circuitous route," Long Feather said. "It's not unusual for a Love priestess to visit with a new empress to discuss pleasuring the emperor and producing an heir."

I met Luc's gaze. The worry leaking from his psyche matched my own. The Jing Temple leaders were worried about the philosophy schools as well as the renegades to go to such measures.

"What triggered the Temples' suspicion concerning the burning of an unoccupied dwelling besides the flames spreading to nearby structures?" Luc asked.

"Human bones were found in the debris," Yar said. "The healers and the Temple of Death are still piecing them together, but four skulls were found. Those fighting the blaze detected both demon magic and generic sorcery, but only at the manse that was the origin of the fire according to the Temple of Balance."

Breath hissed between my lips at this news.

"It could be transients seeking shelter," Jonata volunteered. "A candle knocked over—"

"You don't believe that any more than I do," I said softly.

"You've pointed out repeatedly we must look at all possibilities, m'lady," she replied.

"Gah!" I rose and started pacing. "There's too many possibilities here!"

"But the timing of Wu's escape and the blaze—" Luc started to say.

"I know! I know!" I tossed my hands up. "I'd like to chop off one thread of this entire disastrous journey before the next strangles us."

"I totally agree, Chief Justice," said a new, but familiar, voice.

We all turned to see Yin Li step from mine and Luc's bedchamber. Blades leaving their scabbards hissed behind me.

"Forgive me for not approaching in a straight-forward manner." The Love priestess bowed. When she straightened, an amused smile curved her lips. "His Majesty did promise to show you a passage to escape Cheng-zhou should things go poorly for him during this week."

"You've all had a multitude of state affairs to deal with." I smiled in return. "But sneaking into our sleeping area is a good way to lose your life, my dear."

"I wouldn't have entered if one of you were actually in the room." Yin Li gestured at the bedchamber as she approached us. "I am very aware of your own capabilities, m'lady. Those facts I do not know, my empress has informed me. And anyone who can impress Reverend Mother Xiang is not someone to be treated lightly."

"That's what it took?" I mocked.

She laughed. "I didn't need convincing. However, Reverend Father Biming takes you much more seriously after seeing you blast four demons with lightning. It convinced him how you survived a demon portal."

"He should have taken my word seriously when I was truthspelled in Naha," I grumbled.

Yin Li sighed. "Far too true, m'lady. However, the emperor awaits us, and it's already late. Tomorrow will be a very long day with the opening ceremonies of the holiday. Shall we complete this demonstration before we retire for the night?"

"By all means, Sister."

I followed her into my bed chamber. To my surprise, Yin Li entered the bathing room and retrieved a small conventional lit lantern I knew damn well I hadn't left on the marble shelf near the door. Once all of us crowded into the tiny room, she pulled on the left sconce attached to the far wall. Now, I understood the real reason for the curled end of the gold-plated fixture. The cloth and string Knowledge lantern remained attached to the curved metal when the hinge was in its down position. I smiled at the very clever trick.

One of the thin slabs of marble opened outward into a dark corridor.

"Shang and I have been checking the secret passages for any impediments to Luc and his crutches." She chuckled. "We've also cleared out any spiders we found."

Yar shuddered. "Thank you very much for that small grace, m'lady."

I didn't tease the Light warden about his fear. More than one spider had bitten me during the decade Luc and I were on circuit in the eastern portion of the Duchy of Orrin. I wasn't a fan of the eight-legged creatures either.

"Whatever you do, don't use a light ball or any other magic illumination in these passages," Yin Li added. "Anyone with natural talents or educated at the schools of philosophy will detect the magic. However, there's a few places where you will need to activate a spell. The magic is presumed to be part of the alarm system. At least, that's the story Thief tells if anyone notices them."

"Just a moment." Long Feather raced out of the bathing room. A moment later, he returned with a small oil lamp, the kind most untalented people carried on journeys. A white flame flickered at the end of the wick. He noticed my attention and shrugged.

"No insult to Lady Yin Li, but you've taught us to be prepared," he said. I merely nodded and entered the passage after Jonata.

I couldn't help but notice the wardens kept Luc and I between each of them as we followed Yin Li in a single file. We also didn't need to be told to keep silent.

I also remained quiet about being able to see in the corridor. Only Luc knew about this aspect of my odd sight.

Like the closed off tunnels beneath the Temple in Orrin, a lavender light shone from the incredibly tiny living things clinging to the passage's walls. With all the chaos surrounding the reappearance of the demons, I hadn't had a chance to borrow a magnifying glass to examine the beings to know whether they were a type of plant or animal.

Balance Herself foretold the war between humans and demons would last a thousand years. If She was right, the struggle would end before I died of old age. Maybe, just maybe, if I survived the conflict, I could indulge my curiosity about the things only I could see.

We made one left turn and then a right. At twenty paces, Yin Li stopped in front of another brick wall. This time, she murmured the same spell we used in Orrin to access the Temple tunnels. The bricks folded out of the way, opening another passage.

Or rather what appeared to be a dead end. The room we entered was slightly larger than our suite's bathing rooms. To my surprise, Reverend Father Biming waited for us. He also carried a conventional lantern.

"Come. I'll explain everything when we return here." He touched the section of brick wall to our left and whispered the spell. Like before, the bricks folded back. He gestured for us to follow him.

"But Yin Li," I whispered.

"Will be fine until we return," he said.

This passageway we traveled through was a little wider than the first one. It also grew colder the further we walked. I memorized the paces and turns, but I also marked the wall with my finger. I regretted killing the tiny creatures living on the wall. However, in an emergency, I wanted to be sure we had a back-up system for finding our way out of the palace.

The Reverend Father brought us to a section where the palace's aqueduct entered through the stone walls. The moving liquid hummed through the huge clay pipe. However, there was simply no method anyone larger than a third-winter child could slip through the pipe itself, assuming they didn't drown. From the vibration, the pipe was completely full.

Biming demonstrated the spell to widen the opening around the pipe to allow a full-grown person to exit before he had Luc and me practice it.

"What do we do if we lose them or they are unconscious?" Long Feather murmured.

"You need to trust your own abilities to keep one of them alive and conscious," the Reverend Father said.

"But the horses we borrowed—" Jonata started.

"If our new emperor dies this week, Chengzhou will fall. I mean no ill will to you Issurans, but you may not have help from us." Biming shook his head sadly. "And if things go so badly that we can't help you, you're going to need to do anything you have to in order to get your charges back to the coast and aboard the *Mars Tranquilus*. If you can't do that, you are all lost, Warden."

His bald statement sobered all of us. We knew Po's position as heir to the throne of Jing was precarious, but Biming drove that point home. If the emperor died before we could leave this nation, we were well and truly doomed.

CHAPTER 32

"Thank you for your honest, if brutal, assessment, Reverend Father," I said. "My wardens needed to hear your words."

"After seeing your skills in action, I'm sure they have faith you will pull them through any trouble," he replied.

"No, Reverend Father," Yar rumbled. "The high brother and chief justice have taught us to work together. And they trust us to watch their backs. We will not fail them."

"Have you shown Sister Darys and her wardens this exit?" Luc asked.

Biming shook his head. "Yin Li showed them a different one."

Another concern joined the others wriggling through my mind. "Two secret exits are more than enough to allow any demons and skinwalkers into the palace."

"We're sure there are more than Po and I found as children." Biming chuckled at the memory, but he quickly sobered. "Chengwu joined us in mapping all the ones we could locate. I fear there is one that only Wu knew about."

"The skinwalker who wore Emperor Chengwu's concubine—" Luc started.

"High Brother, let us go back, and then you can question me all you wish." Biming made a show of rubbing his hands together. "Winter still has claim on this side of the world until First Morning."

"I second the Reverend Father's suggestion," I murmured. "I've become used to the warmth of the South Peaceful Sea and the mild weather we've experienced since we left the coast."

Luc snorted. "What you really want is a hot cup of Jing Tea."

"Both can be true," I retorted.

With that, we followed Reverend Father Biming to the room where we met him.

Wu groaned in frustration and disappointment. His head ached so badly he wanted to bang his head on the bricks in front of him. His hands itched as if stung by a hundred wasps, but the impenetrable spell on this section of wall refused to crack. It had to be a doorway to the wing that housed the imperial family. His precocious son had brought those damnable frauds to the palace, instead of someone from one of the rival philosophy schools.

Temple magic wasn't just power, or so the priests said. They claimed it was the belief in the Twelve that formed the foundation of their magics' strength.

Wu snorted. It had more to do with all their being resting in one particular talent, instead of using a variety of talents as his school had taught. In fact, his rejection by the Temples was the best thing that ever happened to him. It allowed him to stretch himself in ways he could have only imagined as a youth.

Burning the remaining School of Sorcery's grimoires had been foolish in hindsight. The library in the School of the Phoenix and Dragon would be the next best resource, but the masters there wouldn't voluntarily assist him. That didn't mean one of the apprentices wouldn't help.

He smiled to himself. It was time to visit the young gentleman who hexed Quan. With everyone out for the Spring Rituals tomorrow, he should be able to access the grounds of the rival school.

Wu started back toward his hidden rooms, planning his disguise for tomorrow's venture in public. Time was short. He needed to kill the bastard and consolidate his power over Jing before the demons and renegades made their next move.

CHAPTER 33

A third magically sealed door was hidden in the anteroom where we'd met Biming. When we passed through that doorway, Po and Shi Hua waited for us inside a room about the size of the anteroom, along with three pots of steaming Jing tea.

The pillows for sitting were silk. Two lacquered tables had been pushed together to make room for everyone. The only tension came from Shi Hua, but the angry glances she shot at Biming left no doubt as to the reason for her stress.

Sister, if he gives you any more grief, I will come back to Jing and take care of him for you. I sent her a crude image of blasting off his manhood with lightning before taking his head.

Shi Hua burst out laughing, and she nearly dropped the cup she was handing to Yar.

"What is so funny, m'lady?" Biming asked. "I could use a good joke."

"Nothing that concerns you, Reverend Father," she said smoothly. "At least, nothing that concerns you yet." She shot him a wicked smile.

When he opened his mouth, Po held up his finger. "For your own sake, my old friend, don't ask and don't even think about asking."

"Why not?"

"Because the chief justice probably just threatened to do something unpleasant to you if you give the empress any more manure." Luc accept his cup from Shi Hua. "Thank you, m'lady." He turned back to Biming. "The last time she laughed like that, both Anthea and Mateqai promised to do me harm for the way I treated the lady while she was with child."

Biming blinked. Then his expression shifted to one of joy as he looked from Shi Hua to Po and back again. "Truly?"

Po grinned and nodded. Shi Hua blushed bright orange.

Jonata snickered. "Time to pay up, boys."

Both Long Feather and Yar grumbled, but they reached into their pockets and slid two coppers each across the table to her.

"You were betting on whether I was with child?" Shi Hua's embarrassed expression turned into outrage.

"No, m'lady." Yar cleared his throat. "The bet was whether the chief justice could keep the knowledge to herself before you and the crown prince announced the news."

Shi Hua rolled her eyes. "Of course, she would keep quiet after what happened with Duke Marco and Lady Katarina."

A grin stretched Biming's lips. He reached over and hugged Po.

"My congratulations to you and Lady Shi Hua," Biming said. "I pray the Twelve grant you a healthy pregnancy and delivery, m'lady." He turned back to me. "However, I am most curious about what you did to the duke and his wife."

I sighed and sipped my tea before I answered. "I revealed Lady Katerina was with child. Not only before she told Marco, but before she realized it herself."

"Your different sight?" Biming asked.

I nodded. "I nearly caused them to break their marriage contract." I shrugged. "However, I apologized profusely, and I learned my lesson from that incident. No matter my personal affection for anyone, I need to keep silent until they are ready to reveal their good news publicly."

"I wanted to share the news with you, Anthea—" Shi Hua started.

I waved away her attempted apology. "I love you like a blood sister, but I also understand your new position. My feelings weren't damaged." I bit my tongue to keep from saying she was pregnant too soon after delivering Chao two days after the Winter Solstice. Even though I would never bear a child, I was very much aware of the toll that pregnancy extracted from a woman's body.

Instead, I shot a look at her husband. "However, I am impressed the crown prince didn't climb the roof of the palace and crow like a cock for proving his seed is viable."

Everyone laughed at my jest, even Po.

"Since this is our one last conference before the week's festivities, Luc, you had a question about the skinwalker inside the palace," Biming prompted. We all quickly sobered at a reminder of why we were here.

"Did any of Emperor Chengwu's harem know about the secret passages within the palace?" Luc felt troubled. Whatever he was thinking, he did not share it with me.

"I feel like I'm gossiping." Biming grimaced. "Once Chengwu was married, he had no relations with anyone, man, woman, or *berda*. To my knowledge, he only told the empress. He may have told his eldest son, Sunshu, but Long was only four winters. I doubt he would have truly understood the danger to him and the potential safety of escaping through the passageways. Our former emperor wouldn't have randomly told anyone else."

"Are you sure he didn't visit the harem, or the women didn't visit him through the secret passages?" Jonata asked.

"I'm sure," Biming said. "His marriage was one of love, not duty." He sighed. "Though it helped that she was noble-born."

But Po cleared his throat. "If we were discussing our grandfather, then yes, some of the harem would have known. My grandparents had a state marriage. There was no love between them. He needed an heir, but Mother was their only surviving child."

Biming jerked at some realization and muttered an obscenity under his breath. "Lady Heng."

Po frowned. "Mother ejected her from the palace before Grandfather's body was cold."

"That doesn't mean the concubine in question didn't know of alternate routes," Biming said.

"Who is Lady Heng?" I asked.

Po and Biming exchanged uneasy glances.

"That was thirty years ago," the Thief priest said.

"She was a former noblewoman who tried to seduce Grandfather into marrying her and making her his new empress." Disgust laced Po's voice. "She thought if she could bear him a boy, her son would replace Mother as Grandfather's heir."

"And?" Luc prompted.

"Her first son was stillborn, and the second son was born with his spine outside of his body." Po shook his head. "She stabbed the healers attending the second birth and strangled the child before the other ladies realized what she was doing."

"Let me guess," I said sourly. "Lady Heng claimed it was pregnancy madness."

"How did you know?" Biming asked.

"My birth mother claimed the same thing when she tried to abort me." I shook my head. "Except she used that as her excuse for the next thirty-two winters."

Biming's eyes narrowed. "I'll have my staff search for Lady Heng when

I return to the Temple. If she wanted revenge, I can't see her waiting until Empress Yu passed."

"Why did Emperor Chengwu keep concubines if he had no intention of . . . using them?" Long Feather asked.

Again, Po and Biming exchanged glances, but this time, it was amusement they shared.

"Appearances," Biming said.

"Mother kept a harem of men for similar reasons, though she only bedded one of them in retaliation for Wu overstepping propriety." Po blew out a deep breath. "Chengwu encouraged her to throw aside his own father for the way he treated Mother."

"If Wu had a secret entrance into the palace, he could have told the skinwalker," Shi Hua said. "Balance confirmed during his trial that he consorted with demons. If he murdered Master Quan for his relationship with Empress Yu, it's likely he had no problem sacrificing his own son and grandsons to force the crown prince back to Jing."

Biming's right eyebrow rose. "That is a lot of conjecture, m'lady."

"No, Reverend Father, it's experience," I said. "My own birth mother went through obsessive lengths to get me executed or kill me herself. She didn't give a damn who stood in her way."

Beneath the table, Luc's left hand clasped my right.

"Chief Justice, you said the skinwalker, who confronted you and the Reverend Father last night, mentioned Wu was hiding the rest of the demon eggs he'd been given. He could have hidden them within the palace, and someone stumbled over them," Yar said.

We all looked at him, and he shrugged.

"The eggs do appear as jewels to those of us with regular sight," he continued. "A concubine would have thought she found a nest egg for when she left the harem."

"How do demon eggs appear to you, Anthea?" Biming asked.

"The handful I've seen have all looked like sapphires," I said.

"The ones retrieved at our southern border resembled sapphires, emeralds, and rubies." Biming noted. "You can't see within a demon egg?"

I laughed. "I can't see through an egg shell or a wall any more than you can."

"If we had time and personnel, we could perform a thorough search,"

Long Feather said. "Perhaps we should stay in Chengzhou after the crown prince's coronation."

Luc laughed. "That would raise more questions about our intentions than solve any of our problems."

"How did the imperial guards know they were dealing with a skinwalker during last winter's attack on the palace?" I asked softly.

"They didn't." Biming's frown deepened. "We only learned after personnel from the Healers Guild and Death arrived. Reverend Father Jun Hie spotted the oddity of the extra skin because with her death, the skinwalker's magic no longer animated the dead flesh. Master Healer Zhi investigated further." He shrugged. "It's not like we can see the effects like you can while the skinwalker is alive, Anthea."

"With all due respect, my lords, someone within the palace let those demons in, or they brought in eggs and used people here to hatch them," Yar said.

"It would have had to been the eggs," Shi Hua said. "The Temple alarm spells weren't designed for eggs. Only the hatched demons,"

"Unless the demons were wearing human skins," I corrected. "That was how they got the eggs into Orrin's Temples last year when Po, Luc, and I were in Tandor."

"My apologies for not being specific." Shi Hua smiled at me. "I deliberately try to forget that incident after what happened to Yanaba." She shook her head, but she projected a sense of wonder, not fear. "Light help us, we didn't even know the blasted creatures reproduced by eggs until the one was smuggled into Orrin a year and a half ago."

"I wonder how they taste with bacon," Long Feather mused.

My warden's odd comment shocked everyone at the table. However, I started laughing at the absurdity of his statement, which was no doubt how he meant it from his grin. Soon everyone, including those from Jing, laughed along with me.

"Leave it to Balance and their black humor to keep us from sinking into circling thoughts," Shi Hua said between chuckles.

When our humor died, Po said, "This will probably the last chance we will be able to speak privately, Anthea. I want to extend my gratitude to you and Luc for keeping me alive long enough to see home again."

"We come to serve," Luc murmured as I found my throat clogged with a multitude of emotions.

"It's more than simple duty," Po replied. "You should know I told Teodora I wanted to request you both to be transferred to your respective Jing Temples."

I frowned. "I'm afraid to hear her reply to you, Your Highness."

Po wore a wry smile. "She said if I'd asked before the demons reappeared, she probably would have agreed."

"But now?" Luc prodded after Po remained silent for a long moment.

"She admitted Issura would have been lost if it weren't for you two, Biming, and the combined Diné and Plains Nations armies." His expression turned stern. "Don't ever think your queen doesn't appreciate your service, even if your Issuran Temple leaders are fools."

I kept myself from issuing my own comments about Reverend Mother Alara and Reverend Father Ferrell. Even if my opinions were appropriate, this was neither the time or place.

"Thank you for your confidence in us, Your Majesty," Luc said.

Everyone looked at me. My eyes stung, and for once, my tongue wouldn't work.

"Where's my chief justice with the sharp blades and sharper tongue?" Po teased.

"I suddenly realized how much I'm going to miss verbally sparring with you, Your Majesty," I choked out.

"But both of you—" Jonata rudely pointed at Po and Biming. "—had better treat Lady Shi Hua correctly and pleasantly, else I assure you that you will have everyone in Orrin on your doorstep seeking redress, my lords."

"That's assuming, Mateqai doesn't deal with you first," Yar added.

"Your warnings have been noted, Wardens," Po said. Biming nodded in agreement.

I reluctantly pushed to my feet. "However, as the Reverend Father said a few moments earlier, tomorrow will be a long day in a longer week. With your permission, Your Majesty, we shall retire for the night."

"Of course," Po said.

Everyone else rose, but Shi Hua circled the table and hugged me tightly. I returned the gesture.

Would it be all right if we talk occasionally, Anthea? I wouldn't have made it through carrying and delivering Chao without you.

Of course! I will miss you, too, Little One.

Thank you, my friend.

We released each other, and we both had to wipe away the wetness from our cheeks.

She turned and hugged Luc. From the soft mental buzz, she spoke privately with him. It was ironic her first babe helped bring Luc out of his melancholy after Gerd murdered his own unborn son.

Shi Hua repeated her hugs and private words with Yar, Jonata, and Long Feather, too. Sadness weeped from the wardens as well. In the span of two winters, the soon-to-be empress had burrowed into all of our hearts.

"I'll guide you back to your suit," Biming said.

"We appreciate your assistance, Reverend Father," Luc said. "However, we won't have you with us if we actually need to use the passageways to escape the city. It's best if we find our way back by ourselves."

Biming nodded. "If we do not have a chance to speak again before you leave, may the Twelve guide you all safely home."

"Thank you, Reverend Father," I said. "May They grant you the courage and patience to deal with the challenges to come."

We all performed the required bows, but Shi Hua hugged us all again. Po followed her lead. It was nice not to have to worry about him groping me and me cutting off his hand for doing so.

I turned and cast the spell to open the door to the secret passage before my emotions made me break down in front of the Jing leaders. It wouldn't help my reputation as a justice to be reckoned with.

This time, Long Feather took the lead while Yar brought up the rear of our column. We were halfway back when he suddenly halted and shielded his lamp. Jonata ran into me.

"I'm—" she started, but I whirled and slapped a hand over her mouth. Behind us, Yar shielded his own lantern, and my companions were plunged into a similar type of darkness I had dealt with the first fifteen winters of my life.

What's wrong? Luc whispered silently.

I reached up for Long Feather's shoulder and repeated the question.

I thought I saw something moving up ahead, m'lady, he replied.

I felt Luc pull Yar and Jonata into our link.

There's a difference between a human and rat, Luc joked.

Except I wasn't laughing.

Jonata, Yar, stay with Luc while Long Feather and I search for whatever he glimpsed. If we don't return in three hundred heartbeats, head back to Po and Shi Hua's private room. This corridor isn't a place we want to be caught in if there's a fight.

At their silent affirmatives, I slipped in front of Long Feather. *I can see in here. I'll lead. You keep an ear out for any unusual sounds.*

He handed his lamp to Jonata and placed his left hand on my left shoulder. I was rather happy we'd gone through the secret passages. The imperial guards would have insisted we were unarmed. I slipped a throwing knife from my wrist sheath. From the faint whisper behind me, Long Feather had also drawn a smaller blade.

Keep your hands off the walls, I ordered.

His golden laughter rang in my mind. *I noticed you marking the way, but I don't think Sister Yin Li or Reverend Father Biming did.*

I wish more wardens than mine noted as much attention to detail, I grumbled.

You taught us, m'lady. Why do you think Chief Justice Elizabeth wanted to poach Gina from Orrin so badly?

If we survive this assignment and the trip home, I'm putting in a transfer to the Wardens Academy, I quipped. *Someone needs to properly train all of you.*

We passed the entrance to the bedchamber I shared with Luc. At twenty more steps, the passageway ended at a perpendicular corridor. I marked the wall with my hand and considered our next move. Walking around blindly in these passages wouldn't do us any good.

From my right came the faintest sound of a pebble hitting a larger stone.

That came from our right, Long Feather said. *Probably a section High Brother Shang and Sister Yin Li haven't had a chance to clear of spiders and debris.*

Did you have to bring up spiders? I complained.

Spiders don't kick pebbles while walking, he reminded me.

I eased forward and to my right, my warden's breath hot on my neck compared to the chill air in the secret passage. This corridor ended at another cross-corridor in ten paces.

I tried to walk how Luc had showed me while he taught me to hunt during our time circuit riding. The last thing I wanted was to alert whatever we were following. Behind me, Long Feather walked on his toes as well.

I reached the second cross-corridor in time to catch a glimpse of a hooded figure on our left. A scraggly blue bread covered the lower half of its face. But at the angry, hot taste of magic, I shoved Long Feather back as I ducked behind the corner. The fireball spell shot past us and scorched the wall where I'd been standing a moment before.

CHAPTER 34

I crouched and peeked around the left corner. A second fire spell whizzed past my head as I jerked back. Thank the Twelve, there was nothing in here that could ignite except me, my warden, and a few abandoned webs. The spells didn't have the rasp of demon magic or the gentle caress of Temple magic.

Long Feather also dropped to a crouch next to me. *A sorcerer?*

That would be my guess. It's definitely not a skinwalker or a demon. At least I knew it wasn't a demon wearing a human skin from the feel of their magic. Demons wearing human skins could pass as a normal person despite my peculiar eyesight, but it wasn't information I let be widely known. I wanted the demons to fear me seeing them. But their particular brand of magic always gave the demons away.

If they used it around me.

He can't see any better than I can, Long Feather said.

We don't know that.

I strained to hear anything. A rustle of their clothing. Another pebble kicked at their approach or retreat. Breath.

Nothing.

I risked another peek around the corner. The figure still stood roughly twenty steps down from where we hid. They didn't flinch at my appearance, so I carefully pulled my head back.

They're still there.

Can you time freeze the section of the passageway? Long Feather asked.

They'll feel my magic before the spell is complete just like I felt theirs, I replied.

What if I offer a distraction? He released his hold on me.

I looked over my shoulder. He reached into the tiny pocket on the exterior of his vest and produced a copper coin.

Is the next hall about the same width as this one? Long Feather asked.

Yes, I said. *What do you intend?*

Skipping a coin on a wall instead of a stone on water. Would you mind stepping back, Chief Justice?

We exchanged places as silently as we could. However, we must have made some noise. Another fireball hit the corner of the opposing wall at roughly the height we crouched.

Before a fourth fireball could fly, Long Feather jumped to his feet and launched his copper. From the chime of metal, it hit the opposing wall, bounced off the wall where we hid, and smacked into something far softer than rock. A low cry of pain followed the dull thud. Then footsteps retreated away from us.

Fast.

That wasn't a rat, I said dryly. As I took a step around my warden to cast my time-freeze spell, he grabbed my arm.

We need to capture him, I snapped.

Long Feather jerked at the force of my silent speech. *No, Chief Justice, I'm not letting you pursue him*, he said with all seriousness. *We've confirmed it was a human sorcerer in the secret passageway. If it's Wu as we believe, he will have traps in here if we try to follow him. Could you or the high brother create the same for him near our suite? I suspect he was searching for the entrance to the crown prince's quarters.*

Long Feather laid out my own worries. Worse, I wondered if the treasonous sorcerer placed demon eggs near our own suite to infect and kill us and the new emperor of Jing.

Fine. I won't run after him, but we need Shang and Yin Li's opinion, I said. *They know both Wu and the demons' tactics here in Jing better than we do.*

Long Feather slumped against the wall. *So much for getting a good night's sleep before the opening ceremonies of the Spring Rituals.*

Let's retrieve your copper so you have some spending money for the festivities, I quipped.

You hope there's a trace of skin or blood on my coin, don't you?

I'll trade your copper for one of my coppers if that will make you feel better, I said.

I'd prefer the renegade's heart on my sword, but I want two coppers for the one you plan to destroy, he teased.

You have a deal, Warden.

After we retrieved Long Feather's coin and I placed it in a silk evidence bag, Luc, Jonata, and Yar met us at the hidden door to my bedchamber's bathing room. No one spoke until we were back in mine and Luc's bed-chamber.

"Shang's coming here though the conventional hallways," Luc said with a scowl. "Yin Li needs to be up early to help Shi Hua prepare for the day. I told him we needed to ward the damn bathing room."

"Well, I don't like the idea of being unarmed in a massive crowd tomorrow," I snapped back.

"You're both more upset we need to place the chamber pot near your bed," Yar said. "Don't knock it over in the middle of the night. I am not cleaning up your mess."

Luc and I stared at the warden. Yar rarely objected to anything, but when he did, it usually regarded Luc or I putting ourselves in harm's way. Even my own wardens froze at Yar's words.

I turned to Luc. "Did Yar just tell his first joke?"

"I was not joking," Yar growled in Issuran. "I'm homesick, I'm exhausted, and I'm damn sick of everyone trying to kill you. With my luck lately, you'll spill your chamber pot, contract some illness, and die in a foreign land. And this entire mission will be for naught!"

He stormed out of our bedchamber. A moment later, the door of the other bedchamber slammed.

Luc stared at the ceiling and blew out a long breath. "Am I truly losing two wardens in this idiotic assignment?"

"Do you want me to speak with him?" I asked softly.

"No!" Jonata and Long Feather exclaimed at the same time with the same energy.

"It's nothing personal," she added. "We haven't had a break in nearly three months." She held up her hands when I opened my mouth to protest. "None of us blame either of you. You haven't had a break any more than we have. But Yar is feeling the pressure of Mateqai resigning in the middle of our journey, and he fears one mistake will cost the high brother his life."

"Nor do any of us blame Mateqai," Long Feather added. "Sister, ur, Lady Shi Hua needs someone she can trust to help her keep Emperor Po alive."

"And we know what you're going to say, Chief Justice," Jonata continued. "You were both clear about the risks, and we understood them." She shrugged. "Now, we have to worry about someone sneaking into your bathing room to slit your throats. Most of all, all three of us know we've been incredibly lucky that hasn't happened the last two nights."

I sighed and started unlacing my robes. "I can't speak for the high brother, but Yin Li's appearance tonight created the same worries in me. Anyone without talent could enter through the bathing room's secret door."

"Should we create pallets in the wardens' room and sleep in there?" Luc asked.

"There's probably a blasted hidden door in their bathing room, too." I pulled off my robes and tossed them on the bed. "The sitting room is no safer if the imperial guards break down the door. Or more likely, Wu and his allies murder them and break in."

"More likely, it would be another demon attack," Long Feather mused. "The demons can simply change their shape and slip through the space between the main door and the floor."

"What would you like us to do, Chief Justice?" Jonata asked.

"For tonight, we're not doing a thing except warding the bedchambers," I stated.

"You're going to trap us in our room?" Long Feather stared at me as if I'd lost all my faculties.

"View it this way," Luc said. "You won't be trapped if someone manages to slit mine or Anthea's throats."

"That is not remotely funny," Jonata said.

"Then give me a better solution, Warden," I replied.

She huffed for a handful of moments before her shoulders sagged. "I don't have one, m'lady."

I stepped closer to Jonata. "Yar's not the only one feeling the pressure on his head. We're all experiencing our own and everyone else's in this blasted city. But I beg you—" I glanced at Long Feather. "—all of you, to keep your wits until the end of this week. Let us talk to the Skoloti about covering each other so you can enjoy yourselves for a bit. But for us, will you two agree to let Yar go first?"

Jonata nodded. "That is a plan we can agree to, m'lady. Thank you for listening. And we understand why you and the high brother feel the wards are necessary. Can you please give us a few moments to carry out our nightly ablutions first?"

"Of course." I smiled. "Thank you for helping me sleep by knowing you won't be disturbed."

Once my wardens departed our bedchamber, Luc crossed to stand behind me and rested his chin on my shoulder. *Are you feeling all right, m'love?*

What do you mean? I leaned my head against his soft curls.

You've never begged anyone for anything before.

I playfully jabbed him in the ribs. *I don't have to beg you when you do everything quite willingly. I hope Shang doesn't take too long. Yin Li isn't the only one who needs some sleep.*

Wu fumed as he took a circuitous route through the imperial palace's secret passages. By the First Emperor! Who else had been in the passage that close to the emperor's quarters?

Whoever it was didn't use magic. Did demons have the discipline not to attack with magic? Their claws, teeth, and shape-shifting abilities were formidable on their own.

Whatever they hit him with made the center of his forehead ache abominably. From the metallic sound of the projectile, he was damn lucky it hadn't pierced his skull or eyes.

After more than a candlemark, he deemed it safe enough to return to his hidden room. He lit the oil lamps and examined his injury in a small mirror.

Purple was replacing the red mark. But what disturbed him the most was the profile of his own son embedded in his skin.

Wu shivered. He never believed in the ancient tales about spirits of those who died horrific deaths roaming the world, seeking vengeance.

While he may not have been the one to take Chengwu's life, he had told Bing which concubine would be the easiest to replace within the harem. His actions made him complicit.

No! No, it was the bastard's fault. Wu wouldn't have been driven to such extreme measures if he'd killed the boy when he had a chance. And by heaven and earth, Wu would make Quan Po pay for ruining his and his son's life.

CHAPTER 35

Shang arrived at our suite shortly after our party changed into our nightwear. None of us felt like standing on ceremony after the stress of the last two full days in Chengzhou. As soon as he entered, he circled and warded the sitting room.

"What happened?" he demanded.

We laid out everything since Yin Li entered our suite from the secret passage and our suspicions.

Shang scowled at the news of someone else roaming unseen through the imperial palace. "The possibility of your initial assessment could be correct. It might be Wu, or the person could be an acolyte of the School of Sorcery Wu allowed into the palace prior to his arrest."

The Conflict priest sighed and rubbed his face. "Too bad you couldn't obtain anything from our mysterious prowler for a tracking spell."

Long Feather and I exchanged smiles.

"We might have something." I rose and strode into my bedchamber to retrieve the silk-wrapped copper from my pocket in my robes. When I returned to the common room, I said, "This is the copper with which my warden struck our unexpected visitor."

"You left something out of your tale," Luc teased.

"I fear weariness is dulling my memory." I grinned back.

Shang stroked his own beard. "As much as I want to hunt down the traitor at this very moment, if we cast the spell now without Temple personnel close enough to apprehend him, he might escape. Then we won't know which direction the next attack would come from."

"Warden Long Feather pointed out that our visitor might have traps set for us in other parts of the passageways," I said. "He suggested we do the same for this sorcerer."

Shang's mouth curved into a slight smile. "That's a most excellent idea, Warden. But we need to do it randomly with various Temple disciplines."

"You have Light and Balance in this room," Luc said. "You, Yin Li, and Reverend Father Biming can intersperse yours with ours."

"But not tonight." Shang rose and stretched. "We're all too tired to take the chance of casting any spell incorrectly. Yin Li and I will meet you here after the opening ceremonies—" He winced. "I apologize for making an assumption that you would not participate in the festivities."

I laughed. "No offense taken. This is much too important to ignore for frivolous entertainment. We'll meet you at our suite, say after the midday meal?"

The Conflict priest nodded. "Very well. Tomorrow at Second Afternoon. In the meantime, I suggest warding your bedchambers for the night. Sleep well."

Once he left, Yar rose. "I owe you both an apology for my outburst."

Luc waved his hand. "Warden, how many times did you have to carry me to bed last year when I was so intoxicated I lost consciousness? You've earned more than enough leeway, and you exhibited the same fears we are all feeling. You have nothing to apologize for."

"But I—"

"Warden, I strongly suggest you visit the Temple of Love tomorrow afternoon to . . . release some of your stress," I said. "Jonata and Long Feather can handle guarding the high brother for an hour or three."

Yar's skin glowed red. "I will take your suggestion under advisement, Chief Justice." He strode into the bedchamber the three wardens shared.

My wardens stood and followed him, but Jonata paused at the doorway. She turned to me with a smile and a nod.

I exchanged a look with Luc. He pushed to his foot and crutches and crossed to the other bedchamber.

"Everyone ready for the night?" At the wardens' affirmatives, the pleasant tingle of Light magic danced along my skin as Luc warded the wardens' bedchamber.

While he cast his spell, I stood and crossed to the sitting room's main door. I checked that it was bolted before I dragged a side table with an elegant ceramic vase in front of the door. If someone entered the suite from that direction before we woke, the vase hitting the polished hardwood floor would alert us.

I snatched up the silk bag with the copper sitting on the side table as I passed. Luc closed the wardens' bedchamber door and joined me as I entered our bedchamber. He took a moment to perform his own ablutions. I placed the evidence bag inside my robe's pocket before I closed our bedchamber door and bolted it.

He lay on our bed while I relieved myself for the night and washed my hands. I shuttered the Knowledge lamp, circled the room to cast my own wards, and climbed into bed beside him.

We lay there silently for a long time before Luc whispered, "A copper for your thoughts?"

"I have far too many thoughts for just a copper."

He rolled to his side to face me and propped his head on his fist. "Why didn't you chase Wu tonight?"

"Are you accusing me of shirking my duty?"

"Not at all," he replied. "I'm impressed you didn't rush headlong into disaster, which we both know you're wont to do, my love."

"Truly?" I asked.

"Please."

"I wanted to, but Long Feather stopped me." I sighed. "But I didn't trust myself."

"What do you mean?"

"The last time we face someone from the School of Sorcery, the court sorcerer in question held both a demon and an egg in reserve. I still dream about the screams of the imperial guardsman the adult demon gutted. I couldn't bear hearing the same thing from Long Feather. That's why I gave in to his advice to not follow the sorcerer in the dark."

Luc pulled my yielding body closer to him. "Didn't you hear Jonata tonight?"

"Y-yes," I choked out. "That's my fear. Too many have died in my service. Too many I care about. I don't know how much more I can take."

"Anthea." He cupped my cheek with his free hand and turned my head to face him. "We are at war. People die in wars. How many thousands have died before us while protecting humankind from the demons?"

"Too many," I whispered. A tear rolled down my cheek. Luc brushed it away with his thumb. "And even more innocents have suffered."

"I understand that feeling." He exhaled and wrapped both his arms around me. "I lost myself in drink to dull my own fears and pain. And that's the trap. Intoxicants only dull the ache in our hearts. The pain is still there, and if we don't find a way to turn it into a strength, it will consume us more surely than the demons would."

"I know that too. It doesn't prevent the agony."

"No, it doesn't," he agreed. "All we can do is claim that pain and make it our own. Don't give the renegades and the demons more power over you. Otherwise, they win. Just promise me you won't go hunting for the sorcerer after I fall asleep."

"I wouldn't—"

He laid an index finger over my lips. "That's bull cakes, and we both know it."

"Risking my own life is different—"

"You're not the only one who fears losing the people they love," he said with a sad ache in his voice. "Please don't be foolish for my sake. Not yours."

I sighed again. "Very well. I swear on Balance I won't track down this sorcerer after you go to sleep tonight."

"Thank you." His kiss sealed my promise.

But long after his soft snores filled our bedchamber, I stared at the ceiling wondering what new horror the morning would bring.

CHAPTER 36

The first day of the Spring Rituals dawned beautiful and warm. Despite our worries and fears concerning Wu, renegades, and demons, the feeling of everyone else's anticipation of the holiday permeated the palace.

Since we were guests of Crown Prince Po and ambassadors from the sovereign nation of Issura, our party was seated in the foreign dignitaries' section on the pavilion between the palace and the Temples for the opening ceremonies.

I felt naked dressed in my chiton with no weapons but a single dagger. Though I wore a stole over my formal wear, I had no place to hide additional blades with the gauzy material. Even if I wore my normal Temple uniform, the imperial guards searched everyone thoroughly. Not even our wardens or the other dignitaries' security personnel were allowed to carry any weapons but a single dagger to the opening ceremonies. Luc had tightly braided my hair. He said I could yank out the pins and whip any antagonist with my waist-length tresses if necessary.

Part of me prayed to the Twelve we could have one full day without any dramatic attempted or successful murders. As usual, none of them replied.

The other part of me scanned the crowd, searching for the gray-green flesh of a skinwalker or the empty black of a demon. I only found the yellow and orange faces of human beings.

As we waited for the ceremony to begin, our False Sister Darys sat next to me. Her wardens joined our own in the seats behind us. Like our own trio, the Thief wardens were dressed in their Temple uniforms. However, Sister Darys wore a decorated felt vest over a wide-sleeved tunic and wool trousers. Oddly, the vest and trousers weren't made from the coats of sheep.

"You look like you sucked on a sour fruit, Chief Justice." The Skoloti priestess grinned.

"My entire staff will tell you I'm not sociable until I have my first cup of Jing black tea in the morning." I smiled in return.

"And that's your only bad habit?" She raised an eyebrow.

"The other is chasing demons without my wardens, which they consistently complain about."

"It makes them look bad. We poor delicate magic workers are supposed to let them be our protecters, just like the guards of the noble class." She laughed. "My own wardens have the same complaint about me taking the initiative when we battle those gray, scaly beasts."

She leaned closer and lowered her voice. "Were you planning to join the rest of today's festivities?"

"There is no point in me participating. I cannot bear children," I stated.

"And I don't relish riding all the way back to our tribal territory while dealing with morning sickness," she murmured. "Would you care to continue our conversation after the midday banquet? I'd like to practice my Issuran language skills while I have a native speaker available."

"And it would give two of our wardens a chance to enjoy themselves?" I teased.

"If you don't mind." She grinned.

I laid my fingers on the back of her hand. *What's really going on?*

My purpose is twofold. We heard some strange noises behind our suite walls last night. But I'm also playing matchmaker. Warden Antiope has a penchant for Rus men, and she wishes to seduce your Yar. The priestess's silver laughter tinkled in my mind.

I doubt Yar would object. But he's been eyeing the taller of your wardens—

That is Antiope, she confirmed.

Then I hope they have a pleasant time later today. And if they wish to use your suite, you are more than welcome to join us for our evening meal.

I will let Antiope know.

As she withdrew from our mental contact, Luc nudged my knee with his own. *Should I ask what you two are plotting?*

Merely making sure Yar will be relaxed when he eventually comes back to our quarters later, I said archly.

He's my warden, Luc protested. *Shouldn't I have some say?*

Do you really want him to throw another tantrum?

No, Luc admitted.

Then hush, my love, and let us handle him. I winked at him.

He chuckled but didn't offer any more complaints or comments.

The entire crowd quieted as the procession from the Temple of Love glided into the huge square. The occasional cough and rustle of clothing were overwhelmed by the chiming of the bells on the priestesses' veils and robes. Unfortunately, their sleeves hid their folded hands, and their robes hid their bare feet. I sent another prayer to the Twelve a skinwalker or a demon hadn't learned my secret and were hiding themselves from my odd sight.

The priestesses stopped in the middle of the square. I counted silently to three before the drums started. A solid steady beat at first while the women and *berda* raised their veils from their faces and held the gauzy material studded with silver bells high above their heads. The Spring Rituals were the only time the clergy of Love allowed their true appearance to be seen in public.

When the drums split into the two-count of a human heart, the women shook their veils in rhythm with their steps. They dipped and turned and whirled around, their robes fluttering around their ankles. Thankfully, none of them had the telltale colors of our enemies. Blue and gold melded into a fascinating pattern as the danced in welcome of the fertile season.

The drums picked up their pace, and the dancers followed suit. The blues of hair and clothing lightened to a marbled green and their skin went from gold to a brilliant orange. The frenzy of their steps beat a pattern on the bricks.

For the first time, I realized how much joy I missed in life because of my resentment of my birth mother and my forced station in life. I'd avoided the Spring Rituals since I was old enough to believe I knew their purpose. However, this was the first time I truly watched and understood their meaning.

Luc intertwined his right fingers with my left and gave my hand a gentle squeeze. Of course, he'd picked up on my emotions. We'd shared too much for too long and in more ways than most humans would ever experience. I squeezed his hand in return.

This dance wasn't just about lust as I'd always presumed. This was warmth returning to the world after the bitter cold of winter. This was new life coming into being. This was Balance creating Light to counter Her darkness. And Love was the seed in all people's hearts and spirits waiting to spring into action under the sun, moon, and stars.

The priestesses danced to give thanks that the Twelve allowed them to bring happiness and gentleness into their worshippers' lives. The veils flew from their hands as each row and column exchanged places. With graceful yet frantic movements, they unlaced their robes, imitating the need to bare ourselves to our loved ones. The people who truly accepted us as we are.

Dancers continued their same intricate movements to shed their robes along the edges of the square. Each priestess wore a simple shift with slits to their hips to allow them freedom of movement. The women and *berda* writhed sinuously about each other.

The drums reached a crescendo when the priestesses massed in the center of the square, touched and being touched. With the loud clash of a gong, they gracefully dropped to the bricks, taking care not to injure each other or themselves.

I was caught up in the spectator's breathless anticipation. My chest ached as the priestesses unpeeled themselves from the pile.

A proud dancer marched over to the drummers and took the staff to the gong. She struck the huge steel instrument once. Twice. On her third blow, the crowd cheered. Across Chengzhou, bells rang out the triple signal for Love, not just the Temples. A dull roar of voices swept over us.

Under the light opening notes of flutes, the Love priestesses went into the crowd and drew people regardless of rank from their seats. Two of them approached Po and Shi Hua on their thrones. I could literally see Mateqai's tension increase from where I sat. Shi Hua must have said something to him silently because he didn't draw his sword on the priestess who took Shi Hua's hand and led her to the square. Jing nobles entered the dignitaries' section, inviting them to dance in celebration of the fertility holiday.

People around us accepted the proffers to celebrate from the dukes and duchesses, lords and ladies, and even the bureaucrats. So, it was not a shock to me that Luc and I were the only ones left.

The drums and stringed instruments joined the music of the flutes. Couples stepped and turned in a complex series of motions. The mathematics were intriguing, but I was rather glad no one had asked us to join.

Luc chuckled. "After all this time, I finally get a chance to dance with you, and I can't."

"Maybe it's a good thing." I smiled at him. "I never learned because no one in Balance bothers, and if you and I tried, I could possibly ruin your remaining foot."

We both laughed at the ludicrous situation we found ourselves. No doubt Thief was also having a good time at our expense.

Lord Jia Hao jogged up the steps to our seats, a noble woman in his wake. To my surprise, he held out his hand. "May I have the pleasure of your company for the opening dances, Chief Justice?"

CHAPTER 37

All of my carefully cultivated poise flew away. "I, er, I—"

"Our Balance doesn't teach their priestesses how to dance," Luc interjected. "Would you be willing to teach her?" He held up his specially designed crutches. "I can't without tripping everyone around us."

"That's an excellent idea, cousin." The woman smiled at us. "I can keep the high brother company while you do so." She focused on Luc and bowed. "I'm Lady Caihong, cousin to the illustrious Lord Jia Huo."

"That sounds like an excellent plan, Lady Caihong." Luc nudge me with his knee. "Anthea?" He leaned his head in the young lord's direction.

As much as I didn't like leaving Luc alone with someone I didn't know, I realized I couldn't decline a respectful invitation. Maybe I could do a little investigating of my own.

I took Lord Jia Huo's hand. "I would be delighted, m'lord. But I must warn you that you're risking your bodily integrity by asking me."

"You would be worth any risk, Lady Justice."

"I'll remind you of that when you're forced to call on a healer later." But I smiled and let him draw me to my feet. We descended to the square.

I watched the movement of the other dancers. I could appreciate the artistry, but replicating it? It would be easier to call lightning.

"Might I make a suggestion, Lady Justice?" Jia Huo murmured.

"Please do," I said fervently.

"The justices cannot see, but they memorize their steps and movements to navigate around their Temple and city, correct?"

"Yes, as long as we don't have an overprotective warden." I frowned slightly. "But what does that—"

"Close your eyes, and listen to my voice."

I inhaled deeply and closed my eyes. As he listed the steps to the hymn of granting fertility, I pictured them as I had before I gained my strange sight.

When he told me to step forward, I did. I stuck to the memorized movements and kept my eyes closed. Somehow, I managed not to step on anyone's toes or run into another dancer and knock them over.

When the music ended and I opened my eyes, Jia Huo held me close to him, his gaze intense. I half-expected him to try and kiss me.

Instead, he murmured, "Would you like to get some refreshment, Chief Justice?"

I nodded, not trusting my words.

The Love priestesses had started slipping away from the imperial pavilion while I danced with Jia Huo. We crossed to the southern edge of the square.

"The palace banquet tables are in the opposite direction, m'lord." I pointed.

"I meant no disrespect to you or our new emperor, Lady Justice." The hint of a smile played with his mouth. "I thought to introduce you to the city of Chengzhou. However, if you don't feel comfortable—"

"Trying to slip away without one of us, Chief Justice," Long Feather said from behind me.

I jumped and pivoted in one motion. He stood straight, his palm resting on the hilt of his dagger. But the scowl on his face was definitely aimed at me.

"The fault is mine, Warden." Jia Huo bowed, a deeper one than I expected since he outranked Long Feather. "Your chief justice has been busy with matters of state since she arrived. I'd hoped to show her more of our lovely city beyond the palace and Temples."

"And I hope you realize she would talk you into taking her to the section of the city where the fire occurred?" Long Feather said dryly.

Jia Huo turned to me with a bit of his confusion seeping past my shields. "You planned to use me?"

"Actually, I planned to visit the site later tonight." I glared at Long Feather. "But this morning, I tried to take my wardens' advice to enjoy myself today, only to be accused of deception."

Not one of Long Feather's muscles twitched at my words. "We are in a foreign nation, not the Duchy of Orrin, Chief Justice."

"Then you are more than welcome to accompany us, Warden . . ." Jia Huo said.

Long Feather remained silent.

As much as I wanted to reprimand him here and now, we were a long way from home, and I needed him as much, if not more, than he needed me. But his bad manners gnawed on my nerves.

"Lord Jia Huo, the warden with the atrocious attitude is Long Feather." I smiled. Warden Long Feather, this is Lord Jia Huo, the brother of Empress Meng Yao."

There was a nearly imperceptible flick of my warden's right eyelid before his visage transformed to a more pleasant expression. "Forgive me, m'lord, for not recognizing you. I meant no offense to your character."

"I realize that, but the insult was aimed at your chief justice, and you should apologize, Warden. She is a senior priestess, not a recalcitrant child. And to my knowledge, the ban on relationships for the Temples of Balance and Light have been lifted. Assuming I did suggest a dalliance to the chief Justice, I have no doubt she could kill me if I did not respect her choices. It is the Spring Rituals after all."

Jia Huo's statement caught both Long Feather and me off guard.

"The fault is mine, m'lord," I said carefully. "Warden Long Feather was merely doing his duty since we . . . encountered some trouble last night."

Jia Huo's right eyebrow lifted. "Within the palace?"

"As you said, it's the Spring Rituals." I smiled and wrapped my left hand around his right elbow. "Let us speak of more pleasant things. And you did offer to show me some of the sights around Chengzhou."

Thankfully, the Jing lord nodded and let the subject drop. Long Feather followed us as we entered the boulevard of the Temples.

Is Jonata with Luc? I asked Long Feather silently.

Yes, Chief Justice, he replied stiffly.

Are you taking a knob from Yar's scroll?

We encountered a sorcerer last night and demons and skinwalkers the night before. Anger salted his words. *You may not take your safety seriously, but your wardens do.*

And I hoped to speak with Lord Jia Huo privately. I snapped back. *He is family by marriage to the crown prince. He would know more about the current players in Jing politics. Po has been away from Chengzhou for nearly eight years.*

Long Feather's anger faltered. *You could have simply informed me and Jonata of your plan. I would have followed you discreetly.*

In a Temple uniform? I teased.

If I took the time to change into civilian clothing, you would take advantage of the delay to disappear, he retorted. *And I don't believe you would*

*break the high brother's heart by letting people believe you dallied with
Lord Jia Huo, even if it is the Spring Rituals.*

He was correct on both counts, and it embarrassed me to admit that
fact to myself.

If you must protect my virtue—

Behind me, Long Feather made a choking sound.

—find a privy so I may speak with him privately.

As long as you swear by the Twelve you won't take off without me.

I do so swear.

As much as I wished to explore the city by myself, I wasn't foolish
enough to do so. But given some of my past actions, I could understand
Long Feather's fear, which was why he was furious I tried to leave the
imperial square without him or Jonata. He would make a fine chief warden someday.

Assuming we all survived to the end of the week. That thought made
Long Feather's concerns even more pointed. Luc and my wardens were
correct. I needed to be more careful.

CHAPTER 38

Jia Huo took us to the cross street between Light and Thief. The entire road had been blocked off. Little stalls lined the Temple walls, and table and benches had been placed on the cobblestones. He stopped at a stall that was twice as large as the others and already had a long line.

"Do you trust me?" he murmured.

"Maybe not you specifically, but I appreciate your taste in food." I grinned, and he laughed at my jest.

When we reached the counter, Jia Huo rattled off the items so fast my mind couldn't keep up with them other than the word "tea". Long Feather volunteered to collect our order while Jia Huo and I found an empty table.

"Are all of your wardens so protective of you?" Jia Huo asked as we claimed a free table. Amusement threaded his tone.

"Unfortunately, I've given my wardens cause," I said ruefully as I sat. Jia Huo made a point of sitting across from me, thereby exposing his back. My own paranoia had kicked in when I claimed the bench so I would have the wall of Light guarding my rear. I ignored my discomfort and continued, "My chief warden is only two winters older than me, and my actions have made his hair gray prematurely."

Jia Huo laughed, his first genuine one I'd heard in the few days I'd known him. "No doubt Warden Long Feather was given strict instructions before you departed for Jing."

"I believe he and Warden Jonata were only given two instructions. Do not let me start any wars and bring me home alive." I grinned.

Jia Huo laughed even louder. "If only you weren't Temple—"

At his abrupt silence, I prodded, "If only I weren't Temple, what?"

"How much do you know about the rivalry between the Temples and the philosophy schools here in Jing?"

"Enough to know there shouldn't be a rivalry," I said softly. "Whoever sits on the Dragon Throne needs the assistance of everyone in order to serve their people and survive this war with the demons."

"I was about to say you would make an excellent candidate for the School of the Phoenix and the Dragon, but I feared you would take an intended compliment as an insult." He inclined his head. "Perhaps I am overthinking the differences between our nations."

"Perhaps." I shrugged. "In Issura, any civilians with talent can still attend Temple classes with the novices. Or they can attend a Guild school. If they chose to do neither, the Temple of Knowledge will teach them control and help them find a place in our society."

"In truth or in theory?" he asked.

I sighed. "In truth though there have been some difficulties during the last five decades. Even my own nation became complacent when the demons didn't make an appearance over the last century."

"Despite your own goddess's prophecy?"

"Even then," I agreed. "We had to learn our lesson the hard way by losing the city of Tandor." I shook my head. "I do not wish that experience on anyone."

Long Feather set a large tray on our table. "I beg your pardon, Lord Jia Huo. The proprietress claims your order is complete and correct, but I thought wontons were served in broth."

"They can be served many ways, Warden." He turned to me. "I ordered several items to be shared among the three of us. I hope you don't mind."

"Not at all." My stomach gurgled, and Long Feather stifled a laugh. "I would like to try as much Jing cuisine as possible."

"And she has a healthy appetite when she remembers to eat," Long Feather teased. "The proprietress is also brewing fresh black tea for you, m'lady, in case you don't like the chilled flower tea."

"Flower tea?" I frowned.

"It is chilled hibiscus tea, a favorite during this holiday," Jia Huo said. "Taste it, and if it's not to your liking, I will gladly drink yours and fetch you an entire pot of black tea. But no one should forget to eat."

"It only happens when there's a perplexing case I am adjudicating," I said archly.

"Or when the Assassins Guild tried to poison her two winters ago and she couldn't keep anything down for three days after she awoke from her healing," Long Feather said as he sat dishes on the table. "And don't you dare touch anything until I return with the black tea."

Jia Huo eyed me as my warden returned to the food stall. "Is he serious?"

"Quite so unfortunately." My stomach rumbled again. No one broke their fast on the first day of the Spring Rituals until after Love's opening dance. "Personally, I think my wardens want to get to our cook's excellent almond pastries before I do."

The Jing lord broke out in more guffaws. "Too bad you cannot stay in our lovely country longer, Lady Justice. I've laughed more with you in less than a candlemark than I have in the last ten years." He wiped his eyes. "Thank you for reminding me there are joys to be had even with the loss of my sister and her family."

"You're not the only one who has lost those close to you," I murmured. "I've lost three of my wardens and my own grandfather since the demons returned. It's not an easy thing to live with, and we find ourselves rehashing what we could have done differently to save them."

"Even so," he admitted.

While Jia Huo divided the contents of the dishes onto the ceramic plates, Long Feather returned with a steaming pot and additional cups and sat next to me. He sipped my chilled tea and waited a long moment before he let me taste it.

To my surprise, the tea's tart flavor reminded me of the sweetened lemon juice Po had served at the Jing Embassy last summer.

"This is wonderful!" I exclaimed. "Do you mind if I drink both types of tea, Lord Jia Huo?"

"Not at all." He tried to give me the plate with the tidbits he selected. Long Feather grabbed it out of Jia Huo's hand.

"Warden!" I snapped. "That was rude!"

"If you have an objection, Chief Justice, you may address it to Chief Little Bear when we arrive home. However, I will follow his orders in regards to protecting you." Long Feather stared me in the eyes as he picked up a pair of eating sticks and nibbled a tiny bit from each item. "You'll like the sweetened rice, m'lady." He handed my plate back to me.

I turned to Jia Huo. "I beg your forgiveness, m'lord. Both of my wardens seemed to have taken leave of their senses since we arrived in your fair land."

"Must I remind you of the incident in Naha?" Long Feather's rhetorical question was as tart as the chilled hibiscus tea.

I settled for glaring at him.

"It is quite all right, Lady Justice." Sadness descended upon Jia Huo once again. "There were those that presumed I would flaunt my relationship with our former emperor. Even as I grieve for my family, I also find myself relieved I'm no longer under such scrutiny." He shook himself out of his melancholy and smiled. "However, as you said, it is the Spring Rituals."

While we ate, both Long Feather and I extolled the virtues of Jing cuisine. The fried wontons with goat cheese and herbs were delightful. Jia Huo had chosen several sweet treats before I mentioned Deborah's almond pastries. My favorite was something he called persimmon five-spice cake. The fruit in the cake topping wasn't something that was grown on the Northern Long Continent, nor could it last on the two-month voyage from Jing to Issura. I became determined to acquire some dried fruit and the five-spice mixture before we left the empire. Surely, Deborah would help me replicate the confection. After we finished our repast, Long Feather excused himself while the lord and I shared a second pot of black tea.

"Now that I haven't tried to poison you, does that mean your warden trusts me?" Jia Huo teased.

"No." I leaned closer. "It means either he's headed toward a privy after all the . . ." In that moment, I couldn't remember the correct word for the type of flower that was used.

"Hibiscus?" Jia Huo suggested.

"Chilled hibiscus tea," I said triumphantly.

He laughed. "What happened to the vaunted memory techniques of Balance?"

"Even a proficient juggler will drop balls when there's too many in the air." I chuckled. "I've been learning your language for only three months."

He leaned back. "Only three months? Then I beg forgiveness for jesting with you. I cannot imagine becoming proficient in a whole new language in such a short time." He hesitated for a moment. "May I ask a question regarding one of your cases?"

"You may ask as long as I have the right to decline to answer," I said. "There are matters which must remain private."

"I understand." He hesitated for a moment before he blurted, "I attended classes at the School of the Phoenix and the Dragon. Master Quan Yong Xi was one of my teachers. Is it true that he was murdered?"

CHAPTER 39

I had expected the young Jing lord to ask more about demons, not Po's birth father. I took another sip of my tea before I said, "May I ask why you are concerned about Master Quan's fate other than any affection for a former instructor?"

Jia Huo looked around us. There were curious glances in my direction and more smiles than frowns. No doubt with the Spring Rituals under way, they now viewed me as a foreign oddity one of their noblemen was attempting to seduce.

But the young lord's mien was quite serious as he leaned closer to me. "I . . . disagreed with our former emperor's disposition of the leader of the School of Sorcery, but perhaps it is fortunate he did not listen to my advice. The crown prince's heritage is no secret, nor was the rivalry between their fathers. Have you petitioned to interrogate our former emperor's father?"

Light bless me, the city's gossip network hadn't gotten wind of Wu's escape.

Yet.

I considered my next words carefully. "I would like to question him in regards to Master Quan's passing. However, there are other matters pressing both the crown prince and the Reverend Mother of Balance at the moment. Not to mention, this is a holiday week."

"But you will stay a few days beyond the Spring Rituals in order to make a formal petition to both the emperor and the Temple of Balance?" His expression was oh-so-hopeful.

"M'lord, I must weigh my duties as a justice with those of my role as our queen's ambassador. I cannot guarantee anything to you at this point." I took another sip of the hot tea to relieve my suddenly dry throat. "Is there a particular reason you're so interested in the drama of your family by marriage?"

Again, Jia Huo looked around the street before he faced me and lowered his voice further. "Are you proficient in silent speech, Lady Justice?"

For a moment, I wondered if the man in front of me was a demon wearing Jia Huo's skin. However, I sensed nothing, but a man lost in his own sorrow.

I nodded and laid my right palm on the table. He placed his hand on mine.

Is this better? I asked.

Thank you, Lady Justice. Relief spread through him now I was willing to listen to his story. *I sat on Emperor Chengwu's advisory council. I know about the demon egg caches that were in the possession of the School of Sorcery. I believe Wu Sunshu smuggled some of the eggs into the palace. It wasn't an outside attack despite the current conjecture. I suspect the eggs were hatched using servants within the palace. However, Duke Mengchang refused to listen to me.*

Are you telling me this hoping I will convince the crown prince to execute Wu? I asked.

No, I think your experience with demons make you more adept at questioning him. Jia Huo winced as he realized he'd just insulted his home Temples. *I mean no disrespect to Reverend Mother Xiang or any of her staff at Balance. Master Quan taught us that theory is a wonderful beginning, but there are things only experience can teach us. From what I've heard, the Temples in your duchy of Orrin have far more experience with demons than anyone else in the World at the moment.*

What about the experience of Reverend Father Chen's army? I asked dryly.

Jia Huo's face flamed orange in a mix of anger and embarrassment at the reminder he wasn't the only one grieving a loss. *I believe they relied too much on theory and weren't prepared for reality.*

If Wu hid a set of demon eggs within the palace, where do you think he might leave them? I asked.

Jia Huo's surprise flooded our low-level speaking link. *You believe me?*

The crown prince was with us in Tandor when we were besieged by a demon army. The smallest of smiles curved my mouth. *I'm not the only one with extensive experience dealing with our foes.*

Jia Huo tensed. *I think perhaps I should speak the rest with the crown prince.*

Of course. His sister had told him about the secret passages within the palace. I had to give him credit for not wanting to betray his new emperor. I decided to take a chance.

Lord Jia Huo, with all due respect, I have no wish for Lady Shi Hua, whom I regard as my own sister, to end up as demon fodder as your sister did. *If you know or suspect there are still demon eggs within the palace and where they might be, for the love of the Twelve, please tell me.*

When he hesitated, I took another huge chance. *I beg you to help me save my sister, her husband, and their unborn child!*

Lady Shi Hua is pregnant? Jia Huo blinked in shock at my revelation.

Please do not share this information, I implored him. *They plan to make the formal announcement after the coronation. However, it's no secret many parties who aren't demon dealing desire not to see the crown prince's coronation happen.*

Unfortunate, but true. He nodded thoughtfully. *I must ask your silence in what I'm about to tell you for your sister's protection.*

Of course. I nodded though I suspected what he would say.

There are secret ways through the palace. A wry smile sent the jewels at the ends of his mustachios swinging. *They aren't uncommon in many places in our land to allow trysts between our royals and nobles and their lovers. But the passages in the imperial palace were built as escape routes in case the city is overrun by demons.*

That's logical considering the palace is in the center of Chengzhou.

If Duke Mengchang followed protocol, the passages for Emperor Chengwu and his family have been sealed, just as the emperor sealed the passages allocated for Empress Yu. Jia Huo played with the jewel at the end of his left mustachio. An unconscious gesture so reminiscent of Po that I nearly laughed.

The School of Sorcery had similar passages within their buildings and grounds, Jia Huo continued. *It's not common knowledge, but a few members did manage to escape despite the imperial army and the Temples' best efforts. I suspect after Empress Yu showed Wu those hidden passages within the palace, he might have created his own escape route.*

It would make sense, I mused. *Especially if he was demon dealing during their marriage.*

I apologize, Lady Justice. Jia Huo's expression turned forlorn. *I know my conjectures are insufficient evidence that would not stand up in a Balance Court.*

But it is the starting point for a more thorough investigation. I sighed. *Unfortunately, I have no jurisdiction in Jing. I can make suggestions to my fellow justices here, but I cannot guarantee any answers for you.*

I am all too aware of that. His tremulous smile fought against his grief.

All I ask is that you address the matter with your sister and the crown prince. As I said when we first met, I only want to see those responsible for my own sister and her family's deaths to pay for what they did.

I will do my best to see justice is done for the innocents in this mess. I squeezed the lord's hand before I released it.

"Do you know of a place where I might purchase some dried persimmon and five spice?" I grinned. "I may not fit into my uniform by the end of the Spring Rituals, but I'd like to replicate those excellent cakes."

"Already done, m'lady." Long Feather resumed his seat beside me. He sat an oiled canvas bag on the table before he inclined his head toward the large stall where Jia Huo had purchased our repast. "The proprietress was gracious enough to share her recipe for the spice cakes on the condition you swear to Balance not to give it to anyone else."

I opened the bag and looked inside. From the delicious odor, there were additional cakes along with the ingredients. Plus, more packages I know I hadn't requested, much less thought of.

"I thought you were searching out a privy. Did you spend all your coin in just this market?"

"No, m'lady." My warden grinned. "The cakes are a gift to you from the proprietress. Apparently, you honored her by devouring all the food Lord Jia Huo purchased. As for the rest, Jonata and I had requests and money from everyone at the Temple for items that are normally difficult to get in Issura."

"Perhaps we should help fulfill Warden Long Feather's quest while I show you our beautiful city," Jia Huo suggested.

"That sounds like an excellent idea, m'lord." I grinned.

As soon as we departed our table, other shoppers claimed it. Jia Huo wrapped my left hand around his right elbow. For once, the protocol gesture for a blind justice didn't irritate me. I found I enjoyed the young man's company despite our rather intense conversation.

We set off for the gates to view the rest of the capital of the Jing Empire.

CHAPTER 40

After shopping in Chengzhou's largest market for rest of the requests on Long Feather's list and all of my own, Jia Huo escorted us to view the statutes, monuments, and the architecture in other sections of Jing's capital. Unfortunately, I had to decline his offer to share a late afternoon meal since I had the meeting with the Skoloti delegation, then another with Shang and Yin Li. I would have preferred his delightful company rather than deal with our current problems.

Jia Huo spoke of riding out to the Great Wall with the entire Issuran party for a midday meal later this week. I promised to send him an answer later today once I discussed the matter with my co-ambassador.

"I believe Lord Jia Huo is rather smitten with you," Long Feather said in Issuran as we made our way back to the palace from the inner circle's gate.

"Of course, he is," I remarked. "I am scintillating company."

My warden laughed loudly at my jest, drawing attention from people we passed.

"I admit I would like to see the Great Wall while we're here," I continued. "It's supposed to be the largest human-made construction after the Great Pyramid of Kemet."

"Not with demons roaming the countryside," Long Feather spat.

At my look, he said, "I apologize for my tone, Chief Justice, but neither Jonata or I will allow you such an outing considering the current circumstances."

"But when will any of us have another chance to see things outside of Issura?" I complained.

My warden made the same exasperated exhalation Luc would have done under the same circumstances. "While we are pleased you aren't sulking in your chambers as is your wont to do during the Sprint Rituals according to the high brother, there are other considerations here besides your obsessive curiosity. Right now, you are representing Queen Teodora and Issura, not the Temple of Balance. It means different standards of conduct. Not to mention, even you admitted one of Chief Warden Little Bear's orders was to keep you alive. That includes stopping you from doing something foolish like packing food and traipsing around the countryside after our encounter the night before last."

"You are definitely an unadventurous person, Long Feather."

"I am perfectly adventurous under the right circumstances," he shot back.

"Sister Migina would question that statement," I teased. The Conflict priestess hadn't made any secret that while she was attracted to nearly anything on two feet, she was particularly obsessed with bedding Long Feather. I'd found out last year he often hid in the tunnels below the Orrin Temples before we sealed them to prevent the demons and renegades from secretly entering our city.

"Cornered and attempted coercion are not the right circumstances," he replied with a huff.

"Will you need tomorrow to find your right circumstances?" I teased some more.

"No, Jonata is taking the next turn."

"Should I be pleased or disappointed you are not finding the right circumstances with her?"

He groaned. "You're going to gnaw on anything I say, aren't you?"

"Would you prefer to be lashed for being rude to an extended member of the Jing imperial family?" I shot back.

"No, Chief Justice." After a moment's pause, he added, "If I asked politely, would you please lash me if we're in Orrin for the next Spring Rituals?"

I came to such an abrupt halt the people walking behind us nearly trampled me. "Do you find sexual release in pain?"

"No." His cheeks glowed orange. "I want a good excuse for avoiding Sister Migina."

"My dear Warden Long Feather, I don't believe that would stop her." I chuckled. "In fact, it would inhibit any chance for you to escape her."

Our False Sister Darys and her other warden arrived at our suite a candlemark after First Afternoon along with Luc and Jonata.

"You weren't at the banquet, Chief Justice," she noted. "Did you have a pleasant encounter with Lord Jia Huo?"

"If tasting Jing cuisine applies to your definition of a pleasant encounter, then yes, I had a wonderful time." I smiled. "Would you care to take a seat while I ward the room?"

Luc and our guest sat while Long Feather served the tea I had ordered from the imperial kitchens. I circled the room, reciting the appropriate spell. The comforting weight of my own magic settled on my shoulders.

I claimed the chair between the Skoloti women and the couch where Luc sprawled to keep his left leg elevated. Despite the excellent care of our healers in Orrin, his stump swelled when he was upright on his crutches for too long. Long Feather had requested ice chips when he ordered our tea. Jonata placed one towel under Luc's stump and another towel holding the ice chips on his shin.

"Can we not dissemble and speak truly with each other, High Sister?" I narrowed my eyes.

"Of course." She nodded, but she didn't seem disturbed by me using her actual title.

"We know you Skoloti were shown a secret passage to escape Cheng-zhou, just as our Issuran party was," I baldly stated.

She nodded again. "However, what we heard last night was not simply people passing by our suite. Twice in quick succession, there was a distinctive sound of metal on rock. Before that, I also felt someone throw at least three fireball spells. That particular magical attack was a favorite of the School of Sorcery. Warden Urania is a low level-empath, and we both detected someone who was injured, but not severely. I am greatly concerned we have a renegade running around within the palace."

The warden in question made the peculiar gestures Luc referred to as someone rolling their eyes. "I don't know what they thought they would accomplish by throwing fire balls. There's nothing in the passages that would burn besides bugs, spider webs, and other people using the passageway."

"There were people behind your wall," I admitted. "Our party was returning to our suite after being shown a hidden exit from the palace when Warden Long Feather caught a glimpse of someone ahead of us. He and I tried to follow the mysterious person when they started throwing fireballs at us." I grinned and looked over my left shoulder at Long Feather. "I couldn't throw up a ward or time freeze spell without our opponent knowing, so my warden skipped a copper off the walls in an attempt to incapacitate the person." I shrugged. "Unfortunately, whoever it was knew the passage system better than we did. They escaped."

"It's best you didn't try to pursue them." Our False Sister Darys shook her head. "If it were an escapee from the School of Sorcery's purge, they probably have trap spells throughout the imperial family's network of secret passageways.

"That's what my own warden counseled." I glanced up at Long Feather again before my attention returned to our guests. "We can confirm there was no taint of demon magic, so it was definitely a talented human we encountered."

"When the copper hit your assailant, was there any blood or skin on it?" Warden Urania asked.

"Yes," I replied. "High Brother Shang planned to make arrangements for the Temple personnel to be near all known exits before we try the tracking spell."

"When?" our False Darys asked. "And what can we do to help? If it weren't for Reverend Father Chen's trap, that demon army would have overrun the Skoloti territories before we could react. We owe the Jing a debt for that sacrifice."

"We're meeting with High Brother Shang at Second Afternoon." I shrugged. "We won't perform the tracking spell until the Jing Temples are ready. When our suspected renegade bolts, we need to have our nets raised."

Everyone chuckled at my jest, but the laughter quickly died at the knock on our suite doors. The sound was dulled by my wards. A more urgent knocking immediately followed.

Jonata leapt to her feet and raced to the wardens' bedchamber. She returned with her sword in hand and Long Feather's in its sheath. She tossed the weapon to him, and he deftly caught the leather and drew his blade in one smooth motion.

I stood and lowered my wards, a time-freeze spell on the tip of my tongue. Urania silently crossed to the door and drew her dagger. Someone hammered even more furious on the lacquered wood. I nodded, and she yanked the door open.

Duke Mengchang burst into the room, not realizing how close Urania came to slitting his throat. "Come quickly, Sister Darys, High Brother Luc. Your wardens have been attacked!"

CHAPTER 41

"What happened?" Luc demanded.

"We're not sure," Mengchang replied breathlessly. "Warden Yar refuses to allow anyone into the Skoloti suite without yours or Sister Darys's affirmation. And no offense, I'm not wasting the lives of the Imperial Guard arguing with a Rus and a Skoloti!"

"At least one of them is alive for questioning," I bit out.

"I've requested a justice and a Light priest, Lady Justice." Instead of respect, the use of my alternate title was a pointed reminder I was outside of Issuran jurisdiction.

"What about healers?" Luc snapped as he swung toward us on his crutches.

"The palace healer is trying to convince your warden to allow her to enter and tend to their injuries, High Brother." The duke bowed to Luc.

I bit my tongue to keep from commenting. For a nation that allows women to join the Temple of Light, some of their leaders had rather contrarian views. Or perhaps I hadn't mended my relationship with Mengchang as I had thought. On the other hand, something terrible had happened for Yar to react toward the duke in such a manner.

"Let us speak with Wardens Antiope and Yar before any more blood is shed, Your Grace," I said.

"Please, Your Grace," Luc added. "Yar is level-headed in a crisis which is why I selected him for this journey. If he's not letting any Jing into the suite assigned to the Skoloti delegates, he has a good reason."

"I concur with the chief justice and high brother," our False Darys said.

The duke's face muscles twitched at Luc and the Skoloti priestess's emphatic pleas. He finally sighed and nodded. "You're correct, but I do not wish to alarm the crown prince's other guests."

"Neither do we," I murmured.

Our party and our guests followed Mengchang down the hallway and around the corner to the suite assigned to the Skoloti, the imperial guards on our heels. Ahead of us, a familiar woman with a master healer badge on her sleeve stood in front of the appropriate door. We'd met Master Yi prior to the crown prince's welcome banquet. The remainder of the imperial squad surrounded her.

At the duke's approach, Master Yi bowed to him. "My apologies, Your Grace. The wardens wish to speak with their seats before they will allow me entrance."

I plunged between the guards and banged on the lacquered wood. "By the Twelve, Yar, if you don't open this door, I will age it until there's nothing left but dust!" I yelled in Issuran.

The door swung open, revealing Luc's warden with a relieved expression and a sheet wrapped around his waist. However, bright pink blood stained his bare skin and the scarf wrapped around his upper arm.

"Just our parties, Duke Mengchang, and Master Yi, please, Chief Justice," he replied in the Jing tongue. He stepped back out of the way.

To my surprise, Mengchang told the imperial guards to wait outside before he followed us into the suite's common room.

Antiope sat on the hearth tiles, wrapped in a blanket. Like Yar, pink blood covered her hands and the hilt of the sword that lay beside her. My own blood chilled at her defensive wounds from someone wielding a knife.

Master Yi pressed Yar to sit beside the Skoloti warden. When she unwrapped Yar's makeshift bandage, my stomach lurched at the depth of the wound. I could see the darker pink of his bone.

"What happened, Yar?" Luc asked in Jing for the benefit of the duke.

"Our assailant snuck in through the passage in Sister Darys's bathing room." Yar's expression of relief turned into a deep scowl.

"Passage?" The healer's head swiveled as her attention switched from Yar to the duke and back again.

"You have heard nothing of this conversation, Master Yi," Mengchang said rather calmly.

"Of course, Your Grace." She bowed her head and returned to cleaning Yar's injury.

"Did either of you recognize them?" I asked.

Both wardens shook their heads.

"They were masked. Thank Light, their blade wasn't coated in poison, else we would not be having this conversation," Yar said.

"I tried to scratch them, Sister, to obtain a sample for a tracking spell." Antiope shook her head. "However, their clothing was well-padded. There wasn't even a gap between their gloves and sleeves. They fled when I obtained my sword." She looked over at Yar with something beyond affection and lust. "Warden Yar kept them distracted while I went for my weapon. He knows of the Jing unarmed fighting arts which kept our opponent off balance."

Yar shrugged, then winced at the motion. He would have surely blushed if he wasn't in so much pain. "I was fortunate Lady Shi Hua taught us when she was assigned to the Orrin Temple of Light. We need every advantage against the demons and renegades."

I wandered through the suite while Master Yi tended to the wardens, careful not to touch anything. The wardens' bedchambers were a disaster with furniture overturned and belongings scattered during the fight. Blood droplets and smears were distribute through the room.

Mengchang followed me as I crossed to the sister's bedchambers. The furnishings, decorations, and personal property were pristine. When I entered her bathing room, the remnants of a spell tingled against my skin. At least, it wasn't the sharp prick of demon magic.

"What do you think or suspect, Chief Justice?" the duke murmured.

"I don't think the wardens were the original target," I said softly. "But then, this isn't my jurisdiction as you've repeatedly pointed out, Your Grace."

"You are merely giving voice to my own suspicions," he said. "Having one of the ambassadors assassinated within the palace would bring the crown prince's competence into question." He faced me. "Demon or human?"

"Human," I replied. "Why?"

"Duke Zixin and his party didn't arrive at the palace until after the opening celebration banquet."

So, Mengchang suspected deliberate insult from his and Po's cousin, the one who had openly questioned Po's claim to the throne, and Mengchang was outraged on Po's behalf.

"Someone could be using Zixin's late arrival to deflect attention away from themselves," I mused.

"Like Wu." Mengchang's statement wasn't even a rhetorical question.

"It's possible." I smirked. "Especially since he thought he would rule Jing through Emperor Chengwu."

Mengchang grunted.

"Still, none of Reverend Mother Xiang's justices will take anything at face value." I sighed. "Not with everyone in Chengzhou jockeying for position under the new regime."

"I have half a mind to ignore the crown prince's request I remain in the capital. I hear there's good farmland in Issura, and he seemed quite happy while living there." He raised an inquiring eyebrow. "What would be the passage cost if I and my family sailed to your queendom on the *Mars Tranquilus*?"

I cocked my head. "Are you planning to hang the crown prince out to dry?"

"Things were ... peaceful for the most part under both Empress Yu and Emperor Chengwu." He exhaled as his gaze swept the bathing room. "At least, they were until the demon invasion."

I could sympathize with the duke. My life had been turned upside down with my first demon encounter, too. It didn't make the change easier to accept.

CHAPTER 42

To my surprise, Justice Mei Wen and Brother Jian were the clergy who responded to Duke Mengchang's request for assistance. The pair were circumspect enough to bade their wardens to remain outside of the Skoloti suite while they worked. However, our uninjured wardens refused to leave. The duke, false Darys, Luc, and I stayed out of Jing clergy's way while they conducted their investigation. Master Yi focused on healing our injured wardens while Mei Wen rewound time to catalog the events.

And the pair were quite thorough. There must have been something special in Shi Hua's novice classes. She and her friends had risen rapidly in their respective Temples given their ages.

Mei Wen's time rewind showed the circumstances exactly as Yar and Antiope had testified under truthspell. Well, the rewind showed a little more than any of us wanted, especially of Yar, considering False Darys and Urania's giggles and his bright orange blush.

However, it left us with more of a puzzle than before.

"That's not the person who attacked us in the passageway last night," Long Feather said. "Yar's attacker is about your height, Chief Justice, whereas last night's opponent was a handspan taller."

"If you shielded your lantern last night, how would you know?" Jian demanded.

Long Feather shrugged. "In Issura, wardens for Balance go through a series of tests while blindfolded. It's designed to place us in our charges' position so we know how best to serve them." He shot a glance at me. "However, those tests do not prepare a warden for a sighted justice."

The clergy and wardens in the room laughed. Even Master Yi grinned.

However, Duke Mengchang looked puzzled. "How can one judge a person's height when they can't see them?"

"Because we use our other senses," Mei Wen replied. "For example, I know Wardens Yar and Long Feather are the tallest men in the room from the location of their voices. Sister Darys and Chief Justice Anthea are roughly the same height. You are between the chief justice and the high brother. And Warden Jonata is a finger or two shorter than I am."

The duke blinked in surprise. "That is amazing. So, you in Balance train your wardens to act in your stead?"

"Not in our stead, but so they have a better idea of what we are capable of," I said. "Our justices are trained to fight with a sword, but my sisters must be much more careful so they don't accidentally behead their own wardens."

"We haven't trained our wardens in Jing by using a blindfold, but the Temple of Conflict perform such exercises with both their clergy and wardens," Mei Wen said. "Warden Long Feather makes an excellent suggestion that I will pass to Reverend Mother Xiang and the Wardens Academy here."

"Is there anything else you need from us before we depart, High Brother?" Jian said.

"No, I do not believe so," Luc said. "Thank you for responding quickly, Brother Jian. And to you, Justice Mei Wen."

Jian turned to Mengchang. "Do you have any questions or concerns before we report out findings to our Temples, Your Grace?"

"No, thank you, Brother." Mengchang forced a pleasant expression though it didn't quite become a smile. "I appreciate your prompt response to my request for an investigation. Please do not mention the passageways within the walls of the palace outside of this room."

"What passageways?" Jian and Mei Wen said innocently in unison.

Bows were exchanged, and the pair departed.

"You think it was one of Wu's surviving students?" the Skoloti priestess asked.

"It's a possibility," Mengchang grumbled. "Or it could be one of the Bao line hoping to disrupt the crown prince's coronation."

"Where are the crown prince and his wife located within the palace?" Luc asked. "Surely, they aren't sleeping in the former emperor's quarters?"

"No." Mengchang's face glowed a hot orange. "However, the fewer people who know where they are—"

"We're not asking for the information," I interjected. "It adds to our theory that our visitors don't know where the royal couple are either."

"You believe your assailant from last night is searching for them?" False Darys asked.

Luc nodded. "Mengchang followed procedure and blocked off the passages Empress Yu and Emperor Chengwu used. It means Crown Prince

Po can't use them either. So last night's assailant only knows the suites where the royal couple *aren't* staying."

"Today's attack on our wardens is something else entirely," I said.

False Darys nodded. "I am the lowest ranked of the foreign dignitaries with the fewest retainers with me as far as Prince Po's foes are aware. My death would sow further dissension in the palace and cause a stir within the Temples."

"But Chief Justice Anthea would be the higher profile target if the warden's assailant wanted to cause trouble," Mengchang protested.

False Darys laughed. "She has more of an affinity with Thief than I do despite our respective affiliations."

But her conjecture assumed whoever attempted to assassinate her didn't know High Sister Zhanna was pretending to be Darys because they killed the wrong twin. I didn't like the implications, but I wasn't sure what we could do differently to protect her. Despite reconciling with Reverend Father Biming, I didn't dare ask for his assistance. The Temples weren't any safer than the palace.

"After the banquet, you did tell Duchess Jia you were returning to your suite to rest before tonight's events," Mengchang prompted our False Darys.

"I did." The Skoloti priestess glanced at me and I gave her a subtle nod.

She turned back to the duke. "However, I made arrangements with Chief Justice Anthea, so our two wardens could have some private time during the Rituals. Warden Urania and I were resting in the Issuran suite." A wry smile tilted her lips. "If I'd known Wardens Antiope and Yar would be interrupted, I would have stayed here and warded my bedchamber."

"Your Grace, do you believe the duchess's flightiness is an act?" I asked. "Or is she cunning enough to push her eldest child's possible claim to the Dragon Throne?"

The duke pondered my question for a long moment. "If you had asked me a year ago, I would have said no, but now, it's a possibility without my cousin Lixin to keep her in check."

"How many people know of the secret passages?" Luc asked.

"It's only supposed to be the imperial family and the grand chancellor," Mengchang answered. "Plus two trusted servants whose families have served imperial family since the first emperor of Jing.

"Except Wu knows as Empress Yu's widower, and Empress Meng Yao told her brother," I said.

Mengchang's eyes bulged before he blurted, "She what?"

"Lord Jia Huo shared that information with me over a meal after the opening ceremonies," I said. "While he doesn't know about Wu's escape, the lord is concerned about the former empress's consort hiding demon eggs within the palace."

Mengchang grimaced. "And why is he telling you this?"

"Because everyone assumes I have the crown prince's ear," I shot back. "However, I did invoke my relationship with Lady Shi Hua because I don't want her rendered limb from limb by demons like Empress Meng Yao."

Luc swung between us. "Your Grace, Chief Justice, please stop. We cannot be at each other's throats. That's exactly what both Prince Po's detractors and the demons want."

"This whole situation is becoming madder by the moment," False Darys murmured while Mengchang and I continued to glare at each other. "However, the high brother speaks wisely. We need to marshal our resources and search the passageways that are supposed to be secret, but everyone seems to know about."

I softened my mien. "What can we do to assist you, Your Grace? Our goals in protecting the imperial couple are the same."

Mengchang huffed, but his ruffled feathers settled at my offer. "I need to confer with the crown prince before we take the next action."

Antiope leaned over and whispered something to Yar in Rus. He snorted and shook his head.

"If you have something to offer, Warden, please share it with the group," False Darys said.

"I merely said I should have taken Warden Yar's offer to use one of the facilities Love provides during the Spring Rituals," Antiope said evenly. "I feared being too far away from our charges. I never dreamed we would be at the receiving end of some idiot's knife."

Even I had to laugh at that comment.

CHAPTER 43

Once Yar and Antiope recovered from their healings and donned civilian clothing, they left for one of Love's facilities within Chengzhou. I slipped Yar some additional coins for their offering to the Temple of Love for which Luc teased me. But the whole point was to give the couple a day to enjoy the holiday. I couldn't begrudge them a little peace to indulge themselves.

As I expected, the Jing leaders of our respective Temples along with Reverend Father Feng of Conflict appeared at the suite in use by those of us from Issura. It happened sooner than my estimate, and our additional guests made the spacious common room feel crowded once we requisitioned additional chairs.

"Sister Darys, I must insist you move to Thief," Biming said. "You are technically my responsibility while in Jing. If you should be killed—"

"My wardens and the warriors who accompanied me won't have a chance of survival if we give in to fear," she snapped. "Not to mention, the renegades would consider my fleeing the palace as a success. There's one less person standing between their demon allies and your new emperor."

"And when our idiot assassin comes back, another dignitary would be at risk," I added.

Jin smiled. "Balance is as logical as ever."

"Which is why I'm not pressing the chief justice to move to our Temple," Xiang said. "She, Sister Darys, and Lady Shi Hua need to be close to the crown prince. The assailant that snuck into the Skoloti suite isn't the first disruption over the last few days. They won't be the last."

"Chief Justice, could the wardens' attacker been another skinwalker searching for the demon eggs they claim Wu hid?" Reverend Father Feng was a quiet, but intense, man. He reminded me of High Brother Talbert back in Orrin.

"Anything is possible, Reverend Father," I replied. "However, none of us detected any demon magic with either the person sneaking around last night or the wardens' attacker this afternoon."

Another knock on our suite door triggered all the wardens in the common room to draw their blades. They all looked to Long Feather as the senior warden of the hosts.

"Jonata." He inclined his head toward the door.

She eased closer and grasped the lever when a specific pattern was knocked out. I breathed a sigh of relief at the familiar notification.

Jonata glanced over her shoulder at me since she recognized the pattern as well.

"If that's not Lady Shi Hua when you open the door, stab first and ask questions later," I ordered. My fingers tingled as I once again started a time-freeze spell.

My warden yanked the door open.

Shi Hua stood there with an amused expression while Po and Mengchang glowered over her shoulders. "Anthea? Are you having a party without us?"

After retrieving more chairs, the royal couple were told of the events since this morning's opening ceremonies for the Spring Rituals that the chancellor didn't know. Shi Hua turned somber while Po played with the gold beads on his left mustachio. I really needed to speak with him about his tell.

"Are you sure Yar is alright?" he glanced between me and Luc.

"I believe he was so eager to celebrate the Spring Rituals he barely felt the slice to his bone," Luc said dryly. After our guests' chuckles died down, he added, "We have no doubt he and Warden Antiope will sleep deeply between their bedplay and their healings."

"Duke Mengchang relayed your request, Anthea," Shi Hua said. "I was about to send a message to ask Reverend Father Feng the same thing when we learned he'd arrived for an audience with you."

"However, I question the wisdom of your suggestion about closing all access to the palace, Anthea," Po said.

"It's not safe for our guests if we allow vermin to wander into their bedchambers," Shi Hua murmured.

"I don't want to trap you in the palace if the tides turn against us, my love," Po said.

"So, it doesn't matter if the imperial protocols allow spiders and rodents within the walls of the palace, and they bite people?" she said emphatically.

When Xiang, Jin, and Feng did not so much as twitch as Shi Hua's carefully coded statement, I groaned. "Is there anyone in Chengzhou who doesn't know about the blasted passageways?"

"I believe there is a blind flower seller on Yangtze Street who may not know," Reverend Father Feng said. I was really beginning to like the Conflict leader and his dry wit.

Shi Hua turned to Po. "This is what I mean, my husband."

I had the impression this was an ongoing source of conflict between the imperial couple. However, both had good points.

"I don't mean to overstep, Your Majesties, but a domestic convenience-used-by-vermin problem was exactly why we had to close off Orrin's tunnel system," I said.

Po and Shi Hua stared at each other for a long moment, obviously discussing the issue privately. Finally, Po turned to False Darys.

"My lady wife and the chief justice are in agreement. Unfortunately, they have plenty of experience guarding my imperial ass," he said.

Biming had great difficulty choking back his laughter.

"What say you, Sister Darys?" Po continued as if nothing had interrupted him.

"Frankly, Your Majesty, I would feel much better if you would move up your coronation, but we both know that is not going to stop your enemies," she said. "I agree the passageways need to be thoroughly searched." She sighed. "Including the ones Duke Mengchang blocked."

"Do you really believe I would—" the duke started.

"The ladies are not questioning your integrity, Bao Mengchang," Reverend Mother Xiang snapped. "The demon attacks on the imperial palace and the Temples were well thought out. Probably long before Empress Yu's death. Why else was the whisper campaign against Crown Prince Po encouraged for so many years?" She continued in a more conciliatory tone. "Your strength is your devotion to duty, Your Grace, but it is also your weakness." She sighed. "And I'm afraid I am just as guilty. We both must learn to adapt to changing circumstances because the demons and their allies aren't going to give us a chance to breathe, much less come up with a better plan than what Lady Shi Hua and two other priestesses have offered."

"Do you have another idea, Chancellor?" Reverend Father Feng asked.

His words deflated Mengchang's pride.

"No, Reverend Father, I do not," the duke admitted. "However, I share the crown prince's fear of Lady Shi Hua being trapped within the city should another demon attack occur."

"Why would all of you—" Reverend Father Jin started to say when Xiang nudge him with her elbow.

Reverend Father Feng shook his head sadly, and Reverend Father Biming smirked.

"Oh." Jin's expression was comical as he finally added one plus one to come up with three.

I thought I was inept about certain things, Luc said silently to me.

You are, but you are a much quicker study, I teased.

"We need to select clergy and wardens we trust to perform this duty." Reverend Father Feng turned to me. "Would you object to Wildling being recruited for the search, Chief Justice?"

"I have no objection, but as everyone in the room has repeatedly pointed out, I have no jurisdiction in Jing, much less Chengzhou," I said with a self-deprecating spread of my hands.

"You do if I give you emergency jurisdiction," Xiang said. "And given the events of the last three days and the loss of two justices in the demon attack last winter, our situation constitutes an emergency to our empire."

"I agree with Reverend Mother Xiang. You and Lady Shi Hua have much more experience dealing with our foes, Chief Justice," Biming added. "And better still, you have survived all of your encounters."

"Through sheer dumb luck." I laughed. "I believe Thief takes more of an interest in us than the deities we serve."

"The Twelve work in conjunction, Anthea," Xiang mildly chastised. "So must we."

"In that case, to answer your question, Reverend Father Feng, then yes, please, ask Wildling for their help." I inclined my head.

After our Jing guests departed with a provisional timetable for sweeping the imperial palace's secret passages, False Darys eyed me. "For someone who claims not to be at the lead of anything, you manage to accomplish taking over every group you are a part of."

"No, they want a foreign scapegoat in case things go horribly wrong," I muttered.

"No, my love." Luc tightly grasped my right hand. "They want to survive whatever is coming, and you're their best chance of doing so."

CHAPTER 44

I had to give the Chengzhou Temples credit. To keep from disturbing the city's celebrants, all the clergy and wardens wore civilian clothing. One third of their people slowly worked their way to the known exits from the imperial palace's secret passageways. Another third made their way as revelers through the public square before slowly entering the palace. I didn't envy the rest who had to cover the complex's sewer system.

A Jing Wildling accompanied Luc and Long Feather in the shape of a huge snake. The Wildling that joined False Darys and Urania wore the shape of a pig. Brother Fa escorted me and Jonata. Though I'd never admit it to anyone, having a priest in the form of a tiger was far more comforting than any Wildling whose second body was a reptile. The dry musk reminded me too much of the demon's odd scent.

Meanwhile, Mei Wen joined Shi Hua in one of the empress's formal sitting rooms as the pair coordinated all the teams searching through the palace. Knowledge had provided the searchers with paper lanterns. Their magic was subtler than the other orders. I postulated the difference was due to only conventional light produced by their spell as opposed to light and heat from the other Temples like Light, Father, or Love.

After we entered the passage behind mine and Luc's bathing room, I laid a hand on the warm, thick fur of Fa's back and pulled his mind into a link with me and Jonata. We focused on the path our sorcerer ran last night while False Darys's group backtracked the trail Yin Li and Biming had led us through last night. Luc and his party along with Shang and his chosen people searched the passages leading away from False Darys's bathing room.

Yar will be upset he couldn't join in the fun, Jonata commented.

Fa laughed, an odd chuffing sound similar to a domestic cat about to produce a hairball. *I'm sure he's having his own brand of fun tonight. Warden Antiope may have to fight off other suitors for his time and attention.*

What makes you say that? I asked.

Not many Rus men are in Chengzhou for the Spring Rituals. Fa's muscles rippled under his fur as we walked. *Many women think a big, strong son is a blessing. Someone who can care for them in their dotage.*

Jonata snorted. *Unfortunately, a large man can mean a large baby.*

Sometimes, too large. If they don't have a midwife or a healer close by, the results can be fatal for both mother and child.

My own mother would agree with you, Warden, Fa said. *She constantly reminds me the healer had to cut me out of her womb to save the lives of both of us.*

I winced at the young priest's cavalier attitude. Luc and I had been caught in an early blizzard the second autumn we rode circuit, and we'd stayed in Meadow Sweet for four days. The innkeeper there went into labor. Ironically, the healer who served the town had been called to a hunting camp for another woman in labor before the start of the snowstorm.

I tried to freeze time around the innkeeper, but I only lasted a day and a half. In the end, the only thing we could do was ease her pain as she and her child died. We couldn't even properly burn her body right away. We had to freeze her corpse outside the inn as the storm raged. Guilt still racked me after all these years.

My normal reaction to someone making me re-live my failures would be to lash out. But wasn't the difference between the innkeeper in Meadow Sweet and Fa's mother a whim of the Twelve? I couldn't call it balance in any sense of the word since two lives were lost as another was gained at the hunting camp.

I cleared my mind of the wayward thoughts and focused on our task. My dark purple handprints from last night stood out against the pale lavender of the tiny creatures who lived on the passageway surfaces.

Fa paused and sniffed at the stone floors and walls. *I detect the chief justice and Warden Long Feather. The oldest scent is Sister Yin Li. But two others, both human males, aren't men I've met.*

Two? My surprise wasn't echoed by my companions.

It means that the sorcerer you and Long Feather chased last night may not be the person who attacked Yar and Antiope, Jonata said. *Unless you think our stabby friend is Sister Yin Li?*

Are you trying to increase my paranoia, Warden? I snapped.

It's not paranoia when the Assassins Guild have placed a price on your head and renegades are trying to collect the reward, Lady Justice, Fa said.

You would make a lovely warm lining for my winter cloak, I said. *Brother.*

The Wildling danced away from my touch. *I didn't say I wished to collect, Lady Justice.*

Jonata chuckled softly behind me. *Don't concern yourself, Brother. The Chief Justice constantly threatens to lash us for insubordination, but there's no one I trust more to cover my back in a fight.*

Aren't you supposed to cover her back? Fa asked.

Why do you think I never actually lash them? I said dryly.

Jonata and Fa laughed at my jest. Or maybe at my expense. I found I didn't care which case it was.

Especially when there was the slightest scrape of leather on stone ahead and along the right cross corridor. And precisely where my hand-prints ended.

We halted. Jonata shuttered her lantern. Fa crouched low. Instead of reaching for my sword, I drew a throwing knife from my belt.

Unfortunately, Shang and Yin Li's efforts to clear the passageways for the imperial couple and Luc to pass through meant there was nothing to inhibit our visitor.

A series of clicks approached us. A bright red claw appeared around the corner. Fa pounced as the rest of the body eased forward.

The pair rolled once. Twice. They parted glaring at each other.

Longnu, what in Wildling's name are you doing in this path? Fa said.

The Wildling's body was long and sinuous with fishlike scales. What appeared to be a mane framed her head. Her narrow snout ended in two wide nostrils and two fleshy tendrils draped over her multitude of sharp teeth.

We finished our assigned passage and were moving to the next. She snapped her teeth for emphasis.

"Anthea?" a familiar masculine voice whispered.

"Yes, Reverend Father," I whispered back.

Lady Shi Hua, we've met Chief Justice Anthea and her party. The passage behind us is clear, Biming said silently.

He held out his hand to me. We joined our teams into a singular link, but I could feel his strain as he kept his quicksilver ability from shutting us out.

No trace of our visitors? Shi Hua's mental voice carried a sharp edge over her normally sweet tone.

Only old scents on our path according to Fa, I reported.

Longnu says the same for our previous path, Biming added.

I've marked them on our map, Mei Wen said.

Neither the empress-to-be or the justice said anything else. I half-expected them to tell us to be careful, but such a warning was unnecessary.

Jonata and the Thief warden with Biming unshielded their lanterns.

Aren't we going to go over the same trail as Sister Darys? I asked. *We are close to the Skoloti suite because the sister and her wardens heard Long Feather and me.*

Let's see what a tracking spell says. Biming winked at me. *You brought your warden's copper, didn't you?*

Yes, I replied crossly. *However, performing the spell now might give one of our subjects an opportunity to evade us or counteract the spell.*

The chief justice has a point, Longnu said. *I suggest we continue as long as Fa or I can pick up our visitors' scents.*

Fa raised his head from where he sniffed the intersection. *I agree.*

Biming nodded. *Very well then.*

We followed the left path our attacker had taken last night. Fa and Longnu took point. The priest's giant head was close to the ground. To my shock, Longnu rose into the air though she had no wings and trailed after Fa.

What type of animal is Sister Longnu? I asked Biming.

Longnu looked over her shoulder. *I'm a dragon, of course.*

I frowned. *Dragons are imaginary.*

Biming chuckled. *They existed. According to most Knowledge priests and civilian historians the first emperor of Jing was a Wildling whose second form was a dragon.*

That's the reason you call it the Dragon Throne? I asked.

He nodded. *They may be extinct or simply in hiding. The consensus is the latter since dragon Wildlings, though rare, are still born within the eastern part of the Old Continent.*

How can you be sure they existed? I asked.

Because Wildlings north of the Xiongnu Confederation occasionally have the second shape of the furred elephants that lived there before Balance's Revelation, the Thief warden replied. *We know those animals existed because their corpses are still found in the permanent ice.*

There are beasts who look similar to Wildling Himself's true form in the Cradle, and stone skeletons verily alike to a dragon that were discovered in the Gobi Desert, Biming shrugged. *According to Knowledge, all manners of creatures may have lived and died before humans appeared in the World.*

But Child created us shortly after Balance created the World, Jonata protested.

What is the lifespan of one of the Twelve? I gently asked my warden.

Longer than a human's, she said.

The clergy of Kemet have never used their imaginations when it comes to the Twelve, I said. *Yet most scholars today would agree that the animal they use to represent Conflict has not been seen in a multitude of winters. Does that mean it did not exist?*

Jonata sighed. *Forgive me for questioning you, Lady Justice.*

Bing chuckled softly. *Always ask for clarification, Warden. Questions are what keeps us growing. It's your own chief justice's curiosity and determination to find answers that provides much of the information as to the demons and renegades' plans. I must admit I allowed myself to forget that such is a necessary function in life.* He shot me a rueful smile.

I nodded in return. I hoped he had learned to question everything after the merry, homicidal path Ogusuku had led him on in the name of protecting the human race.

Fa stopped, retraced his steps and sniffed at the right wall. *Everyone, halt. Longnu, double check the trail for me.*

He stepped back while Longnu landed and performed the same maneuver. She nodded.

The scent definitely stops here. I think there's a spell, but the magic is almost too faint to be detectable.

Biming stepped forward and touched the stones. *I fear we are at a proverbial dead end.*

CHAPTER 45

I crossed to stand beside Biming and examined the wall. Faint cracks showed in the mortar around the block above my head. Since my throwing knife was still in my hand, I raised up on my toes and inserted it into the crack. No spell repelled the steel, nor was there a retaliatory strike against me. Using the blade, I followed the crack across and down to the floor.

It's not a folding spell, Biming observed.

The Thief warden checked the opposing side of the hidden door. *The crack over here is thinner. I'd say the hinges are on this side.*

Do we need magic to open it, or is there a spell to seal it? Fa asked.

We haven't discovered any of the traps Long Feather feared, Jonata commented. *This could be one.*

Aren't you going to warn me not to touch it? I teased.

She snorted. *Doing so only encourages you to do something foolish, m'lady. Besides, you already did.*

The Thief warden gaped at Jonata, but I laughed.

Biming grinned as well. *So, what is your recommendation, Warden?*

A time-delayed unlocking spell, she stated. *However, there's not a lot of cover for us if it's a flashbang spell or something worse protecting the doorway.*

What makes you think it's not a fake doorway? Fa asked.

Because you don't, Brother, Jonata replied. *And Lady Shi Hua does not associate with fools.*

A wave of embarrassment flooded across our collective link. If Fa had been in human form his skin would have turned a brilliant red at my warden's sharp compliment.

Sound logic, Warden, Biming said. *Wardens and Wildlings get down the passageway to the last alcove we passed.*

The Thief warden set his lantern next to the Reverend Father. As the quartet retreated to the limited shelter, Biming faced me.

Have you ever frozen a spell like this before, Chief Justice?

I smiled. *I thought you would ask me for something difficult, Reverend Father.*

My flippant answer seemed to satisfy him. He turned back to the door and began casting the unlock spell. Nothing from around the hidden door reacted, and I froze time around both it and Reverend Father's magic the instant before the spell did its job.

He snatched up the lantern, and we raced back to the alcove. It was a tight squeeze for all of us. I dropped the time freeze spell and threw up a ward at the same instant.

Contrary to all our fears, nothing happened. At least, nothing obvious.

I dropped my ward over the alcove and stepped toward the secret door. Jonata seized my sword arm.

Wardens first, Chief Justice, she said as she handed me her lantern. Biming's warden shot me an amused look as he followed her with the lantern Biming had handed to him.

I thought my wardens were overprotective, Biming observed.

You're further down the Assassins Guild target list than I am, I replied.

I'll see what I can do to make myself more of a target, he teased.

Except I found nothing humorous in his jest. *It's not worth their lives, Reverend Father. I've watched the corpses of too many of my own wardens burn thanks to the Assassins Guild.*

My apologies, Lady Justice, he said. No explanation. No justification for his behavior. It should have been a relief, but my attention was tied to the wardens as they approached the mysterious door.

Biming's warden bent to set his lantern beside the narrow crack on the left at the same moment Jonata pushed on the right side of the door. A series of clicks came from behind the stone-covered façade.

"Down!" The Thief warden shoved Jonata aside.

He wasn't fast enough. A series of darts erupted from the hidden area behind the door. Both wardens ended up in a tangle on the stone floor of the passageway.

My heart rose in my mouth. I raced for Jonata only to be slammed arse first on the unyielding stone when someone jerked on my robes. I looked over my shoulder to berate the person, but very large, very sharp teeth framed Fa's snarl.

Biming and Longnu sidled past us and crept over to the fallen wardens. Staying low, the dragon Wildling dragged the Thief warden off Jonata. A terrible wheezing sound came from my warden.

"Don't move, Warden," Biming warned in a low voice.

She murmured something between gasping breaths. However, I

couldn't catch her actual words. He slowly pulled her away from the now open doorway. I climbed to my feet, but Fa growled behind me.

Slowly, Chief Justice, he said silently.

The two of us carefully approached the rest of our party. I bent to retrieve the lantern from where it rolled against the left wall. A dart appeared to have punctured the paper, which affected the spell it contained. The magic flickered against my shields.

The Thief warden's body convulsed twice and shuddered before it went totally still. Longnu looked up and met my gaze before she shook her head.

"Jonata?" I said softly.

I'm uninjured, m'lady, she said. *The darts are coated with a faster acting poison than southern blue.*

Biming's hands carefully examined her body and used a piece of silk to pluck tiny, steel-tipped darts from her leather vest and leggings.

None of them penetrated your tunic or bare skin? I asked.

She chuckled. *You would know before I would. Do you see any blood on me?*

Only a couple of splotches on your back, but not where a dart pierced your vest.

Thank the Twelve for the padded leathers you wear, Warden, Biming said. *Else we wouldn't be having this conversation.*

I'm well aware, Reverend Father. Jonata looked over at her fellow warden. *I also owe Muchen a debt. His quick actions also saved me.*

I ground my teeth as I examined the Thief warden. The fatal dart stuck out of his cheek just above the lower jaw. The skin around the wound had already blackened from the poison. Once again, someone sacrificed themselves for me and mine, and I didn't even know his name until Death had taken him. When would I ever learn?

Do you have a mirror, Reverend Father? I asked.

He nodded while he placed the darts he'd removed from Jonata's clothing into a small leather pouch. *I also want to know what's in that hidden room that was worth protecting.*

Biming placed the pouch back within his robes and produced a small piece of glass set in a wooden frame. He held it out to me.

I let my black humor leak through the link. *I can't see reflections, Rever-*

end Father. To me, a mirror looks the same as a window pane. I'd be happy to hold it for someone else.

My apologies, Chief Justice.

But from the subtle change in his expression, he filed away that little piece of information about my peculiar eyesight. All I could do was hope his loyalty to Po superseded his wariness of me. And that his original apology for siding with Reverend Father Ogusuku wasn't false.

I crept closer to Biming, ignoring Fa's warning growl. *I don't detect any magic. Could it have been a conventional trap?*

That's my thought as well, he said. *But without a good look, I can't be sure what is the triggering mechanism.*

Jonata, did you get a glimpse of the dimensions of the room? I asked.

Sorry, m'lady. From the lamplight, I could only see the floor, which was stone like the rest of the passageway.

I considered Warden Muchen's damaged paper lantern still in my hand. *You're not going to get a good look at the space with just your mirror, Reverend Father. Do you care if I sacrifice the damaged Knowledge lamp?*

I felt more than heard his chuckle.

Or I could throw in a flashbang, he replied.

That would more likely get both of us banned from the imperial palace. I laughed silently. *And I'd rather save any flashbangs in case we do discover demon eggs.*

Good point. He held out his left palm. *May I?*

I gave him the flickering lamp. In a deft series of motions, he tossed the damaged lantern through the doorway with his left hand, dropped to his right side with the mirror extended in that hand, and jerked upright once again.

There's eighteen miniature cross bows in a rack on a table, he reported. *They are all pointed at the doorway. A line runs from the inside of the door to the table.*

Trade places with me. My tone wasn't as deferential as it should have been to someone who outranked me. However, we quickly switched places so I was next to the edge of the open door.

I eased my head to the right and peered into the room. The set-up was as Biming described, but there were also two huge iron balls hanging from the ceiling on the left and right sides of the room. Their chains were connected to wires that ran down the walls and to rows of trip wires stretching along the floor from the table to the back of the room. The new trap guarded another door set in an alcove at the back of the room. I pulled my head back.

Well? Biming demanded.

I described the second trap and sighed. *There may be another backup neither of us can see.*

But there's no other wires running across the middle of the room? he asked.

None above a handspan from the floor, I said.

He relayed our status to Justice Mei Wen, including his warden's death. *I'll send two Death wardens to collect his body.* She groaned silently. *You're going in regardless of any logical reason not to, aren't you, Reverend Father?*

Do you have a logical reason not to, Justice?

Only the emperor and empress's displeasure if you get yourself and Chief Justice Anthea killed, Mei Wen retorted.

Then don't tell them, I said.

Another search party distracted Mei Wen from talking Biming out of whatever he was going to do.

I should go instead of you, Reverend Father, Longnu said.

No, Sister. I need you and Brother Fa to escort the chief justice and her warden out of the passages if I'm foolish enough to get myself killed. Biming rose, stepped around me and entered the room.

I peered around the doorjamb once again. To my shock, Biming floated across the hidden room above the table full of crossbows. When he reached the rear of the room, he lowered himself. Once inside the alcove, his feet settled on the floor. He crouched and plucked the closest tripwire.

The iron balls swung down and crushed the table and weapons in a resounding BOOM.

CHAPTER 46

The chains creaked from the huge iron balls swinging from the force of their crash. I handed the intact lantern to Jonata, stood, and took one step across the threshold.

"Stop!" Biming held up his hands.

I froze in place. From the warmth behind me, Jonata and the Wildlings looked around me to see what was going on.

Let me doublecheck the room for any more surprises, he added more gently.

All right, but please be careful, I warned. The crushed wood and bits of metal drew my attention from his odd talent. The damaged lantern flickered wildly under the debris, its Knowledge spell on the verge of dying. The second trap had been designed to destroy the evidence of the first trap as well as any foes. But the reasoning and placement of the tripwires indicated someone with average human eyesight.

Like the skinwalker who had assassinated Emperor Chengwu and his family.

Had Biming already come to the same conclusion? If so, we may be closer to the hidden demon eggs than we thought.

The fine hairs on my skin rose as if a breeze stirred them. Biming's detection spell swirled around the room. Something so minor a sorcerer may not notice it.

But I really wanted to know how Biming floated through the air. He wasn't light like dandelion fluff. He didn't heat the air to carry him aloft similar to cloth or paper balloons. Nor did he have wings like a Wildling who could transform into a bird or a bat. He definitely hadn't transformed into a dragon like Longnu. The technique would be fascinating to learn.

He interrupted my analysis. *Anthea, do you see any more traps? I'm not detecting anything through magic or my own eyesight.*

I examined the stones I would have to step on to enter the room since I could not float across the room as he did. That's when I noticed the three stones that were a slightly different shade of green than the rest of the room. One of them right in front of me. I had been about to step on it when Biming shouted.

Jonata, do you see anything unusual about the floor pattern?

She crouched on my right and slightly behind my legs. She held up our intact lantern. *Three of them appear as if they've been painted to match the rest.* She indicated the same nearby stones I'd noticed before she looked up at me. *Possible spring triggers when someone steps on them. Similar to the ones we wardens planned to install with flashbangs at the Orrin tunnel entrances before the seats decided to permanently close the system.*

I turned to Longnu. *Can you fly over them to the Reverend Father? I don't want to leave him alone if we accidentally set off another trap.*

In a lovely change of pace, the Jing priestess didn't question me. Instead, she rose into the air and shot across the room, neatly avoiding the still swinging chains and metal spheres.

Do you see any others those of us on foot need to be concerned about, Chief Justice? Fa asked.

I carefully examined each stone. It took a great deal of time, and I couldn't view the floor stones covered in debris. Nor did I dare to move the debris. Doing so could set off whatever deadly effects we desired to avoid.

There are two discolored slabs near the right wall and three on the left. We must assume there are others underneath the wreckage we cannot see that could go off at any time. Both of you need to stand back.

Fa and Jonata retreated as I requested, and I unsheathed my sword. Even with the Spring Rituals in full swing and acting as a diplomat in a foreign nation, I'd brought my full complement of blades. I wasn't about to hunt an enemy in tight quarters without being fully armed.

Very gently, I scraped a line in Jonata's suspected paint with the tip of my sword on the spot I almost stepped on. Underneath was wood, not stone. At least, nothing happened, like more darts shot from walls or a flashbang igniting.

Jonata's breath hissed between her teeth. *I swear the Twelve have made you their special project, m'lady.*

Fa chuffed. *Or you were assigned to the wrong Temple. Thief favors you.*

I bit my tongue to keep any facetious comments quiet in the link.

Maybe you three should stay there, Biming said. *The last thing I need is to be responsible for the Issuran ambassador's untimely death.*

What? I retorted. *And let you have all the fun? It would totally destroy the fishwives' tales that I plan to rule Jing through the new emperor.*

Jonata laughed. Fa coughed to cover his own humor. Even Biming and Longnu chuckled.

Warden, Brother, memorize my exact steps, I ordered. *I'll mark the fake stones.*

I sucked in a long, deep breath and released it. Making the gesture for good luck with my left hand, I stepped over the painted wood I'd marked. Slowly, I worked my way around the scattered debris, double-checking the color of each piece of flooring before taking the next step or marking the wood with my sword tip. There were more than the initial six I saw. Sweat trickled profusely underneath my leathers despite the chill air when I reached Biming and Longnu.

Jonata followed, imitating my movements except for marking the painted wood slabs. Fa started to step forward and paused. His huge paws would extend over the edges of some of the safe stones to the suspicious wood slabs.

I cursed myself. None of us had considered that problem.

Brother Fa, go back if you can't— Biming started.

We're overthinking the situation, Reverend Father. Fa stepped back from the room and lay on the corridor floor. Fur receded. Bones crunched. Muscles realigned themselves. When he climbed to his feet, the young priest was in human shape. He grinned at us. *This will be a little easier now.*

A couple of times, Fa had to stand on the balls of his feet. They were as huge in human form as they were as tiger paws. However, none of us could fault the young man's sense of balance as he made his way across the safe stones.

Longnu narrowed her huge eyes. *This had better not be an excuse to impress Warden Jonata.*

Warden Jonata has other plans for the holiday, Sister, my guard replied dryly. *No need to raise your back spines.*

Quit bickering and stand back, children, Biming ordered. *I'm going to open the next door.*

This one wasn't disguised. A conventional lever perched on the right side of the wood. The catpaw feeling of Thief magic caressed my skin as Biming readied his ward. He shoved the door open.

Darts slammed into his ward and dropped to the floor. But it was the loud groan of the ceiling that caused me to shove the Wildlings and Jonata into the alcove and throw up my own wards around our little party. The pulleys holding the chains dropped. The iron balls fell to the floor and set off a series of explosions.

CHAPTER 47

Stone, wood, and iron shrapnel slammed into my wards. Somehow, I held them against the onslaught. However, it wasn't just the physical objects that assaulted me. Alien magic filtered past my shields amplifying the pain in my head. But it wasn't a demon spell.

Dust filled the small room. Biming's wards wrapped around mine as the last two flashbangs detonated when bits of the stone ceiling landed on their wooden triggers. By the time the dust started to settle, I feared I'd gone deaf from the ringing in my ears and the pain in my head.

Anyone have injuries? Biming asked.

Jonata and the young Wildlings chorused in the negative. I, on the other hand, collapsed to my knees from a rush of vertigo. Unfortunately, my wards collapsed as well and the dry scent of the powdered debris filled my nostrils.

Chief Justice! Jonata kept my head from hitting the stone wall of the alcove as I fell onto my left side. *What's wrong?*

In the back of my mind, I could hear Shi Hua and Mei Wen silently shouting. Except I couldn't make anything in me respond mentally or physically, either to them or to my warden.

Biming swore a few Jing obscenities as the strange spell started to affect him as well. His silent speech was swallowed by the miasma of both the spell and the dust.

"What's happening?" Jonata said.

Out loud.

Because neither Biming nor I could keep our connection with the other three going.

"I'll re-establish the link," Fa said.

"No!" A strange female voice. Longnu? It had to be since I'd only known her so far as a dragon. "Can't you feel the sorcery? If we use magic, this spell affecting them could incapacitate us as well."

Did that mean shapeshifting wasn't technically magic? My thoughts considered that question because it couldn't do much else. Not even contemplate how we'd escape because so much rubble covered the hidden doorway where we had entered.

"The Reverend Father's still alive," Longnu reported.

Jonata's fingers touched my wrist before she leaned close to my head to check my breath.

"The chief justice is alive, too. So much for sneaking up on Yar and Antiope's assailants," Jonata bit out. "Everyone in the palace had to hear and feel those explosions."

"So much for keeping our investigation secret as well," Longnu muttered.

"Yes, I hear you, Shi Hua," Fa said. "Longnu, Jonata, and I are uninjured, but some kind of sorcery has incapacitated Chief Justice Anthea and Reverend Father Biming." There was a quick pause before he added, "He raised wards when he deliberately set off a conventional trap, but there was a secondary trigger that detonated a bunch of flashbangs. When the chief justice raised her wards to protect our backs, that's when the sorcery hit both of them."

Another pause.

"Their eyes are open, they are breathing, and their hearts are beating, but neither of them is responsive," Fa said.

A third pause.

"That may be difficult, my friend. There's a great deal of wreckage covering the hidden entrance we found leading from the secret passages." He let out an exasperated breath. "Fine. We'll wait."

"No," I croaked. The single word set off a coughing fit now that mine and Biming's wards were no longer protecting us from the dust.

"Here, m'lady." Jonata held a small flask to my lips.

The cool water was quite welcome to my throat after the abrasive particles in the air. I cleared my throat and took another sip.

I tried to pushed myself up, but I didn't have the coordination. My warden saw what I was trying to do and assisted me upright to lean against the alcove wall. I looked around us, or as much as I could without moving my head. Dust covered the living things on the walls. There was no need for me to mark our path. We weren't going out the way we came in.

"What's in this next room besides poisonous darts?" My voice sounded like I was an elder, not a woman in her prime.

A beautiful nude girl with straight blue hair past her waist stepped past me and retrieved the damaged lantern. Its magic flickered even more rapidly after being buffeted by flashbangs, but perhaps she didn't want to lose the intact lantern that sat near my hip. She returned to the second doorway, held up the torn paper lamp, and examined the next chamber.

"There's a table with a rack of miniature crossbows like the crushed one in here. All have been fired. The darts are lying on the floor. We'll have to assume they're poisoned like the first round." She looked over her shoulder at Fa. "Make sure you don't step on one."

She turned back and continued, "None of them reached the Reverend Father or the rest of us. However, all the wires from the crossbows are connected to the door he opened. There are no other wires or strings, and no chains or other devices are hanging from the ceiling. Nor do I see an obvious door to escape through."

"A-an-any h-holes?" Biming choked out from where he lay on the floor. Jonata pivoted to give him some of her water.

Longnu leaned a little further into the room. Her dragon form must lend its flexibility to her human one. She twisted her head to such a degree I would have injured myself if I tried to perform the same maneuver.

"No, sir." She turned back to us. "I suggest we wait for the assistance Lady Shi Hua is sending to us."

"No, we can't simply wait." My voice still had a gravelly quality, but the sound was closer to normal than a few moments before. "These traps are not only part of someone's protection, but a way to give them warning."

"What do you suggest, Lady Justice?" Fa said.

I considered the situation. "Longnu, did you feel anything strange when you shifted back to human form?"

"No." She frowned. "But then, I wasn't carrying the silent speech link. The Reverend Father and you were."

"I suspect it was both of us raising wards that activated the sorcery," I said.

"That makes sense," Jonata murmured. "A lone person would expect another round of darts when they opened the second door. They'd ward the doorway—"

"And leave their back unprotected," Fa continued. "The sorcery was designed to lower a talent's primary defense."

"Thereby, getting killed by the third measure in the first room," Longnu finished. She shivered. "I should have brought some extra clothes with me."

"Jonata, help me take off my robes." I struggled with untying the laces, which should have been a minor action. "There's no reason for Longnu to catch a chill and ruin her holiday."

"Y-you mean like Warden Muchen's holiday has been ruined?" Biming's hoarse voice held a combination of the effect of the sorcerer's spell and grief.

Jonata was in the process of pulling my robes over my head before I could answer.

"I mean no disrespect, Reverend Father," I said gently as Jonata handed the garment to Longnu. "But right now, we must concern ourselves with the surviving members of our teams. We will mourn Warden Muchen properly once our task is accomplished."

"If I might make a suggestion, Chief Justice?" Jonata's earnest gaze meant she had an idea.

"I'm listening," I replied.

"Cast the tracking spell," she said.

"What if it harms her further?" Fa protested while Longnu pulled my robes over her own head.

I smiled at my warden's idea. "First, we'll discover if the sorcerer's spell is meant to stop other kinds of magic besides wards. Second, our target will know we survived the traps in these two rooms. Jonata thinks to flush them out as we originally planned if they're not already on the run."

"Can you do it, Anthea?" Biming croaked.

"I'll do it," Longnu demanded. Fa started to protest, but she held up her hand. "The spell was subtle and designed to use magic against the caster. If the chief justice is correct about wards triggering it, it won't affect me by casting a tracking spell. If it does—" She shrugged. "You'll know not to activate any spell, and it won't harm the Reverend Father or the chief justice further."

"I can't order you to do it or not do it, Sister Longnu," I rubbed my temples, but the obscene headache caused by the delicate sorcery was already receding. I was more amazed my fingers worked correctly, and I didn't poke myself in the eye.

"I-I can d-damn well f-forbid—" Biming's speech devolved into body-wracking coughs.

"I'm sorry, sir, but I didn't understand a word you just said," Longnu said primly.

I was beginning to like the dragon Wildling.

"May I have the coin, Chief Justice?" She held out her palm.

My chuckles launched another coughing fit, but Jonata grinned and said, "She keeps full evidence bags in the left top pocket in her robes. Do you need a flint? We had plenty of stones to strike."

"No, thank you." Longnu grinned in return as she found the silk-wrapped coin. "That I can handle."

"Longnu, please step back from the doorway," I said. "In case you are affected by the sorcery, I don't want you falling on those Twelve-cursed darts."

"You are right, of course."

Fa and Jonata stepped over my legs to give the Wildling priestess a little more room.

She went down to her hands and knees and placed the bag in front of her. Scales grew and spread across her skin as her body lengthened and her limbs shortened. Fa pulled the Reverend Father away from the second doorway. Jonata did the same with me since my legs refused to cooperate.

Longnu looked rather ridiculous wearing my robes as a dragon. The needle pricks of Wildling magic danced along my skin as she murmured the spell in a strange tongue that wasn't remotely related to the Jing language. To my amazement, she breathed fire from her mouth across the coin. White fire danced across the metal's surface for a moment before it died. Just as I thought the spell had failed, an energy ribbon sprang to life. It flared and settled, leading to a spot on the left wall of the second room.

Jonata looked at the place where I and the other three clergy were staring. "Don't tell me it's another hidden doorway." Her statement was followed by a groan.

"Marvelous," Fa muttered. "We're already down three people. How are you feeling, Longnu?"

The Wildling's mental voice whispered through my mind. *No ill effects, my brother.* A tickle of her humor followed. *It seems the chief justice was correct that the sorcery was aimed at someone raising wards to protect themselves from the conventional weapons in the room.*

"I'd love to stay put until help arrives, but I know damn well that would only happen if I hogtie all of you. I don't get paid enough to put Wildling claws to the test." Jonata crossed her arms and scowled at the rest of us.

Biming's boots flexed and pointed. "I can feel my feet again."

"Shall we discover what's behind door number three, Reverend Father?" I asked.

"Sounds like an excellent idea to me." His voice was as gravelly as mine had been a few moments ago, but he could speak clearly and no longer coughed.

Despite my jovial tone, worry nipped my heels as Jonata helped me to my feet. What if something much worse lay behind the next hidden doorway?

CHAPTER 48

With Longnu's aid, Biming was able to float across the room to the hidden door. Jonata and I walked, but I needed her for support. Fa shifted back to his tiger form. With the intact lantern hanging from his huge jaws, he leapt lightly over the scattered darts.

After Biming and Longnu landed beside the third door, he sighed as his fingers traced the barely discernable crack around this hidden door. "This one also swings inward." Glanced around us. "The sorcery in the second chamber wasn't detectable until Anthea and I raised wards. My head still aches abominably. Can any of you perceive additional magic in here?"

"No, sir," each of the wildlings said.

"I can barely feel you and the Wildlings," I muttered.

"I'm a passive so I would need to know where the spell is to activate it," Jonata added.

As Biming stepped back from the hidden door, something roughly waist-high caught my attention. There was a block where none of the lavender beings grew. "Any of you see something different about that narrow stone on the right side of our possible door?"

Not see, Fa said. He nudged me aside with his huge shoulder. *Let me take a whiff.*

He snuffled the block and the area below it. *It's the same scent Longnu and I picked up in the passageway.*

Biming and I exchanged looks.

"Now we know why one of our suspects came this way," I said. "If you know anything, Reverend Father, now would be a good time to deliver the information."

He sighed again. "I know I've given you no reason to trust me lately, but I knew nothing of these rooms. If you feel the need to truthspell me to confirm my word, I acquiesce to your interrogation."

Fa growled deep in his chest and stepped between Biming and me.

"Stand down, Brother Fa," Biming said sternly. "I would feel the same way as the chief justice if our positions were reversed. And I have given her cause not to take my word at face value." A cheeky grin spread across his face. "Not to mention I've seen the Issurans in action against demons and skinwalkers on more than one occasion. Even if you manage to incapacitate Anthea, I assure you Warden Jonata won't let you live long enough to enjoy your victory."

Only then did I notice Jonata had daggers in both hands as she prepared to defend me.

"Not to mention Lady Shi Hua would be very cross with you for starting an unnecessary fight," I added lightly.

I suggest you refrain from further insult against one of our Temple leaders," Fa said.

I cocked my head. "And what insult did I deliver to the Reverend Father?"

Longnu giggled in the back of my mind while Jonata laughed out loud as she sheathed her blades.

Fa's embarrassment flowed over my aching head. He dipped his giant head. *My apologies, Chief Justice. I shouldn't have allowed my temper get the better of me.*

"We all need to keep cool heads in this situation," Biming said gently as he patted Fa's shoulder. "The stakes are far too high for minor personality issues. And a bit of advice, the chief justice can throw lightning. The odds of you succeeding in harming her are infinitesimal."

The head of Thief turned back to me and raised an eyebrow.

I shook my head. "I'm not going to truthspell you here and now." I smiled. "But I reserve the right to do so in the future."

He inclined his head. "Of course, m'lady."

I eyed the suspected door once again. "What if the darker shade on the block is another pressure plate?"

"I'll do the scraping this time," Jonata growled. She shoved roughly past us and drew her right dagger. "All of you need to step back."

Biming and I immediately shuffled to the side. After a moment, Fa did the same while Longnu floated above our heads.

My warden knelt before the door and eyed the questionable stone. I prepped a time freeze spell. Hopefully, the sorcery that incapacitated Biming and me and our wards would ignore my ability to manipulate time.

She lightly scraped the alleged stone with the tip of her dagger, but the sound was distinctively metal-on-metal. "What the demon?"

"Jonata?" I stepped forward. Steel shone pale green through its covering.

"It's definitely paint over steel and a pressure panel like the wood ones in the first room. I've seen latches like this in some of the newer buildings in Standora." She grunted as she sheathed her dagger before she turned and tossed the intact paper lantern to me. "Get against the wall." She gestured to her left. "When you're clear, I'll press it."

"Jonata, no!" I charged toward her, but Fa stepped in my way.

My warden grinned at me. "I don't have a death wish like some people, Anthea. But everything so far points at a fear of other talents, and I know how to dodge." For her to use my given name showed how nervous she was.

"You didn't out in the main passage," I snapped.

However, Fa headbutted me in the direction of Biming and Longnu.

"Accede to your warden's logic, Lady Justice," Biming said.

"You're making me want to stab you again, Reverend Father," I growled as Fa shoved me past the Thief priest and against the stone wall.

"Don't take the chief justice's words literally, Brother Fa," Jonata called out. "Death threats mean she likes the Reverend Father, but she's angry he's right."

I sucked in a deep breath at the same time Jonata did. She pressed the metal latch and dove into a rolling spin as the door swung open.

CHAPTER 49

My lungs ached as we all waited for something, anything, to happen. Near the ceiling, Longnu floated to the stonework above the doorway. She twisted to peer though and a low whistle came from her elongated throat.

It's a secret passageway like the others we were inspecting. A tinge of amazement filled her silent voice. *The tracking spell continues to the left.*

Jonata rose from her crouch and eased closer to the door. *Clear. Can you pick up the scent again, Sister?*

The wildling floated low enough to clear the stones above the doorway and passed through it. Jonata followed, her steps light and mincing.

From the scent, our suspect definitely passed through here, Longnu reported.

Biming, Fa, and I left the room. Longnu crept back and forth along the floor stones, her long snout at an angle. It took me a moment to realize she tried not to contaminate the scent she tracked as well as avoiding any interference with the tracking spell.

Did the second suspect come through here? Biming asked.

Fa took a deep whiff of the trail Longnu followed. *No, sir.*

The most recent scent is the same way as the tracking spell. Longnu pivoted and headed to our left from the last trap room.

These walls and ceiling were pristine lavender. From the bright glow, no one had disturbed these creatures in months. Possibly years. A single set of shoe prints led in the same direction as the Wildlings' detected scent. Did our suspect know something was on the stones that we didn't?

There were no intersections along this passage. Instead, it curved and wound left and right until we reached a narrow staircase.

Biming chuckled softly.

What is it? I asked.

I know where we are now. Po, Chengwu, and I explored this section when we were children. There is a suite at the bottom of these stairs.

It sounds as if there's a story behind your knowledge, I commented.

I'll tell it to you another night before you leave Jing. The Reverend Father sobered. *Let's deal with our current problem first.*

All of us descended the steps single file, except for Longnu who floated above us while she held the damaged lamp in her left clawed front foot.

I went first. For once, no one questioned the arrangement since my odd sight had been beneficial in the trap rooms.

I raised my hand when we reached the next to last step. The yellowish-green gleam of a copper wire stretched across the last step. This time, I felt the definitive tug of sorcery. There was a sharp right turn past the small square of stone floor after the rigged step. I passed the information to the other.

Longnu, can you go down and see if there's any other impediment after this trip wire? I asked.

She floated over my head without any comment and twisted to see our next path. *There's just a regular door with a normal latch to open it, Chief Justice.*

I looked over my shoulder. *Sneaking around is Thief's domain. Any suggestions on our next step, Reverend Father?*

He grinned. *Only that we shouldn't tread on that trip wire.*

Behind him, Jonata snorted. *I thought the chief justice's black sense of humor was bad.*

Fa chuffed at her comment, but he didn't offer any suggestions.

What does Balance's logic say? Longnu asked.

I considered the possibilities. *If our suspect is here and isn't adept in all types of magic, they may think the trap rooms have killed us. If they are here and are adept, they are waiting to kill us. Or our original plan worked. The tracking spell flushed them out, and even now they are escaping from the palace. None of which precludes any potential traps they might have set to shake off our pursuit.*

Let me go ahead in case there's another debilitating spell waiting for the rest of you, Jonata said.

Not this time, Warden. Longnu landed in the square and shed my robes. *If I'm injured or killed, Fa will avenge me.*

How about we avoid both so we can dance at this evening's festivities? he answered.

She winked at him before she disappeared around the corner. A moment later, she called, *Clear!*

We each jumped over the trip wire and entered a luxurious sitting room. Well, it would have been luxurious if not for the slight layer of dust on most of the furniture. A handful of active paper lanterns were scattered around the area. Between those and the smears on several surfaces and an obviously cleaned table and stool, someone had been here recently. Longnu stood on her hind legs before a lacquered wall panel, sniffing. My tracking spell went through the obstacle.

He definitely has been staying here for a couple of days, Fa commented as he prowled around the room.

Clear! Jonata called. She emerged from a bedchamber. *The bedsheets are still warm, and the towels are damp.*

I peered inside. Sure enough, the covers on the bed were rumpled.

The scent around the door is less than an quarter candlemark old, Longnu said. *But the door has a spell on it I don't recognize.*

Lady Shi Hua, one of our snoops is heading for the main sewer junction on the east side of the palace, Biming relayed.

You were supposed to wait for another team, Reverend Father. The anger ran thick in the soon-to-be empress's silent voice.

It was my call, m'lady, since I had the skin and oil from last night's visitor on my copper, I interjected. *Plus, there were no more traps past the first two rooms after we set them all off.* I detailed the directions from Biming for the teams to bypass the trap rooms. At least, he'd learned some political delicacy when it came to the future empress by letting me speak. *By the way, there is a trip wire at the bottom stairs,* I added. *One we haven't triggered.*

All right. There was a long pause while she passed on our information, but her anger had eased in the link. *Those already stationed in the sewers are waiting, and other teams are going to meet them.*

At Biming's sad expression, I said, "Give her time."

He nodded before he turned his attention to the hidden door.

Fa looked at me, then the Reverend Father, but he said nothing. He knew Shi Hua longer than I had. Even longer than Biming had known her. The closest person who knew me in that manner was Luc. I couldn't imagine having someone who watched me go through my various stages in life. My thousands of questions would have to wait until a more appropriate time.

Biming roared a very nasty Jing obscenity that had no equivalent in the Issuran language.

I whirled to find him on the floor cradling his hands on his knees. Longnu danced back from the hidden opening. A fine purple mist blew through the joint between the panel where my tracking spell disappeared and its neighbor.

"What happened?" I rushed over. Jonata followed and crouched next to him.

"Acid," he spat, his pain burning its way through my mental shields before he dropped the link.

We helped him to his feet and led him to the bathing room. He settled next to the faucet as I twisted the lever for cold water. As Jonata helped him dilute the acid before it could do more damage, I ran back into the sitting room. Fa cuddled against his fellow Wildling and purred.

"Longnu, did you get any acid on you?"

She shook her head. Her fleshy whisker tendrils flew back and forth with her motion.

The Reverend Father took the brunt of the spray. I am uninjured. A low audible growl came from deep in her chest. *The locking spell wasn't on the latch. It was on something else inside the hidden door. I heard glass break, and the acid sprayed from the crack.*

She rose and crawled under the one couch that had been uncovered by the suite's recent resident. She came out with an eating stick between her teeth. Floating across the space to avoid the acid on the floor, she pressed the stick in a hole roughly the size of a human finger. A click sounded, and Longnu floated back as the hidden door swung into the sitting room.

More purple liquid dribbled down the doorjamb in the right. Reds and oranges glowed where the acid dissolved the lacquer and ate the wood and stone.

Lady Shi Hua had to leave for one of the festival events, Mei Wen murmured in my head. *I felt the Reverend Father's pain. Are any other members of your teams injured beside him, Chief Justice?*

The rest of us are fine, I said. *However, the Reverend Father will need a healer for bad acid burns on his hands.*

Are you returning the way you went down to the hidden suite? she asked.

Brother Fa and Warden Jonata will escort the Reverend Father back the way we came. I raised my right index finger when my warden opened her mouth to protest. *Longnu and I will pursue the tracking spell.*

"I must protest, Lady Justice," Jonata hissed.

"Your warden has a point." Biming leaned an elbow on Fa's back and struggled to his feet. "Your warden is not intimidated by me, and there's nothing I can hold over her head." He smiled, but a wealth of agony emanated from him, and even I could see the intense lines on his face. "However, both Fa and Longnu will accompany you, Chief Justice. I will not be accused by my empress of sending you to your death."

We promise to guard your justice with our lives, Longnu said.

I groaned. "Why does everyone think I wish to die?"

"Would you prefer we think you are too much of a fool whenever you rush straight into danger?" Jonata said dryly.

"Y-you are—will be—I swear you'll be cleaning the chamber pots in Orrin for the rest of your life," I finally blurted.

"That's still better than what Chief Warden Little Bear threatened Long Feather and me with if we didn't bring you back to Orrin alive, m'lady." The smug look on Jonata's face made me want to launch a right cross into her jaw.

"Get the Reverend Father to a healer, Warden. That is an order," I snapped.

"Yes, Chief Justice." She turned to collect first an intact paper lantern and then the leader of Thief. Together, they disappeared through the other door.

She's going to kill us if anything happens to you, Fa commented.

"No, I won't! I know who to blame!" Jonata's shouts echoed back down the stairwell and into the suite.

I severed my link with her. She needed to focus on her current mission.

"Let us go," I said to the two Wildlings before I really lost my temper and started frying things and people with my lightning talent.

CHAPTER 50

I carried our intact Knowledge lantern as Longnu led the way along my tracking spell. I couldn't help wondering why the person we followed hadn't found a way to disable my spell. Were they not a sorcerer as we expected? Or were they a passive talent, like some of my wardens? Those who could trigger a spell that had been cast by someone with an active talent?

If that were the case, who supplied them with the spells they used within the palace? The lanterns would have been easy. Both Knowledge and a couple of the philosophical schools provided them to the public.

But the rest?

How would someone acquire a locking spell in Jing if they were a passive talent or didn't have a talent at all? I asked.

Thief would provide one with a donation, Fa said. *However, some merchants request locking spells with lethal consequences. Only a couple of the philosophy schools will provide such a spell.*

So, a death sentence without a proper trial, I muttered silently.

Yes, Fa answered. *That's why they are illegal in Jing.*

Let me guess, I said. *The School of Sorcery was one of them.*

They managed to evade any charges on the deadly locking spells for centuries, Fa admitted. *But then they were caught with demon artifacts, including their eggs, thanks to your investigation of the Issuran sea captain's death.*

Why was someone from the School of Sorcery sent to the crown prince in Issura?

An odd sound came from Fa's feline chest. *Master Wu claimed it was for the crown prince's protection. Jian and I believe Wu used him to confirm Shi Hua was Temple by assassinating her. And with her out of the way . . .*

Wu's plan would have been a masterful double stroke. Take down his son's only true rival for the throne and embarrass the Temples by their failure to protect Po. However, my investigation into Captain Arturo's death revealed the renegades' plan.

So why had the sorcerer and the demon been so sloppy by freezing Arturo to death instead of using a medicine from Vintner that would have simulated a natural death? That was one of many questions I would submit to Reverend Mother Xiang when we captured our escapee.

The odor of human waste grew stronger as we followed my tracking spell. A few side tunnels branched off in alternate directions. When I asked about them, Longnu said, *They are used for maintenance. The aqueducts coming into the city are used to flush the sewer out once a year.*

What is done with the waste that is flushed out? I asked.

Fa chuffed. *It is mixed with the city's animal dung and used to fertilize the fields in the villages surrounding Chengzhou. There is a specially built retaining pond outside of the city where it all goes.*

It's more of a lake, Longnu added. *But with the size of the capital, we produced more human waste than animal waste. The farmers find it suitable for their needs, and in return, it helps to feed the populace.*

Do you mix it with ash? I asked.

Before the younger clergy could answer me, shouting echoed through the passageway. It was quickly followed by the sounds of a struggle. The presence of magic raised my fine body hairs, and I started running.

No doubt, the Wildlings could have reached the fight sooner, but they kept their promise to Jonata and stayed by my side.

Both offensive and defensive spells were being cast. The blade-sharp tang of Conflict magic. The soft kitten paws of Thief. The hammer blows of Father. But the sorcery wasn't the sneaking seduction of the trap rooms. No, the opposing sorcery tasted of the same fiery anger as last night.

The tunnel dead-ended at what could only be called a river of waste that flowed in a general westerly direction. To our left, clergy from the three Temples I'd sensed battled a blue-haired figure in civilian clothing on our side of the maintenance workers' walkway.

The same person tethered the end of my tracking spell.

A series of arcs held up the roof for the drain, and the sorcerer stood between two of them. Yes, those would definitely work as long as our suspect didn't dive into the odiferous sludge.

I closed my eyes and concentrated. With so many spells flying back and forth, our suspect didn't feel my time freeze until I cast it. Three Conflict plasma balls were caught even as our suspect took one half-step toward the waste drifting past him.

"Name yourself!" a male voice roared.

"Chief Justice Anthea of the Issuran Temple of Balance with Brother Fa and Sister Longnu from the Jing Temple of Wildling!"

"Reverend Father Feng of the Jing Temple of Conflict!" The rest of the clergy with him called out their identities as well, but I already knew my rush of nerves wouldn't let me remember them all.

We approached our suspect. He was definitely the man Long Feather and I encountered in the secret passage in the wall behind mine and Luc's bathing room. My party and Reverend Father Feng's stopped just outside of our ends of my frozen time.

"How do we get Wu out without him jumping into the muck?" The Reverend Father's voice was caught in the frozen time, but it carried around the rest of the tunnel. His disembodied voice came from my right instead of ahead. If I weren't used to the effects of a time freeze, it would have unraveled what was left of my nerves from this whole expedition to Jing.

"Do you have spell-threaded manacles with you?" I asked.

"Yes, but how do I cuff Wu without being caught in your time freeze, also?"

"Toss them toward Wu," I said. "I'll do the rest."

Feng did as I asked. The heavy silver and steel hung in midair. At least, he hadn't tossed them so high I couldn't reach them.

I turned to Fa and Longnu. "Don't follow me past the closest arch to Wu, or you'll get caught in my spell, too."

Yes, Lady Justice, they chorused silently.

I parted a sliver of my spell and stepped into silence except for my own breathing. I strode across the bricks and grabbed the chain. The manacles floated behind me as if they were kites and the chain were a string. I left them hanging when I reached Wu.

His round face beneath his beard looked nothing like Po's saturnine features. According to Shi Hua, Po and his half-brother could have been twins if not for their age difference. Did both men take after their mother then?

I turned and laid him face down on the algae-covered bricks, turning his head so he could breathe when I released my spell. I tugged both of his arms behind his back and secured the manacles before I pulled the chain down to rest on the bricks, instead of falling on us. Last, I place my left knee on the spot where his neck met his spine. With a murmured word, I dissolved both the time freeze and tracking spells.

Wu's shock at his new position ricocheted off my mental shields. He followed by shouting obscenities that would have melted the ears of the most hardened sailor on Orrin's docks.

Reverend Father Feng and his people rushed over from one side. My Wildling escort padded over from the opposite direction.

"Excellent job, Chief Justice." Feng flashed a grim smile. "Good to know neither Biming nor Xiang exaggerated your talents."

"The Twelve blessed me with the ability to contrive plans that shouldn't work, but do." I climbed to my boots. I'd definitely need to take advantage of Reverend Mother Xiang's laundry services again, and I could beg her for a new pair of boots with a large donation. But maybe I could use the stench of sewer that permeated my robes in my questioning of Wu.

"I wish to accompany you to the Temple of Balance," I said. "I have presented Reverend Mother Xiang with my request to question the prisoner regarding the murder of a Jing citizen in the Duchy of Orrin in Issura."

Feng nodded. "And you request will be honored, Chief Justice." He continued in silent speech, *Justice Mei Wen, we are escorting Chief Justice Anthea to Balance along with the prisoner. Would you please have her wardens meet us there?*

Yes, Reverend Father. A hint of humor flowed from Mei Wen. *The crown prince extends his thanks to all of you as well.*

I only wish I felt as relieved as the Reverend Father appeared. However, there had been two unknown people in the secret passages. And I didn't for one moment believe the older man the Conflict priests hoisted to his feet was the person who had stabbed Yar and Antiope.

CHAPTER 51

When we emerged from the Chengzhou sewer system, we were in a very narrow alley. A boxy, wood-covered wagon sat nearby, blocking the view of any revelers. It was similar to the type the Orrin peacekeepers used to collect those who got a little out of control during the Spring Rituals or the Vintner's festival.

They loaded Wu into the wagon along with a member of Conflict, Thief, and Father. Longnu volunteered as a representative from Wilding, mainly because Fa would not fit inside as a tiger. Wu had remained silent since his initial outburst in the sewer, but he saved most of his glowering for me.

Not that I cared. No one who dealt in demon artifacts or our foes themselves loved me. And I held them in the same regard.

Once Wu was secured within the wagon, Reverend Father Feng bowed to me. "Chief Justice, would you mind riding double with me for the short distance to Balance?" *I would like to speak with you*, he added silently.

"Thank you, Reverend Father. I appreciate the offer." I bowed in return. *I come to serve.*

He led me to a steed that was shorter at the shoulder than my Nassa, but the beast was stockier through the chest with a broader neck and thicker legs. He climbed into his saddle, kicked his left foot free of the stirrup, and held out his left arm. I clasped his forearm and stepped into the stirrup. Once I was settled on the end of the blanket that cushioned his saddle, I freed my boot and wrapped my arms about the Reverend Father's waist. The horse set out at a steady walk as we followed the wagon.

I got a glimpse of Fa at point. The huge tiger did a better job of getting revelers out of our way than the mounted clergy and wardens would have. I chuckled at the expressions of the civilians, but once Fa was out of sight, they returned to their entertainments.

What is so amusing? Reverend Father Feng asked.

Are non-wildling tigers are big as Brother Fa?

The Reverend Father laughed out loud. His humor vibrated through his muscled body and robes since the festivities nearly drowned out his audible voice.

Actually, wild tigers are twice the size of our brother. One pounce can kill a person from their sheer weight.

His information gave me new respect for Fa. His claws and teeth would be lethal enough in their own right. I could barely imagine encountering a born tiger.

But do not fear, Chief Justice, wild tigers live in the wet forests far south of Jing. Your route back to the sea will be free of wild predators.

What did you wish to speak with me about? I asked.

Did you or Biming's team find any demon eggs?

No, Reverend Father, I said. *The problem is they have no sense of demon magic until the hatch, and by then, you have a very serious problem.*

I felt his grunt through my arms. *I prayed one of the teams would find them before they could be used against us again. Do you think the demons and skinwalkers who confronted you upon your return from Wu's cell were telling the truth?*

The whole encounter was rather odd, sir. I replayed the memory, and I realized why the whole incident bothered me. *I've never met a demon who didn't immediately try to kill me. Skinwalkers like to play games, but not demons. They only killed one of the wardens riding point. Why attack the point riders instead of waiting until Xiang, Biming, or I were within reach? They have to know about my lightning abilities. Too many people have witnessed me using them.* I sighed.

And humans gossip worse than crows. Feng emphasized my own fears.

Exactly, and why in the names of the Twelve would we simply give our mortal foes back their eggs? Surely neither the demons or their human allies truly believe we would do so.

A short bark of additional laughter erupted from Feng. *Oh, my dear, there's not too many who can outthink Biming. No wonder he was threatened by you.*

Jealous? He was disturbed by the crown prince's obsession with seducing me, but that was—

Part of me wanted to say that it was ages ago, but this time last year, we arrived in Orrin after we evacuated Tandor, and Bertrice had destroyed the demons and the city. A wave of grief clogged my throat. Balance, how I missed her. And Tyra, who gave her life to save mine as we raced to raise the chains across the harbor so Bertrice would have a tactile barrier to hold the last resort spells.

What's wrong, Anthea? Feng asked gently.

If it weren't for Biming bringing help to Tandor right before the Spring Rituals, everyone within the city would be dead.

Including Emperor Po, Feng added. *I'm afraid Biming wasn't totally altruistic towards Issura.*

Still, he arrived with aid just in time. But we lost so many clergy and wardens in getting the civilians out through the harbor, including personal friends.

Our lives are the price for the continuing existence of the rest of the human race. No emotion came from Feng. *We have Wu again.* He hesitated a moment. *Is it true you killed a man while truthspelling him?*

He was a renegade masquerading as a Light priest, I said defensively. *They had killed High Brother Kam and abducted High Brother Luc. He could have answered my questions rather than choosing death.*

My own question was not an accusation, Chief Justice. He glanced over his shoulder at me. *Wu has had too much of the soft life as the Prince Consort. I believe you are our best chance at breaking him and finding those damn eggs.*

Through our surface link, I saw his greatest fear, which I shared.

The eggs would be used in two days to kill Po and Shi Hua during their coronation.

CHAPTER 52

To my surprise, Luc, Yar, Darys, and her wardens accompanied Jonata and Long Feather to the Temple of Balance. All of the Jing Temple leaders were there as well. They insisted in witnessing Wu's interrogation.

When Luc and Darys were questioned about their presence, she lifted her chin. "Lady Shi Hua asked me to attend to witness the interrogation since she is no longer Temple, and she is occupied with her new duties."

"And you, High Brother?" Reverend Mother Xiang wasn't accusatory, just curious.

A slight smile curved his lips. "The crown prince requested I keep Chief Justice Anthea from accidentally executing the prisoner until you have tried him on the latest charges against him."

That sparked a round of laughter from the Jing Temple personnel. Leave it to Luc's charm to present what could be perceived as an insult into jocularity. I didn't even mind I was the butt of his jest. But I had no doubt, Po had given Luc those exact instructions.

I stood. "Reverend Mother Xiang?"

She nodded roughly in my direction. "You have a concern, Chief Justice?"

"You've read Chief Justice Li Chun of Huang He's report of our interrogation of the renegade who tried to assassinate Crown Prince Bao Quan Po as he disembarked at the dock?"

Xiang nodded. "You fear Wu will attempt a similar action to kill as many clergy as possible?"

"Yes, Reverend Mother. He is far cleverer than any typical renegade I've encountered," I replied. "He did manage to circumvent his magic-damping manacles within his cell. And he's made no secret of his hatred of the Temples."

"What if we ward the fighting pit within my own Temple?" Feng suggested.

"But we wouldn't be able to hear the actual interrogation," Reverend Father Jin of Light protested.

"Yes, you will." Feng smiled. "I have a novice with the strongest physical wards I've encountered, but his ability allows sound through." He turned to Xiang. "I will reinforce Novice Song's ability. Would that be an acceptable compromise?"

Xiang smiled. "I find the compromise acceptable. Any Temple Leader opposed?"

Not even Reverend Father Jin objected, but from his expression, he was worried.

But then, so was I.

Unlike the city of Orrin, the tunnel system of the Jing Temples was still intact and unblocked. We walked from Balance to Conflict without the civilians on the streets any wiser. It made me miss the ability to use the Orrin tunnels, but the memory of what the demon grimoire had done to me and how my grandmother, my birth mother, and I misused our tunnels quickly quashed my wish.

When I followed Reverend Mother Xiang into the Jing Conflict arena, the sheer size of it overwhelmed me. I could only imagine our own High Brother Han's delight in having such a facility to train in during last winter's unusual snow storms. But even all of Orrin's Conflict clergy and wardens together wouldn't take up more than the smallest row in one quarter of the arena.

"Can all of the members of the Jing Conflict order train here at once?" I whispered to Justice Mei Wen, who stood beside me.

"No, Ambassador."

I bit my tongue from making a tart rejoinder at the reminder of my place and that Jing was much larger than Issura. The younger justice wasn't deliberately cruel, but her answer still bothered me. If Jing was like any other nation, Conflict members were a token percentage of its regular army. When the Demon Wars were over and we survived, would we turn on each other like humans did before Balance's Revelation?

A proposal for diplomatic terms for all nations before the end of the war would be useful. Reverend Alara would ignore any recommendation I made, but maybe Queen Teodora would listen. Perhaps the next time we spoke with Duke White Eagle, I could suggest such a course of action. I wouldn't even care if he claimed the idea as his own as long as Issura was prepared for the end of the war. The last one hundred years without demon incursions had made our race lackadaisical and selfish. It would be far worse when the war was over without some preventative measures in place.

When selected clergy and two squads of wardens escorted Wu into Conflict's indoor arena, I was surprised to feel the hum of his spell-threaded manacles over the essence given off by the Temple personnel. A much more powerful spell lay in the metal. The Jing must not want to take chances after Wu escaped the standard shackles at his prison. Instead of the standard rail box where the accused was placed, the Jing shackled him to a pole near the center of the arena's sandy floor.

The iron doors where we entered slammed shut and the folding stairs to the stands were pulled up from the sands. Novice Song laid his wards over the pit. As Feng promised, we could hear the people on the other side of Song's wards. But with the wards' strength, Wu wasn't escaping this time even if he could levitate like Biming or Longnu.

Above us, I could easily pick out the sinuous form of the dragon Wild-ling. False Darys and her wardens perched on the same bench as Biming. Luc sat with Reverend Father Jin, Yar behind him. Part of me wished my wardens had acceded to my request they stay with Luc and Yar.

I received another reminder of Little Bear's orders to Jonata and Long Feather as the residual magic of the pit seeped through the soles of my boots. There had been accidental deaths here, and violence had soaked into the stones beneath the sand. Could Conflict clergy feel the energy? Worse, could Wu use the essence against Novice Song or the other people assembled here? I trusted my wardens to keep their heads, but what if the leftover psychic muck affected them? Jonata was a passive after all.

The chief warden of Balance called the court to order. The other Temple members fell silent. No one even shuffled or coughed.

Conflict had provided a wooden podium and stool for Reverend Mother Xiang. However, her clerk sat in the first row of benches above us with her portable desk and the rest of her accoutrements.

Xiang unsheathed her sword and banged her pommel against the top of her podium three times before she laid her sword across the wood.

"Wu Sunshu, you stand accused of escaping from lawful custody while imprisoned for life for treason and demon dealing. You are also accused in the murder of Quan Yong Xi, former master of the School of the Dragon and the Phoenix. You will now be truthspelled and interrogated in both matters."

The acoustics of the arena were incredible, but it had to be to hear a trainer over the din of weapons. No doubt her words carried to the top row of the immense room. The acoustics also carried Wu's howl of laughter.

"You self-righteous bitch! You can't even follow your own rules! This isn't Balance!"

"A trial can be held anyplace that is convenient for a justice with jurisdiction," Xiang said calmly.

"There must be a full panel of Temple leaders for someone of my station." Red spittle flew from Wu's mouth.

"You have no station, Wu Sunshu," Xiang replied. "You forfeited those rights when you were found guilty of the crime of treason against the Jing Empire and Emperor Bao Chengwu, your own son. Chief Justice Anthea, please truthspell the accused."

"A justice? Where's a Light priest? She's not even Jing!" Wu roared.

I concentrated, recited the spell, and made the appropriate gesture. My power sank into the sorcerer despite his efforts to deflect it. No wonder Conflict placed him in the stronger manacles.

Before Xiang could ask any question, Wu roared, "I escaped! I admit it freely! I did it to keep from being poisoned by the assassin you sent—"

He doubled over and puked.

I glanced at Xiang. The Reverend Mother pursed her lips, obviously feeling the same disgust I did. Many civilians thought if they told their story instead of answering a question, they could evade the effects of a truthspell. For a sorcerer of Wu's reputation, the error was surprising.

After he emptied his stomach, Wu raised his head and glared at me. "That wasn't a truthspell you cast."

"Yes, it was," Xiang said. "You're the one who decided to start this interrogation with a lie. Was the woman found in your cell the person you claim tried to kill you?"

"Yes," he snarled.

"What was her name?" Xiang asked.

Wu's face twisted as he tried to fight my truthspell. "B-bing."

"How did you meet her?"

"Sh-she was a student at the School of Sorcery." He gasped for breath as the power of my truthspell forced the answers out of him.

"Who sent her?"

"From the stink of demon magic on her, either a demon or a skinwalker decided they needed to be rid of me."

"How did she try to kill you?" The Reverend Mother gave him no quarter.

"The last meal she brought to me was poisoned."

"How did you get her to eat the food she brought you?"

Wu twisted and sweated as he tried to fight my truthspell. "H-hex. I laid a hex on her when she first attempted to seduce me. One I could trigger at a later time to control her. Which was how I forced her to eat the poison."

"How did you trigger the hex while wearing spell-threaded manacles?"

"My former teacher at the School of Sorcery trained me to cast despite your precious manacles," he snarled.

"How did Bing escape capture when the personnel and assets of the School of Sorcery were seized after your betrayal was discovered?" Xiang continued. I was impressed by her continued calmness.

"I-I don't . . ." Wu started to choke. "We had our own tunnels running beneath the city. Any escapees would have used those to escape."

"Do you know where she was sheltering?"

"Yes."

"Where?"

"A manse on the west side."

"What is the street and house number?" Xiang asked.

"Mulberry Lane. The manse takes up the entire 13th block on the north side of the street."

"Did you set the fire two nights ago which destroyed the manse?"

"Yes."

"Why?"

Whatever bravado Wu had left drained from him. "Bing and four other surviving members of the School of Sorcery made the mistake of learning demon magic. I am not sure of the identities of the other four people. I found their skinned bodies on the second floor when I arrived at the house after escaping my cell outside of the city. Not even I'm foolish enough to leave them intact for the demons to animate their corpses."

A collective gasp filled the arena.

Xiang pursed her lips. Maybe I wasn't the only one who questioned Wu's honesty with himself since he had the demons' eggs in his possession at one time.

But the Temples now had testimony about who had started the fire. Wu had been granted a reprieve from Death, but he seemed as determined to court Her as Conflict had been at the beginning of the World.

"Do you know of any other survivors of the School of Sorcery?"

"No," he spat.

"Where are the eggs you hid within the Imperial Palace?" the Reverend Mother asked. Her calm was gone. From the tightness of her voice, she wanted to slice off the head of the former Prince Consort here and now.

Behind me, I heard a door open and close. Another murmured rippled through the crowd.

Reverend Mother Xiang grabbed her sword and banged the pommel of her sword on the podium. "Silence!"

Everyone in the arena quieted immediately.

Shi Hua's spirit touched mine. *It's just me and Po.* She withdrew just as quickly. However, this wasn't my court, so I wasn't about to raise a fuss about her possible interference in a legal interrogation. Nor did I blame Po for wanting to attend Wu's questioning. He and Shi Hua must have made some excuse about her not feeling well or being tired since there was a dinner scheduled with the noble houses this evening in order to come to Conflict.

If it were a trial involving my birth father's suspected killer, I would want to attend, too.

Wu quivered and green beads of sweat broke out on his forehead.

Instead of mentioning the imperial couple's presence, Reverend Mother Xiang demanded, "Answer the question, Wu Sunshu."

He bent over, but dry heaves wracked his frame.

"I-I don't know," he finally choked out. He straightened. Yellow spittle dribbled down his chin.

"But you hid the demon eggs in the palace. Isn't that correct?" she continued.

"Yes, but they weren't where I left them when I checked yesterday."

"Where did you hide them?"

"In the secret passage within the walls of the harem's quarters," he snarled.

"Who else knew they were there?"

"I don't know." An ugly expression lit his face bright red. "Question the skinwalker and the demons who murdered my son and grandsons."

The Reverend Mother turned roughly in my direction. "You may ask your questions now, Chief Justice Anthea."

"Thank you, Reverend Mother Xiang." I bowed to her before turning to face Wu once again.

"Why did you convince Emperor Chengwu to send a sorcerer from your school to the Jing Embassy in Issura?"

"To eliminate the bitch the Temples sent with the bastard," he snarled.

"Did you know he smuggled a demon into the embassy?" I asked.

For the first time, Wu's defiance faltered. "He couldn't have. Not without setting off the Temple alarms."

"Did you know he also smuggled an egg into the embassy?" I asked.

"No." The reddish-orange color drained from Wu's skin to be replaced by a sickly greenish-yellow.

"Did you pay Arturo, captain of the ship *Mars Tranquilus*, to carry a package to the Jing embassy in Issura?"

"Yes."

"What was Arturo supposed to take to the Jing embassy?"

"The sorcerer I assigned to the bastard asked for a casket from his quarters. It was . . ." The truth flashed on his features before the dry heaves at his delay in answering bent him nearly double once again.

"The-the casket contained a range of poisons," Wu finally choked out. "I gave the casket to Bing to deliver to the captain of the Issuran ship before it left Huang He. There was no egg, demon or otherwise, in the casket."

"Was Captain Arturo a renegade?" I asked.

"I don't know," Wu spat, regaining some of his animosity.

Part of me hoped to clear Arturo. I didn't want to believe he'd betrayed Duke Marco and the entire human race, but now it seemed only Arturo, the demon, or this Bing could tell the truth of how Arturo ended up frozen solid in his cabin as his first officer and crew brought the *Mars Tranquilus* into port.

I didn't want to strain Reverend Mother Xiang's patience, so I tuned to the actual reason for my petition to interrogate Wu.

"When Master Quan Yong Xi arrived in the city of Orrin in Issura two winters ago, the Healers Guild and the Temple of Child discovered a spell had been cast on him to mimic the symptoms of the Child's Curse. The sworn and sealed statements of those who examined him have been filed with the Jing home Temple of Balance. This spell caused Master Quan's recent death in Orrin despite the healers and clergy's best efforts to break the magic." I pushed back my hood and stepped toward Wu. "Did you cast this spell?"

"No."

"Do you know who did?"

"Yes." A sick smile split his visage.

My heart sank. If it were another member of the School of Sorcery, then there might not be any satisfaction in bringing the culprit to justice. However, I continued. Po needed to know the truth more than I did.

"Who cast the spell?"

Wu didn't even try to resist my truthspell. "Lord Jia Huo, brother of Empress Meng Yao and a student of the School of the Phoenix and the Dragon."

CHAPTER 53

Shock rippled through the audience. I wanted to scream every obscene word I knew. The cunning little worm had been kind to me to obtain information about Po and Shi Hua. We had been so worried about Po's cousins ousting him we never considered it might be another noble. Yet, Jia Huo had been truly grieving for his sister and nephews when we spoke personally while breaking our fast.

"Did you order Lord Jia Huo to cast the spell that eventually killed Master Quan?" I said.

"No." His smirk did nothing to alleviate the feeling I was missing something. But without further evidence, I couldn't pursue the matter. At least, not until Lord Jia Huo was questioned under truthspell.

I turned to Xiang. "I have no further questions for the prisoner at the moment, Reverend Mother, but I reserve the right to question him once you've investigated his claim about Master Quan's true murderer."

"But you wish to amend your request to question Lord Jia Huo?" Her lips twitched as she tried not to laugh at the twist in my own case.

I wished she was Issura's Reverend Mother of Balance. Her black sense of humor matched my own.

"Yes, Reverend Mother." I inclined my head. "I would like to settle the matter of Master Quan's death before I leave Jing. To ease the minds of those who cared for Master Quan if nothing else."

"Very well then." Reverend Mother Xiang stood. "Wu Sunshu, this court granted you clemency based on the testimony of our late emperor and your son Bao Chengwu. Given your stated intention to repeat the same crimes of treason and demon dealing and this court's finding of your guilt in the new charge concerning the murder of the woman Bing, your stay of execution is hereby lifted. However, you will have a minor reprieve until Lord Jia Huo is located and questioned to confirm your testimony concerning Master Quan's death."

She shifted in my direction. "Please release the prisoner from your truthspell, Chief Justice Anthea."

Which I did.

When she no longer sensed my magic, she raised her voice slightly. "With your permission, Reverend Father Feng?"

The leader of Conflict rose. "We live to serve, Reverend Mother Xiang."

"Please escort Wu Sunshu to the Conflict gaol until it is time for his execution." She grasped her sword and banged the pommel on the wooden podium. "This court is adjourned."

Feng nodded to the novice sitting beside him. The boy was much younger than I'd expected. At Feng's indication, the wards on the pit dropped. No one so much as twitched until Wu was removed from the arena.

I pivoted and looked up. The imperial couple, dressed in full royal regalia, sat on the bench next to the Balance clerk. Captain Huizhong was with them along with five additional imperial guards, but not Mateqai.

Interesting. Luc's former warden wouldn't have left Shi Hua's side without good cause, even she merely traveled to one of the Chengzhou Temples.

At the same moment I turned, Po stood. "If it pleases the Temples, may I address this assemblage?"

The Balance chief warden assisted Reverend Mother Xiang to face in the direction of Po. "Aye."

To my surprise, each of the eleven other Temple leaders voted to hear him out. There was a time when Queen Teodora and her foremothers could have made the same request, and it would have been answered positively. These days, the queen and the Temples danced in silence, neither trusting the other.

With the concerns in Issura after the loss of Tandor, how much had I painted Jing with the same brush?

"There are two matters I wish to address." He scanned the attending clergy. "First of all, thank you. Those words are not enough to convey my gratitude to the Temples. Nearly three months ago, you saved Chengzhou from a demon invasion. You saved Jing and its people from total annihilation."

He glanced down at Shi Hua before his attention returned to his rapt audience. "I see your worth and your service to this land and this people. Anything in my power to give that will not harm others is yours. That includes assisting the wardens in protecting the individual members of Knowledge as they travel this empire to teach our children. I have heard of your problems in our villages. Contrary to others' beliefs, we need an educated populace to face the final onslaught of the demons."

His expression grew darker as he stared at our little group on the sand. "Reverend Mother Xiang of Balance, I, Bao Quan Po, Crown Prince of the Jing Empire, hereby request the responsibility of execution within Cheng-zhou upon my ascension to the Dragon Throne."

CHAPTER 54

Another collective gasp carried through the arena. Very rarely did any nation's leader volunteer to be the executioner of those guilty of capital crimes. Part of the reason was to keep the proverbial hands of the rulers clean.

Humans could be so irrational when it came to a loved one losing their head after admitting their crimes under truthspell. Justices performed the function of absorbing that fury by being both judge and executioner in the name of Balance. The people may be angry at the Temples, but they rarely dared to raise their hands against those sworn to uphold the laws that each and every nation shared.

"Are you sure that is wise, Emperor Po?" Xiang asked. "The whisper campaigns against you—"

"Have been working since the day of my birth," he responded. "There are those that have shirked their duty within the empire, whether out of greed or a misguided sense familial duty. That cannot be said of the Temples. I merely wish my late brother had listened to your counsel when it came to the School of Sorcery, but he spared his birth father out of loyalty to our late mother. He felt executing Wu Sunshu would call Empress Bao Yu's personal judgment into question, even though the nobility were the ones who drew the line in the sand in regards to her choice of consorts."

Po smiled as he scanned his audience once again. "Being the asshole everyone expects me to be will give the Temples a chance to rebuild their membership, their morale, and their influence. The loss of Reverend Father Chen and the combined Temple and Imperial armies in the western desert was a deliberate strike to weaken us. I will do my best to rectify those decisions that led to their loss. The demons will not allow us anymore grace, as shown when they accosted Reverend Mother Xiang and Reverend Father Biming a few leagues outside of the capital when they were investigating Wu's escape."

No rustling or murmurs followed his statement. The Temple leaders had informed their orders of the recent confrontation.

"May I ask one question?" asked a female voice from my right.

I turned to find Jing's Reverend Mother of Vintner standing, but her skin color remained yellow calm.

"Of course, Reverend Mother Ah Lam." Po inclined his head.

"Is it true Chief Justice Anthea, the ambassador of Issura, can produce lightning?"

A chill ran threw me. I couldn't expect the Jing clergy who witnessed me throw lightning bolts, whether during our sea battle with skinwalkers or the confrontation with the demons and skinwalkers the other night outside of Chengzhou, to leave such information out of their reports.

That didn't mean other clergy wouldn't consider a previously unknown talent as a threat.

Po eyed me. "I believe it's best if the chief justice answers that question herself."

I drew a deep breath and turned to the Reverend Mother of Vintner. "Yes, it is true."

Rustling and movement came further to my right.

"Would it be acceptable if you and your party stayed in Chengwu a few extra days so we may study this talent?" asked a female voice.

I tuned a half circle to face Reverend Mother Xiao Mei of Knowledge. "I would be honored, but we cannot stay longer than four days. Our ship is waiting in Huang He as we speak. The duke of Orrin will be vexed for us to keep the captain and crew of his flagship idle during the prime trading months. Especially since he took the risk of allowing us use of the ship to bring your new emperor home during winter."

A series of chuckles ran through the assembled clergy. The Reverend Mother of Knowledge grinned.

"Perhaps we could speak during tomorrow's midday meal so my Temple can plan the best way to use your limited time in Jing."

"I would be delighted, Reverend Mother." I bowed. "The invitation is extended to Reverend Mother Ah Lam and any other Temple."

"Is there any other business we must attend to at this moment?" Xiang said.

"No," the Jing Temple leaders chorused.

"Then we shall meet once Lord Jia Huo has been apprehended in order to discover the truth of Master Quan's death," she proclaimed.

"Ambassador Anthea, would you and Ambassador Luc accompany me and my lady wife back to the palace?" Po's voice rang out over the shuffle of people standing to leave the observation benches of the arena once the imperial couple departed.

I inclined my head. "Of course, Your Majesty."

I could feel Luc's curiosity mix with my own. I don't know what Po expected from us. Wu hadn't attempted to evade my questions regarding Master Quan's death. I just didn't understand why Jia Huo would want to kill a master from the order he studied with as a youth, and that question vexed me greatly.

A few moments later, I discovered one thing I detested for sure. Riding in a palanquin carried through the streets of Chengzhou made me feel filthy by treating other humans as beasts of burden. And I said such bluntly to Luc in Issuran.

"The Plains Nations used dogs before horses, camels, and oxen were introduced to the Northern Long Continent," Luc replied in kind.

"So did the Inuit," I snapped. "Not to mention the peoples of the Southern Long Continent use llamas and alpacas, but none of them rode on the shoulders of people. What is your point?"

"You're passing judgment where you have no say as an ambassador," he pointed out.

I reined in my temper at his observation. "I'm not trying to pass judgment. However, this feels too much like slavery," I murmured.

"With the crowds on the street for the Spring Rituals, an animal conveyance runs the risk of harming an innocent," he said. "Especially a child who doesn't understand the danger hooves represent."

I sighed and leaned against the huge cushion that lined the rear of our conveyance. "Why must you pick at my psychic scabs?"

"Because I have some of the same ones, my love." He smiled and intertwined his fingers with mine. "And my guilt would be as deep as the seas if my steed accidentally trampled someone's child."

"I should have asked Wu more questions about Jia Huo and why he would be involved in Master Quan's death," I grumbled.

"It would be hearsay and you know it, Anthea," Luc said sharply. "Wu wants to disrupt the current civil and religious structures in order to take the throne himself, and he had no issue with using the demons to obtain that goal. Why else set Bao against Bao? Why else hide demon eggs within the palace? Why else arrange for his own son's death?"

"That's the part I do not understand." I shook my head. "The Jing regard children as valuable as we Issurans do."

"Important, yes." Luc exhaled deep and long. "But not for the same reasons."

I cocked my head. "What do you mean?"

"The reason Shi Hua's mother never had her tested even when it was obvious she had talent was to keep her working on the family farm. The family had already lost Yin Li to the Temples. And her father died from blood poisoning when his foot became infected after one of their oxen stepped on him and crushed his bones because they felt they couldn't afford to go to a healer. They literally couldn't afford to lose another family member."

"The children in Issuran society perform jobs," I said.

Luc raised an eyebrow. "From First Morning to First Morning?"

"That's ridiculous! Children need time to play."

"Which you and I provide for our squires. Which Mya provides for those under her care, like Cat and Dog," Luc said.

However, I winced at the thought of the two street urchins Mya had taken in. They suffered from my birth mother Gerd's depravity simply because I had fed them and in return, they kept their ears open for information regarding my criminal cases.

"But our wardens have said nothing about the children working in the bowels of the palace because they know you would want to fix things to your sensibilities without any regard to your actual role in Jing at the moment."

"Which role?" I asked wryly. "The queen's command to act as her representative, or the role of making sure Po takes the throne that the Skoloti Reverend Mother of Balance prophesized."

Luc grinned even wider. "Yes."

I laughed and shook my head at his flippant answer.

Our palanquin halted and settled on the ground. The curtains parted, and Long Feather announced, "We have arrived, Chief Justice, High Brother."

I climbed out and held Luc's crutches while Long Feather and Yar assisted Luc to his foot. However, it was Long Feather and Yar's expressions that raised the fine hairs of the back of my neck when I handed the crutches back to Luc.

"What is it?" I whispered in Issuran.

The two men exchanged looks before Long Feather said, "Your suspect has disappeared from the palace."

CHAPTER 55

Captain Mateqai met the imperial couple at the bottom of the palace steps. Our group and the Skoloti representatives remained silent as we followed the Jing party up to the palace's main entrance. Luc's former warden whispered to Po, Shi Hua, and Captain Huizhong as we climbed.

Or the captain of the empress's guard could have been shouting for all I knew. Between the musicians and the crowd laughing and dancing in the palace square, I had barely heard Long Feather's initial words at our arrival, much less the Temple bells ringing out First Night.

Duke Mengchang met us in the palace foyer. With the main doors closed, I could hear his murmured report to Po. Apparently, Shang, Yin Li, and their teams, along with other Temple searchers, had stayed in the secret passages while we were at the Temple of Conflict. They searched for and disabled a great many more traps than the handful Biming and my teams had discovered. When the duke completed his report, the crown prince indicated the Issuran and Skoloti parties follow him. The duke tagged along behind us.

We were ushered into what looked like a receiving room. Mengchang looked at me, a deep frown on his face. After servants brought several pots of tea and the imperial guards departed, Huizhong and Mateqai closed the doors. They tested each of the pots before they allowed any of us to take a sip.

I relaxed in my chair, thankful for the warm ceramic and astringent taste after too many sweets and too much running about throughout the day. Exhaustion stalked me once again.

However, the duke remained standing as he continued to glare at me. "What plan did you concoct with Lord Jia Huo, Chief Justice?" Mengchang deliberately changed my title into a slur.

"What in the World are you blathering about?" I snapped.

"You were seen breaking your fast with him and traveling through the city together this morning. Admit it!" He jabbed a forefinger in my direction.

"I do not deny those actions," I said more calmly. "I also danced with him this morning after the opening ritual, and I dined beside him during the welcome dinner the crown prince hosted when we arrived in your lovely capital." I shrugged. "The only plan I made with him was to dine again at his request before I left Chengzhou. He wished to show me your Great Wall."

"By the Twelve, that was my mistake!" Po snapped his right fingers. "I'm too old for you." His statements produced laughter from everyone in the room.

Well, everyone except Mengchang.

"I must say Lord Jia Huo is charming, but without your very public predatory edge, Your Highness," I teased before I turned back to Mengchang. "If I'd known he was the suspect I sought in Master Quan's death, I would have treated him quite differently, Your Grace."

"And all we have to go on as far as Lord Jia Huo's guilt is the word of a condemned traitor," Po added.

Mengchang's mien abruptly changed. "Please tell me you will not make the same mistake as your brother," he pleaded.

I regarded the duke and tasted his emotions. Like before, it wasn't anger that emanated with his behavior. It was rare, unadulterated fear. So, I answered before Po had a chance to.

"The crown prince officially requested the responsibility of execution from Reverend Mother Xiang."

"If you pardon Wu as your brother did—"

Po held up a hand to stop Mengchang. "He's already been found guilty for escaping custody, murder, additional demon dealing, and another charge of treason. There's no further reason to spare his life."

"And Jia Huo?" The duke dropped the honorific in his presumption of the young man's guilt.

"I will honor Reverend Mother Xiang's pronouncement, regardless of the outcome of his trial," Po declared.

"If—" I said, making sure to emphasize there had been no trial for the young man yet. "—Lord Jia Huo is guilty of Master Quan's death, I will submit a request for extradition."

"As long as you understand, I will petition Reverend Mother Xiang to deny your request if it is proven Jia Huo is the one who took the demon eggs Wu hid within the palace," Po interjected. "I cannot indicate to the Jing populace that demon dealing of any kind will be tolerated."

I inclined my head. "That is your right, Your Highness, but what makes you think Jia Huo took the eggs? Meng Yao and her children were of his blood. He grieves for their loss as much, if not more so, than you do."

Po's eyes narrowed. "If you could cast a spell insidious enough to torture and kill a master sorcerer like my father, what would you do to the man responsible for your sister and nephews' deaths?"

I hoped he was wrong the young lord planned to murder Wu using one of the eggs. But from my brief contact with Jia Huo's mind, I had no doubt he would concoct the most gruesome way to destroy Wu in his desire for revenge.

Meanwhile, the duke gasped and wiggled like a beached fish now that we imploded his suspicion of my morning with Lord Jia Huo. "What in the names of the Twelve is going on?" His attention flipped between Po and me. "I literally received the request from the Temple of Balance to produce Jia Huo for questioning a half candlemark before you returned to the palace, Your Majesty. I've only begun investigating his whereabouts. What does he have to do with demon eggs or Wu's escape?"

"According to Wu while under truthspell, Jia Huo cast the curse the resulted in my father's death," Po said. "Wu also admitted to hiding the demon eggs within the palace prior to his initial arrest. However, he couldn't find them when he returned to the palace and hid in the Kexin suite."

Mengchang blinked rapidly. "I-I thought that secret chamber was a myth."

Po chuckled. "So did I until Chengwu, Biming, and I stumbled upon it when we were children."

"Y-you were playing in the secret passages as children?"

"Very few locks could hold me or the Reverend Father back then," Po admitted.

"Where was this vaunted talent when we were captured by the renegades in Tandor, Your Highness?" Luc drawled.

"I wasn't going to waste my talent and have the renegades slap spelled manacles on me before you devised a method to escape the city, High Brother," Po replied archly.

"Do I need to have Captain Mateqai fetch me a measuring stick to end this contest between you two once and for all?" Shi Hua snapped.

I bit my lip to keep from laughing. Perhaps the two men simply enjoyed irritating each other, which I'd be perfectly happy to let them do as long as

I wasn't at the center of their mutual antagonism. However, we needed to find Lord Jia Huo first.

"If I may, Your Grace, did anyone see the lord in question return to the palace after he and I parted ways shortly after First Afternoon?" I asked.

Mengchang's frown deepened. "No, your captains of the guard questioned everyone as thoroughly as they could without truthspelling them, but no one saw him return."

I bit back a groan. "Part of me hoped he had. If he had been the one who attacked Warden Yar and Antiope, it would have limited our suspect list."

"What if Lord Jia Huo snuck into the palace through the sewers like Wu did, Chief Justice?" Long Feather suggested.

This time, I let out the groan I resisted a moment ago. "I do not relish traipsing through any sewer for a second time in one day."

"He does have a permanent suite in the palace as Empress Meng Yao's brother," Mengchang offered. "Could one of you perform a tracking spell?"

Po and Shi Hua turned to Luc and me. I didn't need one of Luc's lectures. No matter how much I wanted to find the young lord and smack him for using me to discover information.

"We are going to this the proper way, Your Majesties," I stated. "You will answer Reverend Mother Xiang's request and ask her for an immediate tracking spell to be performed on the belief Lord Jia Huo has fled upon hearing Wu has been recaptured."

Po nodded and smiled. "Which is exactly what I was thinking myself, Lady Justice."

CHAPTER 56

After Duke Mengchang left with the formal request to Balance Po had drafted, Shi Hua warded the receiving room.

"We moved both the Issuran and Skoloti parties to new quarters after the attack on Wardens Yar and Antiope this afternoon," she said.

"Thank you for doing so, my lady," False Darys murmured. "However, that may not provide the protection you believe it does, for either us or you and your husband."

"I hope you didn't move us further from your quarters," I protested. "Not when we have the possibility of multiple suspects roaming your Balance-damned secret passages!"

"I wish both of you would give us a little credit." Po wore an amused expression. "The only times my lady wife allowed me to sleep in the same place more than one night since she became my bodyguard nine years ago was aboard my ship, the *Mars Tranquilus,* and the Jing Embassy in Orrin."

"Well, there are limited sleeping quarters onboard any ship," Luc drawled.

"Unless the couple in question has a major fight," I added.

Shi Hua held up her index finger. "Stop. Just stop. Unless you want me to broadcast my morning sickness throughout the palace."

When we all remained silent at her threat, she continued, "As my lord husband started to say, we haven't spent more than one night in the same room since we arrived at the palace. That's the real reason he demanded all the bedrooms in the imperial family wing be prepared."

"We're not in the family wing?" I asked.

"Actually, you were on the other side of the wall from us," Po answered. "Mengchang made some assumptions he should not have."

"What assumptions?" I bit out.

He hesitated, but Shi Hua blurted the answer anyway. "He thought since the ban on Balance and Light having relations had been lifted, you were both sleeping with my husband."

I couldn't help laughing. The idea of Po and Luc together was so ludicrous!

However, my love didn't find the idea as humorous. "The duke—he thought—is he out of his Vintner-blasted mind!" Luc finished loudly.

I was rather glad Shi Hua had warded the room so the rest of the palace staff couldn't hear him.

Po glared at his wife. "I'm not sure which of their reactions I should be more offended by."

"We-we are in the concubines' quarters?" I roared even harder. Tears streamed down my cheeks.

"You're in what will be the new concubine quarters," Shi Hua admitted. "The old ones were closed off after what the demons did to the women—"

I abruptly stopped laughing as she and I stared at each other with dawning realization.

"If one of the women found the eggs while meeting another lover, she would have thought they were jewels," Shi Hua started.

"That could be how the skinwalker got a hold of them," I added. "It couldn't have found them otherwise—"

"—because they're human, and we can't feel them until they hatch," we finished in unison.

"Surely, the demons who confronted you the other night would have known their offspring were responsible for last winter's attack," Luc sputtered.

"What if the demons can't sense their own eggs until they've hatched?" Po suggested.

I leaned my elbows on the table and stared at my no-longer-steaming cup. "Could we possibly get that lucky?"

"Lucky?" Luc blurted. "If no one knows where these eggs are, we're asking for more humans to be slaughtered!"

"No, Po's theory makes sense," Shi Hua said. "If they can sense an egg after it's hatched like us, they would also know how many eggs are left."

"But if we find the eggs before they hatch, we'd destroy them," I said.

"The confrontation with you, Biming and, Xiang was a fact-finding mission," Po said.

"You believe the demons and skinwalkers were testing their reactions to learn if the rest of the eggs had been found and destroyed?" False Darys said.

"Exactly," Po replied.

I stood and rattled off a few of the more colorful obscenities my half-brother Pecos had taught me in his mother's language before I started pacing.

"Anthea, what in the World—" Po started.

"Before you and your wife arrived at Conflict, Wu admitted under truthspell to starting the fire in the city because he discovered four members of the School of Sorcery skinned in one of the school's hiding places," False Darys said.

"Anthea, for the love of the Twelve, please sit down," Shi Hua snapped.

I whirled to face her and threw my arms up. "You don't understand. I revealed everything to those-those—"

"Sit down, Chief Justice." Long Feather grabbed me by the shoulders, guided me back to my chair, and pushed me onto the seat. "They didn't just fool us. They fooled the Jing clergy and wardens as well."

"We must assume the demons and skinwalkers from the other night also used silent speech to relay the information to those wearing the skins of the slaughtered sorcerers before you blasted the ones confronting us," Jonata said.

"But we don't know who the dead sorcerers were," Yar murmured. "Wu didn't even know who the rest of the survivors were besides the woman he killed when she tried to poison him in his cell."

"What do we do, other than dangle the crown prince as bait?" False Darys asked.

Luc and Shi Hua exchanged looks, and I leapt to my feet once again. "Are you two mad? You can't be seriously thinking to use the leader of a sovereign nation to fish for demons!"

"Actually, we would propose the proverbial killing of two birds with one stone." Luc's wild grin scared me.

My eyes narrowed. "What do you mean?"

"You are at the top of many lists for extermination, my friend." Shi Hua's smile matched Luc's. "We're proposing to use you as bait."

"How?" I sank into my chair once again and took a large swallow of my cooled tea.

"If the Temple of Knowledge wants to know how you throw lightning, we'll make sure everyone in the city knows that you will be performing an exhibition the last night of the Spring Rituals," Shi Hua said.

"You want me to what?" I choked out.

"My lady, you're simply trading one target for another," False Darys protested.

"True," Jonata said. "But we won't have to worry about the chief justice going off half-cocked if she's the center of attention."

"You make me sound like a spoiled, conceited noble." I glared over my right shoulder at my warden. "And controlling lightning isn't easy. The last thing we need is me accidentally killing half the citizens of Chengzhou!"

She shrugged. "But if the skinwalkers within in the city are focused on eliminating you, they won't necessarily notice armed, talented civilians."

"You can't possibly be thinking of recruiting the philosophy schools, Warden," I growled.

"Why not?" Yar said. Everyone turned to look at him. Even Antiope had a startled deer expression. He met each of our gazes in turn. "You and the high brother have constantly complained how hard it is to get humans to combine their skills even when it is in their best interests as a whole." He shrugged. "Give the philosophy schools a chance to prove their loyalty to their new emperor by helping to set and spring the trap. If they refuse, Crown Prince Po has his answer of whether they can truly be trusted."

I groaned. "I was the one everyone thought would start a war. What you wardens are proposing could very well start a civil conflict within Jing."

"Maybe. Or maybe not." Po played with the gold beads on his left mustachio.

You must stop playing with your beads, Po, I said silently. *It tells me every time how worried you are. How many others have picked up on your affectation?*

He abruptly released the beads and shot me a perturbed look before he reached across the table and seized my cup. For a brief moment, I thought he'd throw the cup at me. Instead, he refilled it and set it in front of me again.

"Chancellor Mengchang mentioned you had a rapport with Master Ma about my father," Po said. "If you do not mind going to the School of the Phoenix and the Dragon tomorrow morning, Anthea."

"Not by herself," Luc said.

"I'll go with her," Shi Hua said. "Between Mateqai and Jonata, we should be fine."

"I'll be going instead of Jonata," Long Feather said fiercely. "Tomorrow was supposed to be her day of rest and relaxation."

"No, I'll go." Jonata's grin was as nearly as wicked as Luc's had been a moment ago. "The sorcerers will underestimate me because of my size, and the chief justice can provide me with a time freeze spell and other measures that I can activate. I've noticed the schools have a tendency to look at everyone as talented or not talented. They won't consider me as a passive dangerous until it's too late."

Too bad Jonata had been born sighted. She would have made a natural justice.

I looked over my left shoulder. "Besides, Long Feather, you need a break, too, and it is the Spring Rituals."

"But—"

"If it will make you feel better, I can send Antiope with Warden Jonata," False Darys said.

"What about your own protection, Sister?" Luc said.

"Urania is sufficient for me just as Yar is sufficient for you." False Darys smiled. "Also, I sat beside Master Bolin of the School of Nature during the welcome banquet. I think I can best serve our cause by delivering some seeds from our own Temple of Child and requesting his school's aid."

"The other schools can be handled through Biming," Po said. "I believe you all should get some sleep."

"What about the tracking spell on Lord Jia Huo?" I said.

"My dear, I assure you I can handle the matters of the empire on my own." Po's old smirk was back.

My initial reaction was outrage, but he was correct. He would be crowned emperor the day after tomorrow. I would be leaving Jing in less than a week. And this nation was not my responsibility.

I released a deep breath and inclined my head. "Please forgive my thoughtless words, Your Majesty. I shall work on viewing you as the sovereign that you are, not a diplomat I am obliged to protect. Or a friend I care about."

"Things change, Chief Justice." His smile turned sad. "And we must adjust with them."

CHAPTER 57

Our steward Chin escorted us to our new suite. However, none of us were surprised when Shang stepped out of mine and Luc's bedchamber once the steward left.

I dropped into a chair and shook my head sadly. "Brother, with all due respect, it's nearly Second Night. May I please get some sleep before you or Yin Li drag us through your no-longer-secret passages again."

He chuckled, a dry sound that reminded me I hadn't drank enough water today. Or rather yesterday.

"Our empress-to-be suggested I place my palm on the walls to mark your path rather than escort you to the new exit." He demonstrated how he angled his hand to show a straight path and turns.

Luc lowered himself into the chair next to mine during Shang's explanation.

"That doesn't help the rest of us with normal eyesight to find our way," my love said.

The wardens nodded in agreement.

"I'll show you in the morning." I was having a hard time staying awake. "It's up to the Jing Temples to find Lord Jia Huo. We've done more than our share of risking our lives on this mission."

Everyone, even Shang, turned to stare at me.

"I'm acknowledging my limits like you all wanted," I snapped. "Quit giving me those looks."

Shang cocked his head. "Duke Mengchang believes you are in league with the noble in question. You are not reassuring me, Chief Justice."

I waved my hand as if flicking away his comment. "I've been constantly reminded I have no jurisdiction here today. That I am merely the Issuran ambassador." A lump grew in my throat. "Today, one of your Thief wardens died saving Jonata when I offered my services. And then, Lord Jia Huo played on my sympathies regarding your former emperor, his wife, and his children to glean information from me. And I'm no closer to knowing for certain who murdered Master Quan with a foul bit of magic than I was in Issura."

I tried getting air past the growing clog in my throat. My vision blurred, and I squeezed my eyes shut to clear the tears. Warm drops trickled down as I opened my eyes.

"I beg your forgiveness for my outburst, Brother." I blinked more wetness from my eyes. "It has been a trying time since we arrived in Chengzhou."

His mien took on a haunted air. "There's nothing to forgive, Anthea. You and the Temples in Issura managed to save the citizens in Tandor while destroying a demon army, which is more than I could do here."

I slowly stood, crossed to him, and wrapped my arms around him. "We each did the best we could. The difference is Tandor had help from our neighboring nations. You were caught in an uninhabited section of Jing. The fact that any of you survived is a miracle."

Shang hugged me in return. "Surrender would have meant death. The greatest way to thumb our noses at our enemies is living long enough to find a way to defeat them."

We released each other.

"Get some rest, Shang." I patted his shoulder.

"And all of you as well." He stepped back. "The door to the passages is in each of your baths like the last suite. You might want to ward them."

"We will," Luc said.

I didn't notice he had stood and swung over next to me.

Luc shifted his right crutch to hold out his arm. Shang and he clasped wrists.

Silently, the Conflict brother departed through the secret door in our bath.

Our party didn't say much, except for Jonata threatening me if I warded the wardens' bedchamber so they couldn't get to us. All of us prepared for bed before Luc warded the wardens' bathing room. I warded mine and Luc's. This suite had a large armoire for weapons' storage. Yar and Long Feather shoved the heavy wood in front of the suite's main door. It wouldn't stop a renegade with moving talent, but it was the best we could do under the circumstances.

Luc and I retreated to my bedchamber. We checked our personal belongings. In each of our bags was a note from Yin Li, written in Issuran, that she, Shang, and their son had personally confirmed everything was accounted for and had been packed properly. It was a good thing we traded personal items and reading material during the two-month sea voyage. Otherwise, we might be missing some important things, like our weapons.

Only then did I realize my uniform still stunk of the Chengzhou sewer system. I must have nauseated anyone I had been in close proximity to tonight. I stripped off my clothing and carried the garments out to the common room.

A man leapt up from the floor. The pink and white glow of the fire silhouetted his huge figure. I let out a bleat of alarm, dropped my clothes, and grabbed an ornamental vase.

"Is everything all right, m'lady?" Yar's voice.

I sucked in a deep lungful of air in an effort to calm my racing heart.

"Why aren't you in bed?" I snapped.

"I had two naps today." He stepped away from the fire. Yes, it was definitely the Light warden, though I wasn't sure why I depended on my odd vision when I could easily feel his presence. Maybe, I simply didn't trust anyone or anything anymore. Especially with skinwalkers and/or demons running around Chengzhou. Though if one of them could slip the skin to a demon outside of the outermost city walls, we were doomed. Very few people knew my sight couldn't penetrate a demon wearing a human skin the way I could with a skinwalker.

"I took the first watch so Long Feather could get some sleep since he's been traipsing through the city with you," Yar continued. "Jonata will take the second." He cocked his head. "However, you didn't answer my question."

I sighed. "My uniform stinks from chasing Wu through the damn sewer system."

"Ah." He grinned. "So, I must take the brunt of the odor since I enjoyed the holiday with Warden Antiope?"

"I can put them in the bathing room." I bent to gather my clothes.

"I was merely teasing, m'lady. Please get some rest."

I straightened, leaving my uniform, and nodded. "Very well. Good eventide, Yar."

I shuffled back into my bedchamber and climbed into our bed. My groan gave voice to my aching leg muscles. I'd gotten too used to riding a horse over the last two weeks.

Luc rolled over on his side and laid his right arm across my waist and stroked the bare skin of my belly. "You are exhausted if you didn't have the energy to lecture Yar for startling you."

"You heard?"

"Um-hmmm." Luc's breath tickled my neck.

"How can I chastise him when I failed by letting Jia Huo use me?" I complained.

"Stop," he murmured. "I know you. You wouldn't betray a confidence. And it's entirely possible Wu said just enough of the truth to not trigger the spell's pain threshold. We've both seen defendants tell outright lies at the beginning of an interrogation in an attempt to allow half-truths slip through."

"I told Jia Huo that Shi Hua was pregnant."

Luc paused for a moment. I half-expected him to storm from the room. Or at least castigate me for breaking a promise to someone I regarded as a sister. His fingers resumed their caress.

"You wouldn't have done that without a good reason," he murmured. "So why did you?"

"There was so much grief coming from him." I turned onto my side to face Luc. "I thought—I hoped he would see her as someone in his sister's position and help protect her. If I even suspected he was in league with Wu—"

"Stop." Luc laid his right forefinger across my lips. "We don't know his side of the story yet. We already know Wu is foolish enough to demon deal. It's entirely possible he hoped to take an ally of the Bao family down with him."

"It's also entirely possible Jia Huo found the remaining eggs and plans use them to seek revenge on those he blames for Empress Meng Yao's death," I murmured. "If he did—"

"There's nothing you can do if that is the case." Luc kissed my forehead.

"And how is that any different than what I did with the demon grimoire?" I whispered.

"You didn't plan to use the grimoire to seek revenge. You knew it wasn't safe in the hands of the home Temples. You'd been lied to about its destruction. And the renegades did everything they could to make sure it ended up in your possession twice in the hopes it would corrupt you." His fierce tone didn't make my guilt ease.

"But the grimoire did get to me." More tears trickled down my face. "If Ming Wei hadn't s-stopped m-me—" My sob forced its way past my words.

"Maybe the Twelve had a warped plan to save you both, but the good thing is you saved each other." Luc chuckled. "As Mya says, we don't always choose the path of our mental healing."

"We are a pair, aren't we?" I patted his chest.

"Yes," he replied. "We are a pair in desperate need of sleep."

But his good night kiss turned into something more.

And I had to admit his attentions did lead me to sleeping quite soundly.

CHAPTER 58

Anthea!

I tried to ignore the voice. I didn't have court this morning.

Anthea, wake up!

"Get Yanaba to deal with the emergency, Sivan," I murmured. "It's time she learned."

ANTHEA!

At the shout that wasn't from my head of household back home in Orrin, I jerked upright in the bed. For an instant, I didn't know where I was. But Luc was beside me, snoring softly.

Anthea, the Temples found Lord Jia Huo.

Shi Hua?

Yes, the empress-to-be replied. *Reverend Mother Xiang has requested our presence. Duke Mengchang is on his way to gather you and Luc.*

At the same instant, a loud banging came from nearby. Everything from yesterday flashed in my mind. The banging stopped, and voices hummed on the other side of the bedchamber door. I flipped back my covers. Beside me, Luc groaned and blindly sought the blankets at the sudden sensation of cooler air.

He's here already, I said. *Give us a few moments to get dressed.*

Very well. Shi Hua's essence faded from my mind.

I checked our bathing room. No one was inside. I dropped my wards before I returned to the bed and nudged Luc's shoulder. "Wake up. We've been summoned to the Temple of Balance. They found Lord Jia Huo."

Luc's eyes snapped open, and he jolted into a sitting position. "When?"

"I don't know." I circled the bed to search my pack for a clean uniform. "Shi Hua just woke me."

Someone knocked on our bedchamber door. "Chief Justice, Duke Mengchang needs to speak with you," Jonata called out.

"Let us get dressed," I yelled back. "We'll be out in a moment."

I hurriedly donned my clothes before I assisted Luc to the chamber pot. He dressed while I performed my morning ablutions. My braids were still tight despite yesterday's activities, so I simply tied them back with a leather thong. It said how exhausted we both were if neither Luc nor I thought about combing out my hair last night.

When we entered the common room, Duke Menchang paced back and forth. He made our wardens nervous from the tight lines of their shoulders.

"When was Lord Jia Huo found?" I asked before the duke could get a word in.

He blinked. "A little over a candlemark ago. They found him at the Temple of Love."

"Of course. Where else would anyone go if this were their last Spring Rituals?" I grumbled as I finished buckling my harness.

"I would have left the city," Mengchang said dryly.

I stared at the noble. "Did you just make a joke, Your Grace?"

"My apologies, Chief Justice." A smirk reminiscent of Po's tilted his lips. "My wife constantly reminds me that my sense of humor is not shared by most people."

"No offense was taken," Luc interjected. "Anthea would have made the same remark if your positions were reversed."

"I never would have guessed." However, the duke turned quite serious. "Reverend Mother Xiang has requested your presence. While she normally cancels court for the Spring Rituals, she was adamant this matter cannot wait."

The Reverend Mother must have sent one of the senior justices instead of a member of the household staff or a warden. Someone who the duke would have taken seriously to rouse Po and Shi Hua first.

Other than morning greetings, neither the imperial couple nor Luc and I said anything as once again, we traveled by palanquin to the Temple of Balance. From there, we were escorted through the tunnels to the Temple of Conflict. However, Long Feather and I were led to the pit while the rest of our joint party went up the stairs to the viewing benches.

The Jing clergy performed the same precautions as they had with Wu yesterday evening. Spell-threaded manacles. Locking doors and pulling up the stairs to the gallery. Novice Song warded the pit so the spectators could hear the testimony without the accused escaping. The quiet of the audience echoed through the arena.

This time, the spectators included senior clergy from each of the Temples. The other eleven leaders were lined on the benches behind Reverend Mother Xiang. And a section had been reserved for members of the philosophy schools.

Most of the sorcerers appeared dismissive, but Master Ma looked older. Tired. Sad. I couldn't imagine what he was feeling with one of his school's students accused of murdering one of their most noted masters.

To my surprise, Jia Huo's cousin Lady Caihong sat next to Master Ma. Her face sported the same appearance of anxiousness I'd seen so many times. A family member watching a loved one accused of a crime, on trial, and fearing the worst.

My stomach lurched. This was a full-blown trial. Had the preliminaries been observed prior to our arrival?

I must have accidentally projected my dismay because the Reverend Mother spoke to me silently. *The initial interrogation was performed by my second, Chief Justice Dai Lu. I am not Ogusuku. I promised you would be allowed to question the lord. That is why you are here.*

There was only a touch of vexation in her mental tone. I wasn't sure whether it was my questioning of whether she followed proper procedure or my accidental insinuation she was as unethical as the Ryukyuan leader of Thief.

I inclined my head, even though she couldn't see the gesture, and kept my own tone contrite. *I apologize for any offense given, Reverend Mother, and I thank you for allowing me the opportunity to question Lord Jia Huo in the matter of Master Quan's death.*

You do realize if you petition to have him extradited for Quan's murder, the emperor and the nobles will object?

So the emperor has informed me, but I wouldn't do that to Jia Huo's family, I said. *They've already lost so much, but the emperor has also lost loved ones. I only hope we can give him some peace as he starts his new role in Jing.*

A tickle of her amusement flitted through my mind. *I can see why Reverend Mother Fumiko has taken a liking to you.*

I scanned the sands as the last of the observers took their seats. Realization that I wouldn't be performing the truthspell dawned on me as I noticed the Light Priest on the other side of the pit. The patch of a high brother was sewn on his robes at the shoulders. His hair was drawn high at the back of his head into the Jing version of a warrior's knot, and his face was clean-shaven as was the habit of most Light priests I'd met.

Once again, the Balance chief warden called the court into session. The Reverend Mother drew her sword and pounded the pommel on the podium before she settled on the stool and read out the charges. While she did so, I took a long look at Jia Huo and tasted his emotions. A great deal of what I felt from him was shame. Did he regret what he'd done? Or did he regret getting caught? Maybe he regretted being caught by the Temples.

I couldn't help but wonder how Master Ma would react when the sentence was passed. I had been so sure Wu committed the crime out of hatred for his rival. Had my obsession with finding Master Quan's killer ruined our chances of recruiting the School of the Phoenix and the Dragon to flush out the four skinwalkers or demons within Chengzhou.

"How do you plead, Lord Jia Huo?" Reverend Mother Xiang's voice rang out.

He bowed his head. "I plead guilty to both counts."

Gasps ran through the gallery above us. Lady Caihong let out a loud sob before she buried her head against Master Ma's shoulder. Most of the sorcerers looked fearfully at Po.

Xiang turned in my direction. "Did you still wish to question the accused, Chief Justice Anthea of Issura?"

"Yes, please," I answered.

"Proceed."

I walked over to Jia Huo until I was an arms-length away. "Why?"

That was the only question that wouldn't cause the defendant any pain from the truthspell. A person's reasons were in the eye of the beholder. Therefore, answering the question of motivation wasn't a lie.

He lifted his head. The emptiness behind his eyes scared me. "For which charge, Lady Justice?"

"You took the eggs hoping to use them on Wu in revenge for the deaths of your sister Empress Meng Yao and her two children, your nephews. Is that correct?"

"Yes." His voice broke on that one word.

"What I don't understand is why you cast a spell on Master Quan that mimic the effects of the Child's Curse. Why kill a teacher you respected?"

"He discovered I used that same spell on the Lady Cuihong's husband." The same fury and anguish he'd displayed yesterday over the deaths of his sister and nephews was back.

"No!" Lady Cuihong shrieked above us as she leapt to her feet. "I cast the spell on my husband. Jia Huo had nothing to do with it!"

Xiang banged her pommel on the podium once again. "Silence, or I will have the wardens remove you!"

I looked over my shoulder. Master Ma urged the distraught noble-woman back to the bench. She sobbed quietly, but otherwise, she said nothing.

"What did the lady's husband do to deserve death?" I asked.

"He beat her." His skin was so reddish pink I half-expected it to catch fire. "She lost two children because he beat her while she was pregnant. And then, he told her he would kill her if she lost another child."

I choked out my next question. "Why didn't you take her to the Temple of Balance and file charges for the assault?"

"He'd only have his brothers kill her while he was sitting in the gaol," Jia Huo spat. "I wanted him to know what it felt like to lose his mind and become totally helpless. As helpless as he made Cuihong feel."

"Is Lady Cuihong's husband still alive?"

"In a manner." The deadness replaced any emotion. "Until now, every-one assumed he had the Child's Curse, but my cousin and her staff were no longer living in fear in their own house."

"When did Master Quan confront you about your spell?" I asked.

"Four winters ago." Jia Huo shook his head. "The brothers went to him for assistance when all of the healers who examined Cuihong's husband pronounced that he had the Child's Curse and there was nothing they could do."

"What did he say to you?"

"That he was required to report me to the Temple of Balance for the harmful use of magic." Jia Huo's head bowed again. "That's when I cast the spell on him."

"Did you fear for your life when you cursed Master Quan or Cuihong's?"

"Mine," he whispered, though with the acoustics in the arena, every-one could hear them. "But Balance always evens her scales at the end."

"How did Wu Sunshu find out what you had done to Master Quan?" I asked.

"I don't know." Jia Huo's voice was a hollow imitation of his joy and passion from yesterday. "He said he would report me to Balance if I lifted the spell from Master Quan. And then, he made requests of me from time to time."

"What kind of requests?" I asked.

"To influence the emperor and other nobles to side with him during decisions that would benefit the School of Sorcery."

I turned to Xiang and said silently, *Reverend Mother, may I suggest you ask him the location of the eggs privately? I don't want anyone to grab them before you have retrieved them.*

My thoughts exactly, she replied.

Out loud, I said, "I have no further questions, Reverend Mother. Nor will Issura request extradition in this matter. Thank you for pursuing justice on behalf of Master Quan's family and friends."

I bowed and returned to my place on Xiang's left. Despite my pity for the young lord, he'd done all the wrong things. And his actions showed how deep the distrust of the Temples went within Jing.

Since he was a noble, a vote was taken among the Temple leaders concerning Jia Huo's guilt. However, the poll was unanimous, and Reverend Mother Xiang pronounced his sentence.

When Lady Cuihong screamed in protest, she was escorted from the arena by Child wardens. No one remaining looked or felt particularly happy about the outcome of this trial. While it was a pall on the festival, it was obvious many of the clergy had liked and respected the young lord.

My own anger at Jia Huo faded in the wake of his trial. Only pity at his foolishness remained because I was fairly certain Xiang would have done anything to protect Cuihong if she only had known about the young noblewoman's problems.

CHAPTER 59

I wanted nothing more than to go hide in our suite after the stresses of this morning. Well, maybe my desire for a pot of Jing black tea was greater.

As Long Feather and I approached Luc and the rest of our party, Reverend Father Feng intercepted us.

"Forgive me, Chief Justice, but Master Ma has asked for me to mediate a discussion with you here."

"In a Temple?" I blurted.

"He didn't believe you would be comfortable going to the School of the Phoenix and the Dragon, and he didn't wish to go to the Temple of Balance or the imperial palace over his shame that one of his students had lost his moral compass in such a manner."

I took and released a deep breath. "Very well. I will speak with Master Ma if you are agreeable to host such a meeting."

Feng smiled. "Give me a moment, and I'll ensure you have plenty of tea and he has a bottle of rice wine."

I joined our party. "If you'll excuse me, Your Majesties, I'll be staying here for a bit."

Po narrowed his eyes. "Why?"

"Master Ma wishes to speak with me, and the Reverend Father has agreed to mediate our discussion," I said.

Luc jerked, but Po nodded. "This is as neutral a location for such a meeting as either of you can get."

I hesitated for a moment, making sure my wording in the Jing language was as inoffensive as possible. "May I please invite him to the palace on your behalf after the Spring Rituals? I think you would both benefit from sharing your grief concerning your father."

"If he's willing to come, then yes." Po leaned closer. "Though Captain Huizhong may not be as charming when it comes to the schools."

Behind Po, Huizhong rolled his eyes.

"What if I accompanied the chief justice to this meeting?" Shi Hua said.

"No!" everyone, including the imperial guards and our wardens said loudly. It drew attention from everyone else in the great hallway.

Shi Hua glared at all of us in turn. "So much rudeness when I merely offered to assist the chief justice."

"We cannot take any chances, Your Majesty," I said. "With any of the imperial family."

She made a face at my subtle reference to her pregnancy, but otherwise remained quiet.

"I am leaving a palanquin here for your use." Po held up a finger when I opened my mouth to argue, and he softly added, "If our plan is to work, we need our worm intact."

I didn't appreciate being compared to an earth crawler, but more arguing would just waste our limited time. "I will honor your request, Your Majesty."

"Thank you, Chief Justice." He held out his elbow for Shi Hua, she wrapped her arm about his, and they strode up the hall and turned right toward the clergy personal quarters. Apparently, the entrances to the Temple tunnel systems were the same throughout the World.

Luc's fingers brushed mine before he silently said, *Be careful.*

Long Feather will make sure I do. I smiled.

He swung after the imperial couple, Yar at his back.

A Conflict priestess, a high sister from her badge, approached Long Feather and me. "Do you need to take care of any personal needs before I escort you to the meeting room assigned to you, Chief Justice."

I shook my head, but her attention focused on my warden. No one could miss her female appreciation. It was hard to suppress my smile, but I managed.

Somehow.

The meeting room was empty when we arrived. The Conflict priestess reluctantly left despite her efforts to engage my warden in conversation. When the door shut, I leaned closer to Long Feather.

"What is it about you that attracts Conflict clergy of the female persuasion?"

"I wish I knew, Chief Justice." He shook his head. "I wish I knew."

"Should I start a rumor that you have a disease of the genitals?" I teased.

"M'lady, there is someone at home." His face brightened to a brilliant shade of red.

"There is?" I grinned. "Is it someone I know?"

His right eyebrow arched. "That is my private business, Chief Justice."

The door of the meeting room swung open and saved Long Feather from my teasing. To my shock, Reverend Father Feng carried a tray with a steaming pot, a corked bottle, and cups. Master Ma followed him, leaning heavily on his walking stick. A woman trailed after the sorcerer. Her confident demeanor reminded me of a Conflict priestess, but she wore the leathers and carried the undecorated weapons of a mercenary. A Jing Conflict warden pulled the door shut so it was just the five of us.

"Please be seated, my guests," Reverend Father Feng murmured. He made the introductions of everyone present. The woman Tian was Master Ma's personal bodyguard. However, I didn't remember seeing her at the welcome banquet.

Master Ma and I took seats, but our protection stood behind us and well out of the way of the Reverend Father.

Feng poured a cup of tea and handed it to Long Feather. "For you to test for the Chief Justice. Or I can call in one of my priests you've already met and trust to taste it for you."

"Actually, I wish this was not necessary at all, Reverend Father." My warden took a sip from the cup before he handed it to me. "Thankfully, the chief justice prefers her tea plain, so any sweeteners do not hide southern blue."

"As both Thief and Vintner would remind you, there is more than one kind of poison in the World, Warden," Master Ma said as Feng poured him a glass of the rice wine.

"I am well aware from sad experience, Master. However, southern blue is one of the fastest acting poisons with a small dose." I took a sip from my cup. My tongue would have danced in delight if it could. "Maybe I should use my Mill winnings to buy a tea farm here in Jing."

"Mill?" Master Ma asked.

"A strategy game that's popular in Issura," I explained. "The Orrin Temple of Thief hosted a tournament last winter."

"From your expression, something happened during this tournament," Master Ma said. "May I ask what it was?"

I swallowed my memory of the pain I'd felt from Justice Mei Wen. "That was the night we learned you had lost Emperor Chengwu and his family."

"How did you learn about the attack?" Tian demanded.

"The emperor and his brother have, rather had, a strong affection for each other. And they stayed in contact via a distance speaker." I shrugged. A faint suspicion that Justice Mei Wen was also a distance speaker had been nagging me since that night last winter. But with the recent assassinations of prominently placed distance speakers, I wasn't about to ask anyone in Jing.

"Do not worry, Master. I doubt either our Reverend Mother of Balance or our queen would be happy about the chief justice asking for a dispensation to transfer to Jing and farm," Long Feather said in an attempt to lighten the mood.

"However, if I manage to survive the next twenty years, I will need a new occupation." I grinned at Master Ma and Reverend Father Feng.

"You believe the demon wars will be done as proclaimed by Balance?" Master Ma asked.

"Yes, but I'm under no illusion a victory will be easy." I took a sip of my tea.

"And what is your personal opinion of our philosophy schools?" Tian spat.

"I have no quarrels with any school. Those whose talents do not align with the responsibilities of the Temples still need someone to teach them control so they do not harm themselves or others. However, my personal opinion is that anyone, regardless of their respective talents, magic or otherwise, who demon deals is a fool and a traitor," I stated calmly. "That includes my own birth mother."

That little tidbit startled the three Jing citizens.

"Your birth mother was executed for demon dealing?" Master Ma choked out.

"I beheaded her myself." The steel behind my words reminded me of that terrible day. "She was a renegade. She was casting a spell that would have killed everyone in the city of Orrin to summon demons to replace the army we and our allies destroyed in Tandor."

"The crown prince was one of those allies. He aided us in defeating that demon army and evacuating the city," Long Feather added in a voice pitched lower than his normal speaking voice. As if he dared Master Ma or his bodyguard to speak ill of Po.

"This is why Queen Teodora cherishes her personal and political relationship with Crown Prince Po," I said in a lighter tone. "We owe him a great deal."

"Have you ever met a sorcerer before the welcome banquet at the palace besides Master Quan?" Master Ma asked.

"Only the sorcerer Wu Sunshu convinced Emperor Chengwu to send to Issura to allegedly protect the former Ambassador Quan Po. The idiot sorcerer thought he'd get away with smuggling a demon and a demon egg into the Jing Embassy in Orrin to assassinate the crown prince and his body guard." I took another sip of my tea.

"And did you behead him without a trial like you did your mother?" Tian sneered.

"No," I said.

"Surely, you punished him." Master Ma stared at me in horror.

"Up until that point, my experience with demons were with ones who had been summoned to this plane by a human sorcerer." I shrugged again. "The former Ambassador Quan slit the sorcerer's throat in a vain attempt to end the bond and send the demon back to its own plane. That's when we discovered during the demons' last invasion, they had left thousands of their eggs to hatch here so they're not dependent on a human to stay in our World."

"Twelve help us," Master Ma murmured before he downed the rest of his wine in one swallow. "I know we had differences in opinion on the use of our powers for the benefit of the empire, but this . . ." He shook his head.

"What did you really want to ask me, Master?" I said softly.

He cleared his throat. "I'd hoped you would consider allowing some of my students to attend your class at the Temple of Knowledge."

I frowned. "My class?"

He nodded. "On how you can produce lightning. Not even the weather wizards in my own school can manage such a feat. But given your experiences with Jing sorcerers, I can understand if you refuse."

The Jing gossip network did work at incredible speed. I didn't like the idea of the philosophy schools attending, but this was an opportunity to mend relations within Jing society that I would be a fool to forgo.

"I will allow it on three conditions." I held up my right index finger. "You will need to limit the number to five." I raised my middle finger. "I will truthspell them prior to providing any information to assure their loyalty to the human race. And third—" I raised my ring finger. "—I ask that you visit the palace and speak directly with the crown prince after the Spring Rituals. You are the only one I've met in Jing who speaks highly of Master Quan. The crown prince grieves for all of his family, and a kind word would go far toward healing his heart."

My conditions seemed to shock the three Jing people, especially Tian. I sipped my tea while they all considered my words.

Finally, Reverend Father Feng broke the silence. "Would you extend the same offer and conditions to the other Temples and schools?"

"Of course." I nodded.

"We would appreciate such an opportunity," Master Ma murmured.

I chuckled. "Anyone interested may want to attend the final ceremonies of the holiday before they make their decision."

"Why?" Tian blurted.

"The crown prince has asked that I provide a lightning display in conjunction with your magnificent fireworks."

CHAPTER 60

As I expected, my news shocked the sorcerer and his bodyguard. However, a delighted expression spread across Reverend Father Feng's visage.

"Maybe we cannot reproduce your peculiar sight, but having a new weapon may turn the tides of this damn thousand-year war."

"That's the main reason I agreed to the crown prince and the Reverend Mother of Knowledge's requests." I smiled. "This new talent of mine is why I would appreciate the quiet life of tea farmer."

"Something tells me you would drink all your crops." Feng grinned in return.

Behind me came a muffled cough that sounded suspiciously like an aborted bark of laughter.

"Very well." Master Ma pushed to his feet. Unlike the night of the banquet, he appeared pleased and sad. As if he were relieved the human race would survive this war, but he would not live long enough to see the end of it.

He bowed to me. "Thank you for your words and your time, Chief Justice. I look forward to your display of skill tomorrow night, and your class after the Spring Rituals."

I rose and bowed to him. "Thank you for speaking with me. Master, If you have any further questions or concerns, I will be in Chengzhou until the next First Day."

He left the room. His bodyguard trailed after him with a puzzled glance at me. Apparently, I was not what she expected.

When the Conflict warden shut the door behind them, Reverend Father Feng relaxed. "That went better than I expected. However, I apologize for Tian's behavior."

"Was she a Conflict novice?" I asked.

His startled expression answered my question before he said, "Yes. How did you know?"

"Her body language." I frowned as I resumed my seat. "I don't mean to overstep, but she holds much anger. What happened?"

Feng's right thumb and forefinger framed his jaw as he leaned his elbow on the table. "A training accident resulted in a severe head injury. If we didn't have a master healer teaching basic medical care to a class in the novice wing, Tian would have died before any other healer could be summoned. Even with the healing, she developed sudden intense head-aches, and she lost some of the talents necessary for our Temple."

"And she was dismissed from Conflict." I nodded. "I understand her resentment now. Don't you contract with the Healers Guild for a master on your premises?" I asked. "The home Temples in Standora keep a rotat-ing schedule of two masters on call per month."

He exhaled wearily. "The guild leaders only send us journeypeople." A wan smile appeared on his face. "However, you've given me some point-ers during my next negotiations with them."

"I don't have any special skills, Reverend Father," I said. "I find most people respond to honest, straight talk. Though many say I am too blunt." I held up my left index finger though I didn't turn to look at my warden. "Don't even think it, Long Feather."

Feng chuckled. "I've never seen other clergy treat their wardens the way you do. If I didn't know better, I would have thought you were Con-flict yourself."

"We've become a family of sorts," I said. "I respect my wardens. They all could have requested transfers when the Assassins Guild and demons made it their personal mission to kill me."

"We wouldn't—" Long Feather started to protest.

I pivoted in my chair to look directly at him. "You didn't. None of you did. Even after we lost Aglaia, Tyra, and Mylon in less than a year." I turned back to Feng. "Did you have any other questions for me? I did promise my wardens a chance to enjoy the holiday while we are in Chengzhou. They didn't have any chance to do so in the aftermath of the Battle of Tandor last year."

"Far be it from me to get in the way of anyone having a good time during the Spring Rituals." He chuckled as he rose.

I stood as well. "May I make one suggestion, Reverend Father?"

"Of course."

"Please include High Brother Shang in the five Conflict personnel you send to Knowledge."

His expression turned puzzled. "May I ask why?"

"In my case, anger and pain from the Siege of Tandor triggered my initial display of lightning," I said. "It took some sessions with High Sis-ter Mya to focus those emotions properly to control my new talent. Since

Shang's experiences in the Gobi Desert are similar enough to mine, he's the most likely candidate to produce and control lightning."

Feng's right eyebrow rose. "And the fact I've assigned him to help Sister Yin Li in protecting the imperial couple has nothing to do with it?"

"Both factors have everything to do with my request," I replied.

The Reverend Father crossed his arms. "May we be honest with each other, Chief Justice?"

"Of course." I nodded. "Would you like to truthspell me?"

He grinned. "I was about to ask you the same thing."

"Go ahead and speak. If it's something I don't know or cannot answer without betraying Queen Teodora, I will tell you so."

He regarded me for a long moment. "Why is Issura so interested in placing Bao Quan Po on the Dragon Throne?"

"Are you saying he's not the only surviving child of Empress Yu?"

"No, that is not the basis of my question." He unfolded his arms and looked away for a moment. "There's quite a few people who think he is under Teodora's control."

I laughed. "That is most definitely not the case." I sobered. "Emperor Chengwu charged his brother to develop closer ties with Issura. The queen values our trade relationship with Jing, especially for providing flash powder, which is the only thing that has any real effect on demons besides water and magic."

"And your personal relationship with him?"

"I regard him as a valued ally. We've saved each other's lives more times than either of us like to count or admit prior to his brother and nephews' deaths. I have not violated my vows by having intercourse with him. I cannot have children thanks to the first poisoning attempt on me. And finally, I regard the Lady Shi Hua as my blood sister, so I would not harm her for any reason."

Feng nodded. "Thank you for your honesty, Chief Justice."

I inclined my head. "Thank you for the tea and for your mediation skills."

This time, he laughed so hard his entire body shook. "I didn't do a damn thing except serve drinks. And Anthea?" He cocked his head. "I do understand. I didn't want my position either, but we both have our duties to perform."

I inclined my head again. From Shi Hua's stories, Reverend Father

Chen didn't like anyone challenging his authority. I could see why the assembly of high brothers would elect someone with a modicum of compassion, logic, and natural leadership skills. "As you say. But it doesn't make the deaths any easier, does it?"

"No, it does not." Sadness and grief bled from him. How many members of the slaughtered Jing army had he known personally? Grew up together with them here in Chengzhou as novices? It was far too personal and impertinent to ask.

Nor was I sure I wanted to know the answer. Too many deaths surrounded me in the nearly two years since I was sentenced to the seat of Balance in Orrin. I couldn't throw the weight of my dead onto Feng's shoulders any more than I could handle his grief at the moment.

When Long Feather and I returned to the palace, no one was in our suite. He double-checked their bedchamber and bathing room, though I could have told him no one was here. However, I did the same for mine and Luc's room to make sure someone hadn't messed with our personal belongings.

When I returned to the common room, I eyed Long Feather. "Since neither you or Jonata are needed to escort me to the School of the Phoenix and the Dragon, why don't you take your leave and enjoy the rest of the day at the festival?"

He shook his head. "I'm not leaving you alone, m'lady."

"I thought that may be your answer." I sighed. "If I ward my bathing room, may I take a nap privately?"

"Yes, m'lady." He grinned. "Are you sure you don't wish to eat first?"

I grinned. "Sleep first for me, then we'll go back to the food stall by Light. If you're hungry, summon some food from the palace kitchen. Or you can have the cakes." I waved at the canvas bag of items from yesterday.

"They were gifts to you," he protested.

"They are better fresh, Long Feather. I'll buy more at the stall," I promised.

He laughed. "Fine. Go get your rest while you can, m'lady."

I entered my bedchamber. It was stuffy with the warmth of the day, but I didn't dare open my windows. I untied and pulled off my robes. Last thing I needed was an assassin climbing through the apertures—

Curses rang through my head. I hadn't asked either Wu or Jia Huo about the assassin who tried to shoot Po with a poison bolt the morning after we arrived in Chengzhou or Yar and Antiope's attacker. I was definitely slipping in proper interrogation techniques if I couldn't keep the facts of a case straight in my mind.

Even if the case was not mine to oversee.

I used the water closet before I donned my robes. When I entered the common room. Long Feather looked up with the startled eyes of a fawn. A piece of fruit hung between his lips.

"We're getting food early," I stated. "We have an errand to run at the Temple of Balance.

CHAPTER 61

Long Feather chewed and swallowed his mouthful of cake and fruit before he said, "If this is important enough for you to forgo sleep, have something to eat before we go to the Temple of Balance." He stood and swiped at the crumbs on his lips. "I'll request a palanquin."

"No, you are not," I snapped. "My legs work perfectly fine."

He grabbed the bag of treats and held it out to me. I selected a wrapped cake and gulped it down along with some water. I had to admit I felt a bit better with something in my stomach. Those cakes felt like eating a slice of sunshine.

I had another round with the imperial guards at our door when we exited our suite. The burly one also insisted I take a palanquin or at the minimum take my borrowed horse.

I pointed out both a palanquin and a horse made it difficult to see the city and enjoy the festival. Even the surly steward Chin, who rushed up to us because he had heard us argue, agreed any transportation was counterproductive with the festival crowds.

Once outside under the warmth of the sun, all the fussing about my safety seemed ridiculous when the civilians gave us a wide berth as Long Feather and I headed down the street to the Temples. The murmurs and comments about my eyes still wafted after me, but I heard more stories about Jia Huo's public arrest and Wu's recapture.

I gritted my teeth. I'd thought the fishwives in Orrin were bad, and I said as much to Long Feather in our language.

He pursed his lips and glanced around us before he answered in kind. "With all due respect, m'lady, the gossip was just as bad when you first took the Orrin seat of Balance."

"You mean when I was sentenced?"

He snorted. "That was the primary topic. Half the city didn't understand why the Reverend Mother placed a justice found guilty of murder on the Temple seat. The other half questioned whether there had really been demons at all."

"Until we found the demon in the Jing Embassy?"

"Didn't you hear? That was totally the Jing Empire's fault," he mocked. "They planned to invade Issura, didn't you know?"

"Oh," I said. Chief Warden Little Bear's words came back to roost in my mind. I was so mired in self-pity those first few months as the Balance seat I paid little attention to what was happening within Orrin. If I had, maybe Aglaia and High Brother Kam would still be alive. I swallowed hard. I couldn't afford to wallow in my regrets. Not now, but that didn't mean I couldn't make a conciliatory gesture.

"I am sorry I put you and the rest of the Balance staff and wardens in such an untenable position," I murmured. "That wasn't fair to any of you."

Long Feather waved his left hand. "It's water in the bay as far as we're concerned." He grimaced. "Compared to your predecessor, you excel at your position."

"I'm also getting tired of being compared to Penelope," I grumbled.

"All right." He grinned, which was my tip off that I'd been forgiven. "According to Hogarth, you're as mad as Chief Justice Thalia. Is that better?"

I groaned. "Not really." But it was necessary to take his teasing in stride. During our conversations, High Sister Mya of Child told me I needed to accept the barbed comments my friends dished out if I were to continue to say such things to them.

Thankfully, we reached the steps of Balance before Long Feather could lob any more comparisons at me. Few people were around this particular Temple since most cases were paused due to the holiday. That was the real reason neither Wu or Jia Huo had been executed yet.

The wardens at the main entrance didn't even question my appearance at their doorstep. They opened the huge bronze slabs and bowed to me. The Temple doors were normally left open during the Spring Rituals, but Chengzhou, like Orrin, had learned the hard way that the reappearance of the demons meant taking every and all precautions.

A senior justice I hadn't met approached us from a side hall. Oddly, she didn't have a warden guiding her. Not so oddly, her hood was lowered and her head was shaved like every other Jing justice I'd met so far.

"We come to serve," she said with a low bow. "I am Chief Justice Dai Lu. How may we assist you, Chief Justice Anthea?"

I bowed in return. "I had two questions for Reverend Mother Xiang concerning Wu and Jia Huo's trials. May I please speak with her?"

"She is not here at the moment," Dai Lu said. "Would Justice Mei Wen be an appropriate substitute?"

"Absolutely," I said.

Dai Lu indicated that we follow her, and she turned toward the Temple's office section.

"May I ask a personal question?" I said.

She laughed. "Why don't I have a warden as my eyes?"

"Even so."

"I'm one of those who had sight when I was born, but it faded quickly. I was a danger to myself by the time I reached five winters." She glanced at me. "I can detect colors and shadows after a fashion. You and your warden are black fuzzy rectangles with pale brown blobs sitting on top. I can function within the Temple walls, but I do need a warden to watch out for my own good outside of Balance." She chuckled. "However, the little sight I still have is useful. I startled the demons by calling out their locations to my sisters when the damned things invaded last winter."

"It sounds as if you would be a very good training justice for new wardens."

Dai Lu roared with laughter. "That's exactly what the Reverend Mother thought." She immediately sobered. "Thankfully, my former warden Yichen didn't question me when Justice Mei Wen's original Warden Gang was cut down and I ordered him to protect her. My new trainee is out holiday sowing while he has the chance. The rest of this week will be quite busy. Speak of the demon!"

She approached the door Warden Yichen guarded. "Are you staying out of trouble, young man?"

"I always endeavor to do so, Chief Justice." He smiled shyly.

"Please let Justice Mei Wen know Chief Justice Anthea of Issura is here to ask two questions." Dai Lu leaned closer to Yichen and said sotto voce. "Though I'm sure it will be far more than only two."

Long Feather snickered. Yichen flushed scarlet as he reached behind him to knock on Mei Wen's office door.

"Enter," the justice's sweet, high voice called out.

Yichen opened the door just enough to peer around the edge and repeated Dai Lu's request.

"Show Chief Justice Anthea in, please."

Yichen shoved the door open wider and nodded to me. I turned to Dai Lu. "Thank you for the escort, Chief Justice." I bowed.

"All of you can come in," Mei Wen called out. "Including you, Dai Lu."

"Excellent!" Dai Lu followed Long Feather and me into Mei Wen's office. "Please tell me you asked our cook for persimmon spice cakes for our guest."

As Yichen closed the office door, I laughed. "I thought I was bad for visiting Light in Orrin to eat their almond pastries."

"Is that something special Issurans bake for the Spring Rituals?" Dai Lu perched on the lid of Mei Wen's weapons trunk while Long Feather and I claimed the two visitor's stools.

Long Feather laughed, and my face heated. "Our cook and Light's keep the chief justice in almond pastries year-round. We can't have her sneaking out to her favorite baker's shop these days."

Both Jing justices turned somber.

"We understand." Dai Lu sighed.

"She introduced me to a food vendor named Lan when I was a novice—" Mei Wen started.

"Is it the same Lan who has a stall between Light and Thief during the Spring Rituals?" Long Feather's excitement was palpable in the small room.

"How did you know?" Dai Lu said at the same time Mei Wen said, "You found her?"

"The first day of the Spring Rituals." I wasn't about to mention who led us there. While I'd gotten over my anger, I wasn't sure if the justices would react the same as Duke Mengchang and accuse me of being in league with Jia Hou. "We planned to stop there on the way back to the palace for more cakes and her chilled hibiscus tea."

"Then let us deal with business quickly, so you can return to her stall." Mei Wen placed her folded hands on top of her desk. "You had questions, Anthea?"

"I hope you'll forgive me for my own lapse in logic, but this didn't occur to me until we returned to the palace. Did the Reverend Mother or another justice question either Wu or Jia Huo concerning the assassin who tried to shoot the crown prince the morning after he arrived in Chengzhou, the renegade who shot her after she was captured, or the person who attacked Warden Yar of Issura or Warden Antiope of the Skoloti Tribes in her room at the palace?"

"Wu couldn't have killed the assassin," Dai Lu said. "He was still in custody when she shot the bowl in Captain Huizhong's hands. According to the reports I read, the time rewind in Wu's cell confirmed it."

"But he would have been hiding inside the palace when Yar and Antiope were attacked. Plus, he had contact with the handful of his former students for Balance knows how long before he made his escape." Mei Wen rolled her thumbs about each other. "One moment."

A buzz vibrated against my mind as Mei Wen spoke silently with someone else. "Justice Aihan was present when Chief Justice Dai Lu initially interrogated Jia Huo. I've asked her to join us."

"She was one of the justices who responded to the crossbow attack at the palace," I said.

"Even so." Mei Wen shrugged.

"Is she always assigned to investigate crimes regarding the emperor or the nobility?" I asked.

Mei Wen's thumbs twirled faster, but her skin color didn't change.

However, Dai Lu laughed outright. "I take it the nobility in Issura does not interfere with Temple matters."

"Oh, they certainly try." I chuckled. "But the treason of the former duke of Orrin, his wife, and a cousin of the queen two winters ago has chilled most of the political games. For the moment anyway."

"Especially after we lost Tandor and its port and nearly lost Orrin," Long Feather said. "Cant started to experience the same whisper campaigns Jing and Issura faced, but their society doesn't have quite the Old Continent influence concerning a nobility class. The loss of their border city of Rambla and all of its citizens squelched any further gossip about whether the Temples were necessary."

"To answer your question, Anthea, Aihan is noble born," Dai Lu said. "There's been outside pressure to name her as the Reverend Mother's successor. But she knows how to manage egos to get to the truth of a matter."

I rubbed my temples at my growing headache. Why in the world did Queen Teodora think I was suited to be her representative in Jing?

"Except she has no wish for the position," Mei Wen said.

"She would be one of the very few nobles I've met who doesn't want to acquire more power or influence," I commented.

Dai Lu grinned. "Aihan thought she had escaped the ox turds of politics. She loves investigations for the intellectual puzzles they present."

"Even she wishes we could find some way to stop the whisper campaigns in Jing," Mei Wen murmured. "It would make defending the empire from demons so much easier."

Another knock on her office door interrupted her musings. She called out, "Enter!"

The door swung open, and Yichen announced the arrival of Justice Aihan.

"You need me?" she said brightly as her warden brought in an extra stool, which he set next to mine.

"Don't we always, sweetling?" Dai Lu laughed.

Envy flashed through me at the women's camaraderie. My time at the home Temple in Standora wasn't filled with collegial relations. But maybe it wasn't me. I got along fine with the other three justices in residence in Orrin before I left for Jing.

Once Aihan was settled on her stool, the two wardens exited and closed the office door behind them. Mei Wen warded the room before she and Dai Lu laid out my concerns to Aihan.

"I did ask Jia Huo about the two direct attacks at the palace," Dai Lu said. "He was not involved in any way with them. Frankly, his initial interrogation was the fastest and least complicated of any I've ever participated in. He didn't even try to beat the truthspell. I truly believe he regrets his actions, but he is young and foolish and will unfortunately pay the ultimate price. Is there anything you think I missed, Aihan?"

The younger justice shook her head. "I can only add that the Reverend Mother ran the same questions about the palace attacks by Wu after we gave her our reports. Those attacks slipped her mind from the chaos of this week, as it did yours. It's part of the reason the Reverend Mother has all of us cross-checking with each other about our cases. The more minds, the better, she says."

"I am so glad you all work well with each other and don't allow your pride to interfere with obtaining a fair and truthful result," I murmured. "However, I fear this means we still have a third party running around the palace intent on murdering the crown prince and anyone else who gets in their way. I pray you find those demon eggs before our unknown assailant does." Because if they didn't, my people would die here in this foreign land, too.

CHAPTER 62

Mei Wen answered my most pertinent concern first. "The Reverend Mother is retrieving the eggs as we speak." She made the Jing gesture of good luck. "There was no way Jia Huo could be misleading us about where he left the demon eggs. We can only hope no one else has found and removed them."

"Have any of you considered the attacks on the crown prince and the wardens at the palace could have nothing to do with the renegades or the demons?" Aihan asked.

Long Feather and I looked at her, but she didn't add anything to her question. However, Mei Wen groaned and Dai Lu chuckled.

"The Bao cousins," Mei Wen spat in a disgusted tone.

"Even so," Aihan agreed.

"Duke Lixin and Prince Pu have been assassinated within the last week," I said.

"Doesn't stop their idiot sons or the sons' mothers from pursuing any claims to the Dragon Throne," Dai Lu said. "Power or the idea of it makes humans do foolish things."

"Duke Mengchang is the one possible claimant who has been in the capital this whole time," I said.

"I can confirm he doesn't want to be emperor," Aihan said. "I worked with him in the post-battle analysis, and he found the taste quite bitter as acting regent. He was quite relieved when the crown prince arrived on Jing soil."

"Duke Lixin didn't want to be emperor either," Dai Lu said.

Mei Wen laughed. "Duchess Jia can barely hold her tongue, much less a coherent thought or the throne. And Prince Pu has outlived his children and most of his grandchildren. None of his surviving grandchildren have a better claim."

"Not to mention, he preferred to breed silkworms quietly at his estate before his death," Aihan added.

"The crown prince mentioned Duke Zixin as the family member most likely to challenge his claim to the throne," I said. "What is your analysis of him?"

All three justices grew quiet. There wasn't even the buzz indicating they discussed the matter among themselves.

Finally, Aihan said, "He doesn't have the strongest claim, but he is the most outspoken. Plus, he deliberately arrived to the capital late as a snub to the crown prince."

"That's because Duke Guang would rather sit back and let the other claimants kill each other, then swoop in like a carrion bird," Dai Lu said with disgust.

"Duke Xi has a stronger claim than Zixin or Guang," Mei Wen mused. "But his only legitimate complaint has been the loss of Light abilities in the imperial line. Jing rather prides itself on that matter since Empress Bao De and her prince consort sacrificed themselves to destroy the demon army at the Battle of Jicheng. The question is whether Xi has changed his opinion now that the crown prince married a former Light priestess."

"Too bad none of you can do a rewind at the manor house where the last of the School of Sorcery members were hiding," Long Feather said.

Leave it to my warden to stick a butterfly in their ears to prompt some new ideas. Of course, such a thing had become simple at home thanks my junior justice Yanaba merging herself with the literal city of Orrin.

"Do you think together we could handle the rewind of an entire block?" Aihan said.

"But what do we use as the borders of the spell?" Dai Lu asked.

"The four of us should be able to handle it by working together. We can use the cobblestones of the bordering streets for the two-dimensional coordinates," I said. "We take poles with us to define the third axis."

The three justices babbled in agreement, excited about the prospect of trying something that was new for them. I just hoped this would work, and I wasn't putting my sisters in danger. If I got them killed by trying this insane stunt, I'd destroy my own usefulness to Queen Teodora and Emperor Po.

Thankfully, the Balance kitchen fed us something more substantial than the persimmon spice cakes while messages were sent, and we waited for clergy from Light to join us. They also provided several pots of Jing tea so I could stay alert for this task.

To my surprise, it wasn't just Light who joined us. Clergy and wardens from every Temple volunteered to assist in the rewind. Even an older priestess from Love arrived, though this was their busiest time of the year. They also brought several wagons loaded with goods. It reminded me of my head of household and squire attempting to feed and clothe the orphans who ran the streets of Orrin when our Temple of Mother failed in its duties.

Mei Wen requisitioned horses for Long Feather and me, rather than wait for us to go back to the palace. The Wildings and their wardens took point as we wound through alleys and back streets to get to the gates for the innermost wall of the city.

We turned toward the west side of Chengzhou. I was rather glad to have a horse after all the walking I did the last two days. When we passed through the gates of the third wall, traffic faded to nearly nothing.

The homes and shops in this section of the city were once well-kept, but had fallen into neglect and disrepair. People watched us from open windows, often with suspicion, others with downright hatred. The emotion I felt the most was hunger. This unfortunate section would be a breeding ground for renegades if the Temples didn't help restore the area.

Almost as if reading my thoughts, clergy from Mother, Father, Child, and Vintner broke off from our main party along with most of the wagons to distribute food, medicines, and clothing, but Conflict and half the Wildlings followed. Was this something they normally did?

I glanced at Long Feather, riding beside me. He subtly tapped his temple. I reached out to his mind.

What is it?

Please keep your expression neutral, m'lady, he said.

My expression?

You're wearing your judgmental face. The one you make when you believe a clergy member isn't fulfilling their duties to civilians. He stared straight ahead. *I heard from the Jing wardens the Temple personnel have been attacked the last three times they've come to this section of Chengzhou to minister to those in need. Including the night of the fire and the first day of the Spring Rituals. They weren't gossiping. They wanted to make sure I understood the danger to you.*

Thank you for looking out for my safety, but there's usually a reason for resentment. There definitely was in Orrin, I commented. The status of our city when I became the seat of Balance still gnawed on my spirit. Apparently, my predecessor Penelope thought it was appropriate to slice off the hands of starving children when they stole bread to survive. Appealing to anyone at Mother had led the orphaned children to an even worse fate.

Maybe, he said. *Or the whisper campaigns are behind this.*

It took me longer than usual to follow his train of thought, so he explained. *The civilians aren't doing well. They're told it's the Temples fault. When the Temple personnel arrive to provide for the civilian's needs, they take their anger out on the clergy and wardens. So, the Temples bring additional arms to protect themselves, and the civilians take their actions as aggression toward them.*

And it turns into an ugly, downward-spiraling cycle. I resisted the urge to shake my head in disgust. Po didn't need me starting a riot in his capital, even accidentally.

Unfortunately, Long Feather replied. *It took all of us Balance wardens a few months to trust you. You weren't senile, but—*

Oh, I'm mad, but in a different way than Penelope. I bit the tip of my tongue to keep from laughing at the absurdity of our situation and that of the Jing Temples. My black sense of humor would not be appreciated by the civilians.

Even so. His mental tone conveyed his own humor at my poor jest, though his expression remained neutral.

Two blocks after the first group, Love, Knowledge, Thief, and Death parted ways with us along with the last few wagons. That left Balance, Light, and the rest of the Wildlings en route to the site of the fire, which we reached after three more blocks.

Ash covered the cobblestones and muffled the horses' shoes as we approached. Low walls surrounded what had probably been a merchant's or a minor noble's home. Two sides of the brick façade remained standing, but from the charring and cracks, their balance was precarious at best. Stumps of dying trees in the back garden showed through the gaping holes where windows and doors had been.

I examined our surroundings. The first buildings on the block east of the manse were rubble from the spread of the initial fire. The rest of the surrounding structures showed char marks and damage but were intact. Relatively speaking. It was obvious even to my odd eyesight the homes and shops hadn't been kept up. Bricks crumbled, lacquer peeled, and wood rotted on everything.

To top all the damage, the grating of demon magic irritated my psyche.

Mei Wei, why is the section of the city in such poor condition? I asked.

Fifty years ago, the black plague swept through the Old Continent, she said. *This was the first part of the city struck, and a majority of the original residents died. Surviving merchants bought the properties from the survivors or through the magistrate's auction when no heirs could be found. Except they didn't bother doing any maintenance. They would claim the rental fees until the city seized the property for unpaid taxes.*

Her distaste at the situation flavored her mental voice.

And? I prodded.

I can give you the lecture on the city's bureaucrats and their ineptitude, but simply put, as fast as they evict squatters, more return before anyone can buy and claim a building for restoration or destruction.

I sighed. And no one with the gold to purchase a property wanted to waste their coin in dealing with the squatters. Everyone here stayed out of everyone else's business because none of them wanted the city's bureaucrats or peacekeepers asking any questions. It made perfect sense why the fugitives from the School of Sorcery fled to this section of Chengzhou.

We all dismounted. A Light priest and Balance clerk attended each justice. Two of the wardens watched our steeds while the rest of the wardens and the Wildlings spread out to guard our flanks.

The clerk and Light priest assigned to me followed as I walked through where the estate's gate had been and to the southwest corner of the ruined block. It was a good thing we brought the tall pole with us. The low decorative wall wasn't high enough to show us what was happening on the second floor of the manse. I shoved my pole into the soft ash and top soil in my corner of the property. The three other Light priests led their charges to the other three corners and did the same with their poles.

"Chief Justice, how may I serve you?" The middle-aged Light priest bowed. "I have heard you can see."

I chuckled. "Not in the same way you can. I still need an observer during a time rewind. To me, the past appears as whisps of fog. I cannot identify faces or actions."

The priest nodded. "I am Brother Zi Rui. Do you have any additional instructions for me or Clerk Fulu?"

"This is a standard rewind," I said. "Perform your duties as you normally would for any other justice. All I ask is that you don't lead me around like a prized cow."

Brother Zi Rui looked appalled at my statement, but Fulu burst out in laughter.

I grimaced as I looked at the ash and charred bits covering the yard. Another uniform would be filthy by the time this was done. I really needed to avail on the Balance laundry later today. Using the edges of my boots, I cleared the debris until I could touch the actual rocks that formed a border around the plants that had been growing here.

"Fulu, can you draw likenesses?" I asked.

"Yes, Chief Justice." She nodded vigorously. "All of us picked for this assignment can sketch people." Like me, she attempted to clear a spot where she could sit and use her portable desk."

Are we ready? I asked my sister justices.

Yes, Mei Wen replied.

Are we sure five days is long enough? Aihan asked.

Bing was alive three days ago, and Wu came here that same night, Mei Wen said. *As fugitives, I doubt the other four sorcerers left, but that's a chance we must take.*

We do have something in our favor. With the floors and most of the walls gone, our observers will be able to see everything. Even if someone stays in their room the entire time. Dai Lu laughed. *Just make sure our Light clergy mind the debris-filled basement.*

I looked up at Brother Zi Rui. "Justice Dai Lu said to remind you to be careful where you walk."

"I have done this before," he said tersely.

Of course, I got the humorless priest. As an Issuran ambassador, I didn't dare bite back.

We justices silently recited the spell for a rewind. Our magic danced and melded. As one, we yanked the timelines back five days. It was like working with Elizabeth, Yanaba, and Erato back home. The shared load made everything easier.

We kept the rewind at a one-for-five pace to give the clerks enough of a chance to draw the faces of the five fugitives staying at the former manse. Fulu's graphite stick made small scratching noises on the paper as she rapidly sketched the likenesses, but it was Brother Zi Rui's impatience that grated on my nerves at our slow pace. I did my best to ignore him. This information was too important.

Once each of the clerks called out they had all five portraits, we sped up the pace of the rewind. Nothing interesting happened until Bing left the manse before dawn on the day of her death.

"Hold," Fulu shouted.

I passed the request, and together we justices paused the timeline.

"Four new people have entered the gate," Brother Zi Rui reported.

Underneath our rewind, I tasted the sharp bitterness of demon magic. "Demons in human guises or shapeshifters," I said aloud and silently.

"How do you know?" Brother Zi Rui demanded.

"Residue of their magic within the time line," I said.

Again, the clerks reported they had the sketches. We allowed the rewind to continue.

One of the fugitive sorcerers answered the door and the quartet entered the manse. On the other side of the wall, I could hear Long Feather repeating what I said, which let to muttering among the wardens and Wildlings.

"Didn't they see the danger they were in?" Brother Zi Rui said.

I didn't bother answering. If he was one of those who believed the School of Sorcery was totally innocent, it wasn't worth breaking the rewind to answer him.

"From their demeanor, they knew who and what they were dealing with," Fulu said.

The Light priest witnessed what our foes did next. They gathered the four fugitive sorcerers on the second floor. One of the new figures peeled off its human skin.

A dull roar surrounded us. Not from the spell itself, but from the observers gathering on the streets and watching the events of three days ago. And the civilians were seeing a demon for the first time.

At least, they hadn't forgotten all their learning.

"It's a demon." Disbelief filled Brother Zi Rui's voice.

"Witness, my brother," I murmured. If I'd been by myself, sweat would have been pouring from me at this point.

His voice shook as he described the next actions. The demon tried to show one of the fugitive sorcerers how to use another human's skin. The horror on his face was shared by the other three. One of the other demons cast a spell that froze the four fugitives in place. And they were still alive when the demons peeled off the foolish humans' skins.

Off to my right, I heard Brother Zi Rui lose the contents of his stomach. He wasn't the only one from the choking noises on the other side of the decorative low wall. However, I gave my Light priest credit for quickly recovering. He continued his recitation.

Three of the demons left with their new skins carefully packed in their bags. One remained, no doubt waiting for someone. Bing to return from killing Wu, I supplied. It gave her twice the time to return from Wu's secret prison before it left, too.

We let the time lines slip through our fingers until Wu arrived later that night. He hadn't lied about discovering the four skinned bodies on the second floor or setting the fire. He disappeared down into the rubble filling the basement where the Light clergy couldn't see him.

We ended the rewind. I stretched my arms, back, and neck before I stood.

Brother Zi Rui stared at me. "H-how are there demons in Chengzhou without the alarms ringing?"

Unfortunately, the civilian observers heard him and took up the cry.

Maybe my suggestion to rewind the fire had started the very riot I had hoped to avoid.

CHAPTER 63

"Quiet!"

I jumped at Mei Wen's magically amplified command.

"How—" A woman in a simple, ragged skirt and tunic stepped away from the rest of the crowd. "How can there be a demon in Chengzhou?"

To Long Feather's dismay, I climbed up on the low wall and amplified my own voice. "Because when humanity is not unified, the damn demons can slip through the cracks."

"Are you saying this is our fault?" the woman demanded. Several civilians nodded and murmured in agreement with her outrage.

"Are you saying the people in this neighborhood haven't attacked Temple personnel when they've brought food, clothing, and medicines here?" I replied. Several faces glowed, heated by embarrassment. I hoped my sister justices noted which people exhibited guilty behavior through their warden's eyes. Once again, I was chagrinned I had no jurisdiction here.

"They come armed!" another man shouted.

"We are always armed," I said dryly. "But I would bring extra weapons too if some idiot throws bricks and rocks at my head."

"But the demon—" The first woman pointed towards where the second floor of the manse had been.

"They've been developing new tricks since the last set of invasions nearly a century ago," I said. "Haven't any of you listened to the Knowledge clergy so you know the signs to look for?"

"You're not Jing!" someone I couldn't see shouted.

"And we've been speaking for several moments before any of you noticed my accent." I lowered my hood so the civilians could get a good look at me.

Gasps ran through the crowd, along with murmurs of "The Red Justice". Well, if nothing else, the gossip vines in Chengzhou would help bait our trap for tomorrow night.

"I am Chief Justice Anthea DiBalance of Issura," I said. "I am here at the behest of our ruler, Queen Teodora, for two reasons. To represent our nation at the crowning of your new emperor and to teach your Temple of Knowledge some new techniques in fighting the demons. Techniques we in Issura were forced to develop when a demon army showed up on our southern border at this time a year ago."

The anger of crowd drained from them as fast as it had arisen.

"We have nothing to give to the Temples in trade for their goods," the woman said.

"I am Chief Justice Dai Lu of Chengzhou." Dai Lu had exited through the gate and now stood on the street below me with her warden. "Who in the Temples asked you to pay or barter for help? That is quite illegal."

The civilians murmured among themselves, but their spokeswoman looked thoroughly confused.

"That's the way it's been done since I was a child," she said.

"And I ask again, who did this?" Dai Lu said more gently. "I would like specific names, Mistress . . .?"

"Yan," she said.

From her voice and stature, she appeared to be in her prime, which would be twenty-five to forty-five winters, like me. If she were telling the truth, that would be about the time many people, including within the Temples, started to believe the demon wars were over.

"The clergy who come at dawn never give their names," Yan continued. "Nor do they have the gold or silver embroidery on their upper arms as you do. It's yellow or white."

Damn, just like the imposters who abducted Luc two winters ago. The renegades counted on fear to hide the small imperfections in their uniforms. But were these idiots actual renegades, or simply taking advantage of the whisper campaigns to steal goods and gold from Yan and her neighbors?

Balance wardens guided the other two justices to where Dai Lu stood. The Light clergy and Balance clerks joined us. Around us, more citizens and the personnel from the other ten Temples who had joined us in this little expedition, gathered to hear our discussion. Brother Zi Rui climbed up on the wall beside me. Whether to watch for trouble or pull me down for speaking out of turn, I couldn't tell.

"I am Justice Mei Wen. What do you mean they come at dawn?"

"First Morning. When the sun rises." Yan looked at us like we were idiots.

"Most of us are at prayer service at dawn, Mistress," Brother Zi Rui said.

"Not every Temple," I added. "We justices require extra help to prepare for the day. I can't see what I'm doing in a mirror, so I need my head of household to comb and braid my hair for me."

A smattering of laughter ran through the crowd. At least, they knew most clergy in Balance were blind.

"You are the first justices we've seen in this neighborhood," the man beside Yan said.

"I'm Justice Aihan," she said. "May I ask your name?"

"Jun De."

"Who is the member of Knowledge who teaches your children?" Aihan asked.

"There was a woman who wore yellow robes," Jun De said. "She comes to this neighborhood to teach writing and numbers. Our parents told us we didn't need to listen to her."

One of the Knowledge priestesses pushed through the crowd and stood in front of Jun De. "I still come. Last week, you were one of the men who threatened to rape and dismember me if I came back." She spread her arms. "Do you wish to act now?"

Mei Wen? I whispered silently.

Sister Kexin is assigned to this section of the city. She filed a formal complaint about the matter on Third Day last week, the justice answered. *The matter is under investigation.*

Like everywhere else these days, there were too any asinine squabbles and too few justices to deal with them.

However, the wardens present took the alleged death threat seriously. Their hands went to their weapons.

Instead of arguing with the Knowledge priestess, embarrassment seeped from Jun De. "Maybe some of us stepped out of line."

"By refusing to educate your children?" Dai Lu asked. "How would they know if a merchant cheated them if they cannot do sums? How would they read instructions from a healer to prevent or cure disease? How would they know what the laws are to avoid breaking them? Do they even know how to recognize a demon if it shapes itself into a chair?"

"But she said the demons are changing their ways!" Jun De jabbed an index finger in my direction. Such an action in Jing was incredibly rude and tantamount to calling me out. And after all the dangers over the last three months, my temper broke.

I jumped down from the low wall and strode over to him. "What have I done for you to challenge me?"

Jun De was about my height, with broad shoulders and heavily muscled arms. I had to give him credit. He didn't flinch away from me, or my eyes, like so many others who offered insult over the years.

"The Temples share information, especially when it comes to demons." I waved at our surroundings. "You had four in your neighborhood, and none of you noticed. You are damn lucky none of your precious children were eaten!"

"Maybe they're not as dangerous as you Temple people say," he sneered.

"Maybe you should see what I've seen," I said softly before I cupped his cheek. I showed him my memories. The demons who jumped me nearly two summers ago and wanted to eat me. The frozen corpse of Captain Arturo. The skinned body of Brother Jon of Light. The gift of a jewel to Shi Hua that in reality was a demon egg meant to kill her in order to hatch. The demon that chased Shi Hua and me into the tunnels under Orrin after our desperate rescue of Luc. The siege of Tandor and the aftermath of the battle. So much blood. So much death. And my own desperate belief that Balance Herself was correct—that the war would end in twenty-four years if we could beat back the demons.

"Stop it! Stop it! Stop it!" Jun De screamed as he dropped to his knees in the ash and soot that covered the street.

Yan stepped between me and Jun De, who was openly weeping and gagging. "What did you do to him?"

"All I did was show him my memories of demons in Issura," I said. "I didn't even get to the Battle of Naha in the Kingdom of Ryukyu before I arrived in Jing, or the ones we killed a few leagues outside of Chengzhou to protect your own Reverend Mother of Balance the day before the Spring Rituals."

The faces of most of the people, including the members of the Temples, faded to a yellowish-green. Maybe knowledge of the real enemy was sinking into their minds finally.

"All Sister Kexin wanted to do was make sure your children were armed with the knowledge to survive, just like her predecessors wanted to arm you," I said. The stares of everyone on the street would have bothered me years ago, but now, commanding their attention was a necessity. I tried to meet the gazes of everyone willing to look at me and my red eyes.

"Learning trades or swords mean nothing in the long game," I said. "And that's what the demons are playing. The long game. They live longer than us, decades if not centuries longer. We lose when information is not passed down from generation to generation. Knowledge is the ultimate weapon we have."

I shook my head. "But you're handing our unity as a race to them like a grandmother handing out sweets to their grandchildren. And you were willing to do awful things to Sister Kexin, who only wanted to teach you how to protect yourselves."

"I didn't know," Jun De cried. Yan backed away from him.

"But now you do." I held out my hand to him. "The question is what do you plan to do next."

He grasped my hand and stood on shaky legs.

I turned to Yan. "Please tell the justices what you know about the people who come to your neighborhood disguised as clergy." I looked over her head at the crowd of clergy. "Would someone from Child be willing to attend to Jun De? Truth can be as devastating as any illness or injury."

A Child priest with a gentle smile came forward, took Jun De's hand from mine, and led him away from the crowd. A woman and two young men trailed after them as did two of the Child wardens.

Yan invited the Jing justices to her shop for tea. They agreed. Warden Yichen shot me a shy smile and inclined his head before he and their justices' wardens escorted the women across the street.

Brother Zi Rui joined me and leaned close. "I've never met a justice whose tongue was as silvered as a clergy member from Thief." He smiled before he followed the trio of justices.

Fulu handed me several folded sheets of paper before she made a fist with one hand, placed her knuckles into the raised flat palm of her other hand, and bowed. Thank Balance, Shi Hua had taught me that it was a gesture of great respect. I stuck the papers beneath my left arm before I returned Fulu's salute. She grinned before she trotted after Brother Zi Rui.

Long Feather stepped next to me. "What did she give you?"

I unfolded the papers so he could see them. I couldn't see anything written or drawn on a piece of paper the way everyone else with regular eyesight could.

Long Feather grinned. "The portraits she made."

I nodded, refolded the papers and placed them in an inner pocket of my robes.

"I believe you promised me a meal at Lan's stall, Chief Justice," Long Feather murmured.

"I did, didn't I?" I smiled up at him. "Can you please not tell the rest of our party about this incident?"

"I won't if I am provided with a dozen extra spice cakes."

"Warden, are you attempting to blackmail me?"

"No, Chief Justice." His right eyebrow rose. "I am not attempting."

At that moment, both of our stomachs growled, a complaint that the light midday meal at the Temple of Balance was not enough with all the activity and spellcasting of this day. We laughed and turned toward the wardens guarding our horses.

And the day wasn't even over yet. But what I really wanted besides food was a bottle of Pana red after such a trying morning. After everyone comparing me to my grandmother Thalia, it was good to know I had a little bit of my grandfather Kam in me after all.

CHAPTER 64

Members of Conflict escorted Long Feather and me back through the inner walls of Chengzhou before they returned to assist their comrades in the neighborhood on the west side of the outermost ring of the city. From the cooler air caressing my skin, the sun was low in the sky. Was it that late already? I couldn't see the globe to tell for certain with all the buildings in the way, and bells hadn't rung the hour during our ride back to the Temple District.

I ordered more of the stirred noodles with chicken and vegetables while Long Feather asked for cloud swallows. Lan, the proprietress, remembered us from yesterday. The bowls she set on the counter were twice as full as yesterday.

When I protested, she looked around before she grinned. "I charge the nobles and sorcerers twice as much for half the food, but I serve the Twelve by treating the Temples fairly." She eyed my uniform. "And by the filth on your clothes, you have had a long, difficult day, Chief Justice."

"All right, but I am paying you for another two dozen spice cakes," I insisted.

"Of course, m'lady." She cackled at my poor bargaining, but I was so hungry, I didn't care. And Long Feather's order for spice cakes wiped out her remaining supply.

The merchants with stalls along the street were even busier than they had been yesterday morning. The tables were packed. Long Feather held our tray as we scanned the area for an empty bench.

"Chief Justice Anthea!" Arms waved above the heads of the other patrons. "Over here!" The body connected to the arms climbed on the bench and waved more.

"Novice Song of Conflict," Long Feather murmured.

We threaded our way through the crowd to Song's table. It was full of wide-eyed novices, all of them from different Temples. They rose as Song jumped down from the bench. He bowed and made the same gesture of respect Clerk Fulu had. The other novices followed suite. I returned their salute. Song ordered his friends to make space for me and Long Feather.

One of the novices, a girl from Death spoke in the Peaceful Sea trade tongue. "Welcome to Jing, Chief Justice and Warden."

"Both Long Feather and I know your language." I smiled. "And frankly, I need the practice. I've been told I have an atrocious accent."

The young people laughed as I had hoped, and they relaxed a little. They didn't even question us when Long Feather tasted my noodles before he set the bowl in front of me. Song made introductions before the novices peppered us with questions while we ate.

"Are you coming to the martial arts tournament tomorrow?" Le Le from Death asked.

"I don't know yet." I smiled graciously at the girl. "Between my duties at the Temples and the palace, I've been quite busy."

"Tomorrow is my day to enjoy the festivities," Long Feather said. "I'd be happy to attend." He eyed me. "And you need some time off as well, Chief Justice. Why don't you come with me?"

"We'll save you seats," Song exclaimed.

"It won't be as exciting as the year Novice Shi Hua won the top award by defeating Reverend Father Chen," Runchu, the novice from Light, said.

Song glared at his friend. "One does not speak of the dead thusly."

Runchu shrugged. "I wasn't speaking ill. I stated a fact. And I was at the tournament. You weren't even walking yet."

"What are your thoughts on how Novice Shi Hua won, Runchu?" I asked.

"Are you a novice master in Issura?" Enle from Father asked.

"No." I couldn't help grinning at the boy. "Asking questions and finding answers should apply to all Temples. And I've sparred with Lady Shi Hua."

The novices' eyes widened, and their jaws dropped.

"So have I," Long Feather volunteered. "She is a most capable opponent."

"Have either of you ever bested her?" Le Le asked.

"No," Long Feather answered. "But I've improved my skills in trying to."

"What about you, Chief Justice?" Runchu asked.

"Only once in hand-to-hand and twice with practice swords," I admitted. "As Long Feather said, the lady is a most capable opponent."

Su Yan from Vintner spoke for the first time. "It's hard to believe a novice like us is about to become empress."

"You never know what curves the road of life will bring you." Another idea occurred and I pulled Fulu's drawings from my inner robe pocket. "May I ask your assistance on something?"

"Of course, Chief Justice!" Song exclaimed.

"Look at these portraits and tell me if you recognize any of these people." I held out the papers to him. He examined each sketch before he passed it to the next novice.

"I don't." He looked up at me. "I'm sorry."

Su Yan looked up at me with a stricken expression. "Th-this one is my cousin Zhen Zhu. How do you know what she looks like?" Fat yellow tears rolled down her cheeks.

"The face was seen in a rewind I assisted the Chengzhou Temple of Balance with earlier today."

Le Le hugged her friend before she looked at me. "Zhen Zhu joined the School of Sorcery. Su Yan's family was told she had been executed."

I exchanged looks with Long Feather. It wasn't good if Emperor Chengwu and the Temple Leaders had lied about who from the School of Sorcery had been executed. But on the other hand, I understood why they didn't announce that some of the sorcerer apprentices had managed to evade both the Temples and the Imperial Guard.

"I'm so sorry for causing you more pain, Su Yan," I said in a low voice. "Your cousin is dead. This was a demon wearing her skin."

CHAPTER 65

Su Yan buried her face in Le Le's shoulder and quietly wept from the shuddering of her small shoulders."

"Can you tell us anything?" Song asked.

I shook my head. "The matter is being investigated by the Temple of Balance. It is not my jurisdiction, nor my place to say anymore." I cleared my throat. "I do know these likenesses will be circulated later today. Again, I apologize, Su Yan."

She lifted her head and wiped away the dampness from her cheeks and eyelids with her sleeves. "You did nothing wrong, Chief Justice. As my parents said, my cousin made her own choices, no matter how poor those choices they were."

"If it's any consolation, my mother made the same poor choices," I murmured. "The Twelve gave us free will, but sometimes, we do not use that gift wisely."

Runchu gasped. "Your own mother was executed?"

"Yes." These children didn't need to be burdened with my fury and guilt over Gerd's fall. "I'm sorry I dampened your holiday."

Song grasped my hand. "We grieve with you, Chief Justice." He turned to Su Yan. "And with you, my friend."

The other novices repeated his ritual words. A somber mood had fallen over the table. The festival cheer surrounding us seemed almost obscene.

Long Feather opened his sack of spice cakes and handed out the wrapped packages to the novices.

"We cannot accept these, Warden," Song protested, but his friends appeared pleased by the small gifts.

"It is my pleasure, Novice Song." Long Feather smiled. "It is the Spring Rituals after all."

"And remember to take comfort in the small joys of life once you're ordained," I said.

"Thank you for your gift, Warden," Runchu said. "Lan makes the best spice cakes in Jing."

"We know." Long Feather leaned closer to the novices. "Do not spread the word though, else she won't have any for you or me tomorrow."

His humor spread through the children and they giggled. Even Su Yan despite her tears.

I rose. "Thank you for sharing your table with us." I bowed and made the hand gesture of respect. Despite their initial surprise, the novices returned the gesture, once to me and again to Long Feather.

We collected our belongings and placed our used bowls, cups, and eating utensils on the tray. After dropping off our tray of dirty dishes with Lan's washer girl, Long Feather and I headed back toward the palace.

"It's nearly First Evening," he commented. "Do you think we'll get one undisturbed night for an adequate amount of sleep?"

"Shush." I shot him a nasty glare as we circled around the palace square. Civilians were cleaning the area for tonight's events while musicians were setting up in a corner. "Are you challenging Thief to give us a round of bad luck?"

"We both need slumber, m'lady," he replied. "A rested hunter is more likely to make a successful kill."

Unfortunately, bad luck landed as soon as we reached our suite. Our assigned steward Chin waited in front of the door with a vexed expression.

"Where have you been all afternoon?" he snapped.

"Assisting your own Temple of Balance with two capital cases," I replied mildly. "How may I help you?"

He forced himself to relax. "The crown prince asks that you join him and his cousins for dinner. I apologize for the late notice, but I didn't learn of the crown prince's desire until Third Afternoon." He eyed my filthy uniform. "However, I suggest you take a moment to change, Ambassador."

"That would be best," I murmured. "My warden and I will hurry." I resisted the urge to bite the man's head off. If I had been informed of the invitation before the last moment, I would have been prepared.

As soon as we entered our suite, Long Feather shut the door and whispered, "I'm sorry for tempting Thief, m'lady."

"Do not fret." I shook my head. "You're not the one who issued a late invitation."

I strode to the bedchamber I shared with Luc and stripped off my soiled uniform. I quickly wiped down my face and body with a damp cloth. There wasn't a damn thing I could do with my hair. However, I did rinse the cloth and run it over my braids to remove any ash before I tied them back with the thong once again. Instead of the one clean uniform I had left, I donned my formal chiton, stole, and sandals.

I entered the common room to find Long Feather in a clean uniform. A wry smile split his face.

"Do you think we can avail upon Balance to have them clean our uniforms again?"

I marched over to my equipment bag and pulled out my writing implements. I quickly stamped out our need and pressed my personal sigil and a touch of magic into the sealing wax. If someone other than a justice opened it, I would know.

Granted, this was a standard request, but with four demons loose in the city, I wanted to discover how closely I was being watched.

When we exited our suite, I handed the message to Chin. "My apologies for placing more responsibilities on your already full plate, but would you please have someone deliver this message to Reverend Mother Xiang at the Temple of Balance?"

"Of course, Lady Justice." He turned to one of the imperial guards outside our suite. "You heard the ambassador, and the chancellor explicitly stated any errands are not to be trusted to the palace staff."

The guard bowed and strode at a fast clip down the hallway.

The steward turned back to me. "We should have a response by the time you return from your appointment with the crown prince. This way, Lady Justice."

I recognized the hallways he led us through, but we bypassed the grand banquet room. The steward led us to another set of doors.

He opened them and announced my presence. The smaller dining room held a rectangular table. Po sat at one end on a throne-like chair. Three men sat on the left side. Duke Menchang and Duchess Jia sat on the right. There was an empty chair between Jia and another throne-like chair.

Po gestured at the empty chair. "Please join us, Chief Justice."

I crossed to my assigned seat and found I was placed between Shi Hua and Jia.

"Please forgive my tardiness, Your Majesties." I bowed to Po and then Shi Hua before I sat down. Huizhong, Mateqai, and Long Feather held up the walls.

"Why is she allowed to bring personal security, but your own family is not?" The man closest to Po sneered.

"Because my dear cousin Zixin, you are not at the top of the Assassin Guild's bounty list." Po turned to me. "So, Anthea, I hear we have four demons running around in my capital. Whatever shall we do about that?"

CHAPTER 66

While I didn't like being put on the spot, there was obviously something more going on, probably with his cousins' ambitions, and Po needed to get ahead of it. The irony that I had grown to trust the man about to become the Jing emperor more than I did the Issuran Temples was not lost on me.

"The more important thing is we found the demon eggs Wu hid within the city that the demons were searching for," I said.

Both Jia and the man sitting directly across from me gasped. Mengchang muttered something under his breath, most likely an obscenity of some sort. Zixin narrowed his eyes as he glared at me. The Bao cousin sitting across from Jia simply observed everyone else's reactions.

Po nodded. "So Reverend Mother Xiang reported. I'm glad they have been destroyed."

Relief swept through me. Both that she located the blasted eggs and that they had been disposed of.

"It is only a matter of time before the demons are located," I said.

"How did demons get into the city?" Zixin pounded on the table.

"The same way they entered Tandor and Orrin in Issura," I said mildly. "They walked through the gates."

"But the demon alarms—" the man across from me started.

"As I said, Xi, they now wear human skins to trick the alarms." Shi Hua's voice cut through the duke's tirade like hot steel through chilled butter. "In the past, they merely shifted their shapes, which is how the Temples learned to detect them."

That meant Guang was the quiet Bao cousin sitting between Xi and Zixin. The three Jing justices were correct in their assessment. Guang was the one Po and Shi Hua truly needed to beware of.

"When we rewound the time at the site of the fire on Chengzhou's western outer ring, the Balance clerks were able to sketch the faces of the people the demons were wearing and Wu's four apprentices that escaped the raids of the School of Sorcery. The damn demons did skin the apprentices and took their skins with them when they left. Even now, the clerks are making copies for the other Temples, the peacekeepers, and the army regulars." I picked up my goblet and signaled to Long Feather.

He stepped forward and tasted the contents. "Pana red, m'lady. The '66, I believe."

"Thank you, Warden." I raised my cup to Po. "It was an excellent year. I hope you saved the rest of the case for your coronation, Your Majesty." I sipped the wine. Yes, it was definitely the '66 vintage.

"And why are you interfering in our Temples' business, Issuran?" Zixin snapped.

"Temples rarely interfere with each other's workings, Your Grace," I said, keeping my tone neutral. "However, we do cooperate with each other and share information, regardless of our respective orders or nations. In this case, it was much easier to cast a time spell in unison. Jing is a large nation, so it's rare to have sufficient clergy for a major working like this. Your justices are spread thinly because there are simply not enough of us. But it's not just Jing. Issura and every other nation has the same issue. However, I offered my aid to the Jing home Temple of Balance. While the Reverend Mother led the search for the demon eggs, I assisted her second in researching the fire based on the testimony of Wu Sunshu. We confirmed the presence of four demons within Chengzhou."

Instead of acknowledging my words, Zixin turned to the crown prince. "You need to speak to Xiang, Po. To allow a foreigner be involved in our internal affairs—"

"The demons are everyone's affair," I snapped. "Not just Jing's."

"If you don't want our Temples to learn from other nations' clergy, what would you have me do? Order them not to talk to any other clergy?" Po asked. "That would leave Jing woefully behind on any developments in the fight against the demons."

"That very reason is exactly why the Temples are independent from each nation's rulers," Shi Hua added.

"Yet, this woman is here as an ambassador to Jing from Issura!"

"Queen Teodora asked High Brother Luc and me to escort the Jing crown prince home," I said. "And during the time Crown Prince Po was in Issura, he was both an ambassador and a member of the imperial family. Why cannot I be both a chief justice and an ambassador?"

"He was sent away for a reason," Zixin snarled.

"And why is that, Your Grace?" I said.

Instead of answering me, he turned back to Po. "Do you allow foreigners to fight your battles, cousin?"

"It seems your problem is with me, Duke Zixin," I said. "Not your liege."

"Yes, it is." He pointed his forefinger at me. "I resent you ruling Jing through a man who should never be on the Dragon Throne."

Enough was enough. Po may put up with his cousin's behavior, but it didn't mean I had to accept his insults and challenges.

I froze time in the dining room. Zixin's expression was comical with his eyes practically bulging, his mouth open, and his yellow spittle hanging in midair. I rubbed my temples as I considered my next step. Arguing with Zixin would not be productive. He needed a different type of persuasion.

I pushed back my chair and stood. As much as I would like to strip off Zixin's clothing and push him out the palace's main entrance naked, I doubted simple embarrassment would be effective, nor would the queen appreciate me sabotaging Issura's alliance with Jing through petty retaliation. If power was what Zixin was most concerned about, maybe I needed to give him a display like I did with the civilian Jun De this afternoon.

I drew my dagger as I circled the table to the duke in question. The primary blood vessels of his neck glowed orange under his skin. I wrapped my right arm around his neck and set the tip of my blade against one of them. Then I released the time freeze.

Everyone in the room jerked in surprise, except Duchess Jia, who screamed, and Long Feather, who pinched the bridge of his nose in exasperation. I suspected Captains Huizhong and Mateqai were suppressing their laughter like Shi Hua, but I didn't look behind me to confirm my speculation.

"I wouldn't move, Duke Zixin," I purred. "I'd hate to kill you accidentally as I explain certain facts to you." When he remained still and quiet, I began the lesson.

"You may look at being ruler of Jing as the ultimate in power. It is not. Real power comes with a great deal of responsibility and a very large target on your back, something with which I know of personally and your late emperor Chengwu discovered to his regret.

"I have no interest in ruling Jing through the crown prince or by any other means. Quite frankly, I detested Bao Quan Po when we first met. But facing demons together makes one change their mind. I respect him now. A weak man doesn't survive a skinwalker's torture. And a strong man does not start whisper campaigns to undermine his own sovereign when demons are trying to destroy everything you both love.

"However, I do regard the Lady Shi Hua as a sister of my blood. Should *anything* happen to her, her husband, or any of their future offspring, I will hunt down the person or entity at fault.

"Finally, in your own lust for power, you are not paying attention to reality. Someone is trying to kill everyone in the Bao line. Emperor Chengwu and his family last winter. Duke Lixin and Prince Pu on their way to Chengzhou for the Spring Rituals. And I've lost count of the attempts on Crown Prince Po since we first met.

"At first, I thought it was the demons seeking revenge for your ancestor, Empress De, routing them during the Battle of Jicheng. But now, I have to wonder if it's not a Bao trying to clear the way for their own personal gain. Especially since you seem unconcerned about your own safety except when you falsely believe I am receiving something you are not.

"There was a time near the beginning of the demon wars when civil unrest and corrupt rulers nearly caused the extermination of the human race. Maybe it's time that the Temples do resurrect their interference in politics by picking rulers and eliminating those who are problematic. What do you think we should do, Your Grace?"

Yellow beads of sweat gathered along his neck. His pulse beat rapidly. "Po?" he whispered.

"I'm not the one who offered insult to the chief justice. Nor will I inter-fere if she calls you out for a duel. I will tell you that I've seen her face armies of demons, and you as a mere human cannot beat her." The crown prince sipped his wine and winked at me. "You and Warden Long Feather are right, Anthea. I probably should have purchased another case of the '66 before we left Issura last winter."

The stink of Zixin's fear filled the room, but I didn't so much as twitch. I also realized why he wouldn't succeed in overthrowing Po. Ever. Zixin talked a good game, but at heart he was a coward. He was the type who'd believe the demons when they'd offer a false peace, and he'd die in denial as the demons ate his children before him.

"Is this why you invited us to dinner?" Xi asked. "To kill us?"

Po exhaled deeply as he set down his goblet. "Have I lifted a finger against you, cousin? I even called in favors from the Temples to make sure you arrived in Chengzhou alive after what happened to Lixin and Pu."

I felt Xi's eyes on me. "The Issuran—"

"She's Temple, and she doesn't answer to me." Po turned his attention to the other half of the table. "Is there anything I can help you with, Duchess Jia? Your husband always had a kind word and wise advice for me."

"Thank you, Your Majesty." Jia smiled, but the expression couldn't get past the tears she refused to shed. "As I told Lady Shi Hua, I do appreciate your assistance. She has already helped me make arrangements for a private tutor from Knowledge for my eldest, and Duke Mengchang has asked his second son to help me with managing the duchy until I learn how to be a proper regent for my children."

"If there's anything else you need, my dear cousin, all you have to do is ask. Lixin was very close to me when we were children." Po focused on Mengchang. "I am sorry to ask this of you because I know you'd rather be playing with your grandchildren, but I need you to stay in the capital for the foreseeable future. My brother relied heavily on you, and I've been gone long enough I must do the same."

Menchang inclined his head. "I'm here to serve, Your Majesty."

Po turned his attention back to the three cousins on his right. "Chief Justice Anthea and I have always been honest with each other from the first time we met though we often have differences of opinion. Duke Mengchang and Duchess Jia agreed to allow my wife to truthspell them prior to this dinner."

He raised his hand, but he glanced at me before he reached for his goblet instead of the beads on his left mustachio. Relief that he had listened to my advice gave me hope we would survive the week.

Beside I still had spice cakes in my suite I wanted to eat.

"Will you three be willing to undergo a truthspell?" Po smirked. The expression wasn't aimed at me for once, but it never boded well when he pulled it from his bag of tricks.

"H-here and now?" Zixin choked out.

"Of course," Shi Hua said. "You have nothing to hide, do you?"

"Of course, our cousin has nothing to hide, my love," Po said. "He couldn't even hide his atrocious manners towards another of my guests."

Zixin finally received what Po had been hinting at this entire time. His throat bobbed against my forearm.

"I beg forgiveness for insulting you, Chief Justice. It will not happen again."

I froze time in the room once again and removed my blade from the idiot's neck before I returned to my chair. When time resumed, Jia jumped with a cry dying stillborn in her throat.

"I-I need to get used to you doing that." She followed with a weak smile.

"My apologies for startling you, Your Grace," I said before I eyed Zixin. "I accept your apology, Duke Zixin. This time."

He rubbed the spot on his neck where the point of my dagger had rested. "Understood, Chief Justice."

"Are you ready, Duke Zixin?" Shi Hua asked.

"Let us get this matter out of the way," he grumbled.

Light magic tickled my skin as she laid the truthspell on him. She asked the basic questions about his recent actions, who he spoke to concerning Po, and what he said. There was nothing that was evidence he planned to overthrow Po, just general dissatisfaction with his lot in life. When she finished, she turned to her husband.

"Is there anything else you wish to ask, my love?"

Po settled back in his chair and regarded Zixin. "Why do you resent me succeeding my brother? Empress Yu did everything the nobles wanted, including marrying a noble, who betrayed Jing by demon dealing, and naming Chengwu as her successor, and look at the results of all that scheming."

"Your birth father was a peasant," Zixin spat.

"And how does that affect my ability to rule?"

Zixin breathed heavily as the pain from the truthspell rippled through his belly. "It-it doesn't. I just don't want peasants grasping beyond their place."

"What else don't you like about me?" Po asked mildly.

"You have Thief talent!" Zixin bellowed.

"Not enough to be claimed by the Temples."

"Everyone knows Light is the strongest power against the demons!"

Shi Hua and I exchanged looks before we both broke out laughing.

"What's so amusing?" Zixin demanded.

"I'm not the only one in the room with a trace of Thief talent," Po continued in a patient, almost fatherly, tone. "The only reason Anthea is in Balance is because she was born blind. She has a great deal of her birth father's talent, and he is the current Reverend Father of Conflict in Diné. Our own Reverend Father Biming of Thief admits she has the favor of the

Twelve, especially since she's survived more attempts on her life than I've had on mine."

He smiled at Shi Hua. "Even my own wife was cross-trained in Conflict, Thief, and Love as a novice though her primary talent is Light."

He turned back to Zixin. "Our incorrect assumptions are going to kill us faster than opening our minds to other possibilities. In fact, the Temple of Light in Issura has a dearth of Light clergy because they won't admit women who would have been assigned to our Temple of Light after testing."

Po took another sip of his wine before he continued. "And assuming Light is the only Temple that matters will also kill us. As a former Light priestess herself, my wife would be the first to tell you the only way to defeat the demons is by all Twelve Temples working together along with the nobles, the guilds, and the civilians."

"Are you stealing from my speech to the citizens of Orrin last year?" I asked.

Po shrugged. "It was a good speech, and my stealing your words doesn't make them any less true, Lady Justice."

I chuckled and shook my head as I reached for my goblet.

"However—" Po turned back to Zixin. "—this will be your only warning, cousin. I am not Chengwu. I won't keep you alive out of some sort of misplaced sentimentality. If you commit treason, you will be tried and executed."

Zixin bowed his head. "I understand, Your Majesty." He resorted to the proper address for an emperor or empress. Maybe the Twelve granted him a clue after all.

"For your sake, and that of your immediate family, I surely hope so." Po nodded to Shi Hua, and she dissolved the truthspell.

"Guang—" Po began.

The duke jumped to his feet. His chair crashed against the wall. He shoved Ix over.

Shi Hua dove under the table.

Jia screamed. Again.

Mateqai met Guang's headlong rush.

And I froze the room for the third time in the space of a candlemark.

CHAPTER 67

I took a long drink of wine. At the rate things were going during this alleged dinner, I wasn't going to have the chance to finish this excellent vintage.

I stood and carefully sliced time around Mateqai to excise him from my spell. He stumbled and blinked before he realized Duke Guang wasn't moving. Mateqai turned toward me and chuckled.

"I was wondering why you were invited to what was supposed to be a senior royal family dinner." He eyed the frozen Guang. "Let me guess. He's the one who attacked Yar and Antiope?"

"I suspect he's more likely the orchestrator." I sighed. "Reverend Mother Xiang probably learned through her second, Chief Justice Dai Lu, of my speculation that we had a third party involved considering Wu's students were dead before he came back to Chengzhou, and Jia Huo was more concerned with covering his tracks for the two murders he committed."

"That would explain your last-minute invitation." Mateqai frowned. "Why remove me from your spell instead of Long Feather?"

"Take a good look at Guang's dagger."

Mateqai bent closer and muttered, "Donkey balls." He sniffed and sighed. "What's the renegades' preference for southern blue?"

I shrugged. "I don't know if Guang is an actual renegade, or he simply is willing to kill his family to gain the Dragon Throne. As for southern blue, it works quicker than the deadly mushroom concoction they slipped into the Healers Guild oil supply back in Orrin the winter before last, and it's easily obtainable. But the other reason I pulled you out of the freeze spell is we need someone who's a member of Jing security to apprehend the little donkey ass. And I didn't know how Huizhong would react because I've never pulled him out of a time freeze."

Mateqai shook his head before he took a piece of silk from one of his uniform's pockets. He carefully removed Guang's dagger with the silk, wrapped the blade, and set it on the table. With my assistance, he lowered Guang to the wood parquet floor and manacled the renegade duke's wrists behind his back. Mateqai rested a knee between Guang's shoulder blades.

"Ready, Chief Justice."

I unfroze time in the dining room.

Jia finished her scream.

Guang cursed.

Zixin, Po, and Mengchang leapt to their feet.

Long Feather rushed over to help Mateqai.

Huizhong bellowed for the Imperial Guard.

I crossed back to my chair and downed the rest of my wine before I crouched to look at Shi Hua. "Are you all right, m'lady?"

Her eyes pierced me. "Next time, give a woman some warning before you freeze the room."

The attempted stabbing of the captain of the empress's guard was sufficient to get a senior justice to the palace in record time despite the revelers in the streets and the imperial square. I was a little surprised Chief Justice Dai Lu was the representative of Balance to attend to the matter.

She pulled me aside first, or rather her warden did, and she grinned. "Causing more trouble, Anthea?"

I grinned back at her teasing. "This wasn't my fault. The crown prince and Lady Shi Hua are responsible for starting this round of madness."

Dai Lu lowered her voice. "But what are your suspicions?"

"What I know is Duke Guang knocked over Duke Ix and tried to stab Captain Mateqai with a blade coated in southern blue. I managed to time freeze the room before he succeeded." I exhaled as much exhaustion as I could. "Ask Guang about the attack on Wardens Yar and Antiope."

"Your suspected third party?"

"Possibly." I shrugged. "He feared being truthspelled for a reason. But I don't have jurisdiction."

"He's lucky in that regard."

"You're damn right," I snarled.

"Thank you, sister," Dai Lu murmured. "It gives me a starting place for his interrogation. I will request the Reverend Mother to provide you with a report as well as the emperor. And please asks your warden to be available for a trial as a witness."

Concern flared. "Not tomorrow, I hope."

"No." A wry smile brightened her face. "Trapping the demons are the

Temples' priority until the end of the Spring Rituals. Duke Guang can rot in the gaol for a day."

"As the bait for tomorrow night, I hope you succeed in catching or killing the demons before they kill me."

After Dai Lu, the Light priestess accompanying her, and their wardens took statements and left with a chained Guang in tow, I begged the imperial couple to excuse me. I probably should have stayed and eaten something. Despite our early dinner, both mine and Long Feather's stomachs were grumbling by the time we reached our suite.

Yar leapt up from his chair in the common room, his hand on his sword, but he relaxed when he saw it was me and Long Feather. Luc looked at me in surprise. Or rather looked at the chiton and stole I wore.

"Was there someplace I was supposed to be tonight?" he asked.

I shook my head. "Po and Shi Hua needed my help rooting out a problem, so they sent me a last-minute invitation to dinner with the Bao family."

I joined him on the couch near the fireplace, enjoying the warmth. I removed my sandals and curled against him as I told him and Yar of our day's adventures since Jia Huo's trial this morning.

"Has Jonata returned?" I asked.

"She's already asleep. A couple of wardens from Balance took her with them to Love. Long Feather, I warded the wardens' bathing room for the evening so I wouldn't disturb her later. Like I told Yar, please use the water closet in our bathing room. Yar placed your grooming kit in there for the evening."

Long Feather nodded. "I'll prepare for sleep also. It's been a long day."

"I heard your stomach," I said. "Eat a couple of spice cakes first, and pass them around."

As he grabbed his canvas bag and doled out the treats, I asked Luc, "What were you doing all day?"

"Taking in some of the sights. Buying a few trinkets for my mother, sisters, and the rest of Light at home." He accepted his wrapped cakes from Long Feather. "Reverend Father Jin invited us to dine with him. That's when I heard his second's version of your rewind."

"Was he as disturbed as the civilians?" I asked around a mouthful of spice cake and fruit.

Luc shook his head. "They all knew the demons wanted to get their claws on the remaining eggs. And frankly, it sounds like the civilians needed to be disturbed. You and I have had our share of arguments with Magistrate DiCook and other civilians back in Orrin, but I don't recall anyone threatening a clergy member with rape and dismemberment for doing their blasted job."

"I believe the chief justice's sharing of her memories has dissuaded this Jun De from intimidating anyone else from the Temples." Long Feather licked the crumbs from his fingers, folded the papers that had wrapped his cakes, and rose to his feet. "I'll be quick in your bathing room, Chief Justice."

Yar stood and stretched. "Unless you need something else, High Brother, I will retire for the night as well."

"Aren't you and Long Feather going to shove the armoire in front of the door again?" I teased.

The huge man smiled. "As soon as he finishes his nightly routine."

Once the wardens had finished their last needs of the night and moved the armoire, Luc and I retired to our bedchamber. There was a sealed message lying on my side of the bed. I ran my fingers over the wax. The symbol of Knowledge had been imprinted.

"When did this come?" I asked.

"Shortly before Yar and I left for Light," Luc said. "Maybe half a candle-mark after First Evening."

"We must have just missed you." I broke the seal and ran my fingers over the neatly stamped raised codes. Thank the Twelve, all of Balance used the same system regardless of our spoken or written languages.

"The Reverend Mother of Knowledge has invited us both to break our fast with her at a candlemark past Third Morning." I smiled. "She wishes to discuss my teaching lightning, and she extends her gratitude for backing Sister Kexin against the civilians who had threatened her."

"Hopefully, the palace with let us sleep in a bit." Luc swung on his crutches into the bathing room and closed the door.

Exhaustion dragged on my limbs and eyelids. Perhaps I should make time tomorrow afternoon for a nap. I needed to be alert and rested like any good rodent waiting for the snake to bite during the final rituals tomorrow night.

CHAPTER 68

To my surprise, two of the Temple of Balance's tailors showed up at our suite's door at Second Morning with trunks and a warden escort. They quickly altered new uniforms for Jonata, Long Feather, and me. I was a little surprised they had additional clothing that fitted Long Feather's tall, lanky form.

The elder of the tailors laughed when I said as much. "We have more than a few wardens whose parentage can be traced to the Xiongnu Confederation, the Rus, or the Skandza, all of who are taller than the average Jing. Plus, Warden Yichen gave us accurate physical descriptions of you and your two wardens."

"Your laundry will be returned tomorrow morning by Second Afternoon." The younger tailor bowed.

When I offered a donation for the new clothing and the laundering of our dirty uniforms for the second time in three days, they refused. "You served our Temple yesterday," the elder tailor said. "You will be teaching the justices after the Spring Rituals. And the Reverend Mother said if you argue with us, she will have you lashed for insubordination."

My wardens found the last terribly amusing though they managed to hold in their laughter until the Jing tailors and their escort left.

I tilted my head as I regarded Luc. "Have you and Yar taken advantage of Light's laundry and tailor?"

Luc groaned before he handed out silver coins to each of the wardens.

"We told you, High Brother," Jonata said, followed by a cheeky grin. "She'd noticed your new robes only if a demon were dressed in them."

"That's not fair betting on me like that," I protested. "I cannot see like you can."

"But you can smell, Chief Justice," Yar said. "Can't you?"

"I think the trip through the Chengzhou sewer destroyed whatever sense of smell she had," Luc teased. "Bathing was an interesting experience yesterday."

"Why didn't you say something?" I snapped. "I would have moved that uniform."

"So, your bedchamber or the common room absorbed the odors?" Yar stared at me with a perturbed expression.

"I wouldn't talk if I were you, Yar," Jonata said. "I've shared water closets and chamber pots with you for nearly three months."

I sucked in a deep breath to reprimand the wardens, and just as quickly, I released it at the realization of what was really happening. Apparently, I wasn't the only one worried about the trap we were setting for the demons at tonight's events. If teasing each other released their tensions, so be it.

And if I thought it would make a difference, I would have begged Balance for our wardens' lives.

Duke Mengchang found out Long Feather and I had walked back to the Temple of Balance yesterday morning. Our steward Chin and a squad of imperial guards surrounded the entire Issuran party from the instant we stepped out of our suite to the main palace entrance where the duke delivered a velvet lecture wrapped around steel. With four demons on the loose, Luc, our wardens, and I were not to go anywhere in Chengzhou without a full escort according to the crown prince's strict orders. If we did, it would be the army regulars who would be punished.

Damn, Po knew how to emotionally manipulate me. I relented on the damn palanquins, not just to spare the poor soldiers, but since Shi Hua and False Darys were accompanying us. The soon-to-be empress insisted I ride with her and Luc ride with Darys.

Once we were on our way, Shi Hua grasped my hand. *Reverend Mother Xiang reported the results of Duke Guang's initial interrogation. Your copy will be waiting for you when we return. His second son Aiguo is the one who attacked Yar and Antiope. He has been arrested and questioned.*

Did Guang order the attack? I asked.

Unfortunately. Shi Hua sighed and rubbed her abdomen. *Aiguo thought he entered mine and Po's bedchamber for that day. He had seduced a palace maid. She told him we were switching rooms every night, and we would be in the former Skoloti suite that afternoon.*

But you've been in the family section, I said with a scowl.

Obviously, she lied to him, but he claimed to have paid her in gold for the information.

Please tell me she's been arrested and questioned, too, I begged.

She's disappeared. A slight smile curved Shi Hua's mouth. *According to both Aiguo and the head of housekeeping, her appearance didn't match any of the skins we know the demons harvested.*

I frowned. *When was she hired at the palace?*

Right after the demons attacked the city last winter. Shi Hua grinned. *Want to hear something even more odd?*

I nodded.

Reverend Mother Xiang found a note with the eggs. It said, "Aiguo did not find these. Please destroy them." Signed "A Friend".

"He was looking for them?" I blurted aloud.

According to the Reverend Mother Xiang, Guang was told by an unknown person there was a treasure hidden within the walls of the imperial palace. She shrugged. *He sent Aiguo to find the so-called treasure and to kill us.*

I chewed on my lower lip. *None of that makes sense.*

I know. She cocked her head. *Unless the skinwalkers were grooming a new contact at the palace after they lost Wu.*

But who's the mystery maid? I considered the situation. *It almost sounds like she set up Aiguo to be caught by the wardens.*

That was Po and Biming's thoughts as well. Shi Hua smiled. *But they are more concerned about this unknown person who gave Guang the information. How could they know the eggs were there and where Jia Huo had hidden them after he took them?*

The Reverend Mother couldn't get a description or a name of this person from Guang? I asked.

There's a memory block on him. She's working on dissolving it without destroying Guang's sanity in the process.

It wasn't that Xiang cared about Guang's mind. But she wasn't going to execute someone if there was a chance that the person had been manipulated through magic into performing an illegal act.

I scrubbed my hands down my face. *I don't like leaving you and Po alone here.*

"Such is the burden of duty." Shi Hua rubbed her abdomen again.

"Is something wrong?"

She shook her head. "I assure you it's only morning sickness, sister. We need to spend a few hours together before you leave. I am going to miss you."

Before I could answer, the palanquin stopped its peculiar movement, and we were lowered to the ground.

"We've arrived at the Temple of Knowledge, Your Majesty, Chief Justice," Mateqai announced as he pulled back the curtain.

I exited first. Mateqai assisted Shi Hua to her feet.

The Knowledge wardens appeared more concerned about Luc climbing the steps to the entrance than their future empress's well-being. However, Luc had become quite adept at getting around with his crutches. Even to the point of climbing the rigging on the *Mars Tranquilus*, much to Captain Titus's horror. Once the Jing wardens were assured, Luc didn't need assistance, they nodded at us and opened the doors to the Temple.

In the foyer, Sister Kexin smiled broadly at us. "Welcome, welcome. It is so good to meet you, Lady Shi Hua." The priestess bowed deeply. "And you, High Brother Luc." She performed another deep bow. Instead of the traditional greeting, Kexin performed the fist-to-palm gesture to me. "And my profound thanks to you, Chief Justice, for settling my duty to teach children on the western outer ring."

"It's not settled yet, Sister," I murmured. "The real test is when you go back after the Spring Rituals."

"For once, I'm not fearing for mine or the children's safety. Whatever you showed Jun De plus seeing demons so close to their homes has convinced Yan and the other neighborhood leaders to take the threat to their well-being seriously."

Kexin held up her hand. "That does not mean I want to see what you've been through." She pulled up the right sleeve of her robes. The scar of a long, deep laceration showed pale green against her yellow-orange skin. "I've been close enough to a demon to regard them as life-threatening."

"Last winter's battle?" I asked.

"Yes." She pulled down her sleeve. "I was more fortunate than many of our sisters and brothers."

"We grieve with you." I bowed to her.

I recognized her effort to shove away the dark memories. It explained her anger and passion when confronting the civilians in her assigned district for teaching.

"Come, come." Kexin gestured for us to follow her. "It's the Spring Rituals. Time to enjoy the warmth and companionship after a long, hard winter." She set off at a brisk clip down the right hallway and took the second side corridor to the left where most home Temples had their classrooms for the novices.

We followed her into one of the larger rooms. The tables and stools had been rearranged into a large rectangle to accommodate all the senior Knowledge clergy and our party from the palace. Platters and large bowls lined the center of the tables. My stomach rumbled loudly as Reverend Mother Xiao Mei approached us.

"Welcome, my guests." She bowed. "You have my gratitude, Chief Justice. You made inroads in the western, outer section of Chengzhou we haven't been able to for decades."

"I'm only sorry it took my memories of past experiences with demons rather than logic to convince anyone," I said.

The Reverend Mother chuckled. "Fortunately, neither the civilians nor the demons expect mere scholars to know how to fight, much less actually combat them. But Sister Kexin smacking around a group of civilians wouldn't convince them to educate their children."

"I am more concerned the civilians threatened her life, Reverend Mother," Shi Hua interjected. "My duties have meant I've been out of the country for the last eight years. Does this type of behavior happen in Jing often?"

"More than we want to admit, Your Majesty," she conceded. "It took Child, Vintner, and Death withdrawing their support in Xie Han Province to convince Duke Guang to intervene with his farmers." She smirked. "However, new leadership in Xie Han may make a difference."

"The crown prince plans to meet with each of the Temple leaders, starting the next First Day," Shi Hua said. "If you would, please have a list of concerns and needs to present to him."

Reverend Mother Xiao Mei inclined her head. "Such assistance is much appreciated, Your Majesty."

The head of household for Knowledge rang a small copper bell. "Please find your seats. You can continue your conversations, but the food is growing cold."

I was a bit surprised to find they laid places on the table for Captain Mateqai and the visiting wardens. Reverend Mother Xiao Mei smiled at our expressions.

"If your people are going to taste your food anyway, Chief Justice, they might as well be comfortable while doing so."

Once the dishes had circled the tables and plates were full, the conversation quickly turned to how I discovered my new talent and learned to harness it. Most of the clergy were concerned about the safety of the students since we were dealing with lightning.

"Since we cannot let the chief justice leave the Orrin gates without wardens, we learned to stay as far away from her as possible while she practiced," Jonata volunteered.

"And don't stand under any trees," Long Feather added.

"It doesn't help that you are as tall as one," I teased.

The Knowledge clergy laughed at my jest.

"And Warden Long Feather was lucky all he lost was his boots in that incident," Luc said.

His comment made the Knowledge clergy laugh even harder.

"It sounds as if trees would make good practice targets," one of the high brothers said. "There are the woods south of the city scheduled to be destroyed to make way for the fifth wall. Father and the Woodcutters Guild has already harvested the trees healthy enough for their use. If Chief Justice Anthea takes students out there to practice, the civilians can collect precut wood for drying for next winter's fuel."

"As long as you realize this wood is exploded, not cut," Yar said dryly.

A high sister sitting across from him said, "It wouldn't be any different than a tree struck by natural lightning or one blown down in a storm, Warden. And the civilians' work would be cut in half."

Another round of laughter followed the high sister's atrocious pun.

"Reverend Mother, would it be acceptable to integrate the Temples' lessons with those of the philosophy schools?" I asked.

She smiled. "Master Ma approached me about doing so. I told him he needed to ask you. If you're willing to teach the schools as well as the Temples, I have no objection."

"There will be no issues with any rivalry?" Luc asked.

"Last winter's attack shook most of the school's headmasters out of their singular views of the World." Reverend Mother Xiao Mei leaned her elbows on the table and folded her fingers over her bowl. "At Lady Shi Hua's suggestion, Reverend Mother Xiang called all of the headmasters together to watch the destruction of the demon eggs. It was a hard lesson that our greatest enemy is not the demons, but a human who believes the laws don't apply to them."

CHAPTER 69

◇

Reverend Mother Xiao Mei assured us she would extend invitations to all the Temples and schools of philosophy with a limit of five students per Temple and school. As I told her, once one of the Jing students learned the basics, they could teach additional students.

After the lesson plans and places were settled, we returned to the palace. Shi Hua asked me to accompany her to her suite in her preparations for the coronation.

"I hope you're not angry with me for talking to Reverend Mother Xiao Mei before you did," Shi Hua said in Issuran as we headed toward the imperial family's wing of the palace.

"By the Twelve, no!" I exclaimed. "Why would you think that?"

"Because you get bent out of shape when you're not in total control," Mateqai said behind us.

Jonata snickered.

I was rather glad I ordered Long Feather to get some extra rest if he wasn't going to take advantage of his day to enjoy the afternoon's festivities. I didn't need his jests on top of everything else. Caterpillars already crawled through the excellent meal I'd consumed at Knowledge. It wasn't like demons or their human allies to refrain from sowing discord to distract us from their real objective, which only made the proverbial caterpillars crawl faster in my gut.

Which begged the question of whether we were wrong about their real objective in Chengzhou.

Shi Hua relaxed when I didn't lose my temper at Mateqai or Jonata. "I'm still trying to get used to this new role."

"You're doing fine. Unless it was your idea to use me to flush out which cousin was conspiring against your husband," I said. "Then I might have a problem."

She emitted a weak, deprecating chuckle. "That was all on the emperor. He says you are better than any hunting dog."

Both of our guards laughed outright.

"Pardon me?" I stopped and glared at her.

Shi Hua's bright, mischievous grin was back. "He's right, and you know it." She sobered as we continued down the hallway. "I'm going to miss all of you. And I'm terribly sorry I haven't spent more time with you since we arrived in Chengzhou."

"There's nothing to apologize for, my sister." I sighed. "We both knew what you were getting into. As I said before, the emperor needs someone he knows and trusts. I didn't realize how true my words were until last night."

"Reality has struck Duchess Jia, too," Shi Hua murmured. "I liked Lixin. I feared she'd fall apart with his death, but she has strength I never suspected."

"She fears for her children's lives," I said. "That was obvious last night. Just as it is obvious in you now."

"The only redeeming thing about my choices is Chao won't be in the middle of the blasted political cow cakes of Jing," she muttered.

"You know Jeremy will do right by your son."

"Until Chao is old enough to start training at Light." She looked up at me. "He'll be ordained before the thousand years are finished. Do you really believe we humans will win this stupid war?"

"I do." I glanced at her pensive face. "And no, I'm not saying what you want to hear. I truly believe we will outlast the demons and seal them back on their plane of existence. I just wish I could guarantee our friends and family will be alive at the end of the war."

Except I didn't have a Twelve-blessed clue of how we would accomplish such a feat.

And if I was wrong . . .

Well, then, I would know I hadn't truly met Balance or Death a month ago.

I didn't have to do anything for Shi Hua regarding her preparations for the coronation. The ladies of the empress's personal staff had everything under control. I was merely there to keep her calm as she faced the biggest challenge of her short existence. Yin Li was the primary conductor of bathing and dressing the new empress.

And when they were done, Shi Hua looked truly regal. Definitely not the barely dressed courtesan she'd portrayed or the roof-running scamp she had been when I first met her as a Light priestess.

Reverend Father Jin visited to give her the traditional blessing of Light to new rulers. He was a little surprised to see me there since only the maids and the empress's closest female family members were permitted to be with Shi Hua prior to the coronation. Or maybe he hadn't really believed we had a close relationship.

Afterward he finished the blessing, he asked to speak with me. We stepped out into the hall and away from the Imperial guards. Both Long Feather and the Reverend Father's warden stayed back to allow us the illusion of privacy.

"How is she truly doing, Anthea?"

"Reverend Father—"

"Please address me by my given name." His smile was bittersweet.

"Very well—" I hesitated because never had someone higher ranked in the Temples been this magnanimous. "—Jin. She would be this nervous even without my performance later."

He nodded, but he was lost in the past, as if trying to reconcile something. "I first saw her in sword practice a decade ago. Even though she was so much smaller than her peers, she had a fire in her. She never gave up. When I asked her novice instructor about her progress, Brother Lin said she was meant for more than a life in a quiet village temple. I agreed, but this—this was even beyond my imagination."

"I think the crown prince saw her potential long before any of us did," I murmured. "All I know is she has been the closest friend I've ever had. Beyond rank or affiliation or blood."

"Do they actually love each other?" Jin whispered.

"It depends on your definition." I smiled. "Do they have mutual respect and affection? Thankfully more than any other political marriage I've witnessed. But they are not in love. They both are too aware of what Jing needs. She will guard him with her last breath, but she needs the rest of you to watch her back."

He nodded again. "Thank you, Anthea. I will speak to you after the coronation."

"You're welcome, Jin."

As I watched him walk away, I wondered if he regretted training Shi Hua to be a bodyguard for the imperial family. She might have had a more fulfilling life as the local Light priestess in some obscure village after all.

I returned to our new suite to bathe and change my own clothes. As warm as the morning had been, donning my chiton and sandals was a relief. However, not having my sword strapped to my back made me supremely uncomfortable. If the demons struck during the coronation—

"You will freeze time in the courtyard and square long enough for reinforcements to arrive," Luc said as he entered our bedchamber.

I sighed "Was I talking to myself again?"

He chuckled and swung over to kiss my forehead chastely. "More like thinking a little too loudly. Do you want me to braid your hair?"

"No, thank you." I set aside the towel I used to dry my tresses. "I asked Jonata to wrap it into a Diné warrior's knot and assist me with my cosmetics."

"Let me get undressed, and help me into the pool before you call her in here." He winked.

"Are you trying to tempt me as I'm preparing for a major event?" I teased.

"It is the Spring Rituals after all," he mocked. "We supposed to be having fun."

If we survived long enough to board the *Mars Tranquilus* and head for home, I would talk Captain Titus into staying in the Kingdom of O'ahu an extra week. Surely, we deserved a little bit of peace and joy after the last two years of chaos.

CHAPTER 70

The stands were set up in the palace square as they had been the morning of the first Spring Ritual. Once again, Luc and I sat with False Darys in the diplomatic section. I was a little surprised to see Lady Caihong with Duchess Jia as they and the two guards they were permitted climbed the steps to our row.

"May we sit with you, Chief Justice?" Jia murmured.

"Of course, Your Grace." I nudged Luc to scoot over. He and Darys obliged me, and we made enough room for the two nobles. The wardens did the same behind us for the two guards.

"Thank you," Jia whispered. "I wasn't subjecting the poor woman to our so-called people."

"I truly wish things had worked out differently for both of you." Luc listened through me since there was enough noise to cover our conversation.

"As do I." She forced a smile she obviously didn't feel. "Have you met Chancellor Mengchang's son Shoi-Ming?"

"I haven't had the pleasure. Is he the one assisting you in your province?"

She nodded. "I shall introduce you before the banquet. If you do not mind, I would like your opinion of him."

I glanced around her at Caihong. The noblewoman stared at her clasped hands resting on her lap, nothing like the convivial person she had been two mornings ago.

"A possible match?"

"She has . . . confided certain things to me. I don't wish to subject her to anymore pain. She's had enough. After hearing your defense of the empress and then Cuihong's opinion of your treatment of her cousin, I prayed you would assist her"

I bowed my head. "I would be delighted to help her find peace and happiness." The feeling of Luc's approval spread through me.

If Jia was asking for my assistance, it meant things were far worse with Cuihong's husband than Jia Huo had said during his trial. And her cousin would pay for his misguided help with his head. There was ancient saying about bad deeds being punished even though the person's intentions were good. In this case, it showed how deep the whisper campaign against the Jing Temples had burrowed into the citizen's psyches if Jia Huo thought murder was an appropriate action instead of reporting the abuse Cuihong suffered at her husband's hands.

The first beat of the drummers startled me out of my musings. The huge drums lined the sides of the palace grounds. The skins were a single piece of leather. For something of that size, they had to be harvested from the huge beasts of the southern Old Continent or the Cradle. Each drummer held two sticks that were easily as big around as my forearm. The tops of the sicks were round and covered in leather as well.

I could see the drummers and their instruments because instead of viewing stands at the north end of the square, a dais raised to the level of the low wall sat between the palace and the square so everyone had a good view of the coronation.

Frankly, I didn't like the openness around the dais, And I found myself scanning the nearby roofs. Humans were watching the proceedings, but at this distance and angle, I couldn't make out any insignia.

I touched Luc's arm. *Can you make out the people on top of the surrounding buildings?*

Wardens and mainly Conflict clergy, though there's a few from Thief and Light scattered among them, he answered silently. *Don't worry. It's part of what I was doing yesterday.*

I kept my attention on the procession of the Temple leaders up to the dais. *Giving advice on roof climbing?*

I was trying to keep you from fretting, he grumbled. *Reverend Father Feng joined us for dinner and asked me about Reverend Father Kilchii's tactics during the Siege of Tandor and the evacuation.*

Why? I was honestly puzzled.

While Reverend Father Chen was good at running a Temple, his thinking could be . . . limited. Luc's amusement tickled my mind. *It's how Shi Hua defeated him in the hand-to-hand combat during the Spring Rituals from eight years ago.*

I choked back a laugh. Ten of the Temple leaders had taken their place on the dais. The priests of Father surrounded Po and matched his stately, graceful walk. With so many people present, I couldn't pick out his emotions, but his skin had a greenish cast. So, there was more than torture at the hands of skinwalkers that could unsettle the former ambassador.

I couldn't blame him though. Not when the demons would most likely strike here or at the final holiday ceremony later tonight.

As Po and Reverend Father Da of Father took their places, the priestesses of Mother entered the square, surrounding Shi Hua. Their racks of gold bells jingled merrily in counterpoint to the massive drums. The percussion built into a crescendo as Reverend Mother Bai of Mother guided Shi Hua to her place on the dais. The drums and bells abruptly silenced the instant they both turned to face the public.

"I present Bao Quan Po, son of Empress Bao Yu and brother of Emperor Chengwu as the heir to the Dragon Throne." Magic amplified Reverend Father Da's voice so there was no mistaking his words.

"I present Bao Shi Hua, wife of Bao Quan Po, a former priestess of Light, who shall share the Dragon Throne with her husband," Reverend Mother Bai announced.

A murmur ran through the crowd. I'd have been worried if I didn't already know Po planned to make Shi Hua his joint ruler. Doing so would cut down any arguments of who would succeed him, who would be regent of their first child, and on any unknown children trying to lay claim as Po's true heir.

Though he swore on the Twelve he'd been careful in all his amorous adventures prior to his and Shi Hua's marriage. Unfortunately, all the care in the World didn't stop humans from lying.

Or accidental pregnancies from happening.

Reverend Father Jin stepped forward to replace the Temple leaders of Mother and Father. Po and Shi Hua turned to face him, and they knelt on the red silk pillows at his feet.

"Both Bao Quan Po and Bao Shi Hua have been truthspelled." Jin's voice rang out. "Their intentions are to rule Jing wisely and well for the benefit of all living things the Twelve have brought into being. Are there any objections from the Twelve?"

One by one each of the eleven Temple leaders stated there were no objections to the Baos from taking their thrones.

"May the Twelve watch over Bao Quan Po and Bao Shi Hua," Reverend Father Jin continued. "May They guide those who occupy the Dragon Throne. And may They protect the people and land of Jing."

"So be it," the spectators said in unison.

Luc covered my hand with his own. Only then did I realize I held my fingers in the childish gesture for good luck. I sent my own silent prayer to the Twelve they would protect the couple and their unborn child.

Reverend Father Jin held out his hands to them. Po and Shi Hua joined hands before they turned to the crowd.

"We present the new emperor and empress of Jing!" Reverend Father Jin called out "Long live Emperor Bao Quan Po and Empress Bao Shi Hua, the rulers of the Jing Empire!"

A cheer went up from the crowd. Ushers entered the stands to escort each row of spectators to the new imperial couple. Anxiety raced along my nerves as a line of high-ranked nobles formed a single line to approach Po and Shi Hua to give them their congratulations and good wishes. I scanned them, looking for the telltale green-gray of a skinwalker or the black of a demon.

It's done, Anthea, Luc whispered in my mind. *We did what the queen asked of us. Po is home, alive, and officially the Jing emperor.*

Not yet, I answered. *He and Shi Hua are not safe until we find the four demons within the city.*

CHAPTER 71

❖

The rest of the afternoon was fairly quiet. Well, quiet for the last day of the Spring Rituals. The Imperial Guard were the only ones not having any obvious fun. Clergy and wardens in civilian clothing wandered through the crowd, pretending to enjoy themselves but keeping eyes and ears on the crowds for any discrepancy.

The formal banquet for nobles and diplomats was held on the palace grounds. While the bird's nest soup may have been considered a great delicacy, I gave mine to Long Feather. I just couldn't eat it after learning the truth about Jia Huo. I'd never felt sympathy for a murderer before, and the young lord's mistakes unnerved and saddened me. However, I don't think anyone noticed my warden enjoying the delicacy since he was tasting all of my food anyway.

It didn't help that the caterpillars plaguing my stomach earlier had transformed into butterflies trying to force their way up my throat. My nerves must have driven Luc mad because he suggested we walk down to Lan's stall after the banquet.

The Skoloti party came with us. I couldn't help but to notice Warden Urania flirting with Luc despite Yar's looming presence. On the other hand, Antiope was all business. I could see why her dedication would attract the Rus warden's attention.

False Darys brushed her hand against mine. *Do you wish me to speak with Urania about overstepping?*

It's the Spring Rituals. I sighed. *With it comes all kinds of amorous activities.*

I had the impression you and the high brother—

I cannot bear—

—children, she finished. *So you've told me, but the mating edict doesn't mean you cannot enjoy yourself. Especially with the holiday.*

The edict. Cow cakes. All my work with High Sister Mya back in Orrin and my past still haunted me. I tried to blame my mood on exhaustion since we arrived in Chengzhou when it was my former issues coming back to roost on my shoulders. The Spring Rituals had been a curse to me since I was conceived.

When the edict came down, Luc did his duty. I glanced at Darys. *I was granted a dispensation because I couldn't. However, my birth mother killed his unborn child last summer by stabbing Sister Claudia of Love who bore the babe. Sometimes, I wonder if it was the Twelve's way of punishing him for daring to have romantic feelings for me.*

Stop right there. Darys slid her fingers between mine and squeezed. *Your birth mother is the reason you cannot have children.*

A statement, not a question.

Yes, I admitted.

You cannot keep blaming yourself for what that wicked woman did to you and others. Her empathy poured through our link. *Just like I am not to blame for my sister's death. We are not responsible for other people's bad choices.*

Something one of Child's clergy said to you?

She laughed silently. *Actually, it was the aunt I was named after. She's the chief warden for the Reverend Mother of Balance.*

Your aunt is a wise and logical woman, High Sister. I smiled at Zhanna, daring to think her real name since the first time she told it to us. I hoped the Twelve wouldn't strike me down for my presumption.

Lan was already out of her spice cakes when we finally reached her stall, but she had plenty of chilled hibiscus tea and delightful almond butter cookies. We ran into Justice Mei Wen and Warden Yichen. While he wore his uniform, Mei Wen was dressed in a matching top and skirt made of stiffened silk. Silver birds and flowers were embroidered in a lovely pattern along the edges of the material.

Apparently, she had the same affection for Lan's spice cakes, and like me, she was disappointed there were no more. Instead, she selected some lemon cakes for her and her warden. However, we couldn't find a table that would fit all of us, much less two free tables.

"I know a place where we can sit," Mei Wen announced. "Back to Balance, my good warden."

We threaded the throngs to cross the main avenue. Seven novices from different Temples gathered on the bottom three steps of the building. All of them were sharing sweets, and they had drinks with them. None of them could have been older than twelve winters.

"Move over, young ones!" Mei Wen ordered.

All of the novices except the one from Balance exchanged looks before grabbing all their treats and rising.

"We apologize, Lady Justice," the blind girl said while bobbing her head in our general direction.

"I said move over, not leave." Mei Wen sighed in an exaggerated manner. The pair of wardens at Balance's main doors chuckled.

"That has been Justice Mei Wen's spot for people watching since she was a novice herself," the female warden called out.

"B-but she can't watch people," one of the Mother novices sputtered.

"I can," I said sharply. "Now, sit down."

Each of the novices dropped to their bottoms exactly where they stood.

"Please guide me to a place where I can sit next to Anthea, Yichen," Mei Wen said.

The warden led her up to the fifth step beside the Balance novice, and I followed them. A Death novice on the second step moved over so Luc could sit beside him. The rest of our party grabbed seats in between the other novices.

"I didn't know you sat here, m'lady," the poor Balance novice whispered. "I'm so sorry."

"Stop apologizing," Mei Wen gently chided. "You're smart enough to know this is the best spot to enjoy the festivities. Chief Justice Anthea, may I present Novice Baozhai? Novice, this is Chief Justice Anthea from Issura. She escorted Emperor Po home after the attack last winter."

The girl's mouth fell open. The other Mother novice who hadn't spoken yet whispered in Baozhai's ear.

"I-I'm honored to meet you, Chief Justice," Baozhai murmured.

And I'm honored to meet you, Novice Baozhai." I leaned across Mei Wen's lap. "But it's the Spring Rituals. Let us dispense with the titles for the rest of the holiday."

Baozhai giggled, and her friend from Mother stared at me in amazement.

"I told you Mei Wen would be here," a familiar male voice called out.

I looked up to see Brother Jian of Light, Brother Fa of Wildling, and Sister Longnu of Wildling approach Balance along with their own wardens. They greeted everyone as they climbed the steps. The clergy sat behind Mei Wen and their wardens sat on the steps above them. The Balance wardens at the temple's main doors found the whole thing terribly amusing.

The old friends talked about one of their own becoming the empress of Jing. When the novices gathered the courage to ask questions, the trio of Shi Hua's former comrades regaled their audience with tales of their own antics as novices.

Jian was in the middle of a story about Shi Hua substituting ground Szechuan pepper for powdered cloves in retaliation for another novice's prank when their novice master sprinkled some in his morning tea. "So, Master Lin takes this huge gulp, and his face turned—"

A scream rent the air.

Magic surged through stone beneath me an instant before the temple bells rang the distinctive pattern for "demon".

We were all unarmed except for daggers. Now, I had another reason to add to my list of why I hated the Spring Rituals.

CHAPTER 72

Over the panicking civilians, I bellowed, "Novices, get inside Balance!"

Surprisingly, the youngsters listened to me. The girl from Mother assisted Baozhai up the stairs. They disappeared through the doors right before a huge crash echoed up the street. It sounded like a rockfall Luc and I barely avoided in the Gray Mountains one spring on circuit. A billowing cloud of dust floated our way.

"That came from the gates at the inner wall," Jian yelled.

"We need weapons," Zhanna shouted.

Inside, Mei Wen said silently. *We have spares in the armory.*

Yichen practically carried her as we raced up the steps. Fa and Longnu shed their clothing as we ran.

Some civilians realized where they were in the city. The panicking crowd surged toward the perceived safety of the Temples. We would have to let the wardens deal with them.

A enemy feint? Luc asked silently.

Or desperation, I said. Even if the terms of the Skoloti prophecy said Po was safely the emperor of Jing, we couldn't let the demons rampage through Chengzhou.

In the main court room, Mei Wen joined the justices gathered around Reverend Mother Xiang, who stood before the statue of our goddess.

"This way, Anthea," Dai Lu called. She stood near the door to the administrative offices and waved. I headed in her direction, the Issuran, Skoloti, and non-Balance Jing parties trailing behind me.

She stopped a squire who couldn't have been more than seven winters. "Get the laundry that's supposed to go back to the palace for the Issuran ambassador and bring it straight to the armory."

"Yes, Chief Justice." The girl whirled, and raced in the opposite direction.

Inside the armory, we selected from the Temple's extra weapons. The Skoloti went for shorts swords and bows. My people selected the mid-length swords they were used to, except Luc who grabbed a crossbow and a quiver full of quarrels.

I grinned when I saw the scimitar among their collection. The curved blade from the desert tribes in the southern section of the Old Continent was unique. High Sister Dragonfly had lent me hers one time and taught me how to use it. White sparks crackled along my fingers as I picked up the weapon.

"Do you know—" Dai Lu said just as I took a few experimental swings. She sighed. "Nevermind."

I had also pulled a few throwing knives when the squire appeared with my clean uniforms. I quickly changed. Despite the screaming that penetrated the very walls of the temple, I delighted in the feel, and smell, of clean leathers and silks. While I yanked on my robes, I tried not to think about how filthy my fresh uniform would be by the end of the day.

"High Brother, would you please join the Thief shooters on our roof?" Dai Lu had the unfocused quality of listening to someone else not in the armory. The plan made sense. The innermost wall was more of an oval than a true circle. The design limited the approaches to the palace, and any enemy would have to pass the last four Temples to reach the ruler of Jing.

"Anthea and Sister Darys will ride with Balance," Dai Lu added.

Another crash shook the very walls of the Temple. The stones cried a mournful note. If they didn't like what was happening outside, it was bad indeed.

Dai Lu ordered the squire to escort Luc and Yar to the lift and take mine and my wardens' clothing to her office before the chief justice gestured for the rest of us to follow her. The Wildlings had shifted in the few moments it took for us to select weapons. Fa padded beside me, Longnu floated above us.

Thankfully, no one who hadn't seen a dragon before asked any questions. Now simply wasn't the time.

We ran out the rear door of the temple and to the stables. Reverend Mother Xiang, the justices accompanying her, and four squads of wardens were mounted in two columns and waiting for us.

Yang and two other squires held the horses assigned to us. With a grin, she gave me the reins of the horse I'd borrowed yesterday.

"Good hunting, m'lady."

"Thank you, Yang." I mounted the well-trained steed. Unlike most other equines, Temple horses were bred for their intelligence and calmness. They ignored the scents and emotions swirling around them and simply waited for a command.

At the Reverend Mother's signal, I nudged the sides of my assigned horse with my knees. The mare trotted in time with the other steeds as together we exited the back gates of Balance.

And therein lay the difference between the Temples and the civilians. Would the noble ambassadors from the Fire Islands, the Kingdom of Ryukyu, or the Kingdom of Gojoseon join in the defense of a foreign nation? I smiled at my own rhetorical question because I knew the answer.

The columns split at the street between Balance and Knowledge. The left column I was with turned toward the main boulevard. The right column with Zhanna took the back street in a pincher move. Longnu flew after them while Fa ran next to me, his giant paws silently eating the yards in time to the steel horseshoes on the cobblestones.

The main boulevard was relatively clear of civilians as horses from the other Temples poured into the street. At the signal from Death, we commanded our horses into a canter. Buzzing filled my mind as orders were given silently and passed along.

The clergy at the gates say their foe is one gigantic demon, Reverend Mother Xiang said.

You mean a giant army of demons? one of the other justices asked.

No, Reverend Mother Xiang snapped. *One humongous demon. Larger than a Cradle elephant. Taller than a giraffe. Balance forces, we're taking pointing. Brother Fa, with us!*

As the other Temples split apart to allow us through, Fa surged ahead of the Reverend Mother's horse. Xiang gave the signal for a full gallop.

My eyes teared as more dust filled the air. In the miasma of grit ahead of us, steel clashed, magic flashed, and people shouted. Not in panic, but blood-curdling screams punctuated the sounds of battle.

Demon magic rasped against my mental shields. It was far more powerful than anything I'd felt from our enemies before. Not even the collective demon army that invaded Tandor felt like this.

For the first time, I wished I hadn't given myself vision. The monstrosity we galloped toward was something out of my nightmares. A single demon the height of a two-story building besieged the people guarding the inner wall.

The massive iron gates were simply gone.

No, not completely gone. One metal slab cut one of the bureaucracy buildings in half causing its roof to collapse. The other had crushed the tiny security office, gouged deep into cobblestones and grass before landing on the statuary in the remembrance park I had visited two days ago. That explained the crashes and dust.

I ignored the shades of pink liquid and objects smeared around the vicinity of the giant demon. I had to. If I did, I would curl up in a wailing ball, and more people would . . .

I shoved my thoughts ruthlessly aside.

As we galloped toward the monstrosity, catapults on the wall launched round clay objects at it. A series of explosions engulfed the demon's head in a cloud of smoke. Flashbangs. Huge flashbangs.

The giant demon swung around, and its right arm swept across the rampart. Bodies and pieces of the war machines flew in all directions. The flashbangs hadn't damaged the demon at all.

Justices, spread out! Reverend Mother Xiang ordered. *We'll use the intersection and debris as our template for a time freeze.*

The Balance wardens guided their charges into position. Mine simply followed me. As the last justice in the file, I ended up next to the Reverend Mother at the head of the arc. The surviving Conflict and Light priests on the wall kept the monstrosity distracted with charged arrows, fire balls, and plasma bolts, but their magics seemed to have little effect.

On my mark! The Reverend Mother's voice bellowed in my brain. *Three! Two! One! Mark!*

The solid feeling of Balance magic spread across our semicircle toward the giant demon. As if sensing the danger to itself, its talons lengthened into tendrils, which inserted themselves into the many cracks of the innermost wall. Someone shouted, "Retreat!", and the personnel on the rampart above the entrance raced for safety. Just as our spell reached the demon, it roared and heaved. The demon's talons thickened and ripped apart that section of the wall. Without three dimensions as its basis, our time freeze spell died.

"Balance, help us," Reverend Mother Xiang whispered.

To my horror, the demon slapped its giant palm on the justice closest to it.

Only her horse had time to scream.

CHAPTER 73

Retreat! Reverend Mother Xiang ordered.

A wave of charged arrows and crossbow bolts flew over our heads while Balance wardens guided their charges away from the demon.

Something wasn't right. The monstrosity held so much magical power, yet it relied on purely physical attacks. So where were the four demons we knew about . . .

Bile surged in the back of my throat as I realized what the demon magic was doing.

That thing isn't just one demon, I silently told the Reverend Mother. *The demons in the city somehow used their talents to combine into one entity.*

How do we break it apart? she asked.

How do you break apart fog? I responded.

BIMING! She roared.

What? His quicksilver talent felt like trying to catch a fish with only one finger.

The Reverend Mother relayed my observation.

Only the sun's heat can do that, Biming said. *How do you propose—*

Use something that's just as hot, I said. *But I need the rest of you to hold it down so I don't lay waste to the entire city.*

His laughter rang like a gong. *Oh, is that all we need to do?*

I'll distract the monster. Get the movers in place. Po's mental voice was just as smooth as his physical voice. Shi Hua acted as her husband's conduit. *Peacekeepers, send the civilians inside the inner wall toward the palace. Get the civilians outside away from where the gates used to be.*

Your Majesty, get to the palace yourself! Biming shouted.

My people, my responsibility, old friend, Po said. *Anthea, how much space will you need?*

As much as you can give me, I said. *And try to keep it in the damaged section of Chengzhou. I've never attempted to blast something this big, and I don't want to destroy any more of your capital.*

Buzzing filled my mind as orders were relayed to the other Temple personnel.

Reverend Mother, Aihan and I have an idea to help the emperor with his distraction, Mei Wen said.

Get to him, Xiang commanded. *Have the rest of your column join me.*

We took cover behind a bureaucratic building and dismounted. The monstrosity roared a challenge as another wave of charged projectiles hit it.

And once again, they did no perceivable damage.

"I'll need every clergy member to raise wards around that thing once the movers have it down," I said to the Reverend Mother. "It's not going to help the situation if I set Chengzhou on fire."

Someone ran down the boulevard faster than humanly possible. I leaned around the corner of the building.

Po.

Mei Wen and Aihan had sped up time only around the emperor.

He slowed his headlong rush enough to shout something to the demon. I couldn't understand a word because he spoke so fast he sounded like a furious rodent squeaking. My heart caught in my throat when the giant demon raised its fist to smash him.

But it was too big. Too slow.

Po darted behind the demon and fired his entire quiverful of arrows at the demon's tendon that connected its right ankle to the leg muscle. He finished by thrusting his sword into the tendon before he darted away from his foe.

Light magic caressed my skin. Shi Hua had charged his arrows. The spells ignited at the same time. With a horrendous shriek, the giant dropped to its upper limbs.

"Get ready, Anthea," Xiang ordered.

I mounted my borrowed horse since I wasn't charged with Balance magic to speed me up. I tried not to think about the price Po would pay for that spell.

The demon struggled to shift its form. Tendrils exuded from its body and flailed. The injured leg was absorbed back into its body.

Movers, go! The silent order came from the Reverend Mother of Love.

A mix of Temple magic signatures filled the area. The demon collapsed on rubble as if a giant hand had pushed it flat.

I didn't need any order. I touched both heels to my horse's ribs, and she leapt forward into a full gallop.

"Clear!" I shouted out loud and silently.

Wards sprang up around me and the demon. A tentacle lashed out, grabbed my horse's forefoot, and yanked. The mare screamed as her delicate leg bones broke. The sudden jerk toppled me from the saddle.

I landed hard on my side. My recently healed ribs snapped. I couldn't breathe.

Another tendril wrapped itself around my legs and dragged me toward the black writhing mass. The movers were losing their grip on the demon.

And I was too damn close.

Contrary to my friends and wardens' opinions, I had no wish to die. But I couldn't let this thing eat its way through Chengzhou either.

I closed my eyes and summoned all my fury. Static crackled all over my body. I gulped what little air I could and let the lightning flood me.

Whiteness filled my head.

I could only muse that it was a change from the black as I lost consciousness in the terrible heat.

Chapter 74

A soft growl jerked me awake. I lay on my side, my ribs and chest on fire with every breath I took. I opened my eyes to find I stared at a demon. Their eyes were the only thing that wasn't the Balance-awful black. And its red eyes stared at me with sheer loathing.

At least, this demon was normal-sized.

My head rang with the force of my lightning strike. And below my fiery rib pain was an odd numbness. I couldn't even lift my head to check if I still had my limbs.

A sword cut through the demon's neck. A Light-charged sword. The red eyes dimmed until I couldn't tell the difference between them and the rest of the blasted demon.

Someone crouched next to me and bent over so I could see their face. Brother Jian.

"Stay still, Chief Justice." He smiled. "Healers are on their way."

I licked my cracked, blistered lips and tasted blood. "Get . . . them . . . all?"

"Yes. All four of the bastards."

"Po . . ."

"The emperor is alive and safe," Jian assured me.

"Good." I smiled. Or I tried to. Or maybe I only thought I was.

Despite their care, when Jian, the healer, and his apprentices lifted me onto a stretcher, I screamed and passed out again.

Consciousness came back gradually. First thing I noticed was my very dry mouth. Then my bladder decided it needed attention first.

I blinked. The room was unfamiliar. I wasn't in Orrin.

Of course, I wasn't in Orrin. I was in Chengzhou. In Jing.

My bladder encouraged me to get out of bed and get to the water closet. Luc wouldn't be happy if I relieved myself in our bed.

I tried to sit up. A wave of dizziness and sheer exhaustion told me my actions were not a good plan.

Metal squeaked. A woman entered my line of sight. A familiar woman. Master Healer Zhi.

"Good to see you awake," she said cheerfully. "Can you tell me your name?"

"An-Anthea DiBalance." It took some work to get the words out since my tongue stuck to the roof of my mouth. "Before you continue your examination for head trauma, could you please assist me to the water closet, Master Zhi?"

She chuckled. "The emperor and your friends will be happy to know you are alive and want to pee."

She was still laughing after I finished my business and she helped me back into bed.

When I woke next, I recognized the lethargy of a major healing. Zhi sat in the chair beside me, her attention on something in her lap, but she looked up when I stirred.

"Need to use the water closet, Chief Justice?" She grinned.

"Yes, but where am I? This isn't the suite assigned to my party. The bed's too small."

"We're in the imperial family section of the palace. This was the emperor's bedroom when he was a child," the master healer said. "And the smaller bed is more advantageous in caring for you."

"Why are you still here?" I asked. "There are dozens of injured who need you. The demons—"

She sobered. "Anthea, what's the last thing you remember?"

I blinked and tried to pull my memories from the mush of my mind. "I called lightning on the giant demon. It broke apart." I paused as I tugged on the next event. "Luc, no, it was Brother Jian from Light who executed the demon lying beside me. He said healers were on the way. I rebroke my ribs when I landed on some rubble. When they picked me up, I passed out from the pain. You helped me to the water closet a little while ago." I sighed. "I'm sorry. That's all I can recall." I rubbed my sternum at the remembered agony.

"The battle with the giant demon was three days ago," Zhi said softly. "I helped you to the water closet yesterday morning, but you fell asleep before I could call for food for you."

My stomach decided at that moment to express its displeasure at my inattention.

Zhi laughed. "Think you can stay awake long enough for the palace kitchen to deliver some rice porridge?"

I smiled. "If I fall asleep again, wake me." My stomach gurgled in agreement.

Once I ate the sweetened porridge and drank two pitchers of water, Master Zhi allowed Jonata into the bedchamber. Yellow tears trickled down my warden's cheeks as she sat on the edge of my bed.

"Stop, Jonata," I murmured before I reached up to brush away her tears. "You are not at fault. Nor was I trying to kill myself. Our plan simply went sideways."

"Don't all of your plans go askew?" she responded.

I laughed, but the residual ache in my chest cut the sound short.

Jonata and Zhi helped me into the bath. It was the first time since we arrived, I could luxuriate in the pool instead of hurrying through the cleansing of my body. Someone had brought my belongings to this room. My warden towel-dried my hair before she quickly braided my long tresses and pinned them up. Instead of one of my uniforms or my formal chiton, Jonata helped me into a tunic and skirt of silk. Balance's scales were embroidered in silver thread along the hems of the garments.

"Is the silk black?" I asked Jonata.

"Of course." She grinned. "The clothing is a gift from Reverend Mother Xiang." Her expression sobered, and she sighed. "Speaking of which, the Reverend Mother and the emperor are on their way here. I think they both feared Master Zhi was lying about your true condition."

I eyed the healer who was packing up her equipment. "How long have you been here?"

"We brought you back here the day of the battle." She shrugged. "Our new emperor insisted a master healer be with you at all times. Your wardens watched you while I slept."

"Thank you, Master Zhi." I made the fist-to-palm gesture and bowed as low as my still aching chest allowed.

"You're welcome, Chief Justice." She repeated the gesture. "Thank you for saving our city."

I muttered an obscenity as it finally sunk into my brain what day it was. "I also need to apologize to Reverend Mother Xiao Mei."

"Don't fret, m'lady," Jonata murmured. She helped me into silk slippers, also a gift from Reverend Mother Xiang. "Everyone's been too busy with the aftermath to think about your planned class. Well, beyond hoping you'll stay for a few extra days to teach it. The emperor also sent messengers to Huang He to let Captain Titus know of our party's delay and the reasons why."

"How-how many casualties?" I didn't want to hear the answer to my question. I'd seen enough at the destroyed gates to make an educated guess how many had been eaten or killed.

Jonata opened her mouth to answer, but Master Zhi snapped, "No."

"Why?" I asked.

"Because you did what you could. What you had to. Just like everyone else during that obscene battle." Her fierce glare could have ignited the room if she had been a fire talent. "I'll tell you the same thing I said to the emperor. You cannot torture yourself with could haves, would haves, and should haves. It's not a productive use of your time, and it will only drive you into melancholy."

"Are you channeling High Sister Mya of Orrin's Temple of Child?" I smiled to take the edge from my words. "Because you sound exactly like her."

"I had to refer many patients from the winter's attack and this one to our own Child clergy," Zhi said mildly. "I can make arrangements for you as well."

"Thank you, but no." I shook my head. "I'll talk to the high sister when I return home. I still remember the exercises she taught me."

"Just remember war is a terrible thing, Anthea, no matter the reason." She slung her bag over her shoulder. "It takes a toll on the body, but a far worse toll on the spirit. If you have any physical symptoms or decide you want to speak to someone at Child, send for me. And for Death's sake, get some rest. She's been far too busy lately."

I eyed Jonata. "My friends will make sure I get plenty of rest."

My warden glowed bright orange, but whether it was from my teasing assessment or that I called her a friend, I didn't know. Nor was I going to pry.

I turned back to the healer. "Thank you, again, Master Zhi. For everything."

She nodded and exited the bed chamber.

"Are you sure you're up for visitors, m'lady?" Jonata murmured.

"Up, no. But I can visit while sitting."

My legs were shaky after the exertion of bathing and dressing. I managed to push myself upright, and Jonata wrapped her arm about my waist to guide me into the common room.

Luc, Yar, and Little Feather rose from their chairs at our appearance. Obvious relief showed on the men's faces.

"Contrary to popular belief, I'm still alive," I teased. However, I was out of breath just crossing the room to the divan near the dark fireplace. All four of my comrades fussed over the arranging of pillows until I snapped.

"For the love of the Twelve, I am not a newborn!"

"I thought I'd lost you." Luc's hug was mix of joy and fear. And it hurt worse than the initial injuries.

"My love, I appreciate the sentiment, but I'm still healing."

He eased his hold. "I'm sorry." He caressed my cheek as tears slid down his face. "They had to heal you in stages . . ."

"I know." I covered his hand with mine. "A healing is just as hard on the patient as it is the healer. Zhi was trying to fix the damage without killing me. I'm just thankful she wasn't foolish enough to burn out her power."

I hadn't forced Bertrice to do so since I was still inside the womb, but thanks to Mya's help, I no longer felt the guilt. But I still missed Bertrice fiercely.

At a knock on the door, Yar strode over to answer it. He bowed low before he pulled the door fully open. Shi Hua rushed to the divan and squeezed me even harder than Luc had. Thank Balance, she released me just as quickly.

And before I bleated in pain.

"What were you thinking, my beautiful idiot!" Anger exuded from the new empress.

"Jonata will tell you I had a perfectly good plan," I said archly.

"Except your plans always go sideways," Po said. He followed his remark with his annoying smirk.

"You're welcome for saving your capital, Emperor Bao Quan Po," I shot back.

Instead of hugging me, he laid a gentle kiss on my forehead. "I'm glad you are alive and intact, my friend. My chancellor was quite petrified of what Queen Teodora might do if you died here. He's become rather fond of Pana Valley wine."

We all laughed at the simple joy of surviving. I would take that small pleasure. And by Balance, I would cherish my gift.

CHAPTER 75

My closest companions were circumspect about my injuries and the aftermath of the battle. However, Luc admitted Guang and his son's trials had been held, and they had been executed with Wu and Jia Huo for their crimes as scheduled the morning after the attack. Po kept his sworn oath to Reverend Mother Xiang, and the emperor beheaded the guilty parties himself.

Other visitors weren't quite so circumspect.

Duke Mengchang chewed me out for not being more careful and lambasted me for setting a poor example for his emperor. If I had gotten Po killed during the battle, Mengchang claimed he would have strung me up by my toes and let the Imperial Army use me for target practice. After his threats, he laughed. "Your display of power put the fear of the Twelve in Ix and Zixin. I doubt if the emperor will have any more trouble from them. Of course, your threat of revenge at that family dinner helped."

Reverend Father Biming said Mei Wen and Aihan's spell to speed up Po's personal time had left the new emperor's glossy black hair liberally sprinkled with silver. Reverend Mother Xiao Mei claimed it looked distinguished. However, she was rather annoyed the other Temples and schools of philosophy wanted more than five seats for my attempt to teach them how to call lightning after seeing what I could do.

High Sister Zhanna of the Skoloti tribes no longer pretended to be her slain sister now that Po was securely on the Dragon Throne. She was also insistent I teach the lightning class before either of us left. "Even if I can't manage to produce it, others within the tribes might be able to. Is there a distance speaker in Orrin if I have any questions?"

I shook my head. "Have a Skoloti distance speaker relay your message to Empress Shi Hua. She'll make sure I receive it, and she'll send my answer to you."

Brother Jian admitted he had fed his power into me to keep me alive long enough for the healers to reach us. In addition to my broken ribs, my lungs had collapsed, and I had severe burns, not from the lightning, but from the burning demon tentacle wrapped around me. Apparently, the four demons had pulled other matter into their spell to combine themselves into one giant demon.

Fa and Longnu told me about the search for any other demons in the city and the surrounding countryside since every Wilding in Chengzhou had gotten a good whiff of the giant demon. So far, they had found two pockets of demons and three of skinwalkers within a two days ride of the capital. Wildling clergy from the local towns and villages spread the word from there.

Master Ma and Master Bolin thanked me for helping the other philosophy masters see the need for working together with the Temples and Guilds. They were putting measures into place to hopefully ensure another schism wouldn't occur after the demons were finally defeated.

Reverend Mother Xiang asked me bluntly if I would consider transferring to the Jing Temple of Balance. "I won't repeat the load of manure Alara of Issura has said about you, but you aren't the troublemaker she described. If she doesn't want you, I'll take you in an instant."

"I appreciate your candor, Reverend Mother, but I cannot disappoint Queen Teodora. She has given me her full support over the last two years, and before we sailed, she was quite adamant I return to Issura alive."

Xiang chuckled. "If you change your mind about a transfer—"

"I promise the empress will pass the message to you if I do."

My final visitor for the day was surprisingly Reverend Father Jin. He was nearly as shaky as I was when he sat down on the chair by my divan. "I can see why the empress values you as a sister of the spirit."

"I regard her in the same way."

"After the attack, the emperor announced that she is with child."

I grinned. "A little blessing of hope for the new year is always a welcome thing."

His eyes narrowed. "She already told you, didn't she?"

"Actually, I knew before she did." I shrugged. "One of the oddities of my peculiar sight. I may be able to see demons, but I can also see the changes start in a woman's body when her child is conceived. I've learned to remain silent after I nearly destroyed the Duke of Orrin's marriage by accident."

Jin roared with laughter. "I can only imagine his poor wife's face when she didn't know herself yet."

I smiled. "They made a point of telling me she was pregnant again before we left Issura though they hadn't made the formal announcement yet. The babe will be born before we return."

He shook his head. "I wish there were a faster way to travel. The empress would appreciate a visit or two from you as your duties permitted."

"There will be quicker ways to travel." I laughed. "Eventually. Once we put this war to rest and are no longer fighting for our very survival, we'll turn human ingenuity loose. It would almost be worth an extra century or two of life to see what we can create."

"What happened to Balance in everything?" he teased.

"She warned us of the invasion of the demons," I said. "Preparing and fighting them has held us back for nearly two millennia. Our advances would be correcting the scales."

He rose. "I apologize for tiring you, Anthea. I will see you at the last rituals tomorrow night."

"Last rituals?" I frowned. "The end of the Spring Rituals was three days ago."

He smiled. "The emperor called a moratorium until you recovered. He said the Twelve would surely understand after putting his people and his friends to the test."

I shook my head and laughed. "What a silver-tongued scoundrel."

"As much resentment there is over his lack of Light talent, I think Thief has made sure Bao Quan Po is the emperor we need in these times." Jin bowed. "Until tomorrow, Anthea."

When he departed, I laid back against the pillows. The demon attack had been terrible, but maybe something worthwhile had been forged in its fire.

I must have dozed off because the next thing I knew, carts with hot containers and delicious smells were rolled into my little suite. Instead of palace staff, Yar, Jonata, and Little Feather pushed the carts. Luc swung over to sit on the chair on the left side of the divan. Bringing up the rear was . . .

I blinked to make sure I wasn't seeing things.

"Lan?"

She bowed making the fist-to-palm sign. "I come to serve, Chief Justice."

"But what are you doing here?"

"I know what kind of garbage the palace serves." She scowled. "Bah! An injured or sick person needs good, hearty food after a healing!" A wicked smile replaced her scowl. "But it's still technically the Spring Rituals per the emperor's decree, so we will start with fresh spice cakes."

Luc insisted Lan join us for the meal. While we devoured the persimmon and spice cakes, the others told me of Lan appearing at the palace to see her best customer.

"The chancellor was threatening to have me arrested when the empress appeared and ordered him to let me in." Lan clucked her tongue. "I remember when she was a novice. It's hard to believe such a skinny, little thing has become such a beautiful and powerful woman. If I'd known you and she were sisters of the heart, I would have treated you much better, Chief Justice."

"Treated me better?" I exclaimed. "Lan, you have a stall to run, and you gave me your spice cake recipe and extra cakes. Yet, you came to the palace to cook for me."

"Bah!" She waved away my protest. "My son needs the experience of running the stall for next year's Spring Rituals."

"You know, Chief Justice, Deborah will need a replacement eventually," Long Feather said.

"Who is this Deborah?" Lan demanded.

"She's our cook at the Temple of Balance in Orrin," I replied.

Lan turned to Long Feather. "Stop your hints to the chief justice right there, Warden. I cannot leave Jing, much less Chengzhou. I would miss my grandchildren terribly."

"I wouldn't dream of separating you from your family," I said. "I'll just need to find another cook who can replicate your recipes—"

"Just one moment—" Lan abruptly started laughing as she realized I was teasing her. "When you come back to Chengzhou, have the palace send me a message. My shop is in the southern second ring. I would be happy to cook for you again."

"Thank you, Lan. I look forward to it."

My stomach gurgled happily in agreement.

CHAPTER 76

The next morning, I moved back to our assigned suite in the old harem section of the palace. I still needed a long nap in the afternoon in order to attend the final ceremonies of the Spring Rituals. The lingering fatigue from the multiple healings told me how close I'd come to joining Death permanently far more clearly than anyone's stories.

Po insisted I sit at his right side on the dais. In the emperor's annual address, he spoke glowingly of my actions and those of everyone else in the city. There was a moment of silence to honor those at the gate who lost their lives.

I didn't like the attention, but I accepted it. It was terribly amusing how everyone in the city's opinion of me changed over a demon battle.

At the finale of the Rituals was a magnificent fireworks display. Po took my hand so I could see the colors each rocket produced as everyone else saw them. The end of the show was the retelling of the Battle of Jicheng and the sacrifice of Empress Bao De to save her nation and her people. The sorcerers used magic to shape the display into the people and demons of that terrible day.

"I have a feeling there will be a new tale next year to end the Spring Rituals," Po whispered after the show finished.

"And I will unfortunately miss it," I whispered back.

We both laughed and avoided the subject that we wouldn't see each other for years, if ever again.

The next morning, I and my potential students met in the arena at the Temple of Conflict. Mostly, I spoke of theory and how my new ability was tied to my emotions.

However, I did one tiny display. One of the Conflict priestesses attack me with a sword. I shot a small static discharge into her steel. She yelped as the sword flew from her hand.

"What do you do about the numbness?" she asked as she tried to shake feeling back into her arm.

"There's not a thing you can do except wait for it to wear off," Long Feather volunteered.

However, the Temple's new master healer did check the Conflict priestess to make sure there was no permanent nerve damage. Apparently, Reverend Father Feng had negotiated a revised contract with the Healers Guild. He approached me with the Chengzhou magistrate after we were finished with my lecture, display, and the multitude of questions from the people chosen to attend.

"May I add five of my own people who are registered as minor talents to your lessons?" the magistrate asked. "While I don't expect them to blow up giant demons with lightning strikes, the little zap you gave that priestess would come in useful for my people during a brawl or a domestic argument that gets out of hand."

"Of course, Magistrate." I inclined my head. "If Reverend Mother Xiao Mei complains, have her talk to me."

The next morning, my students and I rode to the southern woods scheduled for removal to make way for Chengzhou's fifth wall. The citizens were already repairing the damage the giant demon had done to their beautiful city. The debris from the first wall had been cleared while I convalesced from my injuries. Stonemasons were already filling in the huge gap the giant demon had knocked out where the gates had been.

To my surprise, civilians already waited at the woods with their carts and beasts of burden. I was rather glad Captain Huizhong had sent a unit of imperial soldiers to accompany us.

The soldiers set up safety lines and warned the civilians they'd end up dead just like the demons if they got too close to any stray lightning bolts. Apparently, word of the destruction in Chengzhou had spread. The civilians were curious, but they stayed well out of our way.

As I expected, High Brother Shang was the first to produce a decent lightning strike. He felled a rather large, dead tree from its base. From there, he became my teaching second, encouraging most students, berating others. Doing whatever it took to get one of our students to produce lightning.

High Sister Zhanna was the second to produce a decent strike. She split a trunk hollowed by age and disease. From then on, the rest of my students turned the teaching event into a contest to see who could bring down a live tree.

When we ended the practice at noon, only a handful of students besides Shang and Zhanna managed to throw a lightning bolt. Overall, I thought we did rather well, but Reverend Mother Xiao Mei was greatly disappointed.

"The rest of us must not have enough trauma in our lives," she said bitterly.

"Reverend Mother, all I can tell you is that's what triggered my ability," I said. "I don't really understand how or why though. I would have thought a weather wizard would have discovered the ability long before now. I promised you two more days. After that, it will be up to you to develop other methods for finding and working this talent."

"How many clergy have you been able to train in Issura?" Shang asked.

"None," I said dryly. "It's not for lack of volunteers or attempts." I shook my head. "I assumed anyone with a modicum of talent trapped in Tandor would have been able to produce lightning if trauma were the trigger, including Emperor Po. But not even Chief Justice Elizabeth had been able to produce lightning, and she had the worst trauma of all."

Reverend Mother Xiao Mei shook her head sadly. "I saw both yours and her reports when we were cataloguing the events. You both left a lot out if I read between the lines correctly."

"You did." I sighed. "The renegades have been focusing on breaking justices. The Light clergy make more sense, as does the spate of distance speaker assassinations. The justices don't."

Xiao Mei looked around to see if anyone was close enough to hear our conversation. No one was, but she lowered her voice anyway. "Yes, it does. There's a prophecy—"

I groaned, and Shang chuckled.

"You both know about it?" Her blue eyebrows rose.

"I don't put much faith in prophecies, Reverend Mother," I said. "But I will use our foes belief in them to our advantage."

"Chief Justice," Jonata called. "Headman Yuxuan would like a moment of your time."

I nodded, and a stooped elder toddled over to us.

"Reverend Mother, High Brother." He bowed to the others. "Chief Justice, you have our gratitude in defeating the monster in the capital." He performed the fist-to-palm gesture.

"I didn't do it alone, Headman Yuxuan." I smiled as I returned his salute. As Luc said, the expression took the sting from my often brusque manner. "However, I will relay your appreciation to everyone involved."

He nodded. "I also wanted to say thank you for making our work collecting wood to make charcoal much easier."

"I'm glad our students could help. We'll be out here practicing for two more days—"

"Actually, Chief Justice," Shang interjected. "Those of us learning your technique will be out here every day until the woods are cleared." He grinned. "The masters in charge of building the new wall stopped and spoke with the Reverend Mother and me while you were teaching. We're clearing the area faster than they or the local villagers would be able to do."

I cocked my head and regarded Xiao Mei. "And you said the students weren't performing as well as you hoped."

"There's a large difference between clearing some land for building and taking on demons," she said with a huff.

"I will accept your success for shortening our work, High Brother Shang." Headman Yuxuan bowed. "And, Reverend Mother, you often told my children to be patient in learning new things when you taught in our village."

Xiao Mei's face turned bright orange. "I hate it when my own words are thrown in my face, but thank you for the reminder."

Shang and Yuxuan laughed.

"My junior justices and my wardens do it to me all the time, Reverend Mother." I grinned. "Unfortunately, they are often right."

My statement made the men laugh harder and even drew a smile from Xiao Mei.

CHAPTER 77

The last two days of teaching lightning talent in the mornings passed faster than I imagined. At the end, three more clergy, one of the sorcerers, and a peacekeeper managed to produce lightning bolts. I spent the afternoons at the Temple of Balance, discussing and practicing tactical techniques with the justices.

Our last evening in Chengzhou was spent at a private dinner with the imperial couple. They also invited Duke Menchang, Duchess Jia, and High Sister Zhanna.

To our surprise, the emperor presented gifts to each of us as thanks for our service to his empire, including Mateqai. When the captain of the Empress's Guard tried to refuse it, Po chided him.

"I know you've only been a Jing citizen for a month, Captain, but you should know how rude it is to reject a gift, especially from the emperor."

"My apologies, Your Majesty." Mateqai bowed. "I accept your gift in the spirit in which you meant it." He pulled a scroll from the silk casing and unrolled a bit of it. "I beg your pardon, Your Majesty, But I haven't quite mastered the Jing written language yet."

"There's a plot of land north of the city that used to belong to the emperor," Shi Hua said. "It is now in your name, Lord Mateqai. You need a home that is singularly yours for giving up your old life to remain at my side."

"I-I am overwhelmed by the honor, Your Majesties." He bowed to the imperial couple. "Thank you."

"Just save a square league for Anthea's tea farm," Shi Hua teased as she winked at me.

I turned and glared at Long Feather. "Foreign negotiations are not to be discussed outside of the negotiation room."

"Reverend Father Feng did not ward the room in question. Neither did you," my warden said as he feigned innocence.

I found I didn't mind the snickers and byplay of others quite so much.

The rest of us opened our gifts. Po and Shi had chosen something unique for each of us. In my beribboned wooden box were leather wrist cuffs with brand-new steel throwing knives.

"I noticed your current arm cuffs were showing some wear. Shi Hua smiled.

"Lift the top insert," Po said gently.

I eyed the pair as I lifted the velvet lined wood and gasped in shock. Underneath was a gorgeous silver and obsidian necklace. I lifted the jewelry from its framed bed of velvet. It was simple, but elegant. The center was an obsidian pendant with a set of scales carved into the stone and filled with silver.

"It's beautiful," I murmured. "Thank you."

"Just remember you are a woman as well as a justice." Po lifted his goblet to me.

Are you trying to get under Luc's skin? I said silently.

Maybe. Po gave a deliberately lascivious grin, only to be elbowed in his ribs by his wife.

"Behave, my husband," Shi Hau chided. "Or have you forgotten what we gave the high brother?"

Luc's wooden box was much bigger than mine. He flipped the clasps, lifted the lid, and laughed heartily. Inside was a crossbow. He lifted the insert to find a quiver and bolts. The bolts themselves were works of art. The steel tips had been dipped in gold.

He lifted one of the bolts, held it up to the Knowledge lamps, and shook his head. "I've only seen things like this in Knowledge's history section in Standora."

"Empress Shi Hua suggested these for you," Po said. "At the height of the demon wars two centuries ago, gold plate was used in Light weapons because it can hold a larger magic charge than plain steel. I agree with you and Anthea the recent attacks are only the start of their last great offensive against us. It's best that you are prepared, High Brother since our dear Chief Justice attracts demons the way manure attracts flies."

"Excuse me?" I glared at the emperor while everyone else laughed.

The next morning, our party was awake before First Morning since we were traveling with Duchess Jia and her retinue to Huang He. High Sister Zhanna and her people were up early as well. Everyone wanted to arrive at our respective caravanserais before First Night. No chances were taken even though the Temples and the Imperial Army had found no more demons or skinwalkers.

In the rear courtyard of the palace, Zhanna and I hugged almost as tightly as Yar and Antiope. The Skoloti warden already had the faint glow of a second life developing inside of her.

When Zhanna and I released each other, I repeated, "Practice on the way home. And if you have any questions or concerns, have your distance speaker contact the empress. She will relay the message to me."

"I may not have Balance's memory training, but I won't forget. Be careful on the way to Issura."

"And you to the Skoloti lands."

She turned and mounted her horse. Several Conflict priests traveled with the Skoloti party to the border. Roughly half were survivors from Reverend Father Chen's doomed army.

"Warden Antiope," Zhanna barked.

The female warden planted one last kiss on Yar's mouth before she mounted her own steed. I waved until they disappeared around the corner of the palace.

Shi Hua and Mateqai were already astride their horses. The Empress's Guard was riding with us out of the city on the pretense of inspecting the work on Chengzhou's walls.

"Chief Justice?" Po approached me. He made the fist-to-palm gesture and bowed low. "Thank you for your service to me and my empire."

I matched his respect with the same gestures. "Thank you for your service to me and to Issura."

As I straightened, he wrapped his arms around me and squeezed me until my sore ribs complained. "Stay alive, my friend," he whispered in my ear. "I should like to see you again someday."

"The same to you," I murmured. "Take care of my sister and your children."

"I will," he promised.

At the edge of my mind, I could feel Luc's annoyance. To both of our amazement, Po released me and hugged Luc as well. Po whispered something in Luc's ear, but I wasn't going to invade either of their privacy to learn what was said. Whatever was exchanged, Luc was incredibly solemn when the two men released their holds on each other.

Po held Luc's crutches as he mounted his borrowed horse. Po handed up the crutches, and Luc slid them into their holders stitched into his saddlebags.

The emperor helped Duchess Jia, her children, and Lady Cuihong into Jia's carriage. Cuihong had been questioned in relation to her husband's death, but under the truthspell she truly didn't know about Jia Huo's curse on her husband. She believed her prayers to the Twelve were the reason her husband appeared to be stricken by the Child's Curse until her cousin's trial. In a twist that could only be engineered by Thief Himself, her husband died while I was unconscious from my healings.

Jia was gracious in offering the young woman a place and some time to deal with the events of her life and the pain of what both her husband and her cousin had done. The Duchess simply couldn't afford to be the flighty woman I'd first met. And the widows understood some of each other's pain.

Shi Hua rode beside me as we rounded the palace and headed down the main boulevard. Once again, I was shocked. Clergy and wardens stood at attention in ranks outside of each of their Temples. Each of the Temple leaders stood at the forefront. They made the same fist-to-palm gesture of respect and bowed as the Issuran party and the empress passed.

I think you've been accepted as their empress, I said silently to Shi Hua.

That display was not for me. She smiled. *You've made quite an impact in this nation, my friend.*

Citizens thronged the street as we headed for the eastern gates. I was starting to feel distinctly uncomfortable. But the civilians were as silent as the Temple personnel had been except for the rustle and jingle of their garments as we passed. Like Orrin, too much had happened in Chengzhou for the people to ignore the danger the demons and their allies posed any longer.

At the construction site for the capital's fifth wall, Shi Hua and I dismounted and hugged tightly.

"First Afternoon in Orrin on every Rest Day," she murmured in my ear.

"I promise, but if I'm at the Healers Guild again, Yanaba will relay any news."

She eyed Jonata and Long Feather who were still astride their borrowed horses. "Please keep her out of the Healers Guild."

Jonata nodded. "We will do our best, but we cannot promise anything, Your Majesty."

"But if you wish to bribe me with an annual shipment of five spice, I will chain her to the high brother's bed so he can keep her distracted," Long Feather said.

Appalled, I stared at him in disbelief at his insolence. However, Luc, Yar, and Mateqai laughed out loud.

Jonata's saddle creaked as she leaned closer to him. "The chief justice wasn't supposed to know about our plan."

That triggered laughter from the surrounding imperial guards and Duchess Jia's protective detail.

I ignored them and hugged Shi Hua one last time. "Until we meet again, little sister."

"Until then," she whispered.

My eyes stung as I mounted my borrowed horse once again. I waved at Shi Hua until she was no longer in sight.

The rest of our journey held no surprises. Other than we learned both the Temples and the emperor had covered our costs for the trip back to Huang He. We wanted for nothing and the caravanserai masters made sure we were loaded with goods only available in Jing from their local merchants and artisans. We had to hire another wagon at the third caravanserai we stopped at to carry everything.

We ended up staying in Huang He for two additional days at the behest of Duchess Jia and the Huang He Temples. The city's Temple leaders wanted to confirm the accuracy of the reports from the capital.

I was relieved and sad as the *Mars Tranquilus* left with the morning tide on the third day. Captain Titus steered the ship north to stop and trade in the Fire Islands before we caught the northern Peaceful Sea current for home.

However, I didn't have to do much pleading with the captain to stop for a week in the Kingdom of O'ahu.

CHAPTER 78

◈

A month and two days later . . .

Lying on a woven mat at a sandy beach beneath the warm late afternoon sun, I closed my eyes and relaxed. After the last four and a half months, the simple pleasures of life needed to be cherished. And Balance only knew if I'd have the opportunity to visit any of the islands of the Kingdom of O'ahu again.

Prince Alika had invited Luc and me on a state visit to the Island of Mau'i. The port city of Lele was nothing like Orrin's harbor or the one in the kingdom's capital of Kou. Three wooden piers stretched westward into the Peaceful Sea. Now that we were past mid-spring, ships from all over the vast ocean docked and departed frequently. The Sea Peoples' smaller outriggers and canoes were pulled up onto the sand further down the beach.

The small break in duties was a blessing of the Twelve while Captain Titus traded some of the thank-you goods Emperor Bao Quan Po had gifted us back on O'ahu. I had no doubt the king and queen would grant the captain favorable terms based on our respective nations' long-standing relationship.

As for me, I looked forward to the Duke of Mau'i's formal feast tonight. After tasting the pork roasted in an underground oven at the royal palace in Kou, I immediately regretted denying my clerk Lailani permission to build a traditional Sea Peoples' imu on the grounds of Orrin's Temple of Balance. It was a mistake I planned to rectify as soon as we docked at home.

I hated to admit it, but I rather enjoyed wearing the Sea Peoples' clothing. Everyone wore kilts about their waists and not much else. Of course, Temple personnel wore their order's colors, according to my wardens. But Luc let me peek through his eyes at the civilian and nobles' kilts. The colors and variety of plant-fiber fabrics were simply amazing. Some were dyed as yarn and then woven into beautiful patterns. Others were hand-painted with traditional Sea Peoples' designs. But with the much warmer weather in the island kingdom compared to Issura, the kilts were more comfortable than my usual silks and leathers.

Not to mention, it was rather nice to leave my hair loose, rather than wearing braids constantly. Though I silently admitted to myself I felt a little naked without my sword strapped to my back.

Joyous shouting and splashing could be heard over waves whisper-kissing the land.

"It sounds like your High Brother Luc is enjoying himself." Chief Justice Nalani chuckled on my right.

I laughed as well. "In the water, he is not limited by the loss of his foot."

"And he irritates Yar on purpose by swimming past the point his warden is comfortable," Jonata murmured from my left side.

"Please tell me Long Feather is keeping an eye on them both." I didn't want to watch the men acting stupidly after the last four weeks of being cooped up on the *Mars Tranquilus*.

"The Sea Peoples' wardens and priests are watching out for the high brother as well." Though Jonata didn't laugh, I could hear the humor in her voice. "It wouldn't do for one of the Issuran ambassadors to accidently drown himself."

I sighed, my contentment complete.

Until Jonta muttered a Jing curse word under her breath.

I opened my eyes and jerked into a sitting position. "What is it?"

At the same moment, I saw High Brother Makoa of Light speaking to Luc as they bobbed in the waves and felt Luc's grief and alarm.

"Lady Justices!" Prince Alika shouted behind us.

Both Jonata and Chief Justice Nalani's warden leapt to their feet. I looked over my shoulder. The prince ran toward us from the path leading back into Lele proper. His own guards raced after him.

Jonata stepped between me and the prince, her hand on her dagger. The prince skidded to a halt out of my warden's reach.

"What's wrong, Your Highness?" Nalani asked as her warden assisted her to her feet.

"Forgive the intrusion, Chief Justices." Prince Alika bowed. "My father's distance speaker has received instructions for you from Standora. Queen Teodora is dead. Queen Chiara commands you to return to Issura immediately. You are to sail straight to the capital. My own ship is preparing to return to Kou as we speak, and Captain Iakepa and his crew are assisting Captain Titus in readying the *Mars Tranquilus* for departure on the evening tide."

My heart seized in my chest. Teodora was gone?

I didn't notice Luc at my side until he spoke when I could not form a thought, much less words. "Did Queen Chiara say what happened to her mother?"

Prince Alika shook his head. "I don't know. Father may have more information for you by the time we reach Kou."

I gripped Luc's dripping shoulder. *Did we save Po, only to lose Teodora?*

She did everything to prepare Chiara for this moment. Luc sighed internally. *She knows her duties, and she's ready to take the throne.*

I just pray to the Twelve she survives long enough for us to reach home, I replied bitterly.

What will Anthea and Luc find when they arrive in Standora?
Turn the page for a sneak peek at A Barrel of Vintner!

A Barrel of Vintner

I stood on the bow of the Duke of Orrin's flagship, the Mars Tranquilus. The mountains of Issura and the narrow entrance to the Bay of Standora could be made out in the distance. King Keanu of O'ahu had loaned us three of his best wind talents, including his own Senior Captain Iakepa. They managed to shave six days off the month-long sea voyage home from the island nation.

Despite the sun's warmth on this cloudless day, ice coated my heart. The news of Queen Teodora's death had been a bitter reminder of my own goddess's role after we managed to save Emperor Po of Jing from internal dissension, demon attacks, and the efforts of his late mother's husband to destroy him.

Balance in all things had become an ill jest in my life.

Bootsteps came from behind me. My warden Long Feather gripped the railing as I did in our headlong rush to reach the capital.

"Staring at the land will not make the ship sail faster, m'lady."

I didn't look at him. "I'm very much aware I'm not a wind talent, Warden."

"Nor can you turn back time," he replied evenly. "It was no secret the queen was ill before the Winter Solstice. Long before Emperor Chengwu's assassination."

We'd been ordered to escort Bao Quan Po, the former Jing ambassador, home three weeks after Balance's long night. After his brother the former Jing emperor, the empress, and their two sons were slaughtered in a demon attack on the imperial palace, Po was the sole remaining member of the immediate Bao line.

At least until his wife, the Empress Shi Hua, safely delivered her babe.

"And now, we are three weeks away from the Summer Solstice, Warden," I snapped. "What's your point?"

He leaned his elbows on the rail. Sea spray coated his hair and uniform as it covered mine. "My point is Queen Chiara and Prince Consort White Eagle trust you, m'lady. Maybe you should give them a little bit of trust in return. Surely, their distance speaker would have told you if more was going on in Issura."

Long Feather's observation only added to my irritation. Lord Ayatu-lutul's reticence at giving me and High Brother Luc any additional infor-mation on the days we were scheduled to speak annoyed me. He merely said our new queen needed us home as soon as possible, but he never included our new queen or her husband in any of these contacts.

I hadn't been able to speak with Justices Yanaba or Elizabeth since we arrived at the imperial palace in Jing. I hadn't realized how much I'd depended on Empress Shi Hua's own distance speaking abilities.

Of course, that was before she became empress of Jing. When she was Sister Shi Hua of Light and Ambassador Quan's bodyguard. That seemed like yesterday and forever ago at the same time.

"Chief Justice Anthea?"

I turned to find Captain Titus's second officer Little Squirrel approach-ing me.

She bowed. "High Brother Luc says the queen's distance speaker has notified him that a royal escort will be waiting for you at the pier when we dock. Perhaps you would like to refresh yourself before your audience with Her Majesty."

Her statement wasn't a question.

I snorted. "You and I both know you can speak plainer than that, Sec-ond Officer."

The smaller woman shot me an impish grin. "Very well then. We are making a high-speed approach to the bay's entrance. The dock master is clearing traffic for us. And Captain Titus wants you off the deck of the *Mars Tranquilus* because he already doesn't like risking his own people in these maneuvers, much less the queen's ambassadors. High Brother Luc and his warden have already retreated to your cabin, and Warden Jonata said if you don't come down of your own accord, she will assist me in dragging you to your cabin as well."

Beside me, Long Feather failed to stifle his own bark of laughter.

"You are fortunate I don't wish to waste my time charging all of you with insubordination," I snapped before I stomped down the port-side steps of the forecastle.

When I reached the main deck, I strode over to Captain Titus who was bellowing orders. He paused at my approach.

"A simple request is sufficient, Captain," I spat. "Threats are unneces-sary."

He glared at me over his bushy beard that displayed his Old Continent heritage. "Apparently, they are since you're not in your cabin yet, Lady Justice."

I muttered a Jing slur that questioned his mother's choice of bed partners before I whirled on my boot heel and headed for our quarters. His first and second officers had given up their private cabin for Luc, our wardens, and me. However, my temper had become rather short after our abbreviated visit to O'ahu.

Worse, I hadn't had a chance to taste more of the Sea Peoples' famed underground-roasted pig at the Duke of Mau'i's feast.

When I entered the cabin, Luc, his warden Yar, and my second warden Jonata sat at the table. All three wore smirks.

"None of this is funny," I snapped.

"No," Luc said. "It's predictable. I warned Titus you like being on deck whenever you sail to Standora."

"There's no reason—" I started.

"The Bay of Standora is nothing like Orrin's harbor. The captain will be making a sharp starboard turn when we clear the bay entrance." Jonata lifted her chin. "With the nasty currents of the bay, the rocks on the southside entrance, and our current speed, the crew cannot afford to make mistakes. You, as the queen's ambassador, are a major distraction for them." Her skin grew more orange with each word, and her wave of fury slammed against my mental shields.

"Very well then." I sat on the bench beside her. Long Feather took the seat next to me. "What's your recommendation, Warden?"

"We wait patiently, m'lady," Jonata said primly. "As the *Mars Tranquilus* completes her maneuvers, enough of our velocity will be shed the crew can then dock safely. After that, you can run to the palace for all I care, and when you trip over a cobblestone and land flat on your face, I will laugh my ass off."

I blinked. "If I didn't know better, I would say you're Chief Warden Little Bear wearing a glamour."

The three men broke out in loud laughter while Jonata narrowed her eyes.

"My orders from the chief warden were to get you back to Issura alive," she snapped. "He did not specify where in Issura. Nor did he say uninjured. If you feel the need to replace me, tell me now, and I'll report to the Wardens Academy for reassignment as soon as we disembark."

I blinked again. Jonata had blossomed into a wonderful warden in the nearly year and a half since she had been assigned to the Temple of Balance in Orrin. My Temple. And here I was taking out my own fears and anger on someone who had stayed by my side constantly for the last six months. All the gold in the world couldn't buy that kind of loyalty.

I sucked in a deep breath and released it.

"I apologize for my words and actions, Warden Jonata. I have no excuse for mistreating you." I drew another breath. "I don't want you to leave my service, but I understand if my actions make you feel you need to ask for a reassignment."

She relaxed at my words. "I don't wish to leave, m'lady, and I understand I'm one of the lowest ranked Balance wardens in Orrin. However, after everything we've been through, I thought I'd earned your respect."

"You have. But I've lost so many of your fellow wardens, I fear losing you and Long Feather as well. You've b-become dear t-to me," I choked out.

To my surprise, they both hugged me.

"We feel their loss, too, m'lady," Long Feather whispered.

Jonata sniffed. "I didn't know Aglaia, but Tyra and Mylon didn't regret for one instant their service to you or the Temple. And you're are not responsible for any of their deaths. No one could have predicted those events."

"Our predecessors became complacent after a century without demon attacks," Yar said. "It's our duty to rectify that complacency. All of ours, clergy and wardens alike."

"You speak wise words, my friend." Luc clasped Yar's shoulder.

My wardens released me, and we all pretended not to be emotional.

Long Feather rose. "Jonata switch places with me."

She nodded, and they quickly switched seats. I didn't have to ask. The upcoming turn of the ship meant we'd be slung towards the starboard side. Since both Long Feather and I were larger than the diminutive Jonata, we could possibly injure her severely.

The shouted orders of the deck couldn't drown the calls of the gulls. But when Titus's bellow signaled the next maneuver, even my stomach heaved as the *Mars Tranquilus* nearly laid on its side to make the turn toward the Standora docks.

The tingle of magic flowed over my skin as the wind talents guided the ship to its assigned berth at a more sedate pace. My fellow passengers and I stood to wipe the salt from our skins and change clothes. I'd kept one of the uniforms Jing's Reverend Mother Xiang of Balance had gifted me in reserve for disembarking. A month at sea and minimal use of our fresh water supplies left too much of my own body odor for even me to tolerate.

Little Squirrel knocked on our cabin door and poke her head inside. "It's clear to come out, Chief Justice, High Brother."

The crew were lowering the ramp as we exited the cabin. Even my odd eyesight could pick out the queen's guard and the prince consort without the dock workers giving them a wide berth.

Yar hovered over Luc as he made his way down the gangplank with his specially designed steel crutches. I followed with my own wardens right behind me.

Prince White Eagle stood in front of the queen's guard with a wide smile. "Welcome home, Ambassadors."

To our surprise, he hugged both Luc and me. The prince was a giant of a man like Yar. Easily a couple of palms taller than Luc and me.

We're heading straight to the palace. Our queen needs to speak with you at once.

Concern rankled me. Not the prince's use of silent speech. He was former Temple like Empress Shi Hua. But the worry and fear at his mental touch. Something was terribly wrong.

"The queen wishes to honor you for the excellent job you did in Jing," the prince continued out loud.

"We are here to serve," I murmured as both Luc and I bowed to him. Our wardens followed suit. Their tension permeated my own.

Before we could say our farewells to Captain Titus and the crew of the *Mars Tranquilus*, the queen's guard surrounded us, and we were forced to follow the prince to the waiting carriages.

I glanced at Luc. His frown said volumes.

Say nothing, my love, he whispered in my mind. *There are too many ears here.*

So, he noticed the two Thief spies as well. Scanning the crowd, I realized too many people took notice of our arrival.

And for once, they weren't consumed by the usual gossip about my blood red eyes.

A Barrel of Vintner *is coming soon in ebook and trade paperback formats at your favorite bookstore!*

Words and Phrases Specific to the Justice Series

APPRENTICE – lowest rank of a trade or craft guild

BERDA – gender fluid; someone who does not stick to traditional gender roles

BROTHER – title for any fully ordained priest of any Temple that accepts men, except for the Temple of Father

CANT – Issura's neighboring nation-state to the south

CHENGZHOU – the capital of Jing, a nation-state on the eastern shore of the Old Continent

CHIEF JUSTICE – title of the highest ranked priestess at a Temple of Balance

CHIEF [name of trade] – the highest ranking master guild member of a trade in a city or region

CHUMASH WAY – the last town on the Issuran side of Kulshra'jek Pass

THE CRADLE – according to legend, the continent where Child created the first members of the human race

DUKE/DUCHESS – highest ranking noble of a region

FATHER – title for any fully ordained priest of the Temple of Father

GOJOSEON – a kingdom on a peninsula between Jing and the Xiongnu Confederation along the eastern Old Continent

GRAY MOUNTAINS – a mountain range that runs the entire length of the western side of the Long Continents

THE GRAND CANAL – a human-built canal that passes through the isthmus connecting the Long Continents

GUILD – a civil organization for a trade or craft

GUILD MASTER – an expert tradesman's rank based on analysis of his/her peers

HEALER – a person with the magical ability to heal illness and repair wounds

HIGH BROTHER – title of the chief priest of a city Temple, except the Temple of Father

HIGH FATHER – title of the chief priest of a city's Temple of Father

HIGH MOTHER – title of the chief priestess of a city's Temple of Mother

HIGH SISTER – title of the chief priestess of a city Temple, except the Temples of Balance and Mother

HUANG HE – a port city on the east coast of Jing

ISSURA – queendom on the western coast of Northern Long Continent; the Peaceful Sea forms its western border with the nation of Pagonia to the north, the nation of Cant to the south, the nations of the Cliffdwellers and Diné to the southeast and the Gray Mountains to the east

JING – nation-state on the eastern side of the Old Continent

JOURNEYMAN/JOURNEYWOMAN – middle rank of a trade or craft guild

Justice – title for any fully ordained priestess of the Temple of Balance; alternate term of address is Lady Justice

KEMET – nation-state on the northeast corner of the Cradle

KHAZAR SEA – a freshwater sea in the central part of the Old Continent

KULSHRA'JEK PASS – a pass through the Gray Mountains adjacent to Pana Valley, mainly used by Comanche traders in the summer on their way west and Issuran traders on their way east; the pass itself is considered neutral territory

KOU – the capital of the Kingdom of O'ahu

LELE – a port city on the island of Kaua'i in the Kingdom of O'ahu

THE LONG CONTINENTS – the two continents separating the Peaceful Sea from the Panthalassa Sea, they are connected by a narrow isthmus

THE LOST CONTINENT – the southern continent between the Peaceful Sea and the Storm Sea. By Anthea's time, the original inhabitants were believed to be slaughtered by demons 500 years before. Sailors from the Sea Peoples and Maurya who landed there after the inhabitants' disappearance reported screams but found no one. Those with magic talents went mad. Not even the priests and priestesses from Child could save them. Those who tried went mad themselves.

MAGISTRATE – elected official of a city or town in Issura who is responsible for civil and criminal law enforcement and the city or town's defense/care in an emergency

MASTER – senior member of a trade or craft guild; or the clergyperson who is primarily responsible for the training of a novice class

MIDDLE SEA – the shallow sea that separates The Cradle from the Old Continent

MOTHER – title for any fully ordained priestess of the Temple of Mother

MOUNTAIN GATE – a medium-sized town in the Gray Mountain in the east central part of the Ducy of Orrin in Issura

NAHA – capital of the Kingdom of Ryukyu, a set of islands in the Peaceful Sea southwest of the Fire Islands

NOVICE – a person in training to become a priest/priestess of the Twelve

O'AHU – an island kingdom in the Peaceful Sea approximately halfway between the Old Continent and the Northern Long Continent; the other main islands, besides O'ahu itself, are Mau'i, Kaua'i, Hawai'i, Ni'ihua, Molokai'i, Lana'i, and Kaho'olawe

ORRIN – third largest city in the queendom of Issura with the second largest port

PEACEFUL SEA – the ocean that separates the Long Continents from the eastern part of the Old Continent, the islands and archipelagos of the Sea Peoples, and the Lost Continent

PEACEKEEPERS – men and women who act as a city's police force. They report to the city's magistrate. They also act as an auxiliary defense force if their city or nation is attacked.

RAMBLA – formerly the northernmost city in Cant, its people were used to hatch demon eggs during the events of A Modicum of Truth

REVEREND FATHER – senior-most priest of a Temple order, the leader of that sect in the nation in which he resides

REVEREND MOTHER – senior-most priestess of a Temple order, the leader of that sect in the nation in which she resides

RUS – a nation-state on the west side of the Sea of Zalpa

RYUKYU – a kingdom consisting of a set of islands in the Peaceful Sea southwest of the Fire Islands

SEA OF ZALPA – a mixed fresh water and salt water body in the Old Continent between the Middle Sea and the Khazar Sea

SEAT – person holding the highest-ranking position of a Temple that is not the home Temple for a nation

SISTER – title for any fully ordained priestess of any Temple that accepts women, except for the Temples of Mother and Balance

SKANDZA – a sea-faring people of the north-eastern Old Continent

SKINWALKER – a human with talent who performs demon magic; the magic corrupts their physical body to the point they need another person's skin to contain their spirit

SKOLOTI TRIBES – One of the affiliations of semi-nomadic people in the central part of the Old Continent, north of the Sea of Zalpa

STANDORA – capital and largest city of Issura

TANDOR – Issuran city that guards the border with Cant and Diné

TEMPLE – a collection of people dedicated to the service of one of the twelve gods; a building that houses such people; the primary place of worship for one of the twelve gods

THEMISCYREIA – a nation-state of semi-nomadic people in the central part of the Old Continent, south of the Sea of Zalpa

THE TWELVE – the collective name for the twelve deities of the Justice universe

VALLEY OF THE LOST – the desert between Issura, Diné, and the Cliffdweller Territory

WARDEN – security guard of a Temple, they act as supplementary military personnel in the event of a demon invasion

XIONGNU CONFEDERATION – a collection of nomadic tribes north of Jing

The Twelve Temples
MOTHER

Cloak Color – Light blue

Motto – "To give without thought; to forgive with love."

The Temple of Mother is responsible for the teaching of household arts, such as spinning, weaving, food storage and preparation. The order is also responsible for caring for those who have lost their families.

FATHER

Cloak Color – Dark blue

Motto – "All tools are weapons, and weapons tools."

The Temple of Father is responsible for the constructive arts, such as carpentry and smithing.

BALANCE

Cloak Color – Black

Motto – "Balance in all things."

The Temple of Balance runs the judicial system. A justice is the judge in criminal and civil cases.

LIGHT

Cloak Color – Medium brown

Motto – "Light brings truth, for without truth, there can be no justice."

The Temple of Light is responsible for codifying contracts and mediating contract disputes. A Light priest also acts as the bailiff for a justice, and is often the one to truthspell a witness or the accused. The Temple of Light also provides military support to a nation's civilian army.

KNOWLEDGE

Cloak Color – Gold

Motto – "With patience, knowledge comes."

The Temple of Knowledge is responsible for education and for recording historical events. They essentially act as the library system for the Justice universe.

THIEF

Cloak Color – Grey

Motto – "Hiding in plain sight."

The Temple of Thief acts as the intelligence-gathering arm of both the Temples and the civilian leaders. They finance their efforts through gambling dens.

CONFLICT

Cloak Color – Dark Red

Motto – "Destruction is the necessary evil, for it clears the way for new growth."

The Temple of Conflict focuses on strategy and all martial arts. They are the primary support and teachers of a nation's army.

LOVE

Cloak Color – Medium Red

Motto – "Pleasure is life."

The Temple of Love are the holy prostitutes. They also deal with sex education and lead the Spring Rituals, the annual fertility rites which were first used to breed as many humans with magical talent as possible. Don't underestimate them. They fight just as hard and as nasty as their fellow clergy in Conflict.

CHILD

Cloak Color – Light green

Motto – "All things are new once."

The Temple of Child is responsible for the emotional health of citizens. They also develop and teach agriculture and animal husbandry techniques.

WILDING

Cloak Color – Dark green

Motto – "All creatures return to us."

The Temple of the Wildling God deals with management of wild animal populations, forestry, and the protection of ecosystems. They are the only clergy who can shift into a secondary animal form.

VINTNER

Cloak Color – Purple

Motto – "The line between wisdom and madness is one sip."

The Temple of Vintner not only deals with the cultivation of grapes and the production of wine, but they also promote the gathering, cultivation and processing of all medicinal herbs.

DEATH

Cloak Color – Black

Motto – "For every life, there is a death."

The Temple of Death takes care of the gathering of the dead, the last rites, and disposal of corpses. They also act as a repository for the last wills and testaments of all citizens.

Characters

QUEENDOM OF ISURRA
ORRIN

Temple of Balance

CHIEF JUSTICE ANTHEA – a circuit justice for ten winters until her appointment as Chief Justice of Orrin at the age of thirty winters ("Justice")

CHIEF JUSTICE PENELOPE – deceased, predecessor to Anthea as Chief Justice of Orrin

CHIEF JUSTICE THALIA - deceased, predecessor to Penelope as Chief Justice of Orrin, maternal grandmother of Anthea

CHIEF JUSTICE ELIZABETH – chief justice of the Temple of Balance in Tandor, temporarily assigned to Orrin after the destruction of Tandor, later becomes chief justice of the Duchy of Anacapa

JUSTICE YANABA – junior justice assigned to the city of Orrin after the events of *A Question of Balance*

JUSTICE ERATO – junior justice assigned to the circuit of the eastern section of the duchy of Orrin and the southern tip of the duchy of Pana Valley after Anthea is sentenced to the seat of Orrin in "Justice"

SIVAN – personal assistant to Chief Justice Anthea and head of the household staff

DONELLA – senior clerk

LAILANI – junior clerk

CHIEF WARDEN LITTLE BEAR – head of the Balance wardens

WARDEN TYRA – junior warden, killed in the Battle of Tandor (*A Matter of Death*)

WARDEN GINA – junior warden, promoted to chief warden of Balance under Chief Justice Elizabeth when she is reassigned to the new Duchy of Anacapa

WARDEN AGLAIA – junior warden, died in the battle to retake the Temple of Love (*A Question of Balance*)

WARDEN JONATA – junior warden, Aglaia's replacement from the Standora Wardens' Academy, a passive talent

WARDEN LONG FEATHER – junior warden

WARDEN MYLON – junior warden, died during the events of *A Hand of Father*

HOGARTH – former chief warden under Justices Thalia and Penelope, now stablemaster, husband of Deborah

DEBORAH – Head cook, wife of Hogarth

NATHAN – squire to Chief Justice Anthea after he was sentenced to pay reparations for stealing bread, an orphan, age ten winters at the time of his sentencing in *A Question of Balance*

MING WEI – squire to Justice Yanaba, nine winters old at the end of *A Question of Balance*. Originally from Jing, she was sold by her parents to a Jing noble as a sex slave and brought to Issura. When the noble's crimes were discovered, he immolated himself and his slaves. Ming Wei was the only survivor and has severe scar tissue on her face, back and arms.

Temple of Light

HIGH BROTHER LUC – a circuit priest for twelve winters until his appointment as the seat at the age of thirty-two winters between the events of "Justice" and "Diplomacy in the Dark", his father Itzel is a merchant from Cant

HIGH BROTHER KAM – semi-retired, predecessor to Luc as chief priest, poisoned and died during the events of *A Question of Balance*

BROTHER MAT – Second to Luc. His birth name is Micah. He murdered the real Mat on his way to Orrin from Standora. Died under Anthea's truthspell interrogation in *A Question of Balance.*

BROTHER JEREMY – youngest junior priest until he is promoted to Luc's second after the events of *A Question of Balance.*

BROTHER GARBHAN – junior priest who is assigned permanently to Orrin after the events of *A Matter of Death*

BROTHER WOLF RUN – junior priest partnered with Justice Erato on the eastern Orrin circuit

WARDEN MATEQAI – junior warden, becomes Sister Shi Hua's personal bodyguard during the events of *A Modicum of Truth*

WARDEN YAR – junior warden

CHAO – the son of Sister Shi Hua and Brother Jeremy, conceived due to the breeding edict issued worldwide by the Reverend Mothers of Justice and the Reverend Fathers of Light, born between the events of *A Hand of Father* and *A Measure of Knowledge*

Temple of Love

HIGH SISTER GERD – chief priestess, biological daughter of Thalia and Kam, biological mother of Anthea. She was removed from office on charges of fraud, bribery of a public official, unlawful magic, and conspiracy to commit murder. Later, the charges of dealing in demon artifacts and treason were added. Beheaded by Anthea during the events of *A Twist of Love.*

SISTER DRAGONFLY – Gerd's second, *berda* (genderfluid), is acting High Sister after the events in *A Question of Balance*, becomes High Sister after the events in *A Modicum of Truth*

SISTER CLAUDIA – junior priestess, Dragonfly's second, some Light talent

Temple of Conflict

HIGH BROTHER HAN – chief priest

SISTER MIGINA – junior priestess

Temple of Death

HIGH SISTER BERTRICE – chief priestess

BROTHER XANDER – Bertrice's second until her demise during the Battle of Tandor, succeeds her as Orrin's High Brother of Death

Temple of Child

HIGH SISTER MYA – chief priestess

Temple of Wildling

HIGH BROTHER JAX – chief priest, second form is a wolf

SISTER FARRAH – Jax's second, second form is a fox

BROTHER SISQUOC – priest of the Temple of the Wildling God in Tandor, second form is a panther. He's transferred to the Orrin Temple of the Wildling God after the events of *A Matter of Death.*

Temple of Thief
HIGH BROTHER TALBERT – chief priest

Nobility and their retainers
DUKE BENEDETTO DIMARA – father of Marco, Alessa, and Isabella, husband of Cora, convicted of conspiracy to use illegal magic to mind wipe his son Marco during the events of "Justice"; imprisoned at Standora for life.

LADY CORA DIMARA – mother of Marco, Alessa, and Isabella, convicted of treason and demon dealing, executed by the Reverend Mother Alara of Balance during the events of "Justice".

DUKE MARCO DIMARA – duke of Orrin, inherited his post at the age of eighteen winters after his parents were found guilty of numerous offenses and stripped of their titles and property

LADY KATARINA DIMARA (nee' DiLove) – common-born wife of Marco, animal healer. Her mother was Sister Ilina, a priestess of the Temple of Love who died of the wasting sickness the summer before Katarina's eighteenth winter.

LORD KAM DIMARA – eldest child of Marco and Katarina and heir to the Duchy of Orrin, named for High Brother Kam of Light, godson of Chief Justice Anthea and High Brother Luc

ARTURO – former captain of Duke Marco's flagship. His murder is the precipitating event of "Diplomacy in the Dark".

TITUS – captain of Duke Marco's flagship, the *Mars Tranquilus*

Citizens
MALVEN DICOOK – duly elected magistrate of Orrin

CAT AND DOG – the leaders of Orrin's street children, Chief Justice Anthea uses them to obtain information outside of the normal Temple intelligence channels

Guilds
CHIEF HEALER AARON – head of the Healers' Guild

MASTER HEALER DEVIN – second to Aaron in the Orrin Healer's Guild, originally from New Thenos

JOURNEYWOMAN BLY – a junior healer, often assists Master Devin at autopsies, later a master healer in her own right

STANDORA – capital city of Issura
REVEREND MOTHER ALARA – head of Issura's Temple of Balance

REVEREND FATHER FARRELL – head of Issura's Temple of Light

QUEEN TEODORA – reigning monarch of Issura

CROWN PRINCESS CHIARA – eldest child and heir of Queen Teodora of Issura; lady general of the queen's army

Duke White Eagle – former Conflict brother, left the order to marry Crown

Princess Chiara; honorary title Duke of Standora as the future queen's consort; lord general of the queen's army

JING EMPIRE
CHENGZHOU

Imperial Family

EMPRESS BAO DE – ruler of Jing a century before Bao Yu, she sacrificed herself and her consort to stop a demon army

Empress Bao Yu – ruler of Jing until her death from natural causes during "Courting Trouble"

EMPEROR BAO CHENGWU – ruler of Jing until his assassination by demons, succeeded his mother Bao Yu during "Courting Trouble"

CROWN PRINCE BAO QUAN PO, formerly Ambassador Quan Po – half-brother of Emperor Bao Chengwu; son of Empress Bao Yu and Quan Yong Xi; was heir to the throne until his eldest nephew was born; became heir to the Dragon Throne with the assassinations of his brother and nephews

WU SUNSHU – imperial consort of Empress Bao Yu, master of the School of Sorcery, imprisoned for life on the charge of treason for consorting with demons

QUAN YONG XI – lover of Empress Bao Yu, father of Bao Quan Po, master of the School of the Phoenix and the Dragon, died from a spell that imitated the effects of a disease called the Child's Curse during the events of

Staff at the Imperial Palace

CHIN – a steward assigned to serve the Issuran party

MASTER HEALER YI – a senior member of the Healers Guild assigned to the Imperial Palace to care of the residents, guests, and staff

Temple of Father

REVEREND FATHER DA – head of Jing's Temple of Father

NOVICE ENLE – a novice at the Temple of Father; a friend of Novice Song

Temple of Mother

REVEREND MOTHER BAI – head of Jing's Temple of Mother

Temple of Light

REVEREND FATHER JIN – head of Jing's Temple of Light

SISTER SHI HUA – a priestess of Light, who was tapped as Po's bodyguard. She received additional training from Conflict, Thief, and Love. Originally from the town of Yintze in the southern province of Chu.

BROTHER LIN – novice master of Light

BROTHER JIAN – a priest of Light, classmate of Shi Hua during their novice years

BROTHER BOLIN – a priest of Light, often assigned to assist Justice Aihan, he's also the father of her child

BROTHER ZI RUI – a priest of Light assigned to Anthea during the rewind of the fire in Chengzhou during the events of *A Cup of Conflict*

NOVICE RUNCHU – a novice from Light; a friend of Novice Song

Temple of Wildling

BROTHER FA – a Wildling priest, his second form is a tiger, a friend of Shi Hua and Jian during their novice years

SISTER LONGNU – a Wildling priestess, her second form is a dragon

Temple of Balance

REVEREND MOTHER XIANG – head of Jing's Temple of Balance

CHIEF JUSTICE DAI LU – Reverend Mother Xiang's second; she is not totally blind, but so incredibly nearsighted that she qualifies to be a justice

JUSTICE MEI WEN – a priestess of Balance, Shi Hua's closest friend other than Jian during their novice years

WARDEN GANG – Mei Wen's original warden; he was killed during the winter attack on Chengzhou

WARDEN YICHEN – the warden who saved Mei Wen's life during the attack on Chengzhou, he replaced her previous warden when he was killed defending her

JUSTICE AIHAN – a priestess of Balance, one of their top criminal investigators, she's pregnant with Brother Bolin of Light's child

WARDEN CHAO XING – Aihan's personal warden

CLERK FULU – a clerk of Balance; assigned to assist Anthea during the rewind of the fire in Chengzhou during the events of *A Cup of Conflict*

NOVICE BAOZHAI – a novice of Balance, aged eleven winters during the events of *A Cup of Conflict*

YANG – a squire with the Chengzhou Temple of Balance, she has a talent for training and communicating with horses

Temple of Love

SISTER YIN LI – a priestess of Love, Shi Hua's maternal aunt

YIN SHANG – the son of Sister Yin Li and Brother Shang, he's five winters when he first appeared in *A Touch of Mother*

Temple of Conflict

REVEREND FATHER CHEN – head of Jing's Temple of Conflict

REVEREND FATHER FENG – replaced Chen after the disappearance of him and his army before *A Touch of Mother*

HIGH BROTHER SHANG – a priest of Conflict, Shi Hua's instructor when she was a novice; lover of Yin Li and father of Yin Shang; last seen with Reverend Father Chen's army

NOVICE SONG – a twelve-year-old novice in the Temple of Conflict with extremely powerful wards that allow sound to pass through them

Temple of Thief

REVEREND FATHER BIMING – head of Jing's Temple of Thief

WARDEN MUCHEN – a senior warden with the Temple of Thief, he was killed saving Warden Jonata from a boobytrap during the events of *A Cup of Conflict*

Temple of Child

REVEREND FATHER RUNCHU – head of Jing's Temple of Child

Temple of Knowledge

REVEREND MOTHER XIAO MEI – head of Jing's Temple of Knowledge

SISTER KEXIN – priestess assigned to teach on Chengzou's western third ring of the city

Temple of Vintner

Reverend Mother Ah Lam – head of Jing's Temple of Vintner

NOVICE SU YAN – a novice from the Temple of Vintner, a friend of Novice Song's

Temple of Death

REVEREND FATHER JUN HIE – head of Jing's Temple of Death

NOVICE LE LE – a novice from Death; a friend of Novice Song's

Nobility

LADY HENG – a noblewoman who seduced Po and Chengwu's grandfather in an attempt to become empress by providing him a son; her first son with the emperor was stillborn; when her second son was born with his spine exposed, she stabbed the healers attending her before she strangled the baby; she claimed pregnancy madness was the reason for her actions; Empress Bao Yu banished Heng when she ascended to the Dragon Throne

DUKE BAO ZIXIN – a third cousin of Quan Po who believes he has a superior claim to the Jing throne due to his noble birth

PRINCE BAO PU – an elderly first cousin twice removed of Quan Po

DUKE BAO GUANG – second cousin of Quan Po, rules Xie Han Province

LORD BAO AIGUO – the second eldest son of Duke Guang

DUKE BAO XI – second cousin of Quan Po

DUKE BAO MENGCHANG – second cousin of Quan Po, chancellor under both Emperor Chengwu and Emperor Po

LORD BAO SHOI-MING – the second eldest son of Dike Mengchang, he was asked to assist Duchess Jia in administering Huang He Province after the death of her husband Duke Lixin during the events of *A Cup of Conflict*

Imperial Guard

CAPTAIN HUIZHONG – leader of Bao Quan Po's personal security as ambassador, promoted to head of the Emperor's Guard when Po becomes emperor

MA LI – a member of the Emperor's Guard

Guilds

MASTER HEALER ZHI – second to the leader of the Jing Healers Guild, she often assists the Chengzhou justices with investigations

Jing Philosophy Schools

MASTER MA – head of the School of the Phoenix and the Dragon

XIAN – Master Ma's personal bodyguard

MASTER BOLIN – head of the School of Nature

Civilians

LAN – a cook by trade who runs a food stall on the street between Light and Thief in Chengzhou during the Sprint Rituals; her permanent shop in in the southern second ring of the city

YAN – the spokeswoman for the neighborhood on the west side of Chengzhou where the School of Sorcery had a safe house

JUN DE – a man from the same neighborhood as Yan; he threatened Sister Kexin from Knowledge several times she came to the western third of Chengzhou to teach the children

ZHEN ZHU – Novice Su Yan of Vintner's cousin; a member of the School of Sorcery

YUXUAN – headman on one of the villages outside of Chengzhou

HUANG HE

Nobility

DUKE BAO LIXIN – Second cousin of Bao Quan Po

DUCHESS BAO JIA – Duke Lixin's wife

Temple of Balance

CHIEF JUSTICE LI CHUN – the seat of Balance in the city of Huang He

ISLANDS OF THE SEA PEOPLES

Kingdom of O'ahu

KING KEANU – king of the O'ahu island chain midway between the Long Continents, the Old Continent, and the Lost Continent in the Peaceful Sea; his subjects are part of the Sea People ethnic group

PRINCE ALIKA – youngest son of King Keanu, one of Sister Gretchen's worshippers, the father of her unborn child

CAPTAIN IAKEPA – senior captain of the O'ahu trading fleet

CHIEF JUSTICE NALANI – the seat of Balance in the Duchy of Kaua'i in the Kingdom of O'ahu

HIGH BROTHER MAKOA – the seat of Light in the Duchy of Kaua'i in the Kingdom of O'ahu

DINÉ NATION
AJÉÍ (HEART)

Temple of Light

BROTHER BUMBLEBEE – junior priest of Light with the Diné army, Anthea's half-brother by her father Kilchii

Temple of Conflict

REVEREND FATHER KILCHII – head of the Diné Temple of Conflict. When he first met Anthea, he gave his name as "Nizhé'é", which in the Diné language means "your father" because he is her biological father.

PLAINS NATIONS – COMANCHE

HIGH BROTHER PECOS – a senior Conflict priest with the Diné army during the siege of Tandor, Anthea's half-brother through their father Kilchii

THE KINGDOM OF RYUKYU
NAHA

Temple of Thief

REVEREND FATHER OGUSUKU – head of the Ryukyu Temple of Thief

Temple of Balance

REVEREND MOTHER FUMIKO – the successor to Reverend Mother Yoshiko after her death from natural causes while the *Mars Tranquilus* was docked at Naha, the capital of Ryukyu

THE SKOLOTI TRIBES

Temple of Thief

SISTER DARYS – junior priestess of Thief, mistakenly assassinated by the Assassins Guild who mistook her for her twin sister Zhanna prior to the events of *A Touch of Mother*

HIGH SISTER ZHANNA – senior priestess of Thief; according to Skoloti prophecy, she is presumed to be the ally from the west who aids in placing Bao Quan Po on the Dragon Throne of Jing; she assumed her twin sister Darys's identity after Darys was mistakenly assassinated in Zhanna's place

WARDEN ANTIOPE – one of High Sister Zhanna's personal wardens who accompanied her to Jing

WARDEN URANIA – one of High Sister Zhanna's personal wardens who accompanied her to Jing

ACKNOWLEDGMENTS

What a strange time the last few years have been. There's been a lot of ups and downs in both my life and career as well as the world. Frankly, writing stories for my readers and some good people in my life have kept me on the straight and narrow.

Many thanks to my cover artist Elaina Lee and my formatter JW Manus. After ten years, these ladies are not only professional associates, but they've become good friends as well.

Lots of appreciation for my writing buds Candi, Tracie, Angie, Jo, and Jenn F. for their support and listening to me complain when this book seemed to go on forever.

Much love to Darling Husband, Genius Kid, the Princess Pup, and the Grandpuppy. My family is the best!

SUZAN HARDEN transitioned from writing information technology manuals for companies and legal articles for a law enforcement magazine to her first love, fantasy and science fiction in all their forms. She's the author of the Millersburg Magick Mysteries, the Soccer Moms of the Apocalypse series, and the Books of Apep series.

Contact Suzan Harden
Facebook: @Suzan Harden
Email: suzan@suzanharden.com
Website: www.suzanharden.com

Sign up for Suzan's Mailing List

www.ingramcontent.com/pod-product-compliance
Lightning Source LLC
Chambersburg PA
CBHW071147100726
47908CB00002B/282